SCHULTZ

Books by J. P. Donleavy

Novels
THE GINGER MAN
A SINGULAR MAN
THE SADDEST SUMMER OF SAMUEL S
THE BEASTLY BEATITUDES OF BALTHAZAR B
THE ONION EATERS
A FAIRY TALE OF NEW YORK
THE DESTINIES OF DARCY DANCER, GENTLEMAN
SCHULTZ

Plays
THE GINGER MAN
FAIRY TALES OF NEW YORK
A SINGULAR MAN
THE SADDEST SUMMER OF SAMUEL S
THE BEASTLY BEATITUDES OF BALTHAZAR B

Stories
MEET MY MAKER THE MAD MOLECULE

General
THE UNEXPURGATED CODE
A Complete Manual of Survival & Manners

J. P. Donleavy

SCHULTZ

DELACORTE PRESS/SEYMOUR LAWRENCE

Published by
Delacorte Press / Seymour Lawrence
1 Dag Hammarskjold Plaza
New York, New York 10017

A portion of this book first appeared in *Penthouse*.

Manufactured in the United States of America

First printing

Designed by MaryJane DiMassi

LIBRARY OF CONGRESS CATALOGING IN PUBLICATION DATA

Donleavy, James Patrick.
  Schultz.

  I. Title.
PZ4.D6844Sc [PS3507.O686]   813'.5'4   79-15756
ISBN: 0-440-07957-8

SCHULTZ

1

WHEN Lord Nectarine of Walham Green resigned his mastership of foxhounds, got rid of his wife and shut of his children and happily set up as a bachelor again, installing an attractive erudite housekeeper, and a male secretary hard of hearing, in his new commodious town house, Schultz enjoyed to consult, lunch and dine with his Lordship with as much frequency as his Lordship's tight schedule of social events allowed. Discussing with the noble peer how he might cut adrift from his own burdensome spouse.

"Of course Schultz, you know that foul methods such as murder are out of the question. In any event the black eyes your wife has succeeded in repeatedly giving you demonstrate that you might come a cropper in violently attempting her death."

At a quarter to noon each day his Lordship's chauffeur deposited him at Hyde Park Corner where he enjoyed to stroll up and down the slight hills along Piccadilly. Although he limped slightly from a cricket ball having smashed him on the knee, his nordicly blond Lordship was tall, slender, icy blue eyed and handsome to the extent that young ladies daily walked into walls and posts turning to look at him. He had attended some of the finer schools in England and owned one palace and more than one of the bigger and better castles here and there in various of the more prominent counties.

"I do beg to remind you Schultz, that I am not, repeat not, made of money."

His Lordship rarely made such remarks concerning his wherewithal. Unless Schultz particularly irritated him to. For along with his widespread and substantial assets, plus a prized pack of foxhounds, came numerous liabilities and tribulation as his Lordship was smashed reeling by staggering death duties, blistering taxes, and an unending list of old family retainers to maintain. To all of which had now recently been added his wife's vast separation settlement, his Lordship not believing in divorce. And many was the long arduous hour he spent down in the deep sunless rooms of the city in consultation with firms of lawyers and accountants with whom he could at times be more than abrupt, cutting through their smug drawling pomposities by speaking as he frequently did in a no nonsense manner.

"Schultz you do not impress me in the least."

This was Lord Nectarine's statement upon the occasion of his first meeting with Schultz. A winterish gloomy day of pouring rain. And drops were still rolling off a black curly Schultz's head, which had just hysterically rushed across half London by foot, bus and taxi to meet the rich peer. But suddenly and prophetically during their confrontation, it became a spring afternoon as the storm clouds passed and bathed in golden light, the two of them were standing centre room in the chairman's suite of this long established theatrical producing company tucked up a narrow street just off Piccadilly. But the flooding warmth of sunshine did nothing to soften his Lordship's scepticism.

"From what I have already heard of this production of yours Schultz you are entirely wasting your time attempting to solicit funds from me."

Binky, one of his Lordship's oldest friends, and equally rich, had acquired this showbizz operation to amuse himself and make it simpler to meet and wine and dine ladies of the theatre and those eager to be of that calling. But such arrangements did not come about without a little sand in the ointment. For, most unfortunately, upon the company's reconstruction after a bankruptcy and through a typist's error, the company had been named Sperm Productions instead of Spear Productions. And all attempts to explain Sperm as Spear only led to analogies being drawn between these two words as two items one might get shoved up one. Nor did a simple straightforward apologetic explanation always work.

Dear Madam,

Please ignore our rather suggestive company name, and we hope you will understand that it in no way indicates the nature of what we do.

But as Binky selected his dining and bed companions from his tomes of actresses' photographs listed among juvenile and juvenile character women, this dreadful mistake frequently brought outraged replies from the more established actresses in the field who jumped to the nude conclusion that they were being offered a part to play in a porno film. Instead of in Binky's bed. At such tricky times his Lordship would be requested to sit in on these touchy interviews. Which invariably ended up with an actress ready and upon occasion even begging to play any role these heavenly handsome aristocratic gentlemen could think of.

"This is my dear and old friend, his Royal Grace, who has long been charmed by and admired your splendid performances. He has, I am delighted to say, just joined Sperm Productions as one of our senior directors."

However his Lordship refused to have any of his more elevated entitlements listed on the letterhead. But following passionate implorements from Binky that the company desperately required the elite air his title gave, his Royal Grace did finally consent to being included as Lord Nectarine of Walham Green.

"You are an absolute brick my dear, to honor us top of the page like that."

Although far more shy and retiring than Binky, his Lordship did enjoy to witness these tête à tête occasions with London's leading ladies of stage, screen and radio. Secretly savouring to watch Binky, equally as handsome as his Lordship, lay on thick his languid sleepily drawling manner which so captivated the visiting stars as he stood on tiptoe during introductions, ceremoniously intoning his Lordship's long string of titles.

"Allow me to present you to his Royal Grace, Prince Basil, Earl of Eel Brook Common, Viscount Fulhambroadway and Lord Nectarine of Walham Green, MFH who is, I might add, also a fully accredited Fellow of the Royal Academy of Dancing and a paid up Knight of Malta."

His Lordship much disliked his titles being used and preferred wherever and whenever possible to be merely known as plain Mister Basil Bright or Nectarine. But Binky to whom his Lordship allowed nearly any latitude, would upon the merest of occasions boom out his Lordship's honours, styles and distinctions. And although painful to his Lordship he would patiently and good naturedly stand there through the ordeal, always eagerly awaiting the anonymous lighter moments when upon occasion the pair of them were dealing with the going and coming of minor showbizz personalities when they enjoyed to be asked by these upstarts why didn't both of them with their stunning good looks go to Hollywood.

"Ah now what about that Basil, my dear, should we, do you think we really should become film stars and abandon all this, the ups and resoundingly downs of the London theatrical whirl. Ah but I think not. No I think not. The West End needs us."

Even some major female stars who were now and again carefully entrapped into calling, suggested that either, with their matinee idol faces, could be their leading man in their next movie. But Lord Nectarine only smiled upon these overtures just as he did when he erected various follies on his estates and stood then later when they were expensively completed sadly wondering why he had bothered to build them.

"But of course one builds out of nervous hysteria caused by the ochre hue of one's architect's suede shoes."

But then, to his Lordship, amusement, as it was to Binky, was of the highest priority. And now by taking certain relatively modest handfuls of his vast cash flow and backing shows, he was while forsaking his other risky financial evening pastime of gambling, not only amusing himself immensely but also saving money. He particularly savoured to find the musical type of production featuring scantily clad leggy females and especially would wax delirious were the latter darker skinned. But his Lordship was just not all fun and games, he was also a stickler for artistic standards. And where these fell, his Lordship recoiled and retreated.

It was on such an occasion that Schultz was doing his anxious best to convince his Lordship to part with money. Precisely as his Lordship had done a few minutes previously having just returned from having purchased for five figure sums, three rare snuff boxes in one of London's major auction rooms. To which latter he was constantly departing at various times of day. And now in lieu of lunch he had his mouth full of sliced calves' tongue which a secretary had just fetched for him from that marvellously elegant nearby food emporium of Fortnum's.

"Come on your Highness, the chorus line is full of dark complexioned females. It's only a few thou. The only remaining sixteen thousand quid investment left. You get top billing as producer in a size and type of print not less than one twentieth as big as the stars. All other producers would be listed practically unseen underneath you."

"In fact Schultz I think you are a creampuff."

Creampuff was a word his Lordship was fond of using. Especially with people overheating themselves in their efforts to impress him. Or attempting to play upon his private proclivities. But Sigmund Franz Schultz, although his expression took on a corpse like demeanor, never for a second stopped faintly grinning. Hoping in spite of these bolo punch remarks to penetrate his Lordship's recently increasing financial caution and to prise loose this sizeable investment from his Lordship's aristocratic clutches.

"I mean it stands to reason, three flops in a row, even the law of averages says I got to have a hit."

"The law of averages, Schultz, may more likely say you've got to have bankruptcy."

However, showbizz happened to be having one of its momentary upswings at the time. And Schultz unbeknownst to himself, had found his way into Binky's and his Lordship's favour when they came upon an overnight satchel of Schultz's left at the office and which, along with an address book listing some of America's fabled richest men with their private phone numbers, also contained three pure silk shirts. These latter more than anything else improved Schultz's image in their eyes as they back and forth handled the garments between their unbelieving fingers.

"By jove your Royal Grace these are from a good shirtmaker as well, could it possibly be that Schultz is not a man of straw."

"Yes most surprising discovery this."

It was decided then and there that Schultz if nothing else would be most useful as a front of office man who could hold at arms or breath's length the streams of conmen constantly arriving pushily on the scene. Who seemed to enjoy monopolising conversations in the elegant surrounds of the chairman's suite of Sperm Productions thereby cramping his Lordship's and Binky's style with the visiting ladies. And Schultz, who was adept at making the inferior feel even more so, would be ideal in deterring such chaps with a blistering barrage of impolite intimidation.

"I mean to say your Royal Grace let us pop old Schultzy boy in the little cubbyhole next to the telephonist's switchboard. And the numerous arriving unwanted can be shunted in there."

Not that his Lordship and Binky did not thoroughly enjoy the occasional appearance of a brash conman obnoxiously full of his own self importance, who would with assumed accents and social credentials, attempt to divest them of monies or, which was harder, gain their admiration and friendship. But there was also now the increasingly delicate matter of dealing decently and humanely with recently abandoned young lady actresses, from whom his Lordship and Binky, adoring variety, no longer required services and did not want to unkindly turn away.

"Schultz could not only take care of the outflow of ladies but also those numerous purveyors of criminal improprieties we seem to attract."

Happily it was one of those totally unexpected brief periods in London's West End during which those in pursuit of satisfying their vanity in the theatre were in short supply. For many of these overblown smug superior bombasts had in the two previous seasons been socked soundly into bankruptcy and wound up having to sell their cars and houses and in one instance even to putting the wife out to ply an ancient trade on the streets. As Binky had, while perambulating one of London's better known boulevards, recently observed.

"I say your Royal Grace, I could have sworn I saw thing's wife."

"Who."

"You know, thing. Who sold his motor cars, thoroughbreds, and fatally mortgaged his estate to save his miserable play. I am absolutely certain I rather bumped into her lurking in the Park Lane shadows of the Dorchester Hotel last night."

"O dear."

"Yes indeed and she rather used a variation of that expression to me. I think it was dearie she said. One would think that going on the game like that, that she would be somewhat more discreet. And poor woeful chap her husband. He was lurking on the theatrical edge in the lobby of the Comedy Theatre on that awful first night on Monday."

"How distressing Binky."

"Ah your Esteemed Highness, I think there are more than just a few jealous bitter observers about during this currently healthily booked up season."

Binky and his Lordship had also dropped buckets of cash, but their buckets were happily refilled from drips that still dropped gold in profusion from the one or two admirable hard working ancestors of the many previous generations. Plus they also had several shows profitably touring the provinces. And now with the new use to which Schultz might be put, his Lordship was far more accommodating of Schultz's entreaties for money but nevertheless insisted to keep him in his place.

"Not only Schultz do I think you are a creampuff but also a pettifogger."

Such remarks did stiffen somewhat Schultz's cheek muscles but he invariably continued grinning. While not in the least knowing what a pettifogger was. But he certainly knew by heart the tales of his Lordship's ancient family's considerable investments in South American railways, Bolivian mines, Canadian forests not to mention vast cattle ranches in North and South America. Plus the many tales of his Lordship's not only very direct but sometimes totally rude manner. But there was one aspect of his Lordship's personality that one could always depend upon. And that was his kindly indulgence of the lesser advantaged. And he especially lavished a sporting affection on the unmitigated underdog or anyone so unfortunate as Schultz was, to have been born in Woonsocket, Rhode Island.

"Ah Schultz, but let me add however, that although you are a pettifogging creampuff there is I think running through you the golden thread of innocence."

During his younger days his Lordship upon his tutor first making him aware of the industrial revolution, somewhat sympathised with socialism. And despite the fact that this was more than to some faint degree, intellectual, nevertheless it was genuine. But in relation to his more major tax difficulties, his Lordship was fond of jokingly saying that they were the result of a heinous bureaucratic plot hatched by the unionised idle working classes to undo him.

"Of course it is quite unjust for a certain element of the population to own the lion's share of the wealth of the nation but equally it is entirely tiresome for so many pompous damn complicated letters to have to be written by officialdom to extract such sums from me."

However his Lordship now took a wry joy in his complaint since he had over these past three tough years inherited not only from an amply rich father but also, as he had recently discovered, hugely staggering amounts left in trust for him by two great grand aunts. And assets were literally pouring and tumbling into his coffers more quickly than they could be squandered, taxed or spent.

Of course there were many occasions, usually on a rainy Monday or abysmally dull Sunday, when his Lordship lonely melancholy seated in a chair in the damp shadows of one of the great public rooms of one of his great castles, panicked about the endless expense in his life. And deeply down in the dumps, he would then hysterically make a selection of antiques from some long unused gallery, or utensils from some long abandoned kitchen, hire a lorry and have them carted up to a London auction room.

"Ah but then Schultz you do take the fucking cake sometimes. You really do. You are so preposterously bluffing that it becomes quite endearing."

In the plush ornamented chairman's office of Sperm Productions, his Lordship, through the mildly entertaining afternoons, often sat there in his brocaded Edwardian chair just glowing with approval at the sorry financially impoverished mess that Schultz was usually presently in. Needing as he so desperately did not only the sixteen thousand quid requested of his Lordship but also about sixty thousand more. And his Lordship would sit back delightfully amused as the uncontrollable Schultz paced the carpet smacking his forehead with the palm of his hand, repeating over and over.

"Jesus christ, Jesus christ, I got to fly to fucking New York."

"Schultz if I may say so, you are already flying. Over the fucking carpet that you're prematurely and unnecessarily wearing out."

But again too, his Lordship realised that Schultz, even seen in his very worst panics might be the real McCoy. And a genuine man of the theatre. Who knew deep in his aesthetic bones what the unpredictable public wanted. And his Lordship was becoming nervously suspicious that this, Schultz's latest musical attempt following his three previous resounding flops, might be the one which would set the West End ablaze with its glory.

"Ah Schultz you read all the theatre and film trade magazines cover to cover. You know off by heart the current gross of every Broadway and West End theatre. You have on your fingertips the name of every actress's agent as well as the actress's home telephone number. Surely that must impress investors to invest."

"Come on your Lordship, do you want to be fucking well left behind, I'm telling you, it's going to be a big hit."

His Lordship as he often did stood up and changed his seat in this Sperm Productions' most commodious office. With its satin royal crimsons which dripped and draped everywhere. And which did provoke some unfeeling persons to refer to the decor as Whore's Georgian. His Lordship now crossing to sit down on the blue and white striped chaise longue to regard the pleading Schultz benignly as the latter like an all in wrestler stood there in the foreground, waiting to come to grips with his hair carefully combed to accentuate his black curly locks and his foot idly kicking to dislodge little whorls of wool from the new crimson carpet.

"God you are a poor wretched sod Schultz, aren't you."

"Sure sure, O.K. but I'm telling you this is a fucking hit we're talking about."

The wall photographs of past Kings and Queens of London's theatre and of current famous Hollywood stars flashed in the bursts of afternoon sunlight. But through it all, his extremely eccentric Lordship, who upon occasion wore his shirts inside out or even brushed his teeth with the back of his toothbrush, merely seemed to wait for Schultz's anxiety to explode.

"Ah Schultz, if you did but realise it, I do at times expect to find you left in scattered pieces all over the floor."

"Sure. But I get the fucking show on the road every time."

"Ah Schultz, but there are other times, that you can be found to be such a charmer."

"Come on, holy shit your Lordship don't you want to become fucking rich."

Although his Lordship did not hugely enjoy making bad business judgements he would, when he found people at their most abject and in their most miserable moments, back them when no one else would. Taking it all in good grace when later the time came to heartily and most financially regret. But such instances he regarded as adding spice to life.

"Now Schultz, something that intrigues me. Where did you unearth your list of investors. In this morning's post alone came four returned letters marked deceased. I think that might indicate that your list is not quite up to date. Or else you obtained it from some funeral furnisher."

And on this particular day and in this last hour of rapidly hung up telephones, Schultz's every other investing prospect had opted out and the afternoon was ending in real deep horror for this embattled impresario. Yet not once did Schultz offer to increase his Lordship's share of the profits on his sixteen thousand pounds. Which was lucky. As this made his Lordship cautiously conclude that there might be some real possibilities in the deal after all.

"Ah Schultz indeed, perhaps you do have some actual acumen in you."

"Boy thanks a lot."

"Don't thank me. I think you should thank that uncle of yours the diamond merchant."

"Jesus Uncle Werb. Don't remind me. Sometimes I think I should have listened to him. I wish the fuck I had some of the money that bastard has. He'd say, now Sigmund, before your very eyes. That. That is two million dollars worth of diamonds."

"Of course Schultz, didn't he want you to apprentice. To that more than likely profitable trade."

"Holy shit. I didn't want to go haggling around in those black hatted and coated little groups with those yiddish guys for the rest of my fucking life. And hey your Lordship, meanwhile would you mind if I borrowed a cigarette."

"My god Schultz you've got your nerve to ask me for a cigarette at a time like this. And you must not address me as your Lordship unless you merely intend being amusing since it is the style used by those assuming an employee status."

Regarding cigarettes, these same words were used by his Lordship on his first meeting with Schultz and persisted throughout their relationship. As Schultz had given up smoking only during such times as he was not in his Lordship's presence. But whenever his Lordship lit up, Schultz would invariably request a white tube of tobacco to light up as well.

"For god's sake Schultz why don't you buy your own cigarettes."

"Well I don't smoke."

"Well you smoke whenever you see me."

"Well the rest of the time I don't."

"Well I do sometimes wish you would Schultz so you'd have your own cigarettes. And although I myself indulge this insanitary and unhealthy habit I dislike encouraging it in others."

"Now come on, if you won't come in for sixteen thou the least you can do is give me those addresses and phone numbers of these rich aristocrat friends you know all over the place."

"I assure you Schultz that the words rich and aristocrat which were once so inseparable are no longer and it is more than likely you'll find that either word rarely these days becomes the adjective of the other in describing any of my acquaintances."

Their strange compatibility seemed to proceed on these lines. First his Lordship's absolute refusal then a slight weakening and finally after nonstop afternoon's harassment his Lordship's acquiescence. Except that his Lordship always firmly reneged in the matter of Schultz being allowed access to his Lordship's affluent influential friends.

"Come on for christ's sake, how can that hurt you if I meet these other aristocrats you know. Well what about your sisters or

their husbands then. I meant christ, they're family. They'd understand."

"Good god Schultz do you think I would for one second release
you uncollared upon innocent people. To rip and tear at them the
way you do me. Sometimes Schultz you are exactly like a stage
show."

"What do you mean, stage show. What stage show."

"One which ought to be closed."

Above all his Lordship was most relieved that Schultz had not
managed to impress his two younger and stunningly beautiful sisters Lady Audrey and Emeline who from time to time when up to
London shopping, left packages and messages at the offices of
Sperm Productions. And who were contentedly married to gentlemen in the Foreign Office, and Royal Navy respectively.

"Jesus your Lordship I got real starring parts to cast your sisters
in."

"Schultz. I shall cast you. Out the window. If you're not careful."

The many times now that his Lordship sat or stood observing
Schultz, a mild amusement overcame him. For Schultz, upon each
occasion of meeting these two wondrous ladies, slapped himself
repeatedly on the forehead exclaiming.

"Holy shit. Jesus if I only knew you had such sisters I could
have married one of them."

"And thank god for them Schultz that you didn't."

"But Jesus they're so fucking beautiful and so fucking rich."

"And you Schultz in your fucking ridiculous excitement are like
a fucking roaring bullock. With your balls cut off."

But it was upon an afternoon when Binky had the same morning departed in his grey topper, striped trousers and cutaway coat
to take part in a spot of racing at Ascot, that his Lordship had really come to grips with Schultz. A pair of pigeons had nested
together under a water tank out on a back rooftop terrace. And
his Lordship who had been out late lunching with the board of
directors of one of London's larger banks always liked to return to

see if any of the eggs had hatched. And he now appeared at four o'clock out of the lift and cheerfully greeted by the secretaries, came along the hall and took his turning left and was about to turn his usual immediate right when he heard Schultz in the chairman's office talking in a highly British accent.

"That's correct, this is Lord Nectarine. Speaking. Yes, Lord Nectarine of Walham Green."

His Lordship with his movements now speeded up more than somewhat, bounding into the room. With Schultz standing behind the chairman's desk on the telephone. In three large strides his Lordship was across the carpet. And in a lightning grab with his knuckles turning white hot his Lordship had hold of the phone.

"How dare you Schultz. Give me that. What do you think you're doing."

Schultz, inadvisedly attempting further polite remarks into the black instrument, hung on. To suddenly find himself lifted bodily from the floor and before he knew it, with feet aloft, he had already completed one and a half orbits of the room.

"For fucks sake. Don't kill me."

"I'll kill you Schultz."

Schultz luckily on the next circuit, before flying through a window, crashed into the chaise longue. Separating the upright backrest from the lengthier reclining part of this colorful piece of furniture. And he was, with eyes focusing to see straight, now lying on the floor, still holding the phone trailing its broken wire. And crowned with a shattered picture of a female Hollywood star propped on his head.

"I'm only using your title for fucks sake."

"You have no right to do so."

"What is it, going to fucking well hurt you for christ's sake. Look what you've done, broke the furniture and ripped out the telephone. And I got to fucking call New York."

"My dear Schultz let me assure you, if ever you do that again, you'll be calling the fucking undertakers."

And be
Unable
In your
Rigor mortis
To pay
The bill

2

IT was Schultz's crass indifference to the obvious slight that so intrigued his Lordship. Not only how he seemed to arise sprightly from insult and injury but especially the nervy way Schultz would come up on the rehearsal stage to the elbow of a leading actor or actress and attempt to look over their shoulders as they read their personal fan mail.

"Schultz you really do at times behave in the most overly familiar manner."

"Holy shit what are you talking about."

"I'm talking about your sometimes discomforting proximity Schultz."

"What do you mean proximity. What do you want me to do. Stand outside the door. I got to know what the fucking public thinks of the fucking show."

"Ah Schultz you do so easily get hot under the collar."

In his continued association with both his Lordship and Binky in the regrettably named Sperm Productions Schultz was, after much guff and rubbish, as his Lordship was fond of referring t company general meetings, finally made a company director. His Lordship and Binky owning equally between them nine hundred and ninety shares and Schultz the remaining ten.

"Holy shit, ten shares. You guys are squeezing me out already before I've even got in."

"But of course, Schultz, with your three flops surely you don't expect to be invited to be chairman of the board."

"Jesus, you generous guys."

Although his Lordship and Binky were pleased that Schultz had acquired a patina of British upper class habits to practise in the acceptable places, they did rather enjoy when Schultz got overexcited and lapsed back into his hysterical American mannerisms. Which inevitably happened when Schultz, ever eager to gather his show's investment together, would confront his Lordship and Binky, their feet up and saucy magazines open as they late afternoon contentedly perused the latest in filthy illustrated literature.

"Don't you think your Grace that the position this extremely black chap has taken up upon this extremely white lady affords him little opportunity to enjoy the position the other extremely white lady has taken up upon him."

And one particularly peaceful afternoon during a stretch of no phone calls, Binky had on his desk his usual copy of a theatrical photographic reference book featuring actresses and children, a gold ruler weighting open a page displaying juvenile and younger juvenile women. And Binky, holding his head slightly tilted back turned to announce to his gathered fellow directors.

"Now in this Sarah. We have here a red head. Five foot six and a half inches. The way the light is thrown across the bosoms makes for a young lady I do believe our provincial audiences might quite fancy. A most remarkable cleavage. She'd do for replacing Suzie in It's A Long Way To Piccadilly. Obviously the daughter of a parson. Just gave her agent a little call earlier. The good chap just this second rushed over more particulars by hand. Either straight or musical. And ah. Her abilities seem rather extensive. Recently played Putsie at the Palace Theatre, Western Super Mare. How nice. And my word. Schultz."

"Yeah."

"She played Margo in your ill fated and Sperm Productions' ill advised provincial tour of The Best Bloody End's Up."

"Hey Jesus what are you reminding me for."

"It's her efficient agent Schultz, reminding us of her previous martyrdom under our joint banners."

"Christ she couldn't dance to save her arse. But Jesus what a fucking arse."

"Ah Schultz. Then we absolutely must think up something new and naughty to audition her for. One always searches for perfection in the theatre. And therefore it demands that the likes of this young lady must be explored fully. Do you remember the creature, Basil."

"Bottoms do make their impression on me Binky but I don't recall this particular lady's."

"Pity. She'd do for this rather promising recent script here. I mean she does character, tragedy, comedy or farce. Even dialects. Yiddish, Cockney, Lancashire. Even American. What about that Schultz."

"All these god damn girls put down a string of god damn things they can do as long as your arm whether they can do them or not."

"O dear, Schultz. I suppose you're right. That's the thing I hate most about show business. You really do feel sometimes that these girls care only about furthering their careers. And will grossly misrepresent themselves to gullible producers and prostitute their talent in anything just to do so. While we who love the theatre with all our hearts are put upon to suffer such subterfuge."

"Holy shit you fucking guys, come on, look what you're doing, fucking nothing, be serious for a change, let's get the show on the road."

"Schultz. Dear Schultz. What show. What road. And must you refer to us, and especially his Amazing Grace, as you fucking guys."

"Well what else are you, looking at porno magazines when there's work to do."

18

Binky reaching out to stretch and adjust his leg into a new position where it was cradled on a leather cushion in the crescent comfort of a mahogany gout stool. His voice, as it did when taking folk slightly to task, became even softer and kinder than usual.

"Dear Schultz, you are amazing aren't you. Here I am chairman of this old and established theatrical management, beset by stage carpenters, librettists, wig makers, agents, composers, scene shifters, actresses' husbands, theatre owners, guitar players, lawyers, playwrights, contortionists, posture artists and ponces, not to mention the continual stream of hoaxers and conmen, and here I sit, with an accredited reference book of actresses I have here open before me. Utterly sincere in my unending effort to cherish and promote the very highest standards in dramatic entertainment on the legitimate stage. Indeed to put it more briefly. Can't you see I'm casting."

"Of course I can see. But Jesus, every time I look at you fucking guys I'm thinking of the fucking seconds ticking away."

"Schultz, your obtuse devotion to duty is commendable. But dear me, I do think you rather are at times contemptuous of your fellow colleagues and I'm sure you must realise that such terminology as you fucking guys is most unbefitting his Royal Grace."

"Shit, you two were born with silver spoons in your mouths. I had to deliver fucking newspapers."

"But Schultz both his Royal Grace and I are aware that you are the owner of silk shirts."

"Every other stitch of clothing I'm wearing including the shoes, is from the men's chorus line of The Best Bloody End's Up. And what the fuck are silk shirts compared to your silver spoons from babyhood in big god damn castles. I never had chauffeurs, nannies, cooks, god damn grooms. And the way you sit around here doing nothing while I do all the work."

"Ah Schultz, dear Schultz. I think we must pretend that you're just temporarily unable to be calm because of your hemorrhoids. But we would love to hear more of your difficult deprived background. You simply must tell us more. You must. We have so very little to go on."

19

Schultz's immigrant parents had in the clothing business racked up considerable profits in their bargain basement Ladies' Lingerie and Accessories store, first in Woonsocket and later in two other New England towns. While Schultz as a child prodigy with the violin had grown accustomed to being treated as a king by his family and near relations and as that sissy prick by the rest of the kids on his block. But having forsaken the violin and beaten the piss out of the astonished neighborhood bully, Schultz through a magazine advert applied to a school of dramatic art.

"If they hadn't fucking well accepted me I'd be up to my neck right now merchandising ladies' underwear."

But a semester or two of this preparation for the acting stage so terrified Schultz's parents that he might become a raging homosexual that they finally shipped him off to one of the better East Coast campuses to come into contact with brahmin gung ho ivy league type chaps while attending college. And a lacrosse and squash playing Schultz became at least superficially capable of waltzing and drawling in the best prep school manner when he cared to. Which to his credit was seldom.

"But Schultz you do at times quite surprisingly exhibit characteristics one usually only associates with the more refined of the American educated classes."

"Bullshit."

"Indeed I do believe his Royal Grace happened upon you in the middle of the most authentic la de da accent. Is that not true your Royal Esteem."

"And hey for christ's sake your Lordship you ruined the most important phone call of my life."

His Lordship, as he so often was at this time of day, was seated on the chaise longue, leaning forward over a bowl full of gull's eggs, peeling these one by one and anointing each faintly blue spherical whiteness with the tiniest sprinkle of celery salt. And it was not often that he would pause between bites of this sacred seasonal delicacy to raise his voice as he did now to Schultz.

"Schultz you won't have a life if you ever do that ever again."

"Just once I was doing it. An isolated incident."

"Schultz your behaviour is, if I may say so, absolutely saturated with these isolated incidents."

While Binky rather enjoyed recognising Schultz's more gracious tendencies, he also loved embellishing Schultz's background with remarks to the effect that Schultz's folk were in textiles in a very big tycoonish way on the American East Coast.

"Of course Schultz we do in fact know that all the fine silk shirts you wear are afforded because you are the scion of a great textile dynasty with massive sprawling factories throbbing out household linens sold the world over. And we are only left to wonder why you don't heavily invest in your own sure fire hit shows. Especially this, your latest, and I am sure your most promising. Even the title, Too Too Naughty And Not One Bit Nice, reverberates with the promise of massive gross box office returns."

"And you can fucking well bet on that too. I'm going to sock the cunts right out of their fucking seats."

"Did you hear that your Royal Grace. Are we to assume from these vulgar but fighting words here uttered before us by Schultz that he at last has a hit. And take out our cheque books. In spite of the fact that we know he could finance the show himself."

It had been to this rumour of Schultz's massive riches, spread by Binky in show business circles, that Schultz owed his early marriage. His future wife having first got wind of him while working under the title of musical co-ordinator in the employ of a prominent showbizz personality who enjoyed to call at Sperm Productions and sit about baring his innermost feelings.

"Is that bad that I don't want to hurt people. Tell me if that's bad. That I should hold the human race in high regard."

While he was rather unaristocratically referred to as Big Al Duke, the celebrities' celebrity, Big Al was also an outstanding jazz trombonist and composer who occasionally gave recitals on the concert stage. And he also took up and generously contributed to a bevy of charitable causes. Nor was he ever known to refuse help to those eager to step up the slippery ladders of showbizz into the big time.

"Go ahead just ask. What can I do for you."

21

And Schultz, who seemed ripe for just such promotion, always at least pretended to appreciate this older man's sincere counsel, help and heartfelt advice. Which Big Al dispensed freely, especially following attending rehearsals. And which advice, due to Al's deep artistic convictions, invariably possessed one unerring characteristic. It was always wrong.

"Now Sigmund, I'm telling you the show needs less hoofing and more heart. It needs truth. Fine to have love lyrics but the secret of life needs to throb in every dance step. People these days want the truth along with their entertainment."

Big Al, who in juggling his many musical projects was a busy man. He especially had a large turnover of staff with whom he nevertheless frequently made good friends. Which included many of the young female temporary shorthand typists penetrating his portals. In each case fatherly making sure that they did not take the lecherous plunge into the pool of lust swum in by showbizz folk without holding Al's hand. But Big Al when his love life was under particular pressure did make exceptions for the rare girl of unresistible beauty. And in such cases would allow her to stretch her morals in reach of a more permanent place in the glamourised world of showbizz.

"Honey, a girl like you should have the world at your feet. Please, let me put it there for you."

Most listened avidly to Big Al, and invariably, in order to get right away started screwing their way to the top, were eager to be promptly propositioned. Which Big Al did with his carefully chosen four standard words which could easily upon acceptance be further embellished with, from behind, in front, by the mouth, ear throat or between the tonsils.

"May I enter you."

Although pushing unflatteringly beyond middle age, Big Al was in fact with his practised musical lips, his broad shoulders, his trim athletic figure and gruff voice, a charmer. And he took rejection good naturedly when Schultz's future wife, a stunning dark long haired beauty blushingly would not let Big Al, the celebrities' celebrity, enter her neither by ear nose throat rear or front.

"Look I'm too old for you. Right. O.K. Right. Then I know just the right sort of guy for you honey. And I really know, baby, that you're just going to love this guy. So you don't mind if he's wealthy do you. He's also a real hard hitting go getting young impresario making it right up the ladder to the top of his profession. He's going to be the guy wearing the laurel leaf honey.

"You mean laurel wreath."

"Yeah honey, I mean laurel wreath."

On the spot Big Al picked up his telephone. As Schultz's future wife's ears really perked up at the further mention of this suede chukka booted debonair theatre producer, scion of one of the most momentously rich textile families in the United States, who was, according to Big Al, ensconced momentarily lonely and footloose rambling around his little old town house mansion. Which happened to be nicely situated right smack bang just around one of the best corners of ambassadorially elegant Belgrave Square and was described by the estate agents leasing it, as a superb sumptuously fitted period house in immaculate order. And on his Lordship's initial visit, Schultz stood waiting ready for a stream of superlatives.

"You know Schultz after seeing this extremely pretentious residence of yours located in this rather self conscious area, I think you are an even bigger imposter than ever."

His Lordship having just handed Schultz a cigarette was standing at the foot of the main stairs in the imposing entrance hall, off which there was a fourteenth century panelled drawing room, dining room and library. The house, which stood elevated three floors over a basement, was full of mellow hued antiques, crystal chandeliers and for the previous three months had been pervaded by an awful stench.

"It's no big deal, I got it on a short lease for christ's sake. An underground river was flooding the house's foundations with sewerage. And now the fuckers are trying to raise the rent because the County Council found the broken pipe. These are the first few fragrant days I've had."

"And ah, what have you got back there Schultz, exiting down into the basement."

His Lordship's eye had caught amused and appreciative sight of a honey blond beauty who was slipping quietly out of the library and was now scurrying from the hall down the servants' stairs.

"That isn't anybody. Come on. I'll show you around."

"By god Schultz who was that. It looked to me like a very nice little bit of all right. You're a crafty one aren't you Schultz."

His Lordship was very quickly taking a deeper interest in the dispositions of Schultz's household. The bit of all right he had enquired after was an amply curvaceous Dutch au pair girl who having deserted her employers, had the past two weeks been cooking cleaning and submitting her body to Schultz's not inconsiderable passions. But she had just that previous evening been given the message to vacate. And was now spending most of her time in tears. And the previous night had been locked down the basement.

"Now Schultz, what are you up to. Clearly that young lady did not appear to be at all happy."

"Holy shit don't remind me."

Schultz had met the poor creature in the big modern art gallery on the Thames embankment. Having rushed there in a taxi one Sunday afternoon upon the suggestion of a playwright whose script Schultz was considering. This helpful gentleman eagerly maintaining it was where one could with the snap of a finger pick up the best fluff and crumpet on the hoof in all of London.

"I hope to christ you're not kidding me. I'm really hard up."

And on that particular sabbath an insanely horny Schultz ran leaping up the massive stone front steps three at a time to stride in the entrance beneath the enormous pillars and sweep through room after room ignoring these great modern masterpieces and rapidly sizing up the prospects of any unaccompanied innocent female art lover. All of whom recoiled in horror as he made his blatant shoulder tapping overtures.

"How dare you ask me if I should like to come outside for a walk. Certainly not."

And one refined marvellously legged, tweed suited lady, as she rapidly removed herself out of Schultz's accosting distance, made motions to call for protection of the curator. Who luckily for Schultz was absent, as indeed together with his wide artistic knowledge, this elegant gentleman also happened to be not unhandy with his fists.

"Jesus madam, there's nothing to get upset about. I really thought you were someone else."

It was not till Schultz was desolately leaving at closing time, having thoroughly terrorized half the gallery, that his eyes latched on to a blond slenderly buxom sandaled girl standing alone across the street in the pink afternoon sunshine with her back leaning against the flood wall along the Thames. Through screeching brakes and swerving tyres, Schultz dashed over the road.

"Pardon me baby, are you waiting for anybody."

Some of Schultz's brash approach to women could be attributed to his later teenage life in Brooklyn, where temporarily he lived with his Uncle Werb. When girl members of street gangs seemed to prefer being swept off their feet with a sudden tug on the blouse. Plus too, the occasional implacable rebuff Schultz received from the odd lady professionally close at hand. One of which was the gaily attractive Rebecca, Sperm Productions' most comely secretary, whom Schultz in the nearby presence of his Lordship had with a blatant hallway overture once invited to Fortnum's for tea.

"Schultz no one could ever accuse you of being overly romantic in your approach."

Such was his Lordship's opinion having on this occasion just witnessed Schultz's stopping Rebecca in her tracks and sidestepping to block her way as she attempted to sidestep around him. But Schultz promptly replied with his eminently practical excuse.

"I'm in a god damn hurry and if there was time to waste with beautiful endearing words I'd waste it."

And in this case of the young lady standing so marvellously slender legged in the sunshine across from this famed gallery of art, Schultz wasted not a second. Although she could barely manage to speak English, and Schultz's Dutch was meagre, they did by instant sign language and constant toothy smiles talk long enough for Schultz to have her packed into a taxi and back in bed in Belgravia in no time. The only difficulty being the girl's considerable hesitation in the obvious elegance of Schultz's life, to remove her dress and reveal the sorry state of her tattered underwear. And following a long hard night of lust, Schultz caught sight of her dressing in the morning.

"Hey holy shit honey here's a few quid, go out and buy yourself something decent."

Somehow blue eyed Greta understood these words better than she did Schultz's sign language. She also brought back dusters and a washing up mop. Not of course remotely realising that Schultz got really nervous not to say hysterical at the least signs of domesticity. However, the girl's jumping to action each morning at Schultz's first eye opening and then laying an appetizingly laden breakfast tray and newspaper in front of him, made him delay issuing walking papers. But when she sat contentedly darning holes in his socks until three a.m. one morning, Schultz lost control.

"Hey what the fuck are you doing, darning my socks, and always cleaning and dusting. Why don't you go out to the movies once in a while."

It was at this crucial point and on a sombre London Sunday afternoon with Schultz still in his pyjamas while enjoyably perusing a vicar and choirboy scandal in a Sunday newspaper, that a fatal never to be forgotten moment came. At precisely the toll of Big Ben booming four o'clock. Reverberating out westerly across the quiet empty streets of Westminster. Over the Royal residence of the Sovereign. And beyond the roof tops of the once great old mansions of England's once great rich. And right to the white painted elevation of Schultz's town house in Belgravia. This venerable bell knelled. As Schultz bounded down the stairs to the ringing telephone.

"Hey that you Sigmund. It's me Al."

"Hi Big Al. What's new."

"Sigmund. Let me tell you."

"Sure."

"Sigmund she's standing here. Right next to me. She is so beautiful it hurts. I've tried everything, haven't I honey. To enter you. And Sigmund she's turned me down flat. Now I told her. O.K. so you don't want to fool around with these old guys. I'm thirty four minus my four years I got for good behaviour. But still I'm too ancient. So I got a nice young guy for you. Twenty one. Right. You listening Sigmund."

"I'm pushing thirty and feel like I'm pushing forty but I'm listening Al."

"She's gorgeous. Really gorgeous. So I'm sending her over. If I was just ten years younger I wouldn't do it. I'd keep fighting. Now you treat her right. She's a good girl. And she's a real lady."

"Hey Al for christ's sake wait a minute. Thanks a lot but I got a surplus supply already here right down in the basement."

"Sigmund. Have I ever lied to you."

"No."

"Well I'm going to repeat for you just once more. She is the most lovely creature who has ever put foot over my threshold. So don't make me say it again."

"Send her over Al, for christ's sake, but not till Wednesday."

"It's got to be right now Sigmund."

"Now, Jesus, what's the hurry."

"The hurry is her gorgeous beauty. Before someone else discovers it. So let me ask her first. Hey honey you want to go over right away. She's thinking about it Sigmund."

"Well tell her to fucks sake make up her mind. I already got a job trying to kick this au pair out and after what I've been going through, my prick's not exactly knocking the plaster out of the wall."

"She says O.K. Sigmund. And I'm putting her straight in a taxi. Now you treat her right. Remember she still works for me. You got that."

"Got it Al."

Locking the Dutch au pair in the basement with a whole new batch of holey socks, Schultz tore off his dressing gown as he rushed up three steps at a time to his bathroom to shave, shower and dress. When the taxi let the promised gorgeous creature out, Schultz was at his front bedroom window watching the jet black Ambassador across the street board his black chauffeured limousine in his best striped bow tie. And Schultz could see nothing of her under her wide brimmed deep purple head gear.

"Jesus christ almighty she's dressed like she's going to a funeral."

Checking to see his fly was closed, Schultz rushed down two steps at a time to let this female person smilingly in. She was not exactly what Schultz had expected. Dressed as she was in shiny black high heels, a black suit, frills on her purple blouse front and her hat big enough for Ascot. But with her face framed with black gleaming wavy hair to her shoulders and the most amazing large green almond eyes set in the softest creamiest skin, she was as Big Al had said, really gorgeous.

"I'm Sigmund Schultz, come on in."

"I'm Pricilla and I've heard so much about you."

Schultz sat her on the edge of the just barely discernibly imitation reproduction Louis the Fifteenth gilt wood chair in his panelled drawing room. Her nice round knees held together carefully under her skirt and her long pleasant curvaceous legs leaning and overlapping to the side.

"This is a very nice place you have here, Mr. Schultz."

"Well it's just a kind of temporary convenience to rattle around in."

"I think it's very very nice."

"Let me get you something to drink."

"Well just something like a mineral water please."

"Sure."

Schultz who did not dare to unlock the door to the basement kitchen gave this increasingly gorgeous looking creature a sulfurously stale orange flavoured drink fetched out of the dining room cupboard. Which solitary bottle astonishingly had not been overlooked by the owners in their long itemised list of furnishings. Plus one dare not go down into the kitchen for fresher stuff where, while sewing her fingers to the bone, the poor Dutch au pair was also sobbing in despair.

"I especially Mr. Schultz, like your decor and objets d'art."

"Well it serves the purpose I guess."

"No I really like it. But isn't this awfully big, this house for just one person."

This was this gorgeous creature's remark as she looked up from her poisonous drink and at the mellow illuminated panelling. And Schultz catching his breath at the swellings as her jacket opened, took her on a brief tour of the library and dining room, where her appreciative attitude continued. Schultz reassured when she stopped to glance at four icons which were indeed genuine, having been bequeathed to Schultz by his mother's grandfather who had brought them to Woonsocket from Prague.

"I do honestly like the old atmosphere."

They went that evening to dine at the Savoy. Arriving sheltered from the rain, under this hotel's gleaming blue and green neon lighted entrance. Ushered across the soft carpeted spaciousness. To a table where, as the lights of tugboats passed on the river, Schultz discovered this stunning dish had an equally stunning and expensive appetite.

"Hey honey, don't worry a bit, I mean it, go right ahead. The caviar is delicious here. Have a third helping."

And upon returning to the environs of Belgrave Square he also discovered that the Dutch girl had a temper. Thumping and pounding as she now was the kitchen ceiling with a broom handle. Just as Schultz was pushing and pulling his new honey baby, as he temporarily called her, along the hallway and up the stairs towards the bedroom. As Big Ben chimed midnight.

"Come on honey baby. I'm not going to hurt you."

And it took till the booming bell tolled a solitary one a.m. for Schultz on the way to his bedroom, to reach the first landing. Where he stood, panting, with one hand inside her blouse and his other up her skirt.

"Honey baby, come on. You're gorgeous. You really are. Don't let's waste a night like this."

A last desperate frenzied assault upon her virtue was made by Schultz when he tripped her backwards and they both fell. She suddenly flailing and writhing, and not only kneeing Schultz in the testicles but kicking a pilaster upon which a white marble bust of some Roman Emperor perched.

"Holy shit watch out."

The bust teetering and falling and shattering to pieces on the landing. While Schultz unhanded this gorgeous creature who quickly leaped up. And instantly dove into domestic action. Sweeping up the white flaky plaster lumps into a dust tray as Schultz sat on the stairs.

"Jesus I thought the fucking thing was real marble."

> Christ you
> Can't trust
> These British
> Cunts

3

For the moment at least, the odd dilapidation in this commodious town house hardly mattered as Schultz's landlords were frolicking in distant Bermuda. And just as his Lordship's sharp eye had estimated, it slowly turned out that nearly everything in the house was ersatz of some sort.

"Nothing but sham and imitation Schultz, but of course, in their pretentious way, they do rather tart the premises up a bit."

But back that evening Schultz couldn't have cared less about the furnishings. As clearly from the feels he got of this gorgeous creature's upholstery, hers was the real McCoy. And entirely worthy of the further desperate and up to now hopeless pursuit of entry between those baby soft thighs.

"No no you mustn't."

"For christ's sake come on honey."

"No no you mustn't."

"For christ's sake honey, what's the matter."

"I'm not that sort of girl."

Between these nightly caviar gorging visits to London's most elegant restaurants and her usual midnight departure by Schultz's prepaid taxi home, the struggle continued. Each nightly skirmish providing Schultz with a minuscule advance over this enemy territory towards the bitterly defended objective. And as Schultz progressed inch by inch up between her stunningly slender silky smooth legs and was yet again finally halted within a finger length of victory, he was on the phone.

"Hey Jesus christ almighty Al, what the fuck did you send me over this time. Eight relentless days and I can't get to first base."

"Didn't you hear what I said. I told you already, the girl's a real lady. What the hell do you need to do that kind of thing to her for so soon."

"Hey Al, you serious."

"Of course I'm serious. That girl if she only knew it, could have anybody important in London she wants. Respect her beauty for christ's sake."

"Respect her beauty for christ's sake. I should have my wallet respected. In one fucking week she's already cost me three hundred and sixty two pounds."

"So you got it counted, charge it up to production expenses."

"This is no production, this is false imprisonment of my prick."

"Sigmund, don't ring me anymore if that's the kind of attitude. The girl's a lady. Treat her right. She's gorgeous. And if you can't be patient for what she's going to give you in the end then you don't deserve it."

"Holy shit Al, what the fuck's becoming of you."

"Nothing's becoming of me. It's what ought to be becoming of you into a gentleman. That's what ought to be becoming."

Schultz booked a table under the cherub painted ceiling of the Ritz, and ordered a predinner vintage Roederer to be ready for sipping in the Palm Court. And in black tie and in the largest limousine the car hire firm had in its stable, he ferried himself to Notting Hill Gate. Ringing her doorbell among a dozen others on the doorstep of this tall victorian building and lugging a cellophane wrapped corsage and bouquet of red roses up three bleak dark, dog smelly landings to a dour victorian overstuffed sitting room. Where Pricilla radiantly awaited in a black clinging evening gown which made Schultz gulp in his tracks.

"These are for you honey."

"O aren't you so sweet. You are really."

"I thought we might just amble over on our wheels and pop back a drink at the Savoy. The curtain is at eight. We are having supper later at the Ritz."

"O I must give you a little peck on the cheek."

The electrically operated windows, telephone and air conditioning instruments at her elbow did not, as Schultz thought they might, absolutely rivet her attention. But her eyes did open wide as she carefully stepped down the grimy wet steps and was conducted over the greasy evening pavement to the monstrous warmth of this perfumed interior flooding out the limousine's chauffeured opened door.

"Just take a pew anywhere you like honey."

Pricilla sat herself plonk center on the soft grey upholstery and regally proceeded to ignore London's passing evening pedestrians. But she did momentarily pay attention to look down her nose at the bus queues waiting. Who in turn stared at the longest Rolls-Royce in London. And Schultz suddenly had a rapier thrust like feeling that he was some kind of specially stunted footman stationed in the confines of this whirring limousine purring down the Bayswater Road in all its black majesty, transporting this radiant queen untouchable behind the gleaming glass.

At the Savoy she made an entrance. The doorman sweeping the way ahead through the doors. With Schultz nearly left behind on the pavement. At the theatre she was only mildly impressed as champagne was served in their private box with compliments of the stage manager who returned three times to ask was everything alright. And at the Ritz, following further champagne and the usual copious portions of Beluga plus crepe suzettes and the house's best brandy, Schultz sat with his cigar.

"I hope you enjoyed yourself a little honey, this evening."

"It's been very nice Sigmund."

And back in Belgravia, the jet black Ambassador astonishingly gave Schultz the hi sign and a broad, night illuminating smile as both of them appeared simultaneously out of their limousines and up their steps with their respective beauteous creatures clinging to their respective arms. Schultz delighting in this sudden camaraderie.

"Who's he."

"He's the Ambassador honey."

"And what's that."

This latter remark was expostulated by Pricilla a few seconds later in the hallway at the foot of the stairs up which Schultz was just about to begin his nightly coaxing of this gorgeous creature.

"I got a pet monkey down the cellar, that's all."

"Sounds like a woman crying."

"It's a female chimpanzee."

Her mouth did open wider to Schultz's kisses. And her lower legs parted wider for his hands. But whenever, that thing, as she called it, was rigidly pressing towards home, she struggled in resistance. Till half her gown was ripped and wrapped around her ankles and neck. And when this long careful evening was followed now with an heroic continuous battle till three a.m., Schultz finally gave up. Ushering the rose petal skinned future wife into a guest bedroom. And throwing her a towel, and as a poignant afterthought, a bible to read.

"Here honey, the good book, make yourself at home."

Schultz headed downstairs in dressing gown and his custom made slippers. Taking into the basement with him bedding and locking the door behind him. The grateful au pair spouting a stream of Dutch, sobbed with relief and clung and hugged Schultz as he shifted her up on a pillow softened kitchen table and rogered her in continuo glissando till dawn. As his Lordship later remarked to Binky when relating the story.

"I do not think that Schultz's behaviour was of the most chivalrous."

Schultz's future wife had been educated at various convent boarding schools in far off Canada and Argentina and she ob-

34

jected strenuously to Schultz's frequent foul language. She also refused to again stay overnight in Schultz's town house. For following Schultz's having downstairs done the au pair on the kitchen table, he at first light of dawn, came back up to the future wife in the guest room, dislodged her from bed and whipping off his dressing gown, gave naked chase of her with his restimulated perpendicular pointing in all directions all over the chamber. Before he ended up agonizingly stubbing and breaking two of his middle toes.

"Holy Jesus fucking christ."

"You're profaning again."

The Dutch au pair, despite or because of daily increased proddings still refused to shift out of the locked basement. But this did not stop Schultz's future wife from making the upstairs butler's pantry fully operational to provide Schultz and herself with the odd tasty snack. When now late afternoons, departed early from her job with Big Al, and finding herself temporarily safe from Schultz who limped and sported an open ended sandal on his right bandaged foot, Pricilla donned rubber gloves and dusted and polished all the upstairs rooms.

"Hey for christ's sake the place is clean already."

"But this needs doing every day Sigmund."

And invariably during these cleaning sessions and while Schultz was at Sperm Productions, at least one young lady would show up knocking on the door and ask for Schultz.

"I'm sorry Mr. Schultz is out but I'm Mrs. Schultz can I help you."

But when a black leather attired Germanic looking lady with a monstrous thatch of long straight blond hair to her shoulders stood on the doorstep, Schultz's future wife's face became deeply red when to her standard answer she got a gruff,

"Vass bullshit. Mrs. Schultz. Who are you, the maid. I vant Herr Schultz."

"He's not in."

"Don't vurry I vill be back."

Indeed before he returned that day, three more girls had come and knocked in a most familiar manner for Schultz whose photograph along with Binky's and his Lordship's had just appeared in the evening newspaper, announcing their coming season of productions. And that night Schultz's future wife stayed with him in his bedroom revealing all but where a flimsy bit of lingerie still snugly covered the vital objective. And a trembling Schultz in all his showbizz years had never seen a body quite like it.

"Jesus christ, honey, who built you."

"Do you only have to be interested in my body."

"Honey I'm open to suggestions. What else have you got."

"That's insulting that is."

Schultz stretched spreadeagled like an Aztec in sacrifice and staring up into the lace canopy of the phony fifteenth century bed, reminisced about his teenage sex life in Woonsocket while Pricilla pulled his prick twice, and painfully sat on his toe once. In the morning her large almond eyes narrowed and her voice became ominously lighthearted.

"Who are those girls."

"What girls."

"The girls who keep coming knocking on your door. One of them under her macintosh was in halter and shorts on a red bicycle."

"O those. They're just some stage struck kids wanting to get into show business. I get bothered by them all the time especially when my picture gets all over the newspapers."

"And who is this female monkey you keep in the locked basement."

"Look honey, come on, I got lots of troubles. Just forget what's in the basement will you."

Schultz's future wife now took the precaution of steaming open Schultz's late afternoon mail and throwing away those letters and notes signed Abigail, Helga, Shirley or Teenie Eeenie Bootsie Wootsie. She also, on the day she stopped working for Big Al, finally found the key to the basement. And just as his Lordship had come calling and Schultz had already departed to stroll to the office across St. James's Park, Schultz's future wife was shoving the terrorized and sobbing au pair possessionless out the basement door.

"Of course Binky I was aghast, I thought it was Schultz heaving this most charming young lady out. But instead of Schultz it was another even more attractive lady entirely, doing the shoving."

Ever solicitous of stricken damsels, his Lordship had, when his chauffeur deposited him at Sperm Productions, instructed that this little bit of honey blond all right, be ferried back to her original employers somewhere godforsakenly northeasterly of London where they resided between a crematorium and golf course. And two days later a policeman appeared requesting to see his Lordship to assist him in his further enquiries concerning an abduction. But respectfully retreating when he heard the noble Peer's explanation that the poor creature had been found wandering in tears on the street.

"Can you imagine Binky, my motor's licence number taken for having delivered Schultz's au pair back to where she belongs. Most unpleasant."

"Highly unpleasant, your Amazing Grace."

"Yes I agree, highly unpleasant."

"Ah but I think your Grace we must await an opportunity to straighten old Schultzy boy out, don't you."

Holding daily auditions for casting and hoping that penny by penny and pound by pound, he would gather his show's finances and production together, Schultz minus his dependable au pair, was finding his now semicrippled attempts to enter his future wife well nigh unbearable. Even though she became more practised at pulling and was at last now contemplating allowing that disgusting variation Schultz suggested, of entering her by the mouth.

"Let's go, let's go with it. This is a permissive society honey."

"It may be. But I'm not."

"Honey, look, don't worry, I'm convinced you're not. But could you look at it from my point of view for a second. I'm normal. I need outlet."

With the clock of Big Ben booming a desperate Saturday dawn following the umpteenth night of pulling but saying no to blowing or throwing, Schultz, despite his busted toes, jumped up seven feet high off the bed. Banging his head on the crosspiece of the four poster, but remaining conscious enough to shout.

"Jesus christ I'm not going to go through this anymore, get the fuck out. I mean if you take off a stocking or you let me suck a tit, it's like I ought to get down on my knees in thanksgiving like you were the Queen of fucking Sheba. You're driving me nuts. I have to get laid. Come on. Out. Get the fuck out. I've had enough."

Schultz standing by his bedroom door stark naked and fulsomely erected as he usually was, while the future wife sat up in bed like the Queen of Sheba attired in her frilly nightdress and fulsomely prim as she usually was.

"Do you really want to enter me that bad Sigmund."

"What the fuck do you mean do I want to enter you that bad. I need to screw. And I need to screw four times a goddam day. For christ's sake what the fuck do you think I've got you up here for."

"I'd prefer if you didn't use that language to me please."

"Well I'm horny and fucking well exasperated. It's bad for me to suffer this way."

"Couldn't you wait till we're married."

"Married. Jesus christ married."

"Yes married. That would only take a few minutes to arrange. And please don't continue to be profane."

"What are you kidding."

"No I am not kidding."

"You're serious. I mean do you know what marriage means."

"Yes I know what marriage means."

"It's a fucking lifetime contract for fucks sake, honey."

"Well why shouldn't it be. It's that way for everybody."

"It's not going to be that way for me. It makes me nervous. So when I get back I want you gone."

This conversation produced sulking in Schultz's future wife. And while she remained in bed, Schultz hysterically showered, shaved and dressed. To head out for solace and breakfast in that beige stone retreat of the Dorchester Hotel just a hop skip and a jump across Hyde Park. And with both feet in shoes again he attempted to leap down the stairs three at a time. Tripping at the bottom and howling in agony as he sprained an ankle and further maimed his half mended toes.

"Jesus fuck you fucking ducks."

The future wife in her purple flimsy bed apparel, was sitting upright against the pillows in bed, a fashion magazine open across her lap. She frowned with suitable alarm and sympathy as Schultz limped back into the room looking for his sandals. He bent to rummage among his footwear, and when his back was turned he caught sight of the future wife angled in the closet mirror. Her creamy exquisite face was grinning ear to ear.

> And way
> Down
> In Schultz's
> Soul
> It hooted
> Holy shit

4

As were all Schultz's afflictions, the ankle and toes were treated in Harley Street. By a theatrically fashionable doctor who took an easily amused view of the previous bed chamber injury. And came out from behind his massive antique desk.

"Ah now. And what do we have here this time Mr. Schultz."

"Doc you have a repeat of crippled feet."

"Well you're still upright. And although painful, it's not a major sprain. And one hardly breaks a toe, but you have certainly again rather bruised your phalanges a bit."

With Schultz once more hors de combat, his future wife was now saying that soon soon, the moment his toes were recovered, that miracle of miracles would happen and Schultz could enter her.

"Look honey, that better be as soon as you say because you've already wrecked my peace of mind."

The future wife meanwhile who was quite adequate at the stove, cooked up an international menu out of the noonday delivered assortment of goodies from Harrods' meat department and the London grocery emporium of Fortnum's, with both of whom Schultz had accounts.

"Sure honey you just pick up the phone and order what you want, no problem."

But Schultz, usually a late riser, noticing his mail was tampered with, now struggled up to get down stairs to collect it. While the future wife sat like the Queen of Sheba waiting for Schultz to bring her breakfast. And Schultz scalded his hand rushing back up with her tray in order to gather his personal papers together and with his letters, secrete them away locked in the desk in the library. And following another bedroom blow job interruptus finished by hand, Schultz found it but a momentary cure for his intensifying horniness.

"Hey honey, sorry but you got to vacate today, all afternoon."

"Why."

"I'm having an audition. The director's coming over. And a couple of the stars. And some other people. The stars get really on edge if they think laymen are hanging around."

And Schultz awaited the arrival of this hot little number just graduated from Drama School with her long brown hair down the back of her gymnastic bouncy body, whom he'd recently interviewed at Sperm Productions and was to now audition in the peace and quiet of his versatile town house.

"Honey, let me tell you straight off at once, you got a feel for it, maybe even real promise but it needs hard work, real hard work and plenty of polishing. Now just do that number once more."

Schultz, right in the middle of these words uttered to this healthy smiling young teenager in his panelled library and just as the latter was about to commence hoofing and singing, heard what he thought was the squeak of footsteps on the stairs. And following the rendition of the present number he was about to invite the diminutive teenage lady starlet to maybe show more of what she was made of in a more comfortable room upstairs.

"I'm sorry Mr. Schultz, really I am but I have to get to Swiss Cottage. I have a singing lesson there at five."

41

"Sure kid, that's fine. Fine. Some other time."

"But thank you very much. And I can cancel my singing lesson next week if you want."

"Sure, sure. Don't worry about it. We'll be in touch."

Schultz suddenly out his door, escorting the hot little number around the corner to Hyde Park Tube Station. And a few steps down the street, he looked up to see His Excellency the Ambassador at his frequent position at his French window, mysteriously pointing back across the street. And Schultz stopped and turned to face back at his house. To look up and see the future wife there framed between the parted lace curtains of the bedroom, glaring at him.

"Well you don't own me. Get the fuck out and leave me alone."

Schultz shouted this with his one free scalded shaking fist, his other being gently wrapped around a can of beer as they confronted a day later in the library. For as the incidents of girls calling at Schultz's town house continued together with phone calls and communications on slips of paper dropped in the letter box, the future wife was not only snooping but nagging.

"You simply can't have all these strange people working for you. Some of them hardly speak English."

"Honey they're part of my production team. Don't you understand. I've signed contracts. I have five seamstresses working day and night on costumes. And fucking rehearsals are due to start. Don't for christ's sake give me a hassle."

Schultz presenting this reasoned argument, was a moment later behind drawn drapes and the closed door of the library, treated to the future wife slowly removing her matching dark green cardigan and pulling her jumper up over her head. In spite of gritting his teeth and biting his tongue Schultz roared into erection as this tall dark haired lady stripped to the waist. And slowly so slowly heaving her hips, began a hula hula dance.

"O boy honey, Jesus."

Schultz sat with a beer hungrily watching this fantastic body swaying and cavorting, till he would get a hand job sitting back in the leather chair, a linen napkin carefully placed across his thighs. Just as she had done yesterday.

"Now I'll bet you feel better don't you Sigmund."

"I'm adequate honey. I'm adequate."

But there was no question as to her improving abilities in administering this fingertip touching satisfaction or to the astonishing and stunning beauty of her breasts, which still made Schultz gulp and swallow every time he watched them whitely lazily swinging before his eyes, but from which she presently slapped his reaching hand.

"What did you say."

"You heard me. And for the last time, I'm telling you. Get the fuck out and leave me alone. Who needs this kind of fucking frustration."

Despite the thick carpet, Pricilla made a considerable thump. Keeling over sideways and backwards, her knees buckling and somehow getting her to the floor in such a manner that she lay carefully outstretched, one arm across her breasts and the hem of her skirt chastely at her knees. Just as one would imagine a well bred girl might do when pretending to faint.

"Holy shit."

Schultz stood too stunned to move. Except to take a peek at the library shelves which shook with the thud and the chandelier which tinkled. Getting down on one knee, he gently prodded her.

"Hey baby, baby are you all right. Speak to me."

Schultz did what he had always seen medical people do. And lifted the lid of her closed eye. Which seemed to struggle reshut. But his first ungentlemanly thought was to fuck her as she lay which he reconsidered on the grounds that he might be charged with having then fucked her to death.

"Honey, hey I'm sorry for what I said. Hear me honey."

Schultz now held her extremely limp wrist. Feeling for her pulse whose beats seemed even calmer than his own. In a final attempt to revive her he whispered, prodded and took a good feel of her breasts, before finally goosing her. To then stand watching

43

and waiting for this still breathing body to show a sign of life.

"Holy christ, nagging and no ass and now I needed this. A dead body on my hands."

Schultz on his way to the phone found himself rubbing his fingers up and down on his jacket as if he were trying to erase the fingerprints that might now be traced to having killed her.

"Hey Al, it's me Sigmund."

"Hi ya Sigmund, what's doing, what's new."

"Jesus Al she's on the floor."

"Who's on the floor."

"Pricilla."

"You son of a bitch what did you do to her."

"Nothing for christ's sake Al. I mean maybe she's fainted or something."

"I'm asking you. What did you do to her. To make her faint."

"I didn't do nothing Al. For christ's sake, come on."

"Is she breathing. Does she move."

"I don't know. I think she's breathing."

"Well make sure, go find out. Go hold a mirror to her mouth."

"Is that what I should do."

"I'm telling you to. Go do it. And you son of a bitch I'll kill you if anything happens to that girl."

"O.K. Al, for christ's sake you don't have to have kittens and conniptions. I'm just asking what the fuck I should do."

"I just told you. Hold a mirror to her mouth."

"O.K. Hang on."

Schultz found a mirror rummaging through her handbag. And also found four opened letters addressed to him plus extra keys to every door in his house. The mirror when he held it to her mouth became steamed over. Schultz rushing back at the phone.

"Al."

"Yeah."

"The mirror got steam on it."

"She's breathing then."

"What should I do now. What the fuck do you think is the matter."

"She could have a stroke or a heart attack."

"Isn't she too young Al."

"Nobody is too young to die. Call an ambulance. And she better be alright or I'm putting you on my drop dead list."

"O.K. Al O.K. I'll call an ambulance and I'm hanging up."

Schultz took one more look in the library door at the prostrate figure and dialled nine, nine, nine. And a voice clicked in.

"Emergency, can I help you."

"Yes I need an ambulance. I don't know what happened. She just collapsed."

As Schultz sat in the hall staring across at a painting of red coated horse mounted figures and hounds in front of a stately mansion, he heard a groan come from the library. And rushed back in. The future wife's hand was flapping back and forth like a dead fish and then one eye opened.

"O my god, please, Sigmund, take me up to bed. Please."

"Take you to bed. Holy shit honey an ambulance is on the way to take you to the fucking hospital."

On a late morning once more that same week following further Schultz attempts at screaming at her to get the fuck out, ambulance men were seen running up the steps of Schultz's town house only to depart again with their empty stretcher. Each time leaving Schultz to struggle lugging her under the armpits up to bed. And on one occasion nearly killing himself with his unconscious armful falling backwards on the landing on top of him as he tried to head back downstairs again to answer the phone.

"Ah please, do excuse me, sir. Are you the gentleman across from us in number four."

"Yeah."

"Ah, I am extremely sorry to telephone you but I am making such enquiry on behalf of his Excellency the Ambassador to learn if you are all right in your house. As his Excellency sees the ambulance calling."

"O hey sure. I'm O.K. We're just having a little emergency treatment now and again. And tell his Excellency I really appreciate his call."

45

"Of course sir. And thank you sir for your kind information and may we wish you your continued good health. Goodbye sir."

The fourth time Schultz watched the future wife keel over, he left her fainted on the floor and calmly shaved, showered and dressed. Popping in every few minutes to see if she stirred before finally himself popping out the door under white clean clouds blown by a fresh westerly breeze. To walk briskly heading along Wilton Crescent. Passing these handsome grey stone cut houses and the quiet sombre church and then crossing the nose of Hyde Park. The little patches of green, the fish pond and fountain lying before the calm elegance of the Dorchester Hotel. Where the doorman touched his top hat.

"And good morning sir. Nice to see you."

Reading The Times, Schultz took a quiet pew in a far corner of the restaurant and sat back to a marvellously prolonged breakfast.

"Another kipper sir."

"Yeah sure I don't mind if I do."

But upon reaching Sperm Productions, and before he could open his mail in his windowless cubbyhole, his Lordship with suitable grave ceremony confronted him.

"Schultz, my god, where have you been."

"Having a peaceful breakfast for a change for christ's sake."

"Are you aware that a lady friend of yours was this morning hauled out of your house unconscious in an ambulance to hospital."

"Jesus, holy shit."

"It's well for you to say that Schultz but one does have the impression of your town house doors constantly being opened and a series of attractive women either being hurled on to the pavements or carried out by stretcher."

"Hey don't look at me as if you were always fucking innocent and I'm the guy who is always guilty. What hospital."

"Charing Cross and I suggest Schultz you go there immediately."

"Immediately. I can't. In ten minutes I got an urgent lunch appointment."

"Schultz you do really amaze me. Have you no compassion. You've just come from breakfast. And now you're taking lunch while a young lady at this very moment may be on the operating table. Her life hanging by a thread."

"My life is hanging on by a thread. If I don't get my finance. I got a property developer I've been waiting two fucking weeks to meet who's dying to have an investment fling at showbizz."

"Schultz, good god I think you are the most unchivalrous person I have ever met. We've already had an irate lady shouting various distressing words at us over the telephone. Schultz you simply must cancel your lunch."

"Holy shit, cancel, when this rich son of a bitch could be good for ten or twenty thousand."

"Schultz, I may have thought previously that you were a pettifogging creampuff. But now I'm absolutely convinced that you are also an unmitigated bounder."

"Shit can't you see I'm already on my fucking way to the hospital. Jesus christ what do you fucking guys demand of me. Any minute now, believe me, I'm going to become a fucking homosexual recluse."

"And Schultz, if you do, I fully expect to find unclothed and wretchedly abused small boys being flung out of your town house door every morning."

Schultz, just as fast as the wheels of a taxi might carry him found himself wandering along the creamy walled and desolate corridors of this hospital stinking of alcohol. The bells of an ambulance clanging and trolleys of supine human beings rolled hither and thither. Each step he took, hammering in visions of police tapping him on the shoulder. His stomach churning and his head growing faint, as he saw a body wrapped in sheets and soaked in blood wheeled past him into emergency.

"O my god I missed lunch to see this."

Schultz following the receptionist's directions up staircases and down corridors, was again wiping off his fingerprints on his jacket front, his heart thumping and a sweat collecting on his brow. Till he reached and nearly fell vomiting into Pricilla's room. Full of flowers. A young gentleman hairstylist arranging Pricilla's hair. Plus a monstrously fat lady in a black clinging dress shovelling up spoonfuls of pâté de foie gras with truffles into her thickly powdered jowls. And an open ceramic jar with a sturgeon emblazoned on the side at her elbow.

"Mother this is Mr. Sigmund Schultz."

"Well Mr. Schultz, it's about time I met you. After putting my daughter into hospital like this, and putting a strain on my weak heart. You better hope that she recovers all right. And I'll have you know that before my daughter met you she was escorted out to the very best places by the titled son of a Duke."

A further dazed Schultz went wiping his forehead all the way back down the hospital hall. Until running into a nurse pushing a tray of instruments. Reswallowing his kipper breakfast which had also included two fried tomatoes. Reeling along looking for the staircase landing and turning through a pair of swing doors. Stepping further along a hall and through another door and holding his hand up to shield his headaching eyes. Suddenly in a room confronting a battery of bright lights. Peopled with masked faces, the nearest of which were turning to look at him. As a raised voice was heard.

"He's not scrubbed up."

And a nurse touching Schultz on the elbow as he was turning around to retreat.

"Excuse me, are you doctor Romney."

"No, I'm just trying to find my way out of this hospital."

"Well you happen sir, to be in the operating theatre in the middle of an emergency caesarian section."

Schultz staring at the white coated figures. And then beyond between two suddenly parting doctors who revealed a mound of blood and guts heaving on an operating table. A strange soft music played as the world faded. Schultz keeling over backwards

into the arms of this group of medical students. All standing
ready with their stethoscopes.

<blockquote>
To listen
To this
Faint hearted
Schultz
Maybe breathing
His last
</blockquote>

5

OLLOWING his release from hospital that afternoon, Schultz took time out to have a sherry filled hour by himself in a small panelled bar down the hill from Charing Cross. And in the busy dingy thoroughfare of Villiers Street a little life perked back into him looking into the windows of a few dirty bookshops. All nausea nearly gone strolling now through the photographing tourists and the flocks of pigeons in Trafalgar Square.

"Jesus look at all these pigeons just happy fucking and pecking up the popcorn and enjoying life."

Schultz paced himself gently along Pall Mall, cutting a sharp right into the narrow shadowy alley of Crown Passage. And was at last recovering as he made his way up the little peaceful incline of Duke Street St. James's, past the window displays of antiques, books, shoes and paintings.

"Jesus if I had a couple of fucking hits running in the West End I could just walk in there and buy these joints right out and surround myself with beauty instead of anguish."

Five minutes to four, Schultz reaching the Jermyn Street entrance to Fortnum's. Crossing the soft crimson carpet under the radiantly sparkling chandeliers. To sit among these animated bejewelled ladies. Wait while one of these splendid light green aproned ministrating goddesses fetch a silkily soft chocolate stomach soothing slab of Sacher cake and a pot of smoky scented Earl Grey tea. Thank god there are places like this. Where I can fucking well sit suddenly in peace. Gather my wits back together again. Without having the god damn consequences of my prick always on my mind.

Early that evening shoving a weary body down between the cool sheets, Schultz took a nap in his empty town house. Waking again two hours later hungry and energetic to go dine in his favourite small Chinese restaurant in Soho. Topping off his sweet and sour pork with an hour's pleasant play at a Piccadilly pinball emporium. Winning fourteen games and breaking the house record for the machine.

"Ere ere mister, you must be some kind of expert getting a score like that."

Before returning to Belgravia, Schultz on the previous advice of Big Al, slipped into a theatre to take in the last act of a play with a young Debutant actress whom Al thought might hoof, act and sing her way to stardom. Schultz losing no time getting backstage to introduce himself to the blond curvaceous elegant creature.

"I like your act honey. You had some real nice moments out there. You're the best thing this show's got. If it had more like you, it wouldn't be closing. I'm going to send you a script in the morning."

Just as Big Ben boomed eleven over Belgravia, Schultz stepped out of a taxi. Reaching for his key to mount his steps, a loud rapping of a knocker made his recently calmed heart start beating ultra fast again. A monstrous shadow was blocking Schultz's whole doorway. A figure turning and looming above him. Big jowls quaking in the light of the street lamp on the face of Pricilla's mother.

"Don't you just think you can turn your back on us. Just walk out of the hospital like that. Don't you just think you can take that kind of attitude with me or my daughter. Just who do you think you are. You're nobody."

"Hey look Mrs. Prune, it's after eleven o'clock, you're going to wake the neighbors."

"I'll wake the neighbors alright, don't you worry. They'll hear how you put my daughter into hospital."

"I didn't put your daughter in hospital."

"Do you want to hear from my solicitor. You're going to hear from my solicitor. You left her laying on the floor. Half naked. And walked out of your house. My daughter saw you. That's what you did. To have your breakfast while my daughter was unconscious. And everybody in this street is going to hear what you did."

"Holy christ lady. Come on. What do you want money. I'll give you money."

"You'll give me money. Do you hear what he says. He says he'll give me money."

Schultz ducking and falling backwards as Pricilla's mother's furled umbrella whistled over his head. Holding on to the rung of a railing and squatting on his haunches as more swipes rained down across his back.

"Jesus christ lady, what are you doing."

"I'm teaching you a lesson not to turn your back on your betters that's what I'm doing, you cardboard romeo."

Schultz retreating down the steps, across the sidewalk and into the gutter. Followed by this avalanche of irate flesh disturbing the peace. And in spite of all the frontal assault something made him turn his back yet again and look up. To the third floor of the Ambassador's residence. Just above the drawing room. Where the curtains were parted. And the Ambassador stood. His black diplomatic face grinning ear to ear. Just as a haymaker sailed home blotting out half the world seen by Schultz's eyes.

Arriving next noonday at the offices of Sperm Productions Schultz found his Lordship and Binky just finishing their own recent cups of coffee brewed by the comely ever attentive Rebecca in the little office pantry. These two fellow directors animatedly making their usual midday noises to the effect that they were seriously engaged corporate executives actively running their fast burgeoning show business empire and were contemplating momentous deals to be sealed at the end of lunch that day.

"Ah Rebecca fetch in that contract with that awful man who owns that awfully over priced theatre. You know the one I mean."

Binky liked to pretend that his gallant banter with the winsome Rebecca, was only to make her feel at home and part of their well oiled show business team. And before the novelty had worn off, it had often been the highlight of their business day, to hold prolonged conferences on office efficiency with secretaries.

"Ah yes, a good point that, a ceramic roller to wet stamps. Prevent the health risks of licking."

Or in earlier days when bored with these consultations an ad would be placed in a suitably serious but somewhat arty periodical. And new secretarial candidates would arrive. With his Lordship sitting on the crimson love seat just removed fresh out of his personal palace, as Binky enthroned himself behind the broad expanse of the fine George the Third desk not so freshly lugged out of one of his Lordship's castles.

"Now tell me, Miss ah, I didn't quite catch the pronunciation of your name."

"Pots."

"Ah of course Pots, that's P for peter, O for onanism, T for titty and S for slander."

"Well, I suppose you could spell it that way but in that case it might be better to simply call me Rebecca."

"Ah, but of course, how nice, Rebecca. Now Rebecca tell me this may seem to you perfectly irrelevant but did you play hockey at school."

Some of the interviewed girls were then heard running out the corridor, one screaming, another crying and another using foul obscene unladylike language. Of course this was just a little trick his Lordship and Binky were fond of playing on Schultz.

"Now Miss Pots remember that you're to be secretary to theatri-

53

cal producers and you might be called upon without notice in an emergency to stand in for an indisposed understudy to an indisposed star. So we would appreciate if you could, in order to prove your acting potential, demonstrate to the best of your ability an adequately angry exit as if you had just been grossly insulted. We would like you to do this while passing our executive producer's door."

Rebecca had played her part extremely well on the occasion. Leaving Schultz stunned in his cubbyhole scratching his black curly locks. And she had also proved rather something that the other girls weren't, a distinct all rounder when she set about one entire afternoon cleaning his Lordship's trousers of chewing gum where he had sat stickily in same.

And when Schultz in those days had come out of his own tiny cubbyhole office, his Lordship and Binky lounging in their splendour would be waiting.

"Hey what are you guys doing. I mean that was four fucking girls rushing past my doorway like they'd been really insulted or something."

In total and utter aristocratic astonishment his Lordship and Binky would look back and forth at each other and then at Schultz. And then again back at each other and back at Schultz.

"Well look holy shit isn't that right. I mean your Lordship what the fuck's going on. I mean I'm sitting in there wondering whether to go to the rescue or not."

And now on this inclement noonday, Schultz back from his trauma in the hospital and his fisticuffs and umbrella battering on his front steps, had just entered the chairman's office with his nose buried in the just published copy of a showbizz periodical. And a pair of sunglasses over his black eye.

"Ah Schultz, just in time. His Royal Highness and I have just been discussing your production Too Too Naughty And Not One Bit Nice. Isn't that true Rebecca."

"Yes sir."

"Both his Royal Grace and I Schultz have decided to toy with a

54

rather momentous decision. Now wait for it Schultz, don't yet jump up on our backs screaming yippee hi o, just sit down there on our recently repaired chaise longue. That's better. Ah but first do please let me enquire. How is your hospitalized lady friend."

"Boy I'm telling you. I'm not kidding. I'm going to go queer."

"How sensible of you Schultz. But I say. Dear me. Is that a black eye there behind your sunglasses. What a beauty, isn't it your Royal Grace."

"I ran into a door. So don't get excited."

"Ah, But tell us. Your lady friend, how is she."

"She was with her mother and a hairdresser eating god damn caviar and foie gras in a private room I'm paying for and drinking champagne she had sent over from Fortnum's to be put on my fucking bill, that's what she was doing."

"O we're glad to hear your lady friend's well, Schultz. And Rebecca do please excuse our fellow director's sometimes forceful language."

"She's well, don't worry."

"Ah his Royal Grace and I are genuinely relieved to hear that. You know we were rather concerned for you Schultz, as a most irate lady was on to us on the phone. We really did fear she would strike you with her umbrella or something. Ah but let us get back to business. And forget these black eyes and that scratch or two on your cheek Schultz. Now Schultz the fact of the matter is that we are examining the possibility of taking a more than substantial piece of your little show."

"This is a joke."

"No joke Schultz. On the contrary it's absolute gospel. Of course we expect a few preferential terms. But to those, I'm sure you won't object. Rebecca has them down in her splendid shorthand. Don't you, my dear."

"Yes sir."

"I really don't know what we'd do without you Rebecca."

"Ah you dirty cunts. You've heard it haven't you."

55

"Heard what Schultz. And please. Do, in front of Miss Pots, remember your language."

"That I might have somebody who not only has a beautiful face and body but can really dance and sing."

"Dear me, Schultz one hears a lot of things in the theatre. But I can vouch we have absolutely failed to hear such rumour. Which certainly I assure you wouldn't sway us in the least. We actually think your little show on its present merits has a chance."

"Thanks. But it's no fucking rumour. This girl, you watch is going straight to the top."

"Ah how nice for you Schultz. How nice. We rejoice, don't we Basil. We truly rejoice."

"But Jesus, the show at the moment is the least of my worries. I want to know what's the fucking law on assault in this country."

"Ah Schultz, you were attacked."

"No I wasn't, I was shoved. I mean this fucking girl's mother yesterday at the hospital. She must have weighed two tons. I was so knocked out by the sight of her I walked right into the middle of an operation."

"And his Royal Grace and I understand that completely Schultz, especially when there she was, gorging on caviar and drinking champagne charged to your account."

"People don't have morals any more."

"Ah dear Schultz. Do you know that that lady you describe strikes me as your ideal kind of mother in law."

"Holy shit, Binky don't even ever fucking well joke about a thing like that. For christ's sake."

"Schultz you are an utterly endearing cavalier stylist."

"What's that supposed to mean your Lordship."

"Schultz I haven't the faintest idea. But it is so refreshing to hear you talk of morals. We must also hear more from you on chivalry, courtesy and generosity. Especially as you are presently maintaining your lady friend and her mother in such high living circumstances in the hospital."

"Hey look, people don't have to be eating caviar all the time. On somebody else's bill. I'm generous for christ's sake. And don't worry when it's necessary I got chivalry too."

"Ah Schultz, please, both his Royal Grace and I invite you to sit down. Give Rebecca a chance to catch up on the minutes of our little meeting here."

"Minutes. Holy shit. Stop. What are you taking evidence or something."

"No no. And no need to pop up and make fists at us. You see we both thought you totally devoid of the virtues of generosity and chivalry until this very moment. I mean you could have snatched away the pot of caviar and the champagne and returned it to your elegant grocery merchant Fortnum's and said it was all a horrid mistake."

"Come on you guys. What's this about an investment."

"First Schultz you'll be pleased to hear that his Royal Grace and I are having lunch fetched in. So do relax."

"This office with you guys is always like this. Anything to waste time."

"Schultz. Your fly is open."

"It is not. Holy shit it is."

"Rebecca I think at this point you must leave us. Ah now you see Schultz, how often you assume you're being humbugged. And just when his Lordship as you like to refer to him, is attempting to prevent your being embarrassed by your indecent exposure. Now I speak both for myself and his Royal Grace Schultz when I say we are most interested in a piece of your little show."

"O.K. come on, let's go. How much."

"Ah but firstly Schultz, firstly there are a few little matters to be disposed of. And one rather major one. Now this kicking of ladies out of your house one after another is reflecting badly upon the firm."

"Hey what is this a fucking courtroom or something suddenly."

"Rather more like a court martial Schultz. Behaviour unbecoming and that sort of thing. Especially Schultz when you chuck out females and then such ladies need hospitalization."

57

"She sent herself to the hospital where she's sitting up glowing with health in the fucking bed."

"Ah Schultz that may be but I fear there is to one other such incident attached a further and more serious tale. Which it is of some urgency to tell."

"What tale. And holy shit you guys talk. At least I've got principles. These are foreigners I'm kicking out. Whereas you guys send rushing past my door respectable English girls who came to you innocent looking for a decent job. And get insulted."

"Well of course Schultz but it's merely that we lay down stringent standards to weed out the unladylike types."

"Bullshit."

"Did you know Schultz that just the other day one bosomy youngster without the merest encouragment from myself or our esteemed deputy director Lord Nectarine here, stripped. Yes, you heard correctly Schultz, stripped. Totally without invitation I may needlessly add. And stood right where you stand not quite as hysterical as you but entirely naked to the waist before we could jump up and stop her. We implored her to put back on her clothes. Her bosoms were jumbo sized. One didn't want so much flesh to get chilled. His Royal Grace even went to the extreme of tugging down that drape you see there crumpled upon the deck to cover her. She said most loudly don't you dare put that dirty dusty thing on me. In the end we had to use strong arm tactics. Most embarrassing with her large things heaving around slapping one's face. I mean of course she had, like so many others, misunderstood our letterhead and took the literal interpretation of our most unfortunate company name and thought she was being auditioned to take part in the moving photography of some sordidly disgusting obscenity of one awful kind or another. But Schultz, referring to foreigners, you Schultz I fear might be included in that category. But I'm sure his Royal Grace will agree with me, when I say that you have, haven't you, as an American, rather made yourself at home with us here in dear old England. But please do let me put you at your ease Schultz. As you do look more than somewhat fraught this very serene afternoon."

"What a long load of shit I've just listened to. I think you guys are a bunch of fucking philanderers, that's what I think."

"Schultz that's a most serious accusation and could call for an extraordinary board meeting. By jove I don't think we're going to let you look any more at our pigeons sitting out there on their eggs on our roof."

"Fuck the pigeons. What about the investment."

"Ah Schultz. It must be said for you, resplendent as you are in your sunglasses and grey herringbone, blue shirt, black knit tie and those buttons on your collar tips, that you never give up. However, we do have some rather very heavy matters at hand. Now as you must know, a company is regarded as an entity separate from its members. However if one of its members is a loose moraled philanderer or worse, clapped up, then the company itself might easily be regarded as a clapped up company. And having regard for the name of ours, this simply will not do. Especially as we have already attracted the Board of Trade's attention regarding our undesirable appellation. Ah but let me put business aside a moment. Goodness aren't they the most marvellous aromas."

Lunch accompanied by a bushy browed squat white hatted Italian chef was wheeled in. A boy assistant setting the table. As Binky and his Lordship in their usual manner, again looked at each other and back again at Schultz. The traffic sounds in the street increasing at this late noon time, and Schultz taking out and tearing off his usual half stick of afternoon chewing gum.

"Join us Schultz. Put your gum away. There's a good chap. Sit there."

"Jesus christ you guys, why don't you go out to lunch."

"Because Schultz we want to stay in and talk confidentially to you."

"Come on where's this big fucking investment. More bullshit, isn't it. Just like you give the secretaries."

"Now Schultz you are becoming awfully outspoken. And in front of his Royal Grace too. You really are. But what you think Schultz is entirely your own delusion. But we assure you, that neither I nor his Royal Grace are in the habit of being prevaricators. Or indeed lackadaisical with our chivalry towards ladies. It is merely that with our playful attitude towards secretaries we wish to eliminate from this hair raising business those girls who might tend to be squeamish, nerve wracked and unable to cope at a dire time. You know what show business is like, Schultz. Attracting as it does the very worst most awful sort of people. Help yourself to the gull's eggs. And Mario do pour out for the Viscount Schultz some of your specially selected chablis."

"Very good sir."

"Hey Jesus I know you guys, you're going to try and get me drunk."

"Dear me Schultz you are lacking in faith in your fellow company directors."

"Fucking right I am. And why doesn't his Lordship say something, what is this, like you're waiting to spring something on me."

"Schultz outside the skies have cleared. His Royal Grace will speak in due course. Meanwhile lunch is the order of the day."

The sun shining blazing in the window, sparkling upon the glassware and cutlery. The chef with his swift deft moves over his alcohol burners performing at his little auxiliary table covered in dishes and condiments. While the white coated boy, his hair slicked back and parted in the middle, circled serving this noble Lord and two commoner gentlemen.

"Jesus look at you, the pair of you so fucking rich it isn't true. I mean what do you want, isn't it enough that you got everything in the world already, Jesus castles and cooks, that you get kicks out of making innocent working girls miserable and then me guilty because I object."

"Your Royal Grace don't you think that Schultz here is, under his brash American exterior, a great romantic."

"I do actually Binky, I actually do."

"He reads so many showbizz trade newspapers and periodicals that he thinks every legitimate producer sits with his desperately livid cock out waiting for some defenceless girl to come and be requested to perform some resuscitating mouth tiring ministra-

tion upon it. Totally wrong, Schultz. Just as you, we too are dedicated to the theatre. Do have some more of the smoked salmon
Schultz. And only the other day I was saying to his royal highness
here what a rather good figure you cut. And how your silk shirts
become you."

"This fucking thing I'm wearing is nylon."

"O dear. But now the truth of the matter is Schultz. That we
told these prospective secretaries that they would have to, from
time to time, work for you and that on their way out they might
just peek in the office at the end of the corridor. I fear it was from
that point onwards you heard the vituperation and screaming.
And it does not surprise me in the least following his Royal
Grace's most unfortunate confrontation at your Belgravia estab-
lishment."

"What the fuck are you talking about Binky."

"Ah. I think in the interests of hygiene, and the well being of
the board members of Sperm Productions, not to mention widespread epidemic, his Royal Grace will allow me to repeat for him
his sad tale. And do try the asparagus Schultz, Mario, pop some of
those nice tender stalks on to the Viscount Schultz's plate. And
help yourself Schultz to Mario's renowned mayonnaise."

"Hey come on, what is this."

"Schultz now. You must shut up and listen. This is the matter of
the major matter we must resolve before making our substantial
investment in your little show."

"Christ you guys. I knew you were going to go beating around
the bush when this whole god damn production is on my mind."

"Now Schultz you have, haven't you done some really rather
lousy rotten things to ladies."

"Jesus what is this."

"Well the fact of the matter is, and I have your permission your
Royal Grace, ah good. And Mario that will be all for the moment,
till the scampi thank you."

"Very good sir."

"Well Schultz, one inclement morning not that long ago our
dear Lord Nectarine here was motoring into town from a west

61

country direction from one of his westerly located country houses and thinking of your welfare, asked his faithful Hubert to stop a moment at your residence in order that he might give you a lift into the office. And I regret to say his Royal Grace at once became witness to a rather bizarre event. Schultz, do try that sauce that Mario has spent two hours preparing this morning. Indeed it is the most famous sauce in London."

"Come on you guys. You're going to gorge me. I've got important work to do."

"Schultz there was an au pair."

"What au pair."

"Well we assume it was one you were clearly trying to shove out on the scrap heap after the usual twenty one days of nonstop sexual use or abuse of her body."

"Hey come on what is this."

"Schultz it's a case of inhumanity, and do have a slice of wholemeal bread. Good for your hemorrhoids and chew it well."

"I ain't got hemorrhoids."

"You may have them after this tale Schultz."

"Come on what tale."

"The tale involving his Royal Grace when he saw kneeling on the hard paving stones of your basement kitchen, a young honey blond lady in her night shift. Begging and shivering and sobbing not to be thrown out. No need to look goggle eyed behind your sunglasses Schultz. His royal highness was rather cut to the quick as she wailed out in her miserably fractured English that she would clean and scrub, cook and polish, worship and obey Mr. Schultz till death if only he would let her stay."

"This is what you guys do all day. Dream up this bullshit."

"Ah Schultz there is more. Ah but perhaps we should leave it till brandy and cigar time. We have some rather nice pale old stuff been lying in barrel down the London docks from the beginning of this century that my good chaps Berry Brothers and Rudd have just bottled. I think you'll like its gently exquisite finesse."

"Come on, now you got started trying to ruin my appetite, get finished."

"Well as I say there was his Royal Grace on your doorstep. And then suddenly the servants' entrance is flung open and in a veritable blaze of obscenities this honey blond creature in a yellow flowered dress was shoved into the London elements by a raven haired beauty whom his Royal Grace took to be some new member of your household."

"Hey now wait a minute, you sons of bitches. Have you been spying on me or something."

"Schultz you'll choke speaking with a whole stalk of asparagus sticking out of your mouth like that. Ah but allow me to pour you a little spot more of Chablis to have with your scampi. I see we have struck a chord of some admission here. Haven't we your Royal Grace. That the facts put forth are not entirely, to quote you Schultz, bullshit."

"Like hell they're not."

"I mean Schultz naturally, your being a director of this old established firm we must be alert to hygiene and to your well being. And dear me, you've already admitted being shoved about by this young lady's two ton mother. A black eye today. With your toes broken periodically. A limping and thoroughly distraught man when you come in here prick weary of a lunch time. Well I tell you, his Royal Grace and I are alarmed. Even as we are pleased that you rather exaggeratedly uphold the firm's name."

"Come on, so what, I broke my toes and got a black eye. What's all this hygiene and eviction shit."

"We are Schultz about to come to that. Now his Royal Highness did in fact, on this particular faintly drizzly morning, and entirely out of the goodness of his heart, drive to your premises in order that, with the scarcity of taxis on London rainy mornings, you might not have to overexert your recently broken toes on the way to the office. I mean you have indeed been having to make so many trips to Harley Street these days."

"Jesus, that bitch from Rotterdam."

"Ah Schultz, you've jumped right out of your seat, at long last. And out of you has come a truly heartfelt sentiment. Now why."

"Jesus christ she broke every god damn dish in the kitchen,

threw a flower pot through the window. Poured a jar of honey down the stairs. Flung jam on the walls. I'm still discovering what she did."

"And my dear Schultz you are about to discover more. Concerning that bitch from Rotterdam. And I must because of the verbatim quality, I am sure you'll appreciate is necessary, now hand you over to his royal esteem Prince Basil, the well known Earl of Eel Brook Common and London's most fashionable peer, who will take it up from here. I give you without further embroidery his Amazing Grace."

"Ah my dear pettifogging creampuff Schultz. Sit down."

"What for."

"I think it is best advised you do."

"Jesus I'm all right standing. But I could tell you were fucking well sitting waiting there to jump me with something. Give me a cigarette will you."

"As Binky smokes cigars, you're referring I presume to one of mine Schultz."

"Sure why not."

"Well puff deeply Schultz. You're going to need all the nicotine you can get. Firstly, so that you know beyond question that one does not pull your leg, the young lady's legs from Rotterdam were, apart from being extremely attractively shaped, also extensively hairy."

"O Jesus, come on you guys. You really are trying to get me. I got a hundred and twenty thousand pound production hanging over my head."

"Schultz your budget has suddenly doubled."

"Fucking well right it has. Now will you tell me what the fuck's going on and stop bullshitting all over the place."

"Dear me Schultz is your little show going to cost that much."

"My little show, Binky. Well let me tell you. I got a husband and wife team composing who think that combined they're Puccini. A playwright doing the book who thinks he's Shakespeare. And a fucking director who thinks that in his suede shoes he's god. And they all think they should live full time in suites at the Dorchester."

"O dear Schultz. Do sit down. And finish your scampi. In a moment there will be chocolate mousse. And his Royal Grace and I do so hate to add to your troubles."

"Well go on add. Just don't waste my fucking time doing it. Come on, your Lordship."

"Well Schultz when your lady friend was being flung out by this other most attractive but extremely determined lady I naturally assisted the wretched girl. Not knowing of course that she had done the dire dirty to your domicile. She was nearly delirious, tears streaming down her face. My Dutch is extremely rusty but at least I could follow the rudiments of what she was saying."

"O.K. what was she saying."

"Well among other things, that she couldn't return to her employers. Indeed she volunteered she'd do anything for me, work in any of my castle kitchens or meadows. Of course I realised that this meant that you Schultz had been shooting your loud mouth off yet again, and had been telling her all sorts of exaggerated tales about me. I instead took her to one of the better quality West End hotels and gave them your name and address to send the charges to."

"You did like shit."

"Ah Schultz you are a disbeliever aren't you."

"Damn right. This whole story is all the same, one fifth fact, four fifths fiction."

"Well perhaps. And to some extent you are quite correct Schultz. I did have Hubert take her back to Hornchurch to her employers."

"Hey how did you know where she lived."

"Ah Schultz, of course I knew. From her very own lips. I've repeatedly attempted to make it evident to you that you are being told the absolute truth."

"Well come on then tell it. What's it you're driving at."

"Well Schultz in a nut shell. As a result of assisting this lady not only have I been interviewed by the police regarding her possible abduction but also by three extremely worried medical investigators."

"Holy shit what for."

"Now Schultz please, you've nearly upset the entire table, do sit down."

"Holy christ I'm down."

"Ah that's better. Binky pour our dear fellow director some brandy. Now please don't get hysterical, Schultz."

"Hey how fucking tranquil do you want me to get for christ's sakes."

"Well Schultz, extremely tranquil. Since it appears from confirmed bacterial findings that your young lady was evidently suffering from a rapidly spreading and so far untreatable venereal disease from the Orient. Schultz, sit down. And please listen. These medical investigators are desperate to track anyone down who had any contact with her even of the most casual sort."

"Hey, I'm not going to believe one more fucking word of this."

"By all means, don't Schultz. Don't."

The sun glinting on Schultz's sunglasses and his hands spreading out beside him on the chaise longue where in his table toppling anxiety he was now sitting ready to spring up to escape. His adam's apple going up and down in his throat as he swallowed and his tongue flicking out between his lips. As he quietly turned white before turning beet red.

"Hey come on, is this serious for christ's sake. Is this the truth. Come on Binky. This is all a lot of shit isn't it."

"Schultz, as much as one would prefer it to be, unhappily I assure you, it is distinctly not. And I admonish you to heed his Royal Grace's every word."

"Hey come on. From the Orient. That's miles away."

"Alas not for this incurable chronic vesicular chancre, Schultz. Popping from continent to continent is merely a hop skip and jump for it."

"You guys are really just shitting me. There's got to be a cure."

Binky presiding before his glass of brandy, taking up his gold clipper and snipping a piece from the end of his cigar. As his Lordship crossed his legs and sat deeply back in his chair sniffing his very special old pale cognac over the edge of his glass and then holding it aloft in the direction of both the light and of Schultz's increasingly flustered face.

"Schultz, it's you who ought to be shitting. It's so stupidly American of you, thinking everything's got to have a cure."

"That's not American, that's true. There's a day and night struggle that goes on to find a cure for everything. And they find them. Don't worry."

"I do so hate to dash your hopes Schultz. But according to these medical investigators, although you Americans are presently pulling your hair out trying to find a cure for these deucedly severe microbes, which have afflicted some of your far flung military bases, you yet haven't."

"You don't even have a name for the disease."

"Oriental Venereal Plague."

"Hey come on, that kind of plague stuff went out with the middle ages."

"My dear Schultz. Your innocence and faith in man's all conquering abilities is so refreshing sometimes. But some of these microbes which even predate the human race, not only still lurk everywhere but indeed are far more able to survive than man himself."

"Well what the fuck are they doing about them then. It's not right they're loose like that."

"Exactly. Therefore these investigators are tracking down and rigidly enforcing isolation and quarantine of the unfortunate victims. Fortunately I was wearing gloves and did not come into skin contact with the lady. But of course where she sat in my motor, was sprayed and my gloves burned."

"Holy shit. I needed this now. On top of what I got already."

"And now Schultz what on earth are you so suddenly concerned about."

"My fucking health."

"Schultz you ass, that doesn't mean that you become infected merely by a person's presence. The medical investigators were quite clear in stating that there had to be solid if not somewhat prolonged mucous membrane contact."

"Holy motherfucking christ."

"Come come get a grip on yourself Schultz. There's no need for such extreme blaspheming profanity. You really are beginning to take this awfully hard."

"Hard. You want me to rejoice."

"But surely Schultz this young lady was most safely imprisoned in your commodious basement."

"Yeah sure, I kept her locked down there. But I had to let her loose once in a while, didn't I. You can't treat someone like a criminal before you know they are."

"And quite rightly so Schultz. At least you're eminently fair."

"And I wish I wasn't. Boy. When she was trying to wreck it she got all over the house."

"Ah then Schultz of course you'll make sure to get only experienced fumigators when cleaning the jam off your walls especially if she were flinging it about in bare fistfuls. But do remember. Only those who may have actually had orifice contact are at serious risk. Those who touch the girl on her skin or rub up close to her in some fashion are only at moderate risk."

"Hey now wait a minute why the fuck are they calling it venereal if you can get it just touching someone."

"Ah I'm very glad you asked that question Schultz, it's precisely what I thought. And I'm suitably impressed by your medical knowledge. But damn it all, it really does take the cake you know. Evidently these microbes which have reached us from the Far East are of quite an advanced type. Enabling them to withstand greater rigors in their survival. And Schultz please stop dropping your cigarette ash on the cushion."

"Holy shit here he is telling me to stop dropping my ash on the fucking cushion when I could be deeply infected with fucking germs they got no cure for."

"I've already told you Schultz. It doesn't mean that whenever you lightly brush up against one of these heinously afflicted persons that you will automatically pick up one of these fearful microbes. But of course delving into orifices and therein taking your sport is entirely another matter. Then there is no question this most awful evil affliction may befall one."

"Holy shit stop saying that word orifice will you. Here I stand on the abyss of a hundred and twenty thousand pounds and you give me this kind of good news."

"The really unfortunate thing is Schultz, that we hadn't given it to you sooner. In order to save your new lady friend and even her mother from being infected. Of course the medical investigators will want to interview them. And conveniently she's already in hospital. Why are you looking so distraught Schultz."

"I'm not distraught."

"Anyone Schultz would think you were the way you are again jumping up."

"Well I'm fucking well not. Did these investigators tell you what the symptoms were."

"Yes as a matter of fact."

"Well come on. Tell me."

"Good grief Schultz you are indeed exhibiting the most considerable anxiety."

"Never mind what the fuck I'm exhibiting. What do the symptoms exhibit."

"Well anyone would think you'd caught it the way you're pacing around there."

"What are the fucking symptoms. And Binky while you're falling off the chair spilling your brandy and laughing you can fucking well stop thinking this is so fucking funny. Come on your Lordship."

"Schultz you won't believe it when I tell you."

"Come on fucking well tell me. I'm waiting here for christ's sake."

"O god Schultz it's just dawned on me. Could this be a just retribution. For the stream of au pairs you've corrupted in and out of your bed. And Schultz, my god, one is beginning to think that girl wasn't just simply scrubbing your floors. May we assume perhaps that you were rather friendlier with her than master and servant custom usually permits. And were up her or engaged in behaviour akin to being so."

"No I was not."

"Well then why are you sweating."

"Well holy shit I mean you know, you meet the odd girl here and there and so I got to watch out, don't I."

"Well of course quite, we must all watch out. But for a moment there Schultz, you really had me worried. Because my god I haven't yet told you the worst."

"The worst."

"Precisely. The lady was also suffering from another vicious chronic disease as well. In the form of a mouth fungus."

"O hey Jesus, come on, stop."

"And Schultz. And you'll never believe this. She was also thought to possibly have mumps."

"Now I don't believe you. Fungus and mumps for fucks sake. Come on, you're having me on. Next you'll be telling me that the mouth fungus can make you sterile."

"O no it doesn't. That only happens with the Oriental Venereal Plague Schultz. But of course even the mildest form of this plague could make you impotent if it attacks the testicles. But as you know mumps may also lead to inflammation of the balls."

"You're trying to tear my whole god damn life down."

"Not at all Schultz. Simply warning you. The mouth fungus only causes loosening and loss of the teeth."

"Only. Jesus."

"Especially this particular variety known as the Rotterdam Rot. But then I very much regret to say that the fungus will be the least of your worries if this chronic vesicular gangrene chancre in its secondary stage ravages your entrails."

"Gangrene. I got to get to the fumigators fast."

"Of course Schultz the wretched affliction was brought in by sailors to that busiest of European ports. But think of the things you could have caught Schultz. Leprosy. Island isolation and that type of thing."

70

"Jesus I got to sit down again."

"Binky, some more brandy for our fellow director. And you know Schultz it makes one realise what a marvellous and dedicated medical service we have here. Chaps who have through tireless work traced the origins of these dread diseases."

"Holy shit, I don't need brandy I need a drink of fucking water."

"Binky would you mind awfully getting our cherished and esteemed fellow director a glass of water. We shouldn't of course like our chef or secretaries especially Rebecca, to get wind of these matters. Also I'm afraid Schultz is so overwrought he may not be entirely able to see straight and could easily fall down the lift shaft rushing into the wrong aperture."

"But of course your Amazing Grace. I'll fetch water. But dear me does this mean our dear fellow director Schultz here may end up having to wear a Lazarus rattle to warn of his approach. And someone behind him to sweep up his teeth."

"Don't worry the two of you, I may be sitting here looking collapsed god damn it, but I can still see straight and I'm not going to need any rattle either. Or someone picking up my teeth."

Binky at the office door. Pausing to twiddle and tap his fingers as he elevated himself up and down on his toes and released wind in a series of small elegant pops.

"Please don't mind my rear portal's post luncheon fanfare. Asparagus, scampi and Chablis invariably pop out of me like this. I am just having a look see in the hall to make sure none of our staff are listening to this unfortunate discussion we are having. Ah all's clear. And now perhaps Schultz, in view of the grave risk to your future health, you'd like us to take over your production for you."

In the sudden silence the pigeons cooing out on the rooftop. And his Lordship hardly ever the type to lose his composure unwillingly, suddenly standing, turning his back and going to the window to rearrange and straighten his face wracked by his choked up guffaws. His fingers pressing his stomach to stop the muscles from ripping asunder. And looking out across to the

71

other office buildings to contain himself. As Schultz, leaping to his feet, sunglasses suddenly off. His elbows out from his sides as he stood crouched, one eye puffed and black, right fist clenched and disbelieving horror written all over his face.

"Why you dirty rats."

Binky slowly rising on his toes as if to reach his ears further in the direction of some rare bird song.

"I beg your pardon, Schultz."

"You heard me. You dirty rats. Now I know what you're up to. When you see a guy is down. That's what you do. You move right in. Like vultures. To pick the flesh off my fucking bones."

"We'd hardly want to do that with your bones Schultz, poxed up and fungus ridden as they may possibly be."

"Jesus what human beings you are."

"Schultz I feel somehow you're withholding something from us. That in fact you did plunge it eighteen miles or so up the au pair's orifice."

"I did like fucking hell plunge it up her orifice. And what's more you fucking well know I didn't."

"Ah Schultz, at last. Binky and I are relieved. And your terribly anxious upset attitude about this matter is, forgive me, I must say it, no longer highly suspicious. And we can all relax and even consider shaking hands with you again without nasty thoughts of contagion. And we don't think you're down. Temporarily dismayed perhaps. And after you are cured."

"Cured. I'm not sick yet."

"Well just in case you needed to be cured. Then later we would gladly let you back in on a piece of the action. To use one of your more endearing phrases."

"Let me in on a piece of the action. Me. Who's sweated my guts out on a shoestring and with contracts already signed that could hang me. It's still my fucking show. And no diseases from some dirty Dutch bitch from Rotterdam is going to make it otherwise."

"That's unchivalrous of you to say Schultz, she was after all an

72

attractive girl, outwardly at least. And any of us could be forgiven had we taken an interlocking orifice liberty with her."

"Stop saying orifice, will you. I took no fucking liberties with anybody. And I'm just upset because, well I'm just a good citizen that's all."

"You are a foreigner Schultz."

"What difference does that make. I can still behave like a good citizen. Diseases like that bitch brought to town, I'm concerned. It stands to fucking reason."

"Dear me Schultz, you are at the most unexpected of times quite commendable and I am relieved to hear of your fervent sense of civic duty and I think I speak on behalf of all of us here at Sperm Productions who might have risked contagion from you. But of course I do hope you'll understand Schultz if one still keeps one's breathing distance away."

His Lordship in his rumpled dark blue gabardine suit, turning again to confront Schultz. Whose tie knot was now loose and askew at his throat and three of his buttons open on his shirt as he stood, his sunglasses back on, jerking his thumb.

"If fucking Binky I can hear busting his gut laughing out there in the hall caught it he'd find it a lot less fucking amusing, let me tell you."

"Indeed, Schultz, that stands, to use your terminology, to fucking reason. But surely the word fucking is no longer called for as an adjective in this discussion. Especially as you infer you did not do any with the lady in question. And were then and are now, merely an innocent calm citizen."

"Holy shit. I'm never totally calm. Anyway what do you want me to say. Don't I have enough troubles. She was in my house. Eating my food. Taking in milk bottles off my stoop. And touched and had her fingers all over the milk caps. It happens plenty of times. But just in case, I got to know what the doctors say you should do."

"Simply let them know if any symptoms develop. And then to get in touch with them instantly."

73

"What kind of symptoms."

"With three diseases there are quite a number, but I believe thay are all characterised by a mild tiredness towards late afternoon. Or in the mornings a sudden hair loss."

"Hair loss. I thought it was teeth. How much hair."

"A whole lot, evidently. Why Schultz are you putting your hand up to your head like that."

"No fucking reason."

"Well if it's any help, pubic hair loss is just as copious as the head hair loss."

"Pubic."

"Yes. But please don't start opening up your fly to look now Schultz. Of course a damn nuisance in that area of one's anatomy. To suddenly confront a lady friend out of the blue one morning with hairless pudenda when the previous evening it was hairy."

"Jesus."

"Also one has a sense of thirst. Not that your wanting a glass of water a minute ago Schultz could possibly be taken in that context in the least. Now really the way you're down again up again hopping around you'd think one was now suggesting the girl was rabid."

"Don't worry what you've already told me that Rotterdam bitch has got is enough."

"Well Schultz, I see by my watch I must run. Tell you if I hear anything more."

"Tell me if you hear anything more. Hey what the fuck are you talking about. You've already told me enough for a lifetime. And Jesus do you have to go already."

"I'm afraid so Schultz, Hubert's waiting to take me to pick up some antique and rather valuable jewelry items at Christies. And they close in half an hour."

"Christ you can walk there, it's only two seconds around the corner."

"Well it's rather expected of me to, how shall we put it, to arrive in suitable style."

"Jesus you worry about style at a fucking time like this."

74

Under the not unloving gaze of his Lordship, Schultz sitting back down on the chaise longue. The chef Mario and his assistant with head nods and smiles wheeling out his tables. Schultz's elbows planted apart on his knees and face bent down into his hands. Right under Sperm Productions' most prized autographed photograph of a smiling health glowing famed male Hollywood movie star. And then Schultz opening his mouth and with his fingers tugging on his front teeth. And as his left hand ran up through his hair, his right scratched and pinched in the area of his crotch.

"Holy Jesus fucking christ. There's something loose already down there."

"Schultz, do be calm. Here's your water."

Binky holding out a brimming glass to Schultz. Who suddenly jumping to his feet knocks the water from Binky's fingers and rushes out into the hall. Where the water closet door could be heard opening and slamming loudly shut.

"I say your Royal Amazing Grace, those vomiting noises one hears. What do you suppose is wrong with our little theatrical friend Schultzy boy there. He appears to be having a little spot of bother of some sort in the confines of the water closet, poor chap."

Dear me
He is
Suffering
So

6

On that sumptuously lunched afternoon, Schultz wasted no time in getting in touch with Harley Street. Five minutes later having ashen faced reappeared from the water closet and sat a moment wiping his brow, and then jumping to his feet and with fists clenched, he could be overheard screaming at his Lordship's and Binky's beloved curvaceous and statuesque secretary Rebecca.

"Yes, I want a certain kind of doctor in Harley Street."

"What kind sir."

"Didn't you hear what I said, a certain kind. Don't you know what kind that is."

No journey was ever as dark. Or London buildings so grey. This late afternoon up a thronged Regent Street. Schultz, his white knuckles gripped on each knee held on to himself as his taxi rolled around a sombre Cavendish Square. And turned north into Harley Street where one block further on, Schultz found himself along a dark passage in a chilly water closet, pissing into a bottle.

"Christ even my kidneys are hurting now. I can't just let myself die. Not in the middle of what could be my first chance of a big hit. With a fucking eruption of money. Soaking me right through to my skin."

A more than somewhat attractive nurse smilingly taking the urine warm vial from Schultz. And then being led back upstairs, watching her lean shapely legs flexing before him, Schultz tripped. And again aroused the painful maim in his toes. To limp on the arm of the nurse into a large office to sit before this bow-tied and suede waistcoated medical gentleman. Who increasingly creased his forehead, and as Schultz again explained his diseases, deepened his frown and finally removed his glasses.

"Well Mr. Schultz, although I've not heard of it up until five o'clock today, believe me it's entirely possible that something re-sembling this Oriental Venereal Plague you speak of exists. And that our medical service would be most concerned. Of course I'll have it checked immediately. But I hardly think the World Health Organization would fail to signal it to the medical world. Now you say this Dutch lady is no longer resident in your household. Do you have her address."

"Address."

"Yes."

"Hey doc, if you don't mind I'd like not to get into that kind of stuff. And start handing out private addresses. Like you, I've got a kind of confidential occupation."

"Mr. Schultz, I regret to say, it's not only her address I'd like. But I should also require the address of anyone with whom you've had any sexual intimacy of any kind since you met the Dutch girl."

"Wow. This is a kind of a shakeroo, doc."

"Yes I know. And indeed, no doubt, it will be fraught with pos-sible embarrassment for you. But I assure you it's all kept ex-tremely confidential until such time as we discover whether or not you are infected. And that will take at least until the report comes back from the laboratory. It is a precaution we must take for the benefit of others. Anyway for a start let's take a peek in your mouth. Have any difficulty in swallowing."

"No."

"Just open. Yes. I see. Throat glands seem all alright. Well it may be too early but you're not exhibiting the signs of mumps and your mouth seems perfectly healthy. Indeed I've rarely seen a better set of teeth. Well then. So far, so good. But in respect of this other more serious matter, we must know Mr. Schultz, if you have had sexual intercourse or intimacy with anyone else since meeting the Dutch girl."

"Doc, look, I'm in the theatre, you understand. And you kind of sometimes find yourself with various people a lot."

"I see. Does this mean there are others who may be involved in exposure."

"Yeah."

"Might I ask, how many."

"Doe, look, do you want me to be honest."

"That would help considerably."

"Well the truth is I don't know how many."

"I see."

"I mean don't think I'm promiscuous. I mean I can remember some of them."

"I see."

"But doc Jesus don't ask me to make a list of addresses."

"This is Mr. Schultz, I assure you, a medical matter not a moral one. So now if you would just please lower your trousers, I'll examine you."

Schultz stood staring out a parting in the curtain beyond these pale glassed Georgian panes watching the other medical windows lighting up across the street as he was examined. The doctor saying he could as yet see no definite signs of pathology. But would, if Mr. Schultz would just milk his organ in a downward fashion, take a penis tip smear. And then a blood sample. Which latter nearly made Schultz faint. And at the office door came the doctor's parting advice.

"Have a little drink for yourself Mr. Schultz on the way home. And do take care of that black eye."

Evening rush hour traffic was throbbing as Schultz stopped his taxi on the way back to Belgravia. And bought a flask of whiskey. To uncork it and for the first time in his life to take a neat nip from the bare bottle of this spirit burning down his throat. To rush across the carpet the moment he got back into his hallway. Where the phone was ringing.

"Is this you."

"Yeah who's this."

"This is Al. You really lousy son of a bitch."

"What did I do now Al."

"What did you do now. I'll tell you what you did now. You put her in hospital. With the beautiful kid having a nervous breakdown. And her mother hysterical crying on the telephone to me just a minute ago. That's what you did now."

"Hey Al, can I just gently tell you one thing."

"What gently are you going to tell me. That you broke your prick trying to fuck her, is that what."

"No that's not what. I'm going to tell you if you'd listen that she's kidding for christ's sake."

"Kidding. When she had to have X rays and serious tests. You call that kidding."

"Yeah, I'm calling it kidding. Her two ton mother was there eating caviar while her daughter was having her hair done by some Bond Street transvestite and the place was filled with flowers."

"Did you send her flowers."

"No Al, I did not send her flowers."

"Well I sent the girl flowers."

"O.K. Al, so you sent her flowers. I know that was a wonderful gesture, but why didn't you send her also a bible, a rosary, a yarmulke."

"Hey don't you get smart with me wise guy."

"Look Al."

"You look. I don't give a damn about you running some kind of whorehouse you got there. Girls knocking on the door around the clock. But you're not going to do this to that girl."

"Do what and nobody's knocking on my door. I'm a producer for fucks sake. I got to see girls all the time. And hey Jesus Al, just by the way you know, you got fucking girls girls girls coming and going day and night."

"Yeah but there's a difference. I'm mature about it."

"Holy shit Al, I'm not going to get anywhere talking to you. Especially when what happened was that that poor girl's two ton mother was waking the dead and gave me a black god damn eye."

"Ha ha ha hey that's good."

"You think that's funny Al."

"Yeah I do. It's exactly like you deserve. Now you go back to that hospital and apologise. Or else I'll see to it that your name is such mud in this town that it wouldn't be worth scraping off a shoe."

"What is this, blackmail Al."

"You get to that fucking hospital like I'm telling you that's all."

"I just come this second in from the doctor's."

"So what's wrong with you. And what's that noise."

"They don't know yet. And I'm drinking whiskey, that's the noise. It's going to take tests to find out what's wrong. Now hey come on Al, this is all unreasonable."

"What for you to throw this girl out. The most beautiful creature ever to cross my threshold, that I sent over to you."

"Al you're deluded, I'm hanging up. I've had enough of people for one day."

"Well before you hang up you son of a bitch, and let me tell you, you don't deserve what I'm going to tell you."

"Tell me fucking what."

"That's there's an Irishman who's hit town."

"So what am I supposed to do."

"See him, that's what. He's built like a lion, moves like a cat, dances like Nijinsky, sings like Caruso and could act every leading man off the London stage blindfolded in a jock strap while crooning Rule Britannia."

"Al he should be in a circus."

"Look you fucking know it all. Four Hollywood producers right at this moment are gasping trying to sign him."

"Jesus Al, is this no shit."

"It's no shit."

"No kidding, we'll forget the blindfold and jock strap, where can I see him."

"At night he sleeps in Brompton Cemetery."

"Come on Al, I've had enough bullshit for one day. I'm hanging up and going to bed."

"I'm telling you that's where he sleeps."

"O.K., O.K. that's where he sleeps. So you can get him to my office."

"He won't go to offices."

"So how am I going to see him."

"Go to the cemetery."

"Holy fucking christ Al, I've been through hell today. And you're sending me to the cemetery tonight."

"Do you want to have the chance to star a discovery that could give you the biggest hit this town has ever seen in years."

"Sure I do. But you've been wrong before Al."

"I'm not wrong tonight. Go I'm telling you."

"O.K. Jesus Al I must be out of my mind. I'll go. First thing in the morning."

"Go right now."

"Now, Al."

"Yeah, now."

"How do I know where to find him. It's dark any minute and the cemetery will be closed."

"Go just past the hospital and when you get about twenty yards along the cemetery fence, just shout in that Al sent you."

"Thanks Al. This is sure a great way to cast my show. And I'm really going to appreciate it after the day I've already had, to end up yelling my head off into a cemetery. Let me tell you sincerely I don't need more jokes. But believe it or not I'm going."

Schultz hailing the taxi across the street just disembarking two attractive ladies in front of the Ambassador's house. The driver turning around to look at him as he gave his destination.

"Hey Gov. You mean Brompton Cemetery."

"Yeah that's just what I said."

"That's what I thought you said sir. Which entrance. It's got two. Old Brompton Road. And Fulham Road."

"Is there a hospital."

"Yes."

"Near that entrance."

"Sir you do know the cemetery is closed at this time."

"That's O.K."

Schultz alighting by the fence. And looking back at the hospital. Its eminently legible sign up on its wall. Princess Beatrice. Schultz handing the taxi man a crisp ten shilling note.

"Thank you Gov and I hope you find what you're looking for."

Steam escaping from a pipe high up on the hospital wall. And Schultz counting the rungs along the fence. The grey and white shadows of tombs far into the darkness. Trees branching up into the night. A gentle rain falling. Holy Jesus what am I doing persecuting myself like this. On this fucking godforsaken night I could get my head stuck between the bars of the fence looking for somebody I never heard even existed before.

Schultz looking up and down the road. A man across the street walking his dog. On the corner across from the hospital, the welcome life giving lights of a pub. A laden red double decker bus swaying and roaring by. Marked seventy four. And one coming in the opposite direction with ZOO as its final destination. A limping man approaching. Who now veered out near the curb as he passed, flicking suspicious glances at the loitering Schultz. Holy christ that fucker thinks maybe I'm a grave robber or something.

Schultz waiting till the way was clear. Nervously whistling the tune, Marching Through Georgia. The limping man taking one more look back and disappearing around the corner of the hospital. Schultz now cupping his hands up to his mouth. And whispering through the rungs of the fence.

"Al sent me."

Schultz again looking over his shoulder. The limping gent back in sight and again stopped, staring back. Schultz in his best ivy league nonchalant amble walking onwards along the fence. To stop and turn around to still see the limping man standing looking back. Holy fucking christ. Somebody already thinks I'm nuts. If this is some kind of joke. I don't give a shit how fucking weak Al's heart is, in two minutes I'm going to go over there to his place and bust him one right in his middle aged guts.

Schultz walked to the cemetery entrance. Flanked by grey stone gate lodges. And locked from the world by great high impenetrable iron gates. Inside, a straight road disappearing away into the middle darkness between mausoleums and now in a sudden burst of cloud uncovered moonlight, the distant outline of a church. The sidewalk clear again. Schultz walking back towards the hospital. Looming up with its yellow lighted windows. What a place to be looking down at full of gravestones while you're trying to recover. And tonight I got to go home now to see if I'm losing fistfuls of my pubic hair. Shout this time real loud. And wake the fucking dead the place is full of.

"Al sent me."

Schultz waiting. His voice even echoing back as he stood staring around behind. And at a couple across the street. Stopping to look over. Bigger and better and harder rain drops falling. Jesus while I'm getting really fucking wet I may as well throw caution to the wind. And holler at the top of my fucking lungs.

"Al sent me."

Schultz tightly pushing his face to peer between the bars. Removing his sunglasses. Scanning the dark shadows. The white sepulchres. All the broken and leaning tombstones. Al fucking well better say his prayers. Nothing. Not a sign. Of life. Except footfalls. Directly behind me. And somebody else thinking I'm nuts.

"Ere ere, sir, can I be of any assistance to you."

Schultz spinning around. Undoing his fists still gripped to the bars like the inmate of a prison. And scraping the cheek of his face on a black paint peeling rung.

"No that's all right constable. I was just looking in."

"In the cemetery."

"Yes. I heard there was someone who is famous could be in there. I sort of was trying to read the gravestone."

83

"You mean was famous, don't you sir."

"Yeah that's right."

"Well a bit dark now for that kind of thing, sir."

"Yeah I guess it is."

"American are you sir."

"Yeah I am."

"On a visit are you."

"That's right."

"And spending a bit of overtime are you on the sightseeing."

"Yeah."

"Ah well, welcome to England sir. Enjoy yourself. And don't miss the Tower of London."

"No I won't thanks."

Schultz watching the policeman strolling off. His blue cape spread over his shoulders and the thud of his heavy black gleaming shoes on the pavement. Until his easy gait took him further and further safely away. Past the cemetery entrance. Towards the great massive roof on the skyline and a bridge in the distance where the flash of electricity shot in the sky from passing trains.

Schultz gathering the moist evening air and diesel fumes up his nostrils and down in his lungs. To again give one more most impassioned shout.

"Al fucking well sent me god damn it. Will you speak up if you're in there."

Schultz slowly stepping back from the fence. Thinking he was seeing a ghost. Stopping only as he was nearly killed backing off the curb. An approaching bus beeping its horn. Schultz jumping forward again to the safety of the pavement. To there turn shaking his fist at this roaring public transport, which with its big back wheel passing through a puddle sent a full frontal wave of muddy water splashing Schultz head to toe.

"Fucking god damn hell."

Laughter bellowing out inside the cemetery. And a face rising up on top of a massive hulking shape now getting closer and hunched like a gorilla, growling the other side of the rusting fence.

"Who the fuck wants me."

"Al sent me. Al Duke."

"And what the fucking hell do you mean by interrupting my sleep like that sonny."

"Holy christ you really exist."

"Of course I fucking exist, would you think I didn't. Sure what aria from Puccini do you want to hear."

"No aria. Look, would you do me a big favour."

"Ah now that all depends."

"Would you just please come and see me at three o'clock tomorrow afternoon. Here, my address is on this piece of paper and either of these telephone numbers will get me."

"Sure my name's Terence F. X. Magillacurdy and I come to see no man."

"Hey look, it's not to see me. All I want to do is talk to you. In private. And maybe even beg you."

"For what now would you be begging me."

"To take a part in a show. It could mean Hollywood for you."

"Well for a start you can stuff Hollywood straight up your American arse me boyo."

"O.K. that's swell with me. Believe me, I understand completely how you feel. No problem. But christ I nearly got arrested trying to find you here. Please. Just come to my house. Ten minutes of your time. Three o'clock tomorrow. I'm on bended knee to you."

"Ah me boyo bend your knee to no man. But seeing as you've taken a bath in a street puddle to find me, sure you know, you have the vague possibility of being likeable. Stand up now. That's it. Open your ears."

Schultz standing back as Terence F. X. Magillacurdy's lungs inflated. The lamplight through the bars of the fence cutting across this Roman Emperor's face. As exquisite melodious song arose from this giant man's throat. And flooded the length of Old Brompton Road one end to the other. People stopping on the pavement and appearing curtain twitching at windows of a block of flats. The door of a funeral furnisher just up the street opening. A late working mortician in his apron looking down the road.

A shade in the hospital going up. A white capped nurse peering out. And Schultz pushing his address and telephone numbers through the rungs of the fence.

"That's beautiful see you tomorrow and excuse me for running. I can't afford to be arrested here with you."

Schultz turning and trotting away, the Irishman's laughter erupting in his song following him crossing the street. And up along a crescent of houses where Schultz calmed and walked again to reach the blissful anonymity of Warwick Road. Still hearing the Irishman's distant dulcet voice singing over the rooftops.

> O Danny boy
> The pubs, the pubs
> Are calling
> From Piccadilly
> All the way
> To Camden Town

The voice drowned now by the clanging bell of a police squad car as Schultz flagged a taxi. Taking a deep breath as he put his head back resting on the seat. The soothing throb of the taxi's diesel engine motoring between these shadowy massive mansions. Once peopled with servants and rich mercantile families. Now catacombed with Australians. Jesus what a struggle it is to climb up on top like a hero. And soon as you do everybody is pulling open your shoelaces.

Taxi now passing a little park. Earl's Court Square. And into the more sedate streets. The white painted elevations of South Kensington. Theatre goers. In there behind their polished windows, sparkling tables set for dinner. Guests arriving for cocktails. Little children safe upstairs with nanny in nursery. If only I had that kind of a childhood being read bedtime stories before you go to sleep. Instead of sneaking drags of a cigarette up some garbage strewn alley in the bleak depths of America. And now with one's own entrails maybe wracked with clap eating at my guts already.

The brakes squealing as the taxi came to a halt in front of Sigmund Schultz's Belgravia town house. Schultz paying another crisp ten shilling note to the driver wreathed with a big broad grin.

"Squire you had me worried. I'm the one brought you to the cemetery. You got a spot or two of mud on you. And glad to bring you back. Had meself a quiet cup of tea at Earl's Court there and picked you straight up again as my fare. Things all right at the cemetery."

"They were fine."

"That's good, glad to hear it sir, goodnight."

Butler drawing the drapes of the Ambassador's dining room across the street. Schultz up the steps to his own gleaming front door. Two brass keys to turn in two brass locks. And my own drapes closed across the downstairs window. Don't even remember doing it after this fucking long hard day. Of my heart having to suddenly start beating again just when I thought it had no beats left. At least no behemoth is waiting tonight to come charging at me. Jump in a hot enough bath and could kill some of these microbes. If my prick and balls can stand it. And then my god almighty, after a day like today, I hope I can fall asleep.

"Surprise, Sigmund."

Schultz as his hand was about to land on the light switch of the library. Was in a flood of light coming out of the dining room door just behind him. And hands folded angelically and all smiles in a long black clinging evening gown, stood Pricilla.

"Darling. Darling. I'm back."

"Hey what the fuck's going on."

"Darling, come. I've nearly got it all ready. Everything. All for you. Champagne. Caviar. Smoked salmon. Chicken in aspic. Gulls' eggs, everything you love. For us to have a feast. To celebrate."

"Celebrate what."

"Darling, that I've come out of hospital well again, of course. And all safe and back into your arms."

"You looked fine to me on the floor before you went in."

"That's churlish of you to say. Don't be churlish. And meanie. Come in. Into the dining room. Come now. In here. It's all the food mother and I had left over at the hospital."

"I got no appetite."

"You will have soon darling."

"Why."

"Because of what I'm going to tell you."

"Hey what's that fucking thing."

"That's my big teddy bear Boobles."

"You're asking me to come sit down with a fucking teddy bear at the head of my own table with a place all set for him."

"Darling. Please. I want to tell you something. And I'm going to use that horrid word."

"What are you talking about."

"Darling you can fuck me till your heart's content tonight."

"Holy Jesus christ what are you saying."

"You heard me darling."

"Hey wait a minute. This whole transformation is all taking me pretty suddenly."

"And that's how I want you now darling to take me. Naked and suddenly. Tie me up and whip me. Rape me."

"Just a minute. Hold it. Never mind the sadism. Just how come the big change honey."

"Darling what change."

"Your mother was out there only last night trying to beat my brains out on my own stoop with her umbrella."

"O darling darling, things like that are past. Don't you understand. Past. Gone and forgotten."

"Like this black eye I also got from your mother's fist."

"O my poor darling. It's going to be all right believe me. No please, let me kiss it for you. Let me kiss it. I'll kiss you all over tonight. Even your arse."

"So you're going to kiss my arse. Well that's what you can do, kiss my arse."

"Don't say it like that darling."

"I'm saying it just like you said it. Christ I don't even know where the fuck I am."

"Darling you're with me. With me. You are. And here, my little kisses all over your spotty face for my poor little sweetie pie."

"Hold it, hold it honey. Wait a minute. Please. Stop the smothering."

"Why are you pulling away like this."

"I got to understand what's all the big change all of a sudden."

"Nothing has changed darling, I'm simply yours."

"Well I've just been to the doctor's. And he says I got a raging kind of possible pneumonia or something he thinks could be coming on due to strain and overwork. Plus a toothache. I could contaminate you."

"Then darling, contaminate me."

"Jesus baby don't rush me a second. First just let me change out of my wet clothes."

"Darling, you are wet."

"That's what I said. I need a hot bath. I'm going upstairs."

"Of course darling you need a hot bath. Now I know how busy you are. How did you get all spotted."

"That's how I got spotted. Because I'm busy."

Schultz up the stairs two at a time to exercise his thigh muscles. Pricilla holding up her long gown as she followed.

"Yes I know. Al told mother and me. He's been so sweet."

"What did he tell mother and you."

"About your rehearsal. And all how it might be a wonderful hit."

"You mean my show a hit."

"And mother and I think it's so marvellous for you."

"Look honey, nothing's wonderful. And I haven't got anything together yet that even remotely looks like a hit."

"You haven't."

"No. Nobody knows what the fuck's going to happen till after six months it's already a hit and when that's happened and then it's booked out solid for another year in advance you might lean back a bit for two seconds and say you got a hit. Otherwise all you got is a hit on the head."

"Well Al said you had a hit on your hands. And at a time like that mother said she felt you needed me near you."

"Boy your fucking mother knows exactly the time for you to make yourself an adaptable human being."

"And what does that mean."

"Forget it honey, forget it. Jesus the fucking bulb's gone out for the bathroom."

Schultz standing on a chair lugged in from the hallway. Pricilla holding up a new bulb. And her other hand gripping the chair back as Schultz reached to extract by twists, turns and tugs the old bulb from its socket.

"Jesus this fucking thing won't move. God damn it."

"Be careful Sigmund, the chair. O my god the leg is breaking."

Schultz in his sudden downward descent two handed grabbed the light shade as a parachute. His fingers tearing through the blue parchment and eagerly anchoring around the wire frame. A rip and a crack of ceiling plaster. A flash of electricity and smell of burning as Schultz fell bringing an ersatz Georgian ceiling medallion down fragmenting on his head. As the whole house fused into darkness.

"Fucking bloody cunt. This fucking bloody house and all its god damn phony two bit furniture."

"O darling are you hurt."

"No just my fucking toes maimed again. Now how am I going to find the god damn fuse box when I don't even know where the lousy thing is."

"Anger will get you nowhere darling."

"Like fuck it won't boy. I'll kick the shit out of this house. Till I find it. As if enough didn't happen to me today."

Schultz undressed by candlelight. And sipped a glass of champagne, sucking back the delicately oily grey teardrops of caviar. Lying back in the bath covered to the chin in foam. Big Ben tolling eight bells. Pricilla leaning over the porcelain edge on her elbows staring at him in adoration. And in the flickering yellow glow she helped dry.

"My Sigmund you do have such a big prick and balls."

"That's right honey. Inherited from my grandfather."

"Do you like me to do this to you."

"It's swell honey, it's swell."

"Well I'm going to stop because I want to save it all for when we get to bed."

"Hey honey, do we have to have this big occasion exactly tonight. I'm kind of really knocked out from the day's events."

"You're standing there with an enormous erection."

"I know I am honey, I know it."

"Well you're not that tired out then."

"No you got a point there honey."

"It's you who has the point. And it's such a nice big handsome one. And I want you to put it in me."

"Sure honey, sure."

"I really mean that, Sigmund."

"Sure I know you do honey. Don't get upset. It was only that I think we should wait for a real special moment that's all."

"Haven't you been screaming at me. And yelling that you want satisfaction and a normal sex life. Well that's what I'm fucking well going to give you, when you fuck me tonight."

"Hey christ, the language honey. Watch it. What's got into you."

"Nothing. But tonight, you are."

      O.K.
      I'm convinced
      O.K.

7

It was one minute past Tuesday. Big Ben booming midnight echoing over Belgravia. A rising easterly wind and rain slamming at the windows. When Schultz felt he was dying in an explosion. Pricilla on her back wide eyed, thought Schultz screaming so loud was having a combined heart attack, convulsion and brainstorm. When all he was having was an orgasm.

Pricilla lay like some embalmed queen not particularly of Sheba but not far from there either. Schultz wondering when the Oriental Venereal Plague and its vesicular chancres would erupt. As it did in a dream pushing one's own wheelbarrow full of one's gargantuanly swollen testicles towards Pricilla's two ton mother waiting in an abattoir with a sledgehammer upraised. But on the softened linen sheets finally waking feeling unexpectedly good. Coffee brought by Pricilla with the newspaper. Bedroom bathed in sunshine. Black eye fading fast on one's face.

"Darling you had a nightmare. You were shouting don't break them."

"O yeah someone was carrying a big box of eggs."

That mid morning the Ambassador's Secretary telephoned. Asking if Mr. Schultz and his good friend the dark haired lady could come for a small black tie festivity the following night.

"Who is that foreign voice Sigmund."

"Oh just His Excellency across the street, just likes to know that the house isn't being robbed."

"I heard you say no that you couldn't."

"Hey what is it baby you got to hang your head over the bannister listening with your nose in my business."

"I want to know why you had to say no you couldn't that's all."

"Because I'm fucking too busy that's why. He wanted me to go to dinner."

"O that would be nice."

Schultz on his way out the hall to Sperm Productions phoned the Ambassador to accept. And sunshine beaming down warming one's back, detouring along by the big black numerals on the grey stone houses shaping the sweeping curve of the crescent. To pop into the church at Wilton Place. Pray to Almighty god. That I do not have the venereal plague. With handfuls of my pubic hair falling out my trouser leg.

Schultz doubling back around the other side of the crescent and its stately town houses. Turning up Grosvenor Crescent past the offices of the Red Cross whose tireless members rush aid all over the world to the diseased and distressed. Might even have a cure for me. If only I had the nerve to present myself clapped up inside their polished doors.

Up in the elms and cotton ball trees of Green Park, birds chirping merrily. Schultz cutting through the narrow brick alley and dark tunnel passage and turning right down past this hotel and left into sunny splendors of Westminster, St. James's. The noonday gleaming motor chariots steaming up this boulevard of gentleman's clubs. Chaps popping in and out of hat, shoe, shirt and gun makers. The bowlers tipping, the brollys tapping. The town of London indubitably awake. And Schultz, still breathing heavily after a climb up the stairs with the lift out of action, was about to open his mail when confronted at his cubbyhole door by Rebecca.

"Sir, sorry to disturb you but the Metropolitan Police are on Lord Nectarine's private line for you in his office."

Schultz ashen faced rising behind his desk. Bowels loosening, guts churning. Holy fucking christ almighty, I've got the Oriental Venereal Plague. Jesus. This should happen to me so fucking young. After even praying to god in church. Before I even had a chance to have a hit. Pricilla's mother is now going to be chasing me with an axe. To chop my prick off. And fry it with her sausages.

Schultz entering his Lordship's gloomy office along the passage. His trembling hand nearly dropping the phone as he picked it up. Rebecca discreetly retreating closing the door.

"Hello."

"Is this Mr. Sigmund Schultz."

"Speaking."

"This is Bow Street Police Station. We have a gentleman here sir, who says you are his guardian."

"Who's that."

"His name given us is Terence F. X. Magillacurdy."

"Yeah that's right. What's wrong."

"Well he resisted arrest yesterday evening and was bound over to keep the peace which he was disturbing while being apprehended for trespass and contravening certain bylaws in Brompton Cemetery."

On the pavement outside the Magistrate's Court suitably situated across the street from the Royal Opera House, Schultz discovered instantly that the mere sight of the massive mischievously grinning face of Magillacurdy frightened people in all walks of life. Including himself. As the Irish gentleman in his ripped thick blue sweater, his flame bright hair and torn green corduroy trousers, stood open armed gaily greeting the passing young ladies.

"Ah me boyo now. Sure I had one bobby by the scruff of the neck and another by the tunic. And another on the end of me boot. Trying to knock culture into them. Can you imagine. The lack of respect for a Mozart aria I was right in the middle of ren-

94

dering. With every bit of me artistry fully stretched with the fiendish difficulties that that composer Wolfgang Mozart presents to the innocent singer."

"Who's your Agent Mr. Magillacurdy."

"Agent. What are you talking about. And call me Patrick me boyo. I've scrapped me other christian names. And I'm not to be bartered brokered or sold by any man. I'm me own Agent. And I'd be glad at this very delicate moment to negotiate with you as an advance on my ten per cent, a pint or two of stout in that pub needing patronage standing innocently there on the corner."

Schultz elbowing a way through to the bar in the crowded lunch time pub. Jammed with flower vegetable and fruit merchants. Magillacurdy perched massively on a bar stool. As he downed four pints of draught Guinness in a row without blinking. Pausing only to devour with one bite each, six ham rolls, four scotch eggs and five sausages.

"I abandoned reading writing and arithmetic at the age of five. Took up singing acting and dancing. And now it's me life me boyo. I'm fit for nothing else save carnal criminality. No drama school would even have me. They'd take one look at me as I stepped up to give my audition. And said to my face that if I sang anymore or danced another step they'd be compelled to summon the police. That's nearly been the nature of my theatrical career right down to this very moment of washing this sausage down my throat."

"What have you done in the way of stage work."

"Done. What have I done. I'll tell you what I've done. I've loosened many a rafter and floor board raising the great ghosts of me mummer predecessors in any theatre or building that would stand up under the strain. And you will not hear or see the like of me again."

"I believe you."

"Ah with sufficient wool pulled over your eyes, you're already hopelessly prejudiced in my favour I can see that. And we'll drink to it."

"Hey tell me something, Patrick."

95

"Certainly what is it me boyo now that you'd want to know."

"What are you doing sleeping in a cemetery."

"Ah I knew you'd be too intelligent a man not to ask me that sooner or later. Sure it's nothing more than me temperamental impatient creditors. They have no consideration of any kind. It's been the only safe place I've been able to get a decent night's sleep. And I have a grand little mausoleum nearly to meself. The other chap who is in there using it, is the quietest sleeper you'd ever meet this side of heaven."

"There are two of you in there."

"Ah god it's good to be in the company of a man as fierce intelligent as yourself. That's correct. In a manner of speaking. There are two of us. And the other fellow I presume owns our little house, built in the Grecian style and he doesn't pass many remarks. Not since I would think August fourteenth nineteen thirteen when he was laid to rest. A baronet no less. And I don't mind telling you it's a relief to stretch out next to a bit of elegance and not to have to doss down next to the flotsam and jetsam of London society as I've had upon recent occasion to do."

Schultz wasted no time in begging his Lordship to send his faithful chauffeur Hubert to the pub. Now nearly closing time at three o'clock. To ferry them in suitable style back to Belgravia.

"Ah my dear Schultz, of course you can have my motor. So good to hear from you my dear and I trust your balls have not dropped off yet."

"Holy shit don't remind me. But let me tell you everybody in this business is soon going to be in for a big fucking surprise."

"Ah do I take that to mean Schultz that finally your pubic hair has fallen completely out."

"Your Lordship if I didn't at this second desperately need this favour you're doing me I'd tell you to go fuck yourself."

"And I should dearly love to be able to Schultz, as it would save me squandering so much money on reluctant ladies."

As the car arrived purring up to the curb, Magillacurdy bathed in a beam of afternoon sunshine, was on the pavement rendering the soliloquy from Hamlet. With his tree trunk legs astride, several fly buttons undone, bottles of stout stuck in his pockets, arms outstretched, and head jutting forward. Gathering a traffic stopping crowd who were as the last words trembled from Magillacurdy's lips, clapping and cheering in their tracks. Magillacurdy announcing as he bowed and entered the long gleaming limousine.

"Come and see me on opening night, all of you marvellously charming people. Sure it's only here in the fruit market where you can still find decent cultured citizens in abundance."

Schultz with his sunglasses on as Magillacurdy ensconced back in the soft upholstery, his coal miner's boots with their steel studs propped up on the jump seat and pulling off his sweater and turning it inside out.

"Ah it's pleasantly obvious you're a successful producer me boyo and a vehicle like this calls for me best boot forward and in this case it's a matter of me soup stains being put towards me skin instead of out to the world."

The limousine slowly threading through the crowded market of parked and manoeuvring lorries laden with the shiny light brown skins of onions, the fluffy whites of cauliflowers, flame colored carrots, pale emerald cabbages and deep red peppers, all fresh in from the countryside.

"Ah me boyo here I am recently starving and look at this, enough to feed ten million."

The limousine purring through the sweet smell of oranges, lemons and purple plums, crated and stacked. Porters rumbling by with heaped up carts. Others gathered with hands holding their white cups of tea. The brass plates on doorways of publishers, literary agents and tailors along Henrietta Street. Magillacurdy royally waving and grinning murmuring his acknowledgments to inquisitive looks from the passing people.

"Ah to fuck you. And you too. Yes and even you madam. Would be such sweet paradise."

The motor chariot picking up speed along the Strand. Its theatres, hotels, shops and eating houses. Magillacurdy touching a switch to electrically lower his window. And leaning forward out of his seat, to stick his head and shoulders out into the breeze and shout as the car passed through the throngs going to and from the main line station of Charing Cross.

"Help, help. I'm being kidnapped. Help."

"Holy shit Patrick. Jesus. We're going to get arrested again."

"You and the chauffeur are going to be arrested, not me. I'm being abducted."

Folk stopping to stare at the passing glistening vehicle. Hubert wide eyed turning to see what on earth was happening the other side of the glass division in the back of his limousine until he had to slam on his brakes as he smashed luckily lightly into the big red bus in front.

"Ah sure that put you on tenterhooks didn't it now. Every bobby for miles will have his truncheon at the ready for us."

Magillacurdy taking a bottle of stout out of his pocket and ripping the cap off with his teeth. Schultz wiping the perspiration from his brow as they finally drove through Admiralty Arch and sped along the Mall under the plane trees straight at Buckingham Palace.

"Ah now me boyo till you met me you had yourself a nice little life, hadn't you. And I don't mind saying I'm glad we've met as recently as we did. Sure one minute I'm in a cemetery, the next in prison and the next, without a farthing in me pocket and me belly full, sure I'm heading down the Mall sumptuous as you please on a set of velvet wheels. Should we, do you think, pop out now into the palace and give Her Majesty a thrill. Ah sure, with good reason you believe everything I say and I'm frightening you to death there in the corner, I can see that."

At the door of number four on Schultz's town house stoop stood waiting the Director, the Author, the Choreographer, and the husband and wife composing team, all summoned down from the Dorchester. Schultz and Magillacurdy alighting from the limousine just as the Debutant with her script couched in her arm stepped out of a taxi. Schultz, dropping pound notes out of his wallet as he went rushing over to pay for her fare. As Magillacurdy behind picked them up and came looming in over the Debutant's blond shoulder.

"Ah me darling let me greet you."

Magillacurdy sweeping the Debutant off her feet, hugging and kissing her in his arms. And carrying her bodily all the way up into Schultz's front hall where in her neat slightly rumpled grey flannel suit, she was deposited arse first with a thump on the floor. But before she could shed tears Magillacurdy had her up once more on her feet hugging her.

"Ah now my lovely darling pardon me violence but I always like to see if me leading ladies will bounce. That way I can always tell how far I can safely drop them. O.K. where's the script me boyo. Just give me a look at it so's to see it isn't an awful bunch of appalling rubbish and if it is, why don't despair and fuck the author out the door on the end of a boot, for I just so happen to have me trusty pencil here in me pocket to brush it up a bit. A few little phrases and poetic flourishes here and there and I can put quality and beauty into even the most diabolical piece of trash."

Schultz introducing the newly discovered stars to the Director, Author, Choreographer and Composers. Grimaces creeping over their smiles as Magillacurdy's massive fist painfully compressed all the knuckles offered him. Especially the leather coated Director's with his pink cravat and gold safety pin at the neck of his bright blue shirt. With Magillacurdy's massive miner's boots immediately stepping on the toes of this thin gentleman's silver buckled shiny patent leather slippers.

"Ah now, it's you who is to direct us in this is it. And I suppose you think you're the cat's whiskers."

"Not exactly."

"Not exactly is it. Then maybe you think you're able to fart out your arse every masterly word Shakespeare wrote. And are god's gift to the theatre. And that poor ignorant actors like meself will be dying to be told what to do by the nearly bald likes of you. Ah but I can see fear in your eyes. And I can read your mind. That what on earth am I going to do with this monster. Well I'll relieve you of your anxiety. And tell you right here and now that I'm a fair man. And before I hammer the daylights out of you and your pretensions, I will give you a chance to prove yourself. Sure let's get on with the script now."

The warm pink sun sinking beyond the rooftops of Belgravia. At the sacred hour of tea time. Each chair in the mellow panelled drawing room occupied. The Debutant's open script propped demurely atop her uppermost knee of her crossed legs. Magillacurdy stretched back in an armchair, head resting, booted feet akimbo, as he pulled his sweater up and down like a shade on his hairy pink belly while trepidatiously watched open mouthed and wide eyed by the Director, Author, Choreographer and Composers who had just witnessed a series of life chilling imitations of most of the world's reigning stars of all ethnic persuasions and accents.

"Ah now, I challenge any of you to tell me that my mimic and mime isn't more like the man than he is himself."

Schultz, stationed in his corner by the window, hand clapped his appreciation. And was hesitatingly joined by the rest of his production team. And when the blond Debutant started reading her script, Magillacurdy reaching his own lines, suddenly jumped to his feet, arms waving, voice booming as he declaimed and sang back and forth with the delighted actress. The Director attempting to be part of the theatrical miracle, dropped crouching on one knee, and was promptly swept over backwards thumping on his arse as a gesticulating arm of Magillacurdy's whistled over his bald head.

"Ah pardon me you're getting in the way of me words."

Schultz removing his sunglasses at this stunning rendition. The author smiling in astonishment. The Composer and wife team making notes on their pad and regarding each other with blissful reassurance. With the words of this show nearly shattering the windows of Schultz's drawing room. Where this producer now licked his lips by the window drapes trying to suppress his greediest of smiles. As he stood utterly pleased watching people stop to listen awed in the street. After all these months and wakeful distressing weeks. Here before one now. A showbizz team to erupt beyond the footlights. And send critics everywhere. Into dizzy inspired paeans of praise. And dare it ever be said. Even whispered.

Holy shit
I have
A Hit

Which at last
May not be
On the back
Of my
Head

8

VEN as Schultz's audition raged his Lordship was already being besieged by the police regarding urgent particulars and explanations concerning the kidnapping effected in his motor chariot that afternoon in the Strand. And his Lordship as he tried to ring found Schultz's phone busy. For just following his guests' departure with all piling into his Royal Grace's limousine to be delivered to their various destinations, Schultz had grabbed the phone.

"This you Al."

"Speaking."

"Sigmund here. Jesus christ Al, the fucking guy is a genius, I'm telling you. All I can say is my humble thanks."

"I told you didn't I."

"Yes you did Al. Only you didn't tell me Magillacurdy scares the shit out of everybody in sight. Except the Debutant who fortunately thinks he's marvellous. The Director was trembling in his tracks."

"Good. So now you decide why don't you that you're going to

keep your nose clean and treat that beautiful creature I sent you nice."

"Jesus Al do you always have to get back on that subject so fast."

"Look I'm like the girl's father she ain't got. All she's got is a mother."

"Her mother is the size of three fathers already for christ's sake."

"Boy you are a real funny guy you are talking about a woman who has a serious condition."

"She's got a fucking serious appetite, Al, that's what she's got."

"So we all eat too much."

"Anyway Al you got my best four complimentary seats in the house for opening night."

"Don't worry about complimentary, I'm paying for them seats on principle. All I want you to do is take alright care of the girl."

"Don't worry Al I'm taking her out to a party the Ambassador's throwing across the street."

"That's good."

"But Al I got a problem. And Jesus, it really is very personal. Can I trust you."

"Sure."

"You sure I can trust you, really trust you."

"Sure didn't I just say so."

"It's the most confidential thing I've ever said in my life."

"You haven't said it yet."

"O.K. Al I'm going to say it. Well the fucking bloody thing is I might have some kind of Oriental clap. What should I do."

"Why you fucking dirty son of a bitch."

"Jesus Al stop screaming."

"Stop screaming. Why you cunt you. You should be stopped fucking that's what."

"Will you please listen Al."

"Listen, you want me to listen. To this. When you could already contaminate that girl."

"Al if you'd only listen that's exactly what I told her myself. That I could contaminate her. She was begging me Al to."

"Begging you to contaminate her."

"Yes."

"You mean you did it. You contaminated her."

"Shit Al you don't understand."

"Did you contaminate her. I'm asking you."

"Yes Al. I did. I contaminated her."

"Hey just let me tell you. Even with my heart condition I'm coming over there. And I'm going to beat your lousy brains out. You son of a bitch."

"Don't bust a blood vessel shouting Al. You don't understand how it all fucking well was."

"You son of a bitch I understand. You'd put your prick in a fucking mangle if you thought it would squeeze off your rocks."

"Hey look Al I got to hang up somebody's just coming in my door. Believe me I'll explain everything later. I'm hanging up. Goodbye."

Pricilla pushing in the front door with her arm full of packages. Schultz rushing to help. Catching a foot in the telephone cord and clanging the instrument off the table to the floor.

"Holy shit that's all I need now is to break the phone. What have you got here honey."

"O just some things. And did I hear you say I was just somebody coming in your door."

"Yeah. Sorry. You did. What kind of things you got."

"A dress or two."

"Where did you get them."

"Fortnum's. And why don't you put the phone back on the hook."

"Don't worry about the phone. Worry about Fortnum's. You want to watch it. That's an expensive place."

"O not really."

"What do you mean not really."

"Well I put them on your account, I didn't think you'd mind."

"Now hold it baby, how much was a dress or two."

"Well they were only four hundred and eighteen pounds for two. Reduced."

"For two. Reduced. You mean increased. From what you could have got in a cheaper store. Or I could have got wholesale for half what you paid. Four hundred and eighteen pounds, for christ's sakes. That I'm paying for. You could have asked me. And if you did I would have said fucking well no. With a capital N."

"Your shouting is spitting on me. And I'll take them back if that's the way you feel."

"You take them back honey, and quick right fucking well now take them back."

"The store is closed. I thought you wanted me to look nice for the Ambassador's party."

"What. Look nice for four hundred quid. You could look devastating for a tenth the price in a dress you already got. You can't just go in a store and spend that much of my money."

"You can afford it."

"I can afford it. With your mother and the champagne and caviar. What are you, crazy honey. I can't even afford to take a shit at this fucking time of my life."

"Your constant awful language."

"That's right. And what's more it's going to stay constant. Hey Jesus don't start crying. What is it with you. You think money grows on trees."

"You live in this big house. You go to all the best places. You know all the best people."

"I live here and go to the best places because I fucking well have to. I'm a producer for christ's sake. I got to keep up a big front. And I don't know nobody who wouldn't shit all over me the second my back's to the wall. And stop fucking well crying will you."

"I don't feel well."

"Tough tit."

"You're the most inconsiderate person I think I have ever met. And I feel I'm going to faint."

"Faint for christ's sake, there's tons of room. And padding under the carpet. Only don't knock anything over. Like the phone."

"I didn't knock it over. You did."

"Honey it was you making me nervous coming in the fucking door with the packages."

"I've given you dedicated weeks of my life. I've given you the greatest gift a woman can give a man. I've given you my body."

"And it took long enough to get too."

"How dare you say that."

"So O.K. you gave me a gift, your body. O.K. and I already said thanks. But you're giving me a fucking headache now honey."

Schultz bending over. Brushing a whorl of carpet wool from his knee. When the slap landed. Just as the packages hit the floor. His face spun around by the sting. The burn of fingernails digging in his cheeks. The feel of sticky blood on his fingertips.

"Jesus you bitch you fucking well clawed me. Right on top of what your fucking mother already did."

"And that's not all I'll do. You horrid mean person you."

"Goodbye honey. Get you, your dresses, your suitcases and your ass and get the fuck out of here. And for the last time. Leave me to enjoy my fucking life. That I was enjoying. Before you showed up."

Pricilla rushing up the stairs. Schultz standing scratching his head. Until he saw the boxes on the floor and started kicking them ceiling high all over the hall. Pricilla, rushing back down the stairs, jumped on his shoulders, her fingers sinking locked in his hair and tugging him over backwards on to the floor. As the phone rang.

"Jesus let go for christ's sake, it's the phone, this time of evening it could be an important call from Hollywood you bitch, let go."

"Fuck your bloody stupid Hollywood. Kicking my dresses like that."

Schultz knocked on his back got one hand loose and with an almighty right hook his fist caught Pricilla on the jaw laying her backwards unconscious across his legs. Schultz tugging the ringing phone off the table, catching the instrument before it hit the floor and holding his distinctly loosened hair and scalp with one hand and the telephone with the other.

"Schultz is this you."

"Yes. Who's this."

"My god. I've been trying to ring you for the last twenty minutes. This is Basil Nectarine. What have you done with my motor car."

"Nothing."

"The police Schultz are looking for it. All over London. They say it kidnapped someone."

"It kidnapped nobody."

"Where is the car Schultz."

"It's taking the cast and my Director, Author, Choreographer and Composers home."

"O my god."

"What the fuck's the matter."

"Well they could all be arrested."

"Holy shit."

"And Hubert gets awfully upset when things go wrong."

"Jesus. Hubert you worry about. When my whole show could be in jail."

Schultz reaching to pick up his sunglasses. Putting them on as he lay back staring at the ceiling. In the middle of triumph. Here I am on my fucking back in the middle of chaos. Four hundred and eighteen pounds. Add that to the rest of my bills. Jesus christ add it to everything. As well as Oriental Venereal Plague put on my bill of health. And my whole production imprisoned. But what a beautiful punch it was. Be the first time she's ever really fainted unconscious. A minute of silence is bliss. All the dead weight of her on my legs. She's still breathing. But what's that sound. Of dripping.

Schultz shoving Pricilla. Levering her off with his upraised knees as she rolled over and he pulled out his feet. Schultz crawling a few paces and jumping up. Rushing into the library. To see the ceiling billowing downwards with water pouring and dripping over tables and bookcases.

"Jesus fucking christ now I need a rowboat in the house."

Schultz rushing out and up the stairs and into the bathroom.

107

All taps on. The basin, the bidet and the tub overflowing with water. The once beige carpet several shades deeper and squelching underfoot. Schultz turning off the taps and throwing towels around the floor which merely sank soaked into the deluge. The front bell ringing as Schultz closed the bathroom door where water was pouring out into the hall. And at the top of the stairs holding wet hands up over his eyes.

"I should need a flood right at this time of my existence. This fucking bitch is just ruining my life completely by gradual degrees."

Schultz step by slow step down the stairs. The inert body of Pricilla stretched on her back hands upturned. The smell of burning. One dress box stuck on top of the shade of the table lamp where it had landed kicked by Schultz's foot. And the doorbell still ringing.

"Jesus, who now is at the door. Wearing out the bell. Hold it will you, I'm coming."

Schultz opening the door. Stepping back to await the blue uniforms and tall helmets of the London Metropolitan Police to come enquiring in about a kidnap. Instead of the irate red flushed face of Al in heather colored tweeds and bright orange tie. To enquire about a knockout. And whose taxi was just pulling away in the street.

"For christ's sake Al it's you."

"You're god damn right it's me."

"Jesus Al I'm busy. I got a flood. Don't come in. Can you come around later."

Al pushing past Schultz. The wind blowing through the hall and slamming the front door closed, trembling and tinkling the crystal chandelier. As Al wide eyed with horror and hands raised elbowed Schultz aside.

"Hey what the hell happened."

"Take it easy Al. She fainted. She does it all the time. Like I told you."

"Why you dirty no good son of a bitch. She's got blood on her lip. You hit her."

"I did like hell hit her Al."

"You fucking hit her. Look at this. She looks dead. Her jaw and lip bruised. Blood."

"She jumped on me from behind. I'm telling you, she's a wild-cat. And don't worry she's alive."

"You son of a bitch. Come on. Pick on me. A man. Why don't you. Go ahead. I'm taking the glasses off. Put your fists up."

"I'm not going to fight you Al. And all your mid west morals. You're a generation older. I could physically kill you."

"You just try it. Let's see you. With your diseased prick. You contaminate the girl. Then you hit her. Come on. Put em up."

"Al come on, act your age. I got my whole cast and show out in a car in London at this second with the whole police force after them."

"You got clap that's what you got."

"Don't shout that out Al it was confidential."

"Confidential. It's clap. It's contagious."

"I got neighbors for christ's sake. Keep your voice down."

"You no good shit, you no good dirty shit. And hey watch where you're stepping on the girl."

Schultz turning to step back one leg over the prostrate Pricilla who emitted a long low groan. Al lunging. His left arm out to grab Schultz by the lapel. Schultz reeling back crashing into the table. The phone starting to ring. Schultz reaching out with a right hand for the receiver and raising his left to ward off a roundhouse fist sweeping jawwards from Al. Which connected high up on the side of Schultz's head as he ducked. And made him see sparkling exploding stars.

"Shit you bastard you hit me. Al I'll kill you."

Al with a neat skip over Pricilla, wading in, heart condition and all. Sending right crosses and left uppercuts as Schultz shouted into the phone before dropping it.

"Hello whoever you are. I got a temporary problem. Please call me back."

Schultz punching now for his life. Connecting with a straight left ka plonk on Al's nose which instantly cascaded bleeding blood. Schultz momentarily still and aghast at the horrifying crimson sight of Al's face. Al undaunted cutting free with a looping right connecting with Schultz's unblack eye. Schultz hanging on in a clinch.

"I'll kill you Al. If you don't cut it out right now. I'll fucking well kill you. I don't care how fucking near the grave you are already. I'll kill you."

"Try it. Go ahead try it. Let go. And get some more of what you're getting."

"You asked for it Al."

Schultz pummelling lefts and rights into Al's belly, driving him back just as Al again caught Schultz on the side of the head and Schultz fell to the floor. Al momentarily surveying his handy work. Stepping backwards and promptly tripping over the just reviving Pricilla. Crashing down arse and elbows first on top of her. Pricilla letting loose one of her more prolonged blood-curdling screams.

"Now it's you you fucking dumbbell Al who's killing her."

Schultz scrambling to his feet. The sudden sound outside of police car bells and racing engines. Heavy boots pounding on the front steps. Schultz's heart in his chest quivering waiting for the doorbell to ring. His bloodied fists unclenched hanging at his sides. Pricilla groaning hands to her ribs where the backs of Al's elbows had landed. The front door splintering asunder. And smashed wide open limping from its hinges. Two vast London bobbies falling into the hallway. Followed by four more. Two with sawn off shotguns levelled at Schultz.

"Hands up. Don't move."

"Don't shoot, don't shoot for christ's sake."

I'm
A theatrical
Producer

9

PEER'S CAR IN KIDNAP MUDDLE
West End Cast and Production Detained

Pedestrians in the Strand outside Charing Cross Station just after three o'clock this afternoon were witness to a man shouting for help from the window of a Rolls-Royce limousine. The vehicle which had the characteristic blue light of Royal Cars, and whose licence registration number was traced by police, was found to be owned by Lord Nectarine, MFH, old Harrovian and one of England's most outstanding schoolboy and university cricketers.

The car which was not located for several hours was finally stopped by Police on Fulham Road near Brompton Cemetery where it was said one of its occupants who resisted arrest was being delivered. Mr. Hubert Jones, Lord Nectarine's chauffeur, fainted during the incident.

Others found in the car and who were detained at Walham

Green Police Station to help police with their further enquiries, said they were en route to their respective destinations from an audition and that they were members of the
cast, The Director, Composers, Choreographer, and Author of
a soon to be West End production, "Kiss It Don't Hold It It's
Too Hot." The car's occupants were later released but not
before the Police were treated to some song and dance by one
of the male stars.

At the same time, Police on a tipoff that the alleged kidnap
might have political as well as monarchist implications, raided
the house of a Mr. Sigmund Schultz a theatrical impresario
who was thought to have borrowed Lord Nectarine's car.

At Mr. Schultz's Belgravia address Police found a man and
woman who were believed to have been both knocked down
in a struggle with Mr. Schultz. Charged with having caused
actual bodily harm Mr. Schultz was arrested. One policeman
with a dislocated shoulder sustained in gaining entry and two
other persons suffering injuries in the affray, were treated
for their injuries at St. George's Hospital nearby and allowed
to go home. Their names are being withheld by Police.

For the first time in Sperm Productions business history, all
directors were in the office at the ungodly and untheatrical hour
of eleven a.m. The incident which had screamed headlines in the
late editions of London's evening newspapers had percolated into
most of the popular morning papers as well. With Binky overflowing with delight with every edition spread across the chairman's desk.

IRISH ACTOR'S SHOUT FOR HELP
FAMED CRICKETER'S LIMOUSINE INVOLVED
WEST END ABDUCTION A WEST END PRODUCTION
BELGRAVIA IMPRESARIO SOCKS TWO

Schultz the last to arrive came into the chairman's office in his
darkest pair of sunglasses yet. Bloodstains on his shirt, lip swollen,

face scratched and tie knot undone. Rumbles of suppressed laughter rocking Binky as he neatly cut the end off a cigar with a silver penknife. While his Lordship, having lit up his tenth cigarette, was puffing madly away and jigging his foot nervously up and down.

"Schultz, never in a million years am I going to let you have my motor again."

"None of it was my fault."

"Schultz that is what you always say."

"Tell me how am I going to predict this Magillacurdy's going to stick his big thick Irish skull out the fucking window of the car and start shouting he's kidnapped. Anyway Jesus your Lordship, look at the good publicity for the show will you."

"Schultz you are, aren't you, utterly without conscience. I hardly think having my identification dragged into the paper in this manner is good publicity."

"Shit I got arrested. I've just been up in the dock in court before a judge. Blamed for assaulting people. There wasn't even decent toilet paper in my cell where everybody could watch you taking a crap. The media made me look like a criminal. And look it says everywhere you were one of England's best all time cricketers. Isn't that the national fucking sport. I mean if you could play American baseball that well you'd have people asking for your autograph everywhere you went. Anyway I'm dead beat. That police cell all night, people and noise waking you up every five minutes. And Jesus I need a clean shirt. I got to rush right out this second. Where's an extra couple of copies of my budget Binky. This big property developer I was going to meet before you made me go down to the fucking hospital that day is dying at the end of the phone now to get his money into the show."

"Just a moment, Schultz allow me, the sleeves may be a mite too long but otherwise it should fit."

"Hey christ Binky, you're giving me the shirt off your back."

"Schultz, yes, I have that honor."

"Hey christ, wait a minute. I'm touched. I really am. Thanks. And it's silk."

The shirts exchanged across the chairman's desk. Schultz removing his undershirt stained with blood. As Binky, the window light playing over his bare shoulders, turned a page of newspaper.

"Holy shit Binky you're built like an adonis. Isn't there anything you guys weren't born with."

"Of course Schultz over the generations and centuries of selective breeding for muscles, brains and beauty, not to mention land holdings, coal mines and distilleries, such results have given his Lordship and I a few advantages we enjoy over your usual upper-middle classes. And I'm flattered Schultz that you should remark so about my physique but dear me you must not jump overboard. I think both his Royal Grace and I, among many other things, lack your unquenchable fighting spirit. And ah Schultz, you're not even stopping to look at your mail."

"Binky I got no time this morning. My door on the house is busted. Fucking rooms flooded. In court this morning I got fined twenty five bloody quid and told by the Judge I was a menace. When I was the fucking one who was attacked by two maniacs. I'm telling you if I can only stay alive for another month or so, just alive that's all. I'm going to have the biggest smash on my hands that you guys or this town has ever seen. Hey this shirt fits swell. And boy I can use the temporary confidence of these gold cuff links."

"But Schultz before you rush off, perhaps you'd tell your old pal Binky about the prognosis of your Oriental Plague."

"Jesus that worry got crushed right out of existence in the last twenty four hours. No microbe could live through what I've been through."

"Ah but Schultz this is a most interesting development, your socking people."

"That's right. Any shit now from anybody. That's what they get. This. Right in the gizzard."

"But Schultz I must remind you this is England. You can't go around punching people."

"Can't I. Just watch your daily newspapers you guys."

Schultz folding his production agreement and shoving it into his jacket inside pocket. A rapping at the office door. Binky in his lightest airiest vowels saying come in. Rebecca with one of her long elegant hands brushing back a soft curled long blond brown strand of hair from her attractively wide forehead.

"Excuse me sir. O goodness, I'm sorry."

"Ah forgive me Rebecca my momentary state of undress. We're just doing a little experimenting with costuming. Do come in."

"There is an urgent personal call for Mr. Schultz on Lord Nectarine's private line."

His Lordship suddenly sitting bolt upright on the chaise longue highly unamused. Having been lying back not unsmilingly in calm enjoyment of this morning's marvellous showbizz conference.

"Schultz to whom have you given my private number upon which to take your personal calls when there are six other lines."

"Jesus your Lordship, I gave it to nobody. And do you have to get steamed up about such a simple little item like that. Besides you never use the damn thing."

Schultz hurrying out of the office. And back in a moment. Beaming ear to ear. As Binky following a puff of cigar smoke raised his chin enquiringly.

"Ah Schultz clearly good news."

"Jesus that was the laboratory tests. The Doc just got in. You sons of bitches. I ain't got a thing wrong with me."

"Ah how nice to hear that, Schultz. How nice."

Schultz his scratched face with one very black eye and the other fading blue and his rumpled ivy league attire now improved with Binky's silk shirt, swept jauntily out of the office of Sperm Productions. Even popping on his head a fedora his Lordship abandoned on a clothes rack in the hall. As Binky further conferred with his aristocratic associate.

"Ah your Royal Grace we must really admire him I think. Especially in view of the dear boy's ability to convert as it were your limousine into Schultz's personal bandwagon. And in spite of his venereal tribulation."

Binky who quite savoured to take hilarious delight in another's mild misfortune was also as he had amply demonstrated this very morning, possessed of an astonishing magnanimity and humanity and would rush to any downed friend's assistance. And now he especially relished the publicity which had helpfully befallen Schultz.

"Your Royal Grace I think, I really do, that we must now consider seriously buying up Schultz's show."

This previously glowering grey day, now blossoming a bird singing cheerful London bright blue. Pigeons cooing out on the roof. Binky, in Schultz's bloodstained shirt and without his usual oval cuff links flashing gold, sifting and shifting one last time chuckling through the newspapers, laughing outright here and roaring there. And now finally taking up the morning's post. And still convulsing himself with laughter with his somewhat less amused Lordship over this morning's marvellous fun and games, not to mention the contemplated renewed efforts to reawaken somehow Schultz's terror of clap, pox and plague.

"I wonder, your Amazing Grace, if we were lacking in imagination not to throw in some further dread, testicles popping off disease of mid Africa to befuddle his doctor and quake poor Schultzy boy in his tracks. Would you believe it that prior to these present well publicized mishaps that the prospect of throwing further jolts into Schultz, had me popping open the encyclopaedia last night looking for fresh scary medical afflictions."

Binky loungingly tilting back in his chair and raising one foot to rest on his gout stool. His finger idly flicking through the stack of letters. Looking up from time to time as he selected an envelope which he sniffed before more closely scrutinizing. Then raising his smiling face to survey his Lordship who was removing a rather tattered old sock from one of his extremely white narrow feet, which had been encased, as were Binky's and Schultz's feet, in shoes from the male chorus line of a previous failed Schultz production.

"Bills from set designers and builders and lighting companies do have an unerring smell. Or goodness, your Amazing Grace is that perfume I perceive, your foot."

"Now Binky you're not to behave with me as you do with Schultz."

"Of course I wouldn't dream of doing so. But I say. Speak of the poor devil. What's this little item. Addressed to Schultz. Sigmund F. And appended by Esquire if you please. And by god, from, of all places, Buckingham Palace. Well, I think we must look into this. I mean it's just as exciting as spying on the middle classes. And we may indeed have revealed to us further insights into Schultz's character. And just, ah, gently unstick this seal."

"Binky you mustn't do that."

"But your Amazing Grace of course I must, when one confronts an envelope issuing from our Sovereign's London residence to Schultz who simply no matter how one stretches one's imagination, is not quite properly equipped to mingle among even the more shallowly Debrett of London's aristocracy. Never mind, the Queen."

"Binky that really is an outrageous thing to do. You mustn't."

"O pish and pother. Schultzy boy won't mind. I say. Good god."

Binky his nostrils flickering and eyelids fluttering, holding aloft a gleaming gold embossed invitation.

"I say. Good gracious me. How in heaven's name does Schultz rate this. Your Royal Grace, you do realise that here I hold a command from the Sovereign herself to Schultz himself. Albeit through the medium of a Royal employee."

"I don't believe you Binky."

"Ah you Royals are all the same, sceptic to the last. Allow me. To therefore read. The Master of the Household is Commanded by Her Majesty to invite Mr. Sigmund Franz Schultz to an afternoon party at Buckingham Palace."

"Good god, Binky."

"Ah at last I'm glad to see you alarmed your Royal Grace. And I mean to say my dear, to watch Schultz elbow his way about among minor royalty may be an amusement not to be missed. Being as he is so marvellously oblivious to their terribly high social positions.

117

But ye gads. Heaven forbid. Imagine. Schultz. Bloodstained. Black eyed. Face clawed. In personal intimate proximity with the Sovereign herself, Her Majesty the Queen."

With one bare foot wagging loose, his Lordship, rarely one to bestir himself unless in the most dire of emergencies, hobbled over to Binky to take the invitation in hand. Binky slitting open more letters and removing photographs sent by the usual young ladies displaying their particulars. Holding each picture up to the window light, moving the shiny surface this way and that. And with his desk magnifying glass uncovered from its scarlet kidskin case, perusing certain photographs more carefully.

"Ah, yes, just as I thought, this nicely rounded young lady is worthy of an audition. I do love the way they sincerely stare out at me so absolutely intent upon stardom."

"My god Binky, this invitation is absolutely genuine."

"Of course it is my dear, haven't I just attempted to make such an impression upon you. Do you suppose your Royal Grace that someone at the Royal Palace got his hands on the wrong mailing list."

"Binky you must put it properly back in its envelope and reseal it with haste."

"Ah now, my good Lord. Let us not be too hasty. Let us consider a few points first. For a start the palace advisers will with dismay, be reeling with the impact of Schultz's recent publicity. And of course they may, being so formidably possessed as they are with good breeding, not revoke Schultz's invitation. But I mean can we, as directors of Sperm Productions, now allow a grimly certain faux pas to befall Her Majesty. I mean one would not be concerned of course were it just the ordinary royals. But the Queen herself. Ye gads. Tantamount to treason, that would be. I mean even, in the regrettable name of this firm, to bring our warning to the attention of the Sovereign's private secretary is heinous. But now with all this over newspapers. And with our Schultzy boy previously worried to a frazzle as he was over the diseases we made him think he had, he absolutely is bound to commit the most fatal type of indiscretion which will reflect disagreeably upon this company. And I speak as chairman."

"Binky you really must reseal this."

"I shall this second. But my dear Lord Nectarine are you suggesting I allow this travesty to take place. I mean the likes of Schultz rubbing elbows with just your usual Royals, as I've already said, that is highly amusing. But the Sovereign. Who holds what's left of our fading empire together. O dear dear me I dread to think. Dread to conceive. Can you imagine. Hey gee hi ya queenie, glad to make your acquaintance, my whole fucking cast was just fucking kidnapped and got a lot of good fucking publicity, and do you want to invest in my fucking new show, Boom Madam Bang Madam Pop Madam Pop or whatever the wretched thing has just recently been renamed. You, my dearest Royal Grace are only too familiar yourself with his behaviour."

"Binky I think you must calm yourself."

"And let my country and my Queen down, never. Although I'm sure one will much content oneself in knowing and admiring the magical way in which the Sovereign's acolytes will gently sidestep merely without word or motion, the kind of embarrassments presented by the Schultzes of this world."

"Ah god bless poor dear old Schultz."

"What's that. Good gracious Basil, my dear. I mean you Lord Nectarine might imagine that all this is just a great hoo ha over nothing. But I remain most concerned. Did you know that Schultz on a previous occasion of rubbing shoulders in the better circles, not only borrowed a cigarette from a member of the royal family but also requested a match. Did your Royal Grace know that."

"No I did not Binky."

"I was there. And of course I sank immediately downwards under the arches of some nice lady's high heels. And amid the first hushed horror that the first request produced, absolute gasps followed by stunned whispers all over the place greeted Schultz's asking of a light. Hey honey baby you got a light. Fortunately it was given by a nearby equerry. But of course your Amazing

Grace, indeed, not only did this social clanger provoke the usual remarks of how did that person get in here. But most astonishingly Schultzy boy was, by the royal female personage who had given him the cigarette, also invited to lunch. Now how do we account for that. Can you elicit an insight from your long and unhurried moments mingling in such circles. It's taxed my mind to the limit. I absolutely haven't got a clue."

"Times are changing you know Binky."

"Yes and how sad my Lord."

"And Binky we must not overlook the fact that Schultz is possessed of some faculty enabling him to blithely ignore some of the more superficial niceties. And I do think he is rather blessedly oblivious to his either being rejected or accepted."

"Ah. Speak of the devil. You're back Schultz. We were just this moment discussing you."

Schultz with the knot of his tie undone. His Lordship's fedora on his head. Sunglasses gleaming.

"Hey you fucking guys. You're not trying to dream up more shit to put me through. My doctor's bills cost me a fortune. You sons of bitches. And Binky, I suspect it's you who dreamed up my diseases."

"That aspersion you so rashly cast is wounding Schultz."

"You nearly worried me out of my mind. I could have gone crazy if I didn't have so much other fucking god damn things happening to me."

"Ah Schultz, dear Schultz. We were only trying to keep your mind off your production worries."

"Well boy, shit you nearly did. But boy let me tell you this tycoon. Five words it took him. How much do you need. And I told him. And a second later he said I'll take half. Hey any mail for me."

"Right there Schultz. Right there."

"Hey what's going on. Why are you guys looking at me like that."

"Ah Schultz we look at you for three reasons. Firstly to see if any other symptoms of any other dread disease may have become obvious. And then we look at you because we like you. And lastly we look at you because we think you behave exactly like a hungry monkey."

"Thanks a lot. But right now folks who cares what I look like. I haven't a fucking worry in the whole wide world. But when half the show's investment's taken is that all you guys got to say to me."

Schultz opening his Royal envelope. Taking out the stiff white card and after a brief glance, unceremoniously stuffing the invitation in his jacket side pocket.

"Except to say Schultz you don't seem to pay much attention to your mail these days. That letter you just crammed in your pocket looked rather emblazoned with engravings that might incline one to think it was an important invitation."

"Look at you fucking guys playing games while I got things on my mind. Hey why don't the two of you guys get married and have fucking children."

"Ah Schultz you really are, aren't you full of wonderful ideas."

"Well all you do is hang around here like you know where your next million is coming from. And both of you fucking well do. But I don't."

"But Schultz his Royal Grace and I distinctly thought we saw a communication, indeed something which appeared might even be from the Royal Palace."

"So."

"So Schultz we would love to see it."

"Jesus you guys haven't you ever seen a royal invitation before."

"Well I'm sure his Amazing Grace has seen many but such as myself is not always invited to every top occasion and the word frequently could never apply to the number of times I have popped into the palace. Surely in view of my socially deprived situation you can let me in on the royal communication."

"I'm really sorry you guys, you know how it is in those circles, I can't tell you a single thing about it. But you know how everyone over there in the palace is always trying to rub shoulders in show business."

"I must confess Schultz you really do have us stumped. Neither his Amazing Grace nor I know of such inclinations of the Royal Family."

Schultz changing into a new silk shirt he'd bought and towards the waning afternoon following Schultz's smooth telephone conversations with less resisting investors, there nevertheless appeared a certain anxiety creeping over Schultz with his increased visits to the water closet. And it especially became apparent, when Schultz pretending to search the telephone book for new possible showbizz victims, was yet again overheard screaming at Rebecca, his Lordship's and Binky's adored shapely and charming secretary.

"Yes, I want the same kind of certain doctor not a different one in Harley Street. I threw away his number."

"What kind was he sir."

"Didn't you hear me last time what I said, a certain kind. The same doctor I had before."

Binky and his Lordship were now once more hopeful that indeed Schultz might as the afternoon ebbed provide one more good laugh before they repaired to tea. And they were both not unpleasantly instantly alarmed, not to say momentarily stunned out of their privileged minds. To have Schultz with his sunglasses hysterically removed, and with black and blue eyes blazing come charging into the chairman's office just as they were departing for a slap up Fortnum's repast complete with salmon sandwiches, gulls' eggs and topped off with sacher cake and lapsang souchong.

"Hey hold it you guys."

Schultz putting his hands up and down and through his hair which he indeed was unquestionably loosening at the roots. Binky already steamed up with suppressed laughter finally exploding as Schultz's tongue nervously licked his lips as he regarded the dislodged strands in his palm. Plus his back now seemed to lose its straightness entirely.

"Jesus christ almighty what are you laughing about Binky."

"Not a thing."

"You know don't you."

"Know what Schultz."

"What's happened."

"What's happened Schultz."

"I've got the fucking god damn clap. That's what's happened. The Doc this minute tells me on the phone I got all the symptoms. I've got a burning discharge started this afternoon like crazy."

"Please Schultz do then please stand back a bit from his Royal Grace and I. And pray tell who did this awful thing to you."

"I'll tell you who. And I'm telling you too, you can't trust nobody in this fucking world. I got it from the cunt you sent me down to visit in the hospital. She gave it to me. Posing as a vestal virgin. Where's some notepaper. I'm making a record of this. I'm going to sue her and her mother. Come on your Lordship let me at the notepaper."

"You know Schultz you do rather harden one."

"Why. What the fuck's the matter now."

"Well you rush in here. And proceed to open personal desks, fish out personal notepaper."

"I'm looking for some good fucking engraved notepaper you guys keep locked up. Plus I got to give Binky his shirt back."

"But you also handle one's personal desk furnishings without the least concern. Having just announced you're clapped up. And not once, not even once have you exhibited or made any effort whatsoever to avoid handling Binky's or my personal desk gewgaws."

Binky in his undershirt, holding away from him with his pincered fingers Schultz's bloodied garment as he on tiptoe announced.

"And Schultz, please do keep my shirt. Merely give me back my cuff links. Just pop them there on the edge of the desk. I do believe boiling them may be sufficient sterilization. Don't you agree your Royal Grace."

"Holy shit, you guys. Treat me like a leper now. I come from the cleanest country in the world. I mean you only got soft toilet

123

paper in England a few years ago. And now here I am. A wonderful future ahead."

  With only
  The clap
  Holding me
  Back

10

His own comb having been commandeered by Magillacurdy rushing to adjust a curl on some lady's dog in the street, Schultz asked for a loan of his Lordship's or Binky's who both demurred. Especially as at that very next moment Schultz had the effrontery to attempt to also borrow a handkerchief before heading down to his taxi ordered to take him to Harley Street. Where the attractive nurse smiled welcome in the dark hall and led him with her prick stirring legs up the stairs.

"Of course Mr. Schultz it can hit that hard and that fast as you put it. The incubation period can be anywhere from two to ten days. From our previous conclusive tests it is established that you have never had gonorrhea previously. But this does unquestionably look like a particularly virulent case of clap, to use its more common appellation. It could also be a form of non specific urethritis."

"Just cure me Doc just cure me. I really am in a hurry."

"May I enquire if you are likely to be exposed again to the source of this present infection."

"Doc, can you just give me something so I don't get it again."

"I'm afraid Mr. Schultz I can't. You are simply going to have to refrain from sexual intercourse for a while."

"Doc, it's the one thing in my life I can't do without."

"Well Mr. Schultz let me say that that is extremely apparent. As indeed I fear you went right ahead with the intercourse which gave you your present infection without waiting for clearance from me as to your possibly being already infected."

"Doc this girl imposed on me. And gave me this what I've got. I was really trying to control myself."

"I see. Just bend a little forward. Well now let's find a suitable spot on your buttock. Your punishment as it were is ready to be administered."

"Holy shit, excuse my language Doc. You're not going to shove that all the way into me are you."

"You won't feel a thing except a sudden deep jab or two into a very large muscle."

"Jesus Doc I got a special aversion to that kind of pain from big needles."

"You seem if I may say so Mr. Schultz, to take your other injuries rather well. Black eyes, and the rather deep scratches on your face. I hope I'm not maligning you. But I do believe I've been reading about you. You are the Mr. Schultz to whom the papers recently refer."

"Yeah Doc. Regrettably."

"Well the theatre must be becoming a very lively place these days."

Schultz with his pained arse in a taxi heading south across Oxford Street. Down New Bond. Grand emporiums of auction houses. Art dealers and women's fashions. Turn west on a sedate and grey stoned Brook Street. Grosvenor Square and its flat green park. Tall elms. The statue of an American President standing solemn in a cloak with a cane. The Embassy with its great eagle spread high over its entrance. Christ if clap has to get mentioned in the renewal of my passport. Have you at any time had a virulent venereal disease. How often. Caught it from whom. And when infected how many other people did you then give it to. Do you intend to disloyally import it into the United States. In which case can you give the names of those people who will risk exposure to you on your return home.

Down Park Lane. The dear Dorchester radiant in pink rays of sun. Late afternoon whores patrolling. Even thicker than they did when I first came to this town. And spending every cent I had, trying to live like a big time producer. Till I was broke with nowhere to live, without a penny in my pocket. Cold and hungry on a last desperate day. Standing around the corner from Piccadilly Circus in Air Street. Before I was going to deliver myself to the Embassy. For a taxpayers' sponsored ride back to America. Kind hearted Lizzie from Limerick stepped up behind me in the shadows. Supported me for six peaceful weeks. While customers were pounding her in the next room. And I pounded her after her night's work without even getting so much as a cold. She gave me pocket money and the least troubles I ever had from a female. Except when she made me go into a Catholic church on Sunday. To stand around freezing my balls off with a bunch of vacuous mumbling Irish.

Circling Hyde Park Corner. Wellington Statue. The great Arch. And the Artillery Memorial. The traffic in its thickening stream. Slowing bumper to bumper. At least one person in every two cars has got to buy a ticket to my show. Everybody needs entertainment. If only there was no censorship I could sell serial rights of a T.V. film of my fucking life, for a fucking fortune and retire forever from being a producer. Got to keep my mental faculties together. Stick Binky and his Lordship with the rest of the investment. And start paying off bills stacking up at the Dorchester.

The taxi cruising past the ambulance entrance of St. George's Hospital down Grosvenor Crescent. Into Belgrave Square. The cream painted facades. The always shrouded secret park in the middle. Down my nice private quiet street. Lights all lit in all the windows of the Ambassador's house. He's about the only friend I've got in London.

"There you are Squire, Harley Street to Belgravia."

127

"Thanks. Keep the change."

"Thank you sir. And enjoy your stay in Britain."

Schultz looking up at his splintered front door as he pushed open the squealing gate in the railings to the steps down to the basement. In the cold kitchen, sticking a knife in a jar of peanut butter. Suck a big glob of the stuff off the blade. Take a spoonful of strawberry jam. Gnaw on a piece of stale bread. Sustain me till I see what new shit is going to hit the fan. Climb up the stairs. Peek in the pantry. And wince into the library. The front door propped closed with the hall table stacked with wet books. Everything is worse than I thought. Jesus the end of the world can come hidden away in your own life.

On the hall table, atop the soaked books, two envelopes. Hand delivered and shoved down from the letter box. Schultz with his finger ripping one open.

Chary, Leer, Unkanny
Mumchance & Nightingale.

Dear Sir,

Upon certain newspaper reports having come to the attention of our clients Mr. & Mrs. Adams Apple-Apple, they did upon our advice instruct their surveyor, Mr. Johns, to inspect the property of No. 4 Arabesque Street in your absence, which is permitted under the lease which lease we hold no longer valid.

Mr. Johns' report is now in our hands. The general condition he described the house to be in, is to say the least, entirely deplorable. Extensive damage has not only been done to the valuable contents but to the fabric of the building. Walls everywhere are fingerprinted and marked and smudged as if items of food were flung about the premises. Indeed a piece of Gorgonzola cheese was found adhering to a signed and dated eighteenth century painting "Hounds Taking the Scent." And the valuable plaster work on the ceilings of the bathroom and library have been entirely destroyed.

The disappearance has also been noted of the fourteenth century bust of Justinian, from the landing. In this latter matter we would be glad to have your immediate check in the amount of fourteen thousand pounds being the assessed value of the piece. As soon as builders' estimates are in our hands we will advise you of the final amount required to cover other damage. Meanwhile your early check in the amount of ten thousand pounds as part payment is required forthwith.

Aside from the clear evidence of moral turpitude expressly forbidden in the lease, and in other extraordinary circumstances prevailing and in order to preserve that more damage does not take place and, without prejudice to any other remedy we may have in the matter, we are instructed by our clients to hereby serve notice upon you to vacate the premises of No. 4 Arabesque Street, Belgravia within seven days or legal proceedings will be taken against you so to do.

Yours faithfully,

Chary, Leer, Unkanny
Mumchance & Nightingale

P.S. As a personal note from a senior member of this firm, I should like to make the point that this is not what one would expect from a citizen of that country which came to fight beside us so gallantly following our winning single handedly the battle of Britain.

Schultz holding the letter up shaking it. You dirty bunch of British tight assed fuckers just let me give you a fucking point or two. In the first place that bust of Justinian was unadulterated plaster and a piece of lousy cheap junk. In the second place the bathroom faucets all exploded leaking till I got a wrench myself to twist the fucking things shut. In the third place the place was practically a sewer when I moved in. In the fourth place all my

129

fucking problems are caused by women. In the fifth place none of you are going to get a red cent out of me.

Schultz leaning against the wall, momentarily relaxing from his shouting match with the physically unrepresented firm of Chary, Leer etcetera. Taxi diesel engines throbbing by in the street. Schultz's finger slowly ripping open the second envelope. With the same black heavily engraved letterhead. Jesus christ at least no one can accuse me I'm handicapped by my optimism at this fucking time of my life. They've added a really appropriate new partner's name since their previous letter two minutes ago.

Chary, Leer, Unkanny
Mumchance, Voyeur &
Nightingale

Dear Sir,

We are instructed by Mr. Al Duke and Miss Pricilla Prune to act upon another matter separate from the one concerning clients from whom you have leased No. 4 Arabesque Street.

In court proceedings this morning you pleaded guilty to assaulting our clients. Who as a result of such assault were both treated for abrasions and contusions. Miss Prune, who now requires extensive dental work having lost and swallowed her tooth as a consequence of being struck by your fist, also suffered severe bruising to her chest area and will be unable to work for some considerable time. She must also due to dental damage eat slops.

Mr. Duke who so bravely defended the honor of Miss Prune, had to have administered prolonged medication to stop the persistent bleeding of his nose. The clothes he was wearing as were those of Miss Prune were stained with blood and cannot be worn again.

Mr. Duke however, has agreed to waive his right to any damages subject to your fully compensating Miss Prune who had a brand new dress of hers scorched irreparably through your having kicked it up on top of a lamp bulb. We would be glad to have your immediate check in the amount of six hundred and forty nine pounds and ten shillings to cover the above as well as our own out of pocket expenses, otherwise we are instructed to issue proceedings against you for this amount and hold you liable for all costs in so doing.

Yours faithfully,

Chary, Leer, Unkanny
Mumchance, Voyeur &
Nightingale.

P.S. As a senior partner of this firm, one hopes that your unchivalrous treatment of a lady will reach the attention of the Home Office and the appropriate action ensue.

"You fucking sons of bitches I'll give you something to sue about."

Schultz sailing his right foot into a hall chair. Kicking the brocaded seat upwards out of its frame. His left foot sailing through the presently knee high lamp shade on top of which Pricilla's dress scorched. Tearing down a painting from the wall and sending another foot through into the infinities of its rural scene. Schultz as his Lordship would say, was in an excitable state. And foot kicking crazy. As well as foot kicking mad. Till hearing a voice. And fingers widening an aperture in the splintered door.

"Ah let me give you a hand in there me boyo, that's no way now to wreck a house. You'd be hours doing it. Here let me show you now how that's done. As soon as I break me way in."

"Jesus Magillacurdy the door's blocked, go downstairs for christ's sake. Don't do nothing. I'm a ruined enough man as it is."

"Nonsense. Nonsense. Sure what kind of dissident black bile talk is that to oppress the breast. When there are pints of the finest to be drunk off hundreds of mahogany bars all over London. And women to be downed with them. Ruined. Never. Redeemed is more like it."

131

Magillacurdy skipping sideways in through the basement kitchen door. To stand there on the flagstones a benign loving smile across his face.

"Ah now me boyo. I came to apologise I have. For causing you all your trouble. But didn't we hit the headlines with a bang, though."

"We hit them alright Magillacurdy. You're a publicist par excellence."

"Ah now surely that's not all I'm good for."

"Magillacurdy I'll give it to you straight. And you know all this yourself already. You are the biggest genius I've ever encountered in showbizz."

"Ah bless you and may your years in showbizz have been legion."

"But Jesus christ almighty Magillacurdy, never again please will you, shout out the window of a car we're in that you're being kidnapped."

Magillacurdy pulling his blazing red forelock, his eyes welling with moisture. Tears slowly oozing to tumble down his pale cheeks. And go rolling over the corners of his lips dimpled in a smile.

"Ah me boyo, me boyo, me boyo. I'm conscience stricken. Contrite."

Magillacurdy's miner's boots thumping across the kitchen floor. His massive arm reaching around the back of Schultz's shoulder.

"Ah me boyo. Is it not a pity the world has no place for me. Except right at the very top."

"And Magillacurdy do you on top of everything else, also have to be devastatingly charming."

"Ah me worst fault that. When me charm gets the better of me. Sure no one can resist it. And I have victims all over the place."

From up under his thick blue sweater, Magillacurdy pulling his script.

"On closer prolonged scrutiny this is the greatest load of awful shit since vanity in the theatre was invented but me boyo you're sincere, I can see that. So I'm going to accept and take the part for your winningly lovable sake alone. Ah but as I suspected the lyrics did just lend themselves to revisions. So make a fresh script out of this now. And after I've consulted with the Director, Choreographer and Composers and given the author a Welsh miner's boot up his hole, you won't have such a bad little show on your hands after all. Now do you have a bottle of health giving stout handy."

With a glass of whiskey, another rib creaking hug and a resounding kiss on Schultz's cheek, Magillacurdy danced light footed out the kitchen door. And went roaring away up the basement steps having sung four new astonishing numbers he'd written into the script.

Schultz, undressing to soak in a hot wet tub in his wet blacked out bathroom, could still hear the voice of Magillacurdy serenading down Arabesque Street. Warm water lapping at the lobes of Schultz's ears. Silence now. Like a Saturday noonday with folk gone on their weekend ways to the country. Be sued for a big fraction of my whole show's budget. Here I am thinking I've escaped from all the witch and bitchhood of American fucked up womanhood. And right in the middle of England I walk into the worst bitch of my life. Jesus the British secret service could be creeping up on me to bounce bullets off the side of my bath.

Schultz suddenly alert sitting up in the bubbly water. A creak of floor board on the stairs and coming closer out in the hall. Schultz gripping both sides of the tub. Levering himself up half ready to crouch down again submerged behind the porcelain. One hand slipping and Schultz plunging splashing backwards bodily in the bath head under water nearly drowning. Framed in the door the female silhouette of Pricilla.

"That's you Sigmund isn't it."

"Yes it's fucking well me."

"Why are you in the dark. Aren't you ready yet. Well I'm asking you, aren't you."

"To your first question I'm in the dark because there's no light. To the second question. No. I'm not ready. I'm fucking drowned. To your third remark in that tone of voice. I'll get up out of this bath and knock some more of your teeth out."

"Darling please, don't get angry with me. I'm only asking because of the Ambassador's party we've been invited to. And we're late."

"If I wasn't lying down in this bath here taking a much needed rest I swear I'd clip you one right again in the fucking mouth."

"O darling isn't one sock in the jaw quite enough."

"Not for you it sure enough isn't. You got some nerve coming back here. You know don't you you're trying to sue me. In my own house. You and that geriatric creep Al."

"But why should that stop us from going to the Ambassador's party."

"I'll tell you something to stop us. Just tell me who the fuck other than me you're fucking."

"Darling that's offensive."

"Cut the shit. Who else are you screwing."

"I assume you are accusing me of having slept with other men, and I emphatically have not. Besides my past is none of your business."

"You honey have infected me with a dose of the clap."

"How dare you. I have never had such a thing in my life."

"You should have been a fucking actress honey. The way you play those lines."

"How dare you."

"You're just beautiful. Every inflection perfect."

"I'll kill you."

"Hey get the fuck away from me. Or I'll throw this soapy water all over you and that dress I paid for you're wearing. You're clapped up honey."

"No one has ever spoken to me in such an insulting manner before in my entire life."

"Get used to it honey. You're a walking health hazard. The

source of my fucking infection. Jesus I nearly said affection. Wow."

"You foul horrible insensitive thing. I'll have you know that the man to whom I was recently engaged was titled. And was just one among the many men who have adored and worshipped me. Even though he was an aristocrat he followed me about like a faithful dog."

"Woof woof."

"Be smart. Go ahead. You got your clap from one of those common trollops who appear on your doorstep."

"I didn't honey. I got the clap straight from you. And you better go see the doctor and get a big needle up your nice soft white arse."

Pricilla picking up the hem of her long dress, spinning around and tiptoeing out over the sopping towels and squelching wet carpet of the half lit bathroom. Her footsteps down the stairs. Schultz wrapping in a towel. Sticking his feet in his slippers waiting dry, out in the hall. Tip toeing down. To see if Pricilla was further wrecking the house. Instead of sitting as she was in the drawing room reading a fashion magazine open across her knee.

"Hey come on you. Out. This is no fücking private club for you to sit around in. After clapping me up and going to a fucking lawyer. Suing me. With that big bullshitter Al who thinks he's some kind of big father figure and protector of ladies in distress. Look at this place. You turned the fucking faucets on. The library is ruined. They're trying to get me for thousands of pounds for the damage."

"O darling, I'm sorry."

"You're sorry."

"Yes I am. Please forgive me for whatever I've done."

"Well, what the fuck did you do all these things for."

"I don't want to be taken for granted."

"Holy shit. You don't want to be taken for granted so you should then practise inhumanity on me."

135

"You did damage too darling."

"Sure I did when I was so furious out of my fucking mind over the damage you did. So what are you still sitting there all dressed up for."

"And why are you standing there in a towel undressed."

"Because honey soon I'm going to sit smouldering like any good producer should, right where you're sitting, with cigars sticking out smoking all over me in my silver lamé shirt I've got upstairs and a gold medallion clanking on the hairs of my chest waiting for these limey British cunts to come try and get me, a red blooded American, out of this fucking house before my lease is up. So before I get back down here again. You better be gone."

Schultz in his bedroom. Peeking out the curtains to across the street. Cars and limousines arriving at the Ambassador's house. Unloading emissaries, envoys, proconsuls and ministers. Chauffeurs jumping out to open doors. The long radiant flowing dresses of wives and mistresses. The plenipotentiary glamour. Two butlers taking coats inside the Ambassador's black and white marble floored hall. Jesus, what am I alive for. Instead of worrying about legal actions and fucking wasting time going to bed, I ought to bandage over the worst scratches and go over there in my sunglasses and tuxedo and mix in with some of those nice folks. And even though one's going to feel awfully dirty and clapped up, it will be a nice little elegant normal distraction. Amid the pieces of diplomatic undiseased ass, caviar and vaults of unlimited champagne.

Schultz dressing. Snapping up across his shoulders his emerald green braces over his silk shirt. Putting on his cummerbund and polishing his dancing pumps with the sleeve of his tuxedo. Tying a knot in his bowtie with what Binky said was the necessary amount of foppishness. And Schultz heading down into the hall. Picking up the phone from the floor just as it was ringing.

"Hello."

"I'm sorry to disturb you like this, but are you the occupant of what I think must be number four Arabesque Street."

"Yes."

"Well, I don't want to alarm you sir but I'm sure you'll under-stand that in attempting to keep up standards in the area I really thought I should inform you direct instead of calling the Police. My wife has just got a rather nasty shock. I do think you should look out into your garden."

'What's wrong."

"Well sir I don't quite know how to put this but there appears to be a person there. Who does not appear well."

"Holy shit."

"I beg your pardon."

"Sorry it's just a religious expression. Thanks for calling."

Schultz hanging up and heading into the library to look out the window. The tiny fish pond with no fish and a statue of a cherub holding a wand out of which the estate agents said water would come upon depressing a switch inside the kitchen door. And nothing happened even when you hit it with a hammer.

"Jesus I can't see a god damn thing out there. O Jesus. There is something. Come on. When the fuck is my life ever going to get tranquil again."

Beyond the edge of paving stones a garden bench. A lady's silver slippered foot sticking out. Schultz rushing past the pantry and down stairs. Twisting a knee and stumbling as he went. And a grab at the bannister dislodging one end of it from the wall.

"Holy shit something else to get sued for."

Schultz limping out into the darkened confines of the garden. Ivy covered lattice around the walls and dried up rose plants in beds. On a little patch of lawn, in a long gown. Pricilla stretched out spreadeagled on her back in the grass.

"Jesus Fortnum's may as well charge her up to me along with the dress."

Schultz hobbling back into the kitchen and filling a bucket of water. Returning to stand over Pricilla with the brimming white porcelain pail. Swinging it back in order to deliver the entire cold contents splashing on the prostrate body. Pricilla sitting bolt upright and shouting.

"Don't you dare."

Schultz did
And she screamed
Blue bloody murder

As she
Got doused

11

WITH the invitation pushed through his letter box, Schultz proffering it to the Ambassador's major domo. Who stood in his gold braided regalia on the marble black and white landing at the top of the curved staircase. He bent whispering for the lady's name. And the exalted commissionaire's voice booming out identities of these two new arrivals. From just across the street.

"Mr. Sigmund Franz Schultz and Miss Pricilla Prune."

Schultz had one or two additional contusions. Received from Pricilla's pummelling fists and groin kicks uppercutting from her silver slippered foot. Following the bucket of cold water straight splash into her face and all over her bosoms and the rest of her. As she sat propped up by her arms. Schultz grinning for the first time in days. Her pale pink garment turned a darker shade. But on her feet screaming, Pricilla punched, scratched, gouged and attempted to bite Schultz all around the fish pond. Till police came rushing out the kitchen door into the garden.

"Come on honey, move forward, you're holding up the reception line."

Pricilla was now in a cloud of musky perfume and her black clinging see through gown. Her drenched Fortnum's haute couture creation left hanging from the kitchen ceiling to dry. And her brand new patent leather opera bag held up under her left noticeable nipple crested marvellous tit. Smiling with her lower lip stretched over to hide her lower missing bicuspid.

"Come on honey, what are you trying to do, hog the limelight."

"Shut up you."

Schultz pushing Pricilla forward into the large drawing room and pressing his bandages down on his cheeks and also rubbing his knee to realign the ligaments stretched out of place in the rush down his kitchen stairs. As he now straightened up with his slightly lessened limp to confront the beaming dark complexioned face of the Ambassador.

"Ah Mr. Schultz. Please. Enter. It is so good of you to come."

"Thanks Your Excellency. It's swell to be here."

"And of course I have not had the pleasure."

"O yeah, sorry. His Excellency. Pricilla Prune."

"I am enraptured my dear."

"You are very very charming Your Excellency."

The ebony rotund head of the Ambassador lifting away from Pricilla's outstretched hand. His white teeth blazing in a smile. Beyond him stood London's black and white diplomatic corps in their dark regalia. And military gentlemen conspicuous in their gold braid, shiny insignia and medals flashing and jangling. Flowers on the marble topped tables. Seated on Louis the Fourteenth sofas, ladies with long cigarette holders. And a distinct additional babble in the din of voices in the area of the room to which Pricilla navigated. To stunningly take up a position near a painting, Camels in Caravan on the Nile.

"Madam."

A pale faced waiter just managing to proffer a glass of champagne through the throng of gentlemen surrounding her. Schultz squeezed away facing the backs of ministers plenipotentiary, assorted chargé d'affaires, attachés, and first and second secretaries four deep. A smiling gurgling Pricilla bathed in the stream of flatteries wafting her way from every direction. Jesus you'd think these guys had never seen a real beauty before. But holy shit. Be a great way to get rid of this bitch. Just beat it and leave her to hand out a dose of clap to the whole diplomatic corps in London. And leave it to the Arabs to blame it on the Israelis or the Israelis to blame it on the Arabs.

"Ah Mr. Schultz, my dear neighbor. The gladiator of Arabesque Street."

"Your Excellency I got a few little cuts all right. Tripping down the stairs."

"Ah my dear sir never mind, so many things one must be careful of in this city of London which offers so many wonderful pleasures. But it is so good to see you. After all the ambulances, all the Police."

"Yeah they've been a few ambulances and Police all right."

"And all the pretty women. Who come to your house all the time."

"Now and again they do."

"But there you are, already alone, and your beautiful friend surrounded. But was there something again this evening that happened."

"Nothing. Just someone trying to rob me fell in the fish pond. My neighbors living behind me called the Police. But this is a nice party you've got going."

"Yes we do rather pride ourselves on our good parties. But of course the addition of you and your latest lady friend does help you know. She is by far the most attractive of all the attractive ladies. Let me congratulate you. Did you notice, how the entire male assemblage have immediately congregated about her. Such a thing could put a strain on the rafters and send London's diplomatic corps tumbling to the floor below. N'est-ce pas."

"Yeah I notice that, Your Excellency."

"You are not jealous."

141

"Your Excellency, ugly guys like me just have to be patient and wait their turn."

"Ah but you are much too modest Mr. Schultz. You clearly have an incredible way with the ladies. You don't kid me."

"Likewise Your Excellency you don't do too bad yourself."

"Ha ha, Mr. Schultz, it is how do you say, in the nature of the diplomatic profession to keep everyone happy. But perhaps we, the two of us, might keep in touch about such things as beauty and the wonders of London. And perhaps you and your lady friend would come some evening to dine with us. In a more intime situation perhaps."

"Any time Your Excellency wants to give me a tinkle, you just do that little thing."

"I shall Mr. Schultz, I assure you, I shall."

A hush over the gathering. The last glasses clanking on marble tops and clinking against each other. Whispers dying away. All the seated standing. The Ambassador stationed at the white gold leaf embellished open double doors. A drum roll. Bugles sounding a fanfare. And the commissionaire's voice throbbing out over the gathered expectant guests.

"His Royal Imperial Highness Field Marshal King Buggybooiamcheesetoo and Her Royal Imperial Highness."

The King Buggyspendthriftboob, as some chargé d'affaires whispered behind Schultz that he ought to be called, came in massively rotund and slightly rolling on his feet with a large mouthful of shiny gold teeth that looked like they might, if you got too close, take a big bite out of you.

"Hey do you mind telling me who the hell's this making an entrance."

"He is the Emperor His Royal Imperial Highness King of the Sovereign State of Boohooland."

"Jesus, never heard of the place."

"It is sir a few million acres of mountain range, lakes, a deep navigable river to the sea and some hundreds of thousands in population."

"Thanks for the information. It's amazing isn't it how these vine swinging upstarts think they own the world suddenly when they got a few snake infested steamy acres of impenetrable jungle to crow over."

"I think sir that you might find if you cared to investigate that there is more than just some steamy jungle to crow over."

"Well look at the guy, he can hardly stand up with all his medals. His wife looks like she just escaped out of some Harlem jewelry store in the middle of a riot. By the way who are you."

"I am the Foreign Minister of the State whose Sovereign you have just attempted to describe sir."

"O hey I'm sorry. I hope I didn't hurt your feelings."

"Sir while I was at one of the better known schools in England situated on one of its best known rivers, I learned that one must be charitable to those who speak out of ignorance."

"Well Minister, if you'll excuse the undiplomatic language, I put my fucking foot into it didn't I."

"Well perhaps. But a foot at least is not your entire leg sir. And by the way Her Imperial Highness is His Imperial Highness's sister."

"Well at least let me wish you entire luck with your whole nation Minister."

"Thank you sir."

Schultz crushing between his teeth several creamed mushroom and smoked salmon canapes washed down with three glasses of champagne. And watching the African political celebrities, he avoided all further loose talk. Till another fanfare and drum roll. A major domo announcing dinner. The assembled guests following King Buggyboo proceeding down the curved grand staircase. Through crystal chandelier lit reception rooms opening out on a covered terrace and down steps to a vast marquee stretched over a large garden. With even a fish pond and fountain. White tables on which candles flickered. A dance floor built over the grass. Gloved waiters behind long linen counters of heaped up victuals. And on a raised banquet dais a floodlit table gleaming with gold plate.

143

"Boy these rich wog bastards don't fool around when it comes to fucking lavish feasting. They make the British look like the stingy fuckers they really are."

Schultz looking the way his face looked, took up a lonely vigil at a table set amid the thicker shrubberies. Examining the silver George III candelabra decorated with Egyptian female figures, oak leaves and fan motifs. Sipping a glass of champagne. And taking up to his lips a piece of toast heaped inch deep in Beluga, that he was just about to bite.

"Holy shit."

At the high table set for the King. His Imperial Highness carefully peeling and holding up a grape between his fingers. To place the skinless green ripeness between Pricilla's opening lips. Who sat smilingly seated at the King's right elbow which at the moment is nudged deeply into her tit.

"Jesus I get invited and she takes the glory."

The clank and clang of delph and cutlery. The string orchestra at the far end of the tent playing a medley of English boating tunes. Waiters hurrying platters of chicken legs, pigeon legs, pheasant legs, turkey legs and all matter of other parts of roasted and non roasted beeves and birds not to mention lobster, smoked trout, prawns and the endless pouring out of this booming Echezeaux and Chablis grand cru.

A dark shadow hovering near Schultz. A smiling beribboned dark complexioned gentleman bowing and touching the back of a chair.

"Ah sir, may I."

"Sure."

"I should first like sir to present the compliments of His Royal Imperial Highness King Buggybooiamcheesetoo."

"Sure. Who are you."

"I have just had the honor as recently as last week to present my letters of credence as Ambassador Extraordinary and Plenipotentiary from Boohooland to the Court of St. James's."

"Sit down. Great little country you have, Your Excellency."

"Thank you sir. His Majesty hopes you will not be offended for his having rather commandeered your most attractive lady friend this evening. He sends his apologies but she is so striking and it is the custom of our country, that the King always pays his respects to the most beautiful woman present. And he hopes you will not mind."

"Tell the King to help himself and make himself at home."

"Then you do not mind."

"Your Excellency. Just let me take off my sunglasses for a second. And take a look at my face. What do you see."

"Dear me sir."

"That's right. Guess who gave me all this."

"I quite understand sir."

"Hey out of interest. Back in your country. If the King likes a girl he sees."

"It is the custom that he takes her sir. Which of course, being a gentleman as well as a King, he would not dream of doing."

"And if some guy objects you cut off his hands or something."

"No we cut off his ears. Cutting off so many pairs of hands would affect our economy. But I do thank you sir for being so understanding. And I will convey this to His Majesty."

"You do that."

"He will be most pleased. Although His Majesty is a warrior and soldier he prefers not to transgress upon the sensitivities of others."

"But Your Excellency before you go, there's another little thing you ought to know."

"And what is that sir."

"Well it's a rather confidential and intimate matter. And I hope I can rely on you to keep it that way."

"But of course you can sir, you have my word as a gentleman as well as an Ambassador."

"The girl has a social disease."

"Ah. I see. That is most extremely good of you to be so forthcoming sir. But I do not think that will matter in the least. His

145

Majesty's doctors take such things in their stride so to speak."

"Well they're going to have real fun getting in stride with this one let me tell you."

The Ambassador regaining his seat. Schultz tucking into a nice dark bit of turkey and taking a sip of Echezeaux. The Ambassador's silk cuffs each linked with a massive diamond set in an ingot of gold as he folds his black white palmed hands carefully together on the linen. His chin lifting as his eyebrows closed together over his broad shiny dark nose.

"Do please sir, enlighten me further."

"Well this humdinger is called the Oriental Venereal Plague."

"Excuse me please sir I am not familiar with that word. What is this humdinger."

"It means something remarkable. Out of the ordinary. Every doctor in London is trying to cure me at this second."

"Sir you must tell me immediately concerning this."

"That's exactly, as you might say, what I'm doing. My balls are swollen out like grapefruits."

"I must sir, excuse myself and get to the King at once."

"You do that. You wouldn't want the King's testicles to come plummeting off."

Schultz, not a man to imbibe too deeply, drank off his glass of Echezeaux in a swallow and poured another. As the Ambassador, nearly tripping on his face, pushed his way through the throngs of feasting people. Rushing now around a boxwood shrub manicured in the shape of a peacock. And bam. The Ambassador upsetting a lady's drink on her dress. Patting her about with napkins and summoning waiters and flunkies from the royal entourage. And just managing to pay his last apologies to the lady as the master of ceremonies announced.

"My Lords, Your Excellencies, Ladies and Gentlemen. His Royal Imperial Highness will now start the dancing, thank you."

Schultz watching over the rim of his wine glass. As the King of Boohooland led Pricilla by her hand held high out on to the dance floor. The assemblage breaking into applause. The orchestra playing. And the big bellied King and Pricilla gliding about fox trotting cheek to cheek in the many hued splendors of flashing light.

"Jesus now she really thinks she's the fucking Queen of Sheba."

The Ambassador standing at the edge of the now crowded dance floor undiplomatically rubbing his anxious hands together. No doubt contemplating that the King's medical advisers will never find a needle big enough to penetrate deep enough into the royal fat black arse and are really going to have to go digging all over the jungle to find herbs they think are strong enough to cure their Sovereign's humdinger dose of Oriental Venereal Plague.

Six coal dark drummers in loincloths joining the orchestra. Faces streaked with paint, ankles jangling ivory bracelets and hands slapping their double ended tom toms. Bugles blowing. Dancers making room for the King as he erupted into a sweat flying, bug eyed, lip licking war dance hoofing in all directions. With Pricilla, hands wagging over her head, cavorting to the throb of drums, her hips pumping, legs kicking, arms writhing and head flung back and forth like her tonsils were exploding.

"Jesus christ the two of them look like they're going to fuck right there and now. The son of a bitch's big black hand just grabbed her straight on the tit. She smiled. I'll kill her. What the fuck does she think she's doing. Making an ass out of me all here alone like I had leprosy at this table."

On the sidelines, the Ambassador patting his white hanky at his ebony forehead. The King and Pricilla center floor. Surrounded at an admiring distance by the other frenzied oscillating guests. The King's whooping mouth wide open. Medals bouncing on his chest. Fist shaking around his head. The diamond studded gold braid of a Field Marshal hanging askew off one shoulder. Any second now his fly is going to bust open. To treat us to a flash of his big black famous prick.

"And look at that fucking bitch will you. In a hula, a shimmy, can can, belly roll and cha cha cha, all rolled into one. And doesn't even know I'm alive. This is the fucking thanks you get for taking a person to a party."

The Ambassador from Boohooland still waiting for His Imperial Majesty to come in off the dance floor. A military attaché at his shoulder. The two of them in urgent conference. No doubt worrying about their own balls being chopped off and being hung in the sun to dry when His Imperial Highness's private parts go swelling up like canteloupes and clatter off bouncing around their jungle kingdom like stale coconuts. This would be exactly the right time to slip away from this undiplomatic incident. Except no fucking two bit King is going to take a fucking girl away from me. Just throw back a big shot of this excellent cognac. And go cut in on that big black bastard. And maybe get some fucking justice and fair play and peace of mind for one night.

Schultz setting off to the dance floor. Stepping and dodging between the couples and putting his ligament out of place once more. And just as he reached the swirling King and Pricilla with a finger poised ready to tap His Imperial Highness on the shoulder, Schultz tripped over a loose royal foot. Grabbing as he did so a balancing hold on the Field Marshal's gold braided epaulette. Which ripped off as Schultz fell. To suddenly find himself with the aid of five uniformed members of the royal entourage being forcibly air lifted from the floor.

"Hey get your fucking hands off me you cunts."

The Ambassador from Boohooland covering his face. Schultz shaking and twisting loose from the grasping enclosing arms. Regaining his feet. Swinging a looping haymaker. Catching an equerry smack on the jaw. And sending him flat on his arse. As shouts went up and the lights suddenly went out. To the deafening screams of the ladies.

"Assassination."

"Save the King."

"Fuck the King."

Reinforcements called. With members of Scotland Yard's Flying Squad on duty in the street rushing inside. And Schultz immediately overwhelmed by an army from Boohooland, was knocked unconscious dreaming. Of standing one youthful day on an apartment house stoop. With his violin. The pink setting sun flashing on windows. As all the little girls on the block collected to listen. Smiling in admiration. Adoring as they heard.

> This
> One time
> Child prodigy play
> The battle hymn
> Of the Republic

12

POLICE bells clanged around Belgravia that night. Folk who had fled in that dangerous direction, got soaked falling flat faced in the fish pond. Schultz knees cut crawling over crushed glass, slipped under a tent flap, and attempting to climb over a garden wall, was apprehended not only by a spike ripping his tuxedo in half but also by a Scotland Yard detective lurking in an alley. And frog marched back. Pricilla was staring daggers and dirks at Schultz.

"That's right I came with her."

"And that's all you did. You got taught a lesson didn't you. And if you ever try and touch me again the King's bodyguards will kill you."

The host Ambassador, all kindness, protocol and understanding had Schultz, for decency's sake, wrapped in a damask table cloth and looking suitably and suddenly Arabic, he was conducted by a solicitous chargé d'affaires across to Four Arabesque just as Big Ben was booming two in the morning. Picking slivers of glass out of his knee and undressing for bed, he heard car doors slamming. With a painful head, aching stomach muscles, and sore ribs he stood in his pyjamas shaking a fist at the front window.

"Nobody, fucking nobody pushes Sigmund Franz Schultz around and gets away with it. That's fucking gospel you cunts, believe me."

Under umbrellas in the pouring rain His Royal Imperial Highness flanked by flunkies, went down the steps of the Ambassador's house. Pricilla just behind him surrounded by military attachés. Ganged up on. That's what I was. Look at that. That bitch. I even had to claim I came with her. Ratted on me the first opportunity she got. Doesn't even give this house a glance. Heading in clothes I own to that first car in a caravan of limousines. Leaves me in the lurch. Getting right in behind the King. Who's going to fuck her ass now and worry about the Oriental Venereal Plague later.

Schultz this following windy wet day at one thirty p.m. in the office of Sperm Productions. Having dispatched a stage carpenter, scene designer and two assistants to Arabesque Street to effect repairs. Now reading the newspaper under Court and Social.

His Royal Imperial Majesty Field Marshal King Buggybooiamcheesetoo was guest of honour at a banquet given last night by His Excellency the Ambassador of Zumzimzamgazi.

Schultz's bitten fingernail underlining the small print listing attending guests. Pricilla's name first following members of the peerage. And his last, following everyone else. And before that night was over, Schultz had also seen descend from the Ambassador's doorway, along with Her Imperial Highness the King's sister, Pricilla's mother. All two tons of her. Maybe three tons. If she got loose for any length of time among the food.

"Jesus the pair of them are a team of shameless bloody social climbers."

Shiny wet under the lamp light, the stream of chauffeured cars

151

came down the street one after another, stopped, people climbed in under umbrellas and the limousines pulled away towards Belgrave Square. Pricilla's mother getting a vehicle all to herself which lowered considerably on its suspension. That was that. A nice little night of social relaxation. Taught one more lesson I already knew even in Woonsocket. That women go ga ga over kings.

And further down the Court and Social page under Forthcoming Marriages, Schultz's eye alighted upon a familiar title.

Earl of Eel Brook Common and Miss Violet Clutterbutterbucks.

The marriage has been arranged and the wedding will shortly take place between Basil, the eldest son of the late Lord Nectarine, eighteenth Earl of Eel Brook Common and Lady Nectarine and Violet youngest daughter of Admiral and Mrs. S.O.S. Clutterbutterbucks D.S.O. of Castle Cranockity, Moss of Barmuckity, Scotland.

"Ah Schultz early to work are you and as usual, taking up the seat of authority in the chairman's chair. And also as usual looking the worse for wear. Upon how many au pairs did you perform your rite of simulated procreation last night."

"Jesus christ Binky, did you see this. His Lordship is getting fucking well married. Right here in the paper. I knew he'd see sense at long last and fucking settle down."

"Ah Schultz, trust you to use your own inimitable adjectives to describe what is for his Lordship and myself too, a sacred step in life. If you will, please just do cast your eyes further below in the same listing."

Mr. Jeremy Balthazar Binky Sunningdale and Lady Jane Pricklygorse.

The engagement has been announced and the wedding will shortly take place between Jeremy, eldest son of S.U.N. Sunningdale Bt. and Lady Sunningdale and Lady Jane youngest daughter of the Duke and Duchess of Putney.

"Jesus, what are you guys, a fucking team or something. What are you doing this both at the same time for. Getting tied up like that."

"Schultz I hardly think the word tied is appropriate. And did you not express your approval at his Royal Grace settling down. My little lady is quite a nice little lady and his Amazing Grace and I are in fact planning to have a joint ceremony. With religious, gestative and social difficulties permitting of course."

"Jesus Binky, you guys. You do nothing but try to treat yourselves to thrills in life."

"Thrills. Good gracious me. What ever do you mean Schultz."

"The whole thing is like it was preordained. I mean to me, christ imagine going to bed with a girl wearing a tiara right at the top of the peerage and fucking the tonsils and titled tits off her. How did you do it, land a Duke's daughter."

"Ah Schultz you do have the most graphic if not charming way of putting things. Well of course marrying a Duke's daughter does mean stepping up the ladder a wee bit but dash it all Schultz, I do possess a very modest little bit of social standing myself you know. And I did of course further flatter my way into the Duke and Duchess's confidence by getting their daughter absolutely pregnant beyond retreat."

"Then how about an investment from your future mother and father in law for the show."

"Schultz you are aren't you completely without shyness or scruples."

"Come on, with all that's happening to me these days, I got to fast reach that sacred moment when the show is financed, cast, the theatre booked and all that's left is just the ratting, treachery, backbiting and insubordination of rehearsals. Then opening night. And Jesus then may the gross never grieve. And that's one thing I know. That there is nothing, but nothing, more beautiful in this world than the money made out of the box office of a theatre."

"Schultz, you are utterly endearing. Just what one needs for the spirit on such inclement days."

153

"I am also an embattled fucker on plenty of fronts. Do you know let me tell you something Binky. When I first landed in this country I stayed at the Savoy Hotel because I wanted to be somewhere where the roof didn't leak. Three weeks later I could just pay the bill and I was on the street broke with nowhere to go. Nobody wanted to know me. I mean shit, you English seize up like stone walls. I actually began to starve. I was actually hungry standing at a fucking window of a restaurant reading the menu and dying for something to eat."

"O dear Schultz, O dear."

"And you know what happened. A fucking whore came along."

"How nice for you Schultz."

"Well let me tell you something, that girl fucking well saved my life."

"Schultz let us just now suppose that his Royal Grace and I took the remaining half of your little show. Would you make you unbelievably happy. Following all your previous woe."

"What are you kidding. I'd be fucking ecstatic."

"And would you Schultz continue to use the company's stage manager, scene designers and assistants to rebuild your house."

"Hey come on, I had to do some emergency repairs. The guys are sitting around doing nothing."

"How would you like it Schultz if his Royal Grace or I were to ship off a mob of production staff to one of his Royal Grace's castles or my more modest little acres and put them hard at work in our pantries."

"It ain't the same thing for christ's sake. I got to keep up appearances. Which happen to be fucking well falling down around my ears recently. With crummy English landlords suing me. Who go stay in Bermuda on the rent I'm paying them. And by the way. What's that big book in his Lordship's drawer with Nectarine Castle written on it. Full of lists of names under headings like household, gardens, park, farm. With stonemasons, laborers, carpenters, huntsmen, footmen, cooks, parlour maids, grooms. Holy shit, your Lordship, I didn't see you come in, I was just asking Binky here."

"Schultz I shall be terribly angry if you have been again in my office and snooping in my desk."

"Hey I was looking for an eraser. But what is all that. Do you keep all these fucking people employed, eating and drinking and sleeping in beds."

"Schultz I'll thank you to mind your own bloody business."

"All I'm doing is just wondering. I counted thirty seven people. Hey is that for just one guy in one castle."

"I'd appreciate Schultz if you would discontinue your wondering."

"But hey congratulations your Lordship. You're finally settling down. They're going to be two of you now. In one castle."

"I wish you would drop that subject Schultz."

"Why, I'm interested. What do you do when you go there, count them all. I mean how do you know the staff are not fucking off all the time, talking to one another, doing no work, eating your food, when you're not around while you're at one of your other castles where they're probably doing the same thing."

"What a pity it is Schultz you aren't saddled with these problems since you have them so well appreciated."

"Sure why not. I wouldn't mind."

"Well that's precisely what they are doing at my castles, fuck all."

"So you admit you got castles in the plural. With all these retinue."

"I admit nothing of the kind Schultz. Especially as I must rush this moment. Binky, hand me that catalogue. Must pop to Spink's. They have a rather interesting attractively underpriced coin they're offering."

His Lordship gone. Binky as he sat back in the chairman's chair, propping a leg up on his gout stool. Raindrops tapping the window. Schultz seated on the edge of the chaise longue, biting a thumbnail over which he twisted his head back and forth as he chewed.

"Schultz. Ah my dear Schultz. Despite your black eyes, despite your contusions, your scratches and your unforgiveable nosiness.

One can't help liking you. And in your own little way you are a sporting chap. So, as the raindrops fall outside and as this great city of London groans on in lust, I want you Schultz to put me down for, what is it, would it be a quarter, yes I think that's the figure, a quarter, a full twenty five percentum of your little show plus the usual overcall."

"Jesus christ almighty, you mean it Binky."

"I have just said so."

"Hey shit, this is my fucking lucky day. I'm three quarters financed."

"And Schultz when his Royal Grace returns from his coin purchase I think you may find yourself one hundred per cent financed."

"Binky I could kiss you, no shit."

"Well Schultz, that would indeed be nice as soon as your doctor gives you your venereal clearance. But shouldn't we also wait for the reviews. And then if those are not too dastardly, you may indeed kiss me. But no groping please."

Schultz leaping up from the chaise longue, pivoting in a circle smacking his fist into the palm of his hand.

"Jesus, like magic, it's all coming together. My show. This Debutant girl, a sure star. I got Magillacurdy, a genius. Top fucking Choreographer, Composers, Director. I got your weddings. We could have the whole fucking thing happening together. We're going to really kill them. We could have you married on stage between the first and second acts. Nothing can go wrong. It would be an aristocratic sensation. Hey how the fuck did you meet these girls. None of them ever once come in the office."

"Schultz no need to stop in your tracks to wonder why. The reason is not far to seek."

"What because of me. I'm god's gift to women for fucks sake. But Jesus you know what I'd really like in this life, is one of his Lordship's fucking sisters. I could screw one of those marvellous creatures all the way to Mars. You know, Binky, seeing what it does for you guys, I need good breeding and manners in my life. To make my day to day existence sublime just like yours."

"And you know Schultz what we have always admired about you. Your marvellous set of teeth. And your easy ready smile."

"Here let me show you. Now how's that. For an ad for toothpaste."

"And Schultz I do believe I was asked to duly advise you of an invitation from his Royal Grace for a weekend's hunting, shooting and fishing at one of his Lordship's most favourite, and as you Americans are sometimes fond of putting it, little country cottages."

"No shit."

"No shit Schultz."

"But christ I can't hunt shoot or fish."

"Ah you Americans, so dismally unprepared for life aren't you."

"We didn't have a thousand years like you who while squeezing the last best drop out of subjects all over the world, had nothing else to do but hunt shoot and fish. But hey Jesus, this is no fucking trick is it, I can use an invitation like this. I really could."

"That's why his Royal Grace has extended one. We know how hard you have fought. Indeed looking at my watch, might you be ready Schultz to depart towards the countrywards by three o'clock."

"Hey I'm not even packed. But you bet your ass I'll be ready. I just got to go see if I can book a theatre."

"Take my car Schultz. Just purring downstairs. I'll ring down to Tobias. But don't, please don't put on board kidnapped passengers. Tobias will gladly ferry you to your appointment and back to your town house for your weekend sartorial knicknacks. And I shall await with his Royal Grace your return. Telling him meanwhile about this absolutely topping idea of yours of our being wed between acts of Kiss It Don't Hold It It's Too Hot. What could be more delightful for our prospective inlaws and their stuffy relatives. I'm sure that although at first they may be a little sceptical they will finally come to appreciate all the advantages of the marvellous publicity. Why we may even marry nude, what do you think."

157

"Sure, why the fuck not. Hot diggity dog. I'm off Binky. This is the beginning of the greatest few days of my entire life."

Schultz heading out the hall of Sperm Productions, passing Rebecca at her office door. Where she turned her back and her face away red eyed with tears. Schultz hitting his forehead with his palm as he descended in the lift. Holy shit that poor girl, she's shattered that the guys are getting married. What the fuck is it with women anyway no matter what else, they all want to march up that aisle.

A gentle faced grey haired grey uniformed chauffeur saluting as he opened the pearl grey limousine door. Schultz bouncing on the soft upholstery, as the great motor purred left and right and right again. Up St. James's. Turning along Piccadilly. Schultz picking up the phone. Asking Tobias to get him a number. Just as they were passing the Fortnum & Mason clock, with its bells jangling and Fortnum and Mason appearing out the clock door.

"Al."

"Yeah."

"This is Sigmund."

"Yeah."

"I'm sorry about the fight. And ruining your clothes. But what the fuck do you want to go and sue me for Al."

"Don't talk to me. My lawyers are who you should talk to."

"Al look, for christ sakes we were real friends before this bitch came along. But I mean if you want a legal fight I'll fight you right up into and all over the House of Lords."

"Hey tough guy you do that."

"No shit Al come on. What a waste."

"Pay the girl the damages."

"Shit that bitch has already cost me a fucking fortune. I wouldn't pay her the price of a free crap in a public toilet."

"That's the kind of sentiment I expect from you, you philanderer."

"Philanderer, holy shit Al. You keep calling me that. What am I supposed to do fuck holes in walls. And do you know where that girl is right now. Do you."

"No. You tell me: Where is she. And where are you."

"She is right this fucking moment being fucked silly right up between her eyeballs by that big black bastard King Buggybooiamcheesetoo. And I am just passing Fortnum's."

"What are you talking about."

"The King, Al."

"What King."

"Of Boohooland."

"What are you trying to be real funny. Passing Fortnum's. Boohooland. I am cheese too. Or do you need to see a psychiatrist soon."

"Look Al in your newspaper. He's all over it. The guy who's been murdering everybody and chopping off ears and hands."

"He should chop your prick off."

"Jesus I knew the second those words were out of my mouth that that was exactly what you were going to say. No shit. You couldn't resist it could you. You're turning into some kind of geriatric mollycoddler of women for christ's sake. And you know what Al."

"Yeah I got all day to listen to you, you tell me what."

"She's gone. She took off with him. With her mother. That jigaboo King is probably fucking the mother too."

"You are the lowest form of racist creep."

"Jesus now I'm a racist."

"And a two bit phony bullshitter."

"Yeah Al, I know, but you just listen."

"Like hell I'll listen. You listen."

"No Al you listen a second god damn it. You want to hear what really happened. She told me she was giving me the gift of her body. And you know Al what she gave me. She gave me the clap. That's what she gave me. I didn't have it. I have doctor's proof. I got it from her."

"So now you smear the girl. You should have got strychnine. And she should sue you for slander."

"Al there is no use talking to you is there. But I made this last

desperate effort just because I happen to be feeling good to tell
you drop the case."

"Drop dead."

"I'll counterclaim Al."

"Counterclaim."

"Al it's against my principles to pay up six hundred and forty
nine pounds and ten shillings when it was me who was attacked.
The fucking two of you attacked me."

"Why don't you dry up. People like you are a menace to society.
And if you think I'm kidding about what I'm going to do to you,
I'm giving my lawyers the details of what you just said as soon as
you hang up."

"Al, I ask you with my deepest sincerity to forget suing me.
Because so help me god I'll tear you limb from limb, legally or
otherwise."

"Threatening me with violence now."

"Yeah. I am now. And for final and all time. Fuck you Al.
Goodbye."

Schultz with his whitened knuckles gripped hanging up the
ivory phone and popping out of the pearly grey motor car. Looking at his watch. And running up the steps of this victorian building. Impatiently going into a series of wrong doors.

"What the shit is wrong with this building, why do all these
openings lead nowhere."

Until Schultz found a narrow elegantly carpeted staircase heading upwards. Past posters of productions. The paraphernalia of
hits. And into a large reception office. A sour smiling mousy faced
girl looking up from her novel she's reading as she nods and says
parting words into the telephone.

"He'll ring you the first chance he gets. Yes. Thank you. Yes.
Good afternoon. Can I help you."

"I have an appointment with Mr. Gayboy, my name is Schultz."

"O yes Mr. Schultz. At two forty five."

"It's two forty seven right now."

"I'm afraid that he's busy at the moment. Do you mind waiting."

"How long."

"I'm afraid I can't say. He does have his do not disturb auditioning light on, which often means Mr. Gayboy, when he's suddenly busy like this, can be up to half an hour or more."

"I just made this appointment. And come rushing over here. You mean to tell me he's auditioning."

"I'm sorry but I'm afraid that's how it is sir."

"Well you just get on that intercom there and tell your Mr. Gayboy that Sigmund Franz Schultz is out here waiting. And I want to see him."

"I can't do that sir."

"You can't do that. What the fuck are you here for. Like the angel Gabriel stationed at the gates of heaven."

"I don't think I will be spoken to in that manner."

"You just have been spoken to in that manner. Well what are you going to do. You going to tell him I'm here. Or you going to keep me standing here like this."

"You could sit down sir."

"Like hell I will. I'm in a hurry. And I'm fucking well going in there."

"You can't do that."

"Well you just try and stop me baby."

"Sir come back."

"No two bit son of a bitch theatre operator is going to keep me waiting like this."

Schultz opening a door. Into a dark hall. And along another deep carpeted passage lined with theatrical posters. Rapping on a door marked with a prominent brass plate.

PRIVATE

Schultz pushing it open. Entering this large sombre room. Lined with books. More theatrical posters on the panelled walls. A fire glowing in the grate. Sketches and paintings of stage sets. And center room Mr. Gayboy standing, turning to look back over his shoulder. As he spoke to his young lady lying in front of him prostrate on her back across the large desk, her skirt up around her neck and her ample white thighs up over Mr. Gayboy's shoulders.

"You stupid girl you left the door open."

"Whoops excuse me folks I'm sorry. I'm Sigmund Schultz. I had an appointment."

"Well can't you see I'm busy."

"Look, just a second of your time. I wouldn't interrupt you like this if it wasn't really urgent. I want to book the Regent. From the fifteenth. I got a smash hit lined up."

"Please get out. If you don't mind."

"It only takes a second to say yes or no."

"No. Now get out."

"Hey you're crazy. I'll pay eleven weeks rent in advance. Right today. It's a good deal for you. I'm telling you."

"Very well. Leave your check for sixteen thousand five hundred pounds with my secretary outside. We'll call your bank and I'll have an Agreement prepared. You're from that management."

"Yes the one and only Sperm Productions."

"I'd rather you'd go now if you don't mind."

"Sure. Pardon my intrusion. Have a good day."

Schultz smiling at the secretary wide eyed aghast in the hall. And while slowly closing this door so prominently marked private, taking one more fast look at this scene. Of bare bottomed Mr. Gayboy in his striped shirt sleeves and dangling blazing crimson braces. His garters peeking over his trousers down around his ankles. And clearly several miles up the pleasantly chubby blond on his desk. In whom his grunting in and out attention was not once interrupted. Jesus just when everything's suddenly going swell. Everything suddenly starts going even better. And I get one of the best theatres in this town.

> Which
> Not only
> Groans but
> Moans
> With lust

13

SCHULTZ that afternoon leaving the theatre operator's office, stood in utter ecstasy at the top
of the flight of stairs. Clenching fists at his sides and putting his
head back to roar.

"Holy shit I'm off to the fucking races again."

And stepping forth triumphantly at the top carpeted stair,
Schultz tripped. Pitching forward to descend head over heels
tumbling to the bottom. Gasping for breath on his hands and
knees, feeling for injuries and reaching for his sunglasses in the
middle of the lobby floor. As an attractive scarlet suited young
lady dropped a file of papers as she leaned over to assist.

"My goodness can I help you."

"Jesus christ thanks honey. I should sue the owners of this fucking building for negligence. Do you mind giving me your phone
number as a witness."

Pigeons fluttering in a clear blue sky. Fresh big white clouds
floating westerly over London. With new bruises but bones unbro-

ken, Schultz in Arabesque Street carefully alighted from the pearl grey limousine. The door of number four opening once more on its hinges. To reveal an already amazing transformation. The scene designers on Sperm Productions' scaffolding working on the library ceiling. Smiling down at Schultz smiling up.

"Hey Jesus fellas you're doing a real great fucking job, no kidding."

Schultz in his bedroom throwing clothes into the pigskin Gladstone bag. Purchased out of his first management money from his first big London flop. And looking in the mirror. One's scars miraculously healing. Black eyes fading. I might even look human once more. With my career at last taking off in the direction of my golden dreams. That bitch and her clap finally out of my life. A pity her luscious gorgeous white body had to go with her.

Outside Sperm Productions his Lordship's limousine packed purring and ready for the road. Binky's pearl grey motor now taking up the rear with his shotgun cases, fishing rods, riding gear and luggage.

"Ah Schultz après vous. His Royal Grace any moment shall be flying out to be with us. Seat yourself. I trust you found Gayboy up one of his assistants prodding away as is his wont."

"Jesus Binky he actually was. He agreed the deal right in the middle of it. Soon as I offered him the rent."

"Ah I see. Amazing isn't it Schultz, how people's interest in money is so easily aroused when they ought to be otherwise engrossed."

His Lordship one side, Binky the other and Schultz luxuriating in the flashing beams of sunshine. Down Sloane Street and humming along the King's Road. So named for a monarch who once made his way to the edge of Fulham to mount a lady friend. Before there were these drab house and shop fronts. A pottery, cemetery and church. And over the Thames at Putney Bridge. Its mud flats along the river black and shiny at low tide. Playing fields and the greenery of Barnes Common. And the larger more affluent suburban houses. Mortlake and Sheen. And beyond at a mile a minute through Sunningdale. Until at four o'clock they agreeably took tea in a cozy oak tea room of a village. Schultz leaning way back in his chair as he slowly pushed a cream bun into his pleased expression and regarded the tweedy rose growing ladies.

"Jesus, England. Look at this quaint fucking place. Like a magazine advertisement for the good life. Well bred people just hanging around in here eating this Devon clotted cream, hot scones and clover honey and drinking tea in the middle of this secluded picturesque countryside without a single fucking worry in the world."

"Ah Schultz his Royal Grace and I did so think you might like it all."

"Like it, I'm fucking well utterly enchanted. But with this kind of bliss no wonder the country is ruined."

Schultz constantly jerking around in his seat enquiring about nearly every item in the passing landscape. Hubert directed to make a little detour to a tiny village where, nervously hopping out, his Lordship bought cheese and tongue.

"Now Schultz try a bit of cheese wrapped up in this calves' tongue."

"Hey this is really delicious. Jesus to think I was screwing around years in the fucking States missing all this. When are we reaching your cottage your Lordship. We've been heading down this winding narrow road over these hills and through these valleys for half an hour."

"Not long Schultz. In fact just over this bridge and up through the village."

"Hey this is really beautiful. And christ. Did you see her. That girl. Did you see her. She turned around looking at us. Gorgeous. Shit. Everyone is turning around and looking at us."

"Schultz I must warn you. You are not to spread your clap around this place, where I unfortunately happen to be known."

"Hey you have to remind me of that just when I'm enjoying myself. All I'm doing is remarking on the incredible beauty. But don't worry about a thing your Lordship, my prick is temporarily safely bandaged up inside my zipped up fly. Till I start using it on this fantastic girl I met today in the lobby of Gayboy's building."

Up through the high street. A bakery, a grocery, a pub and neat grey stone houses. A saddlers. Seed and grain merchant. A book shop. Tall elms surrounding a triangular green. A hotel The Lord Nectarine. Past some ancient stone cottages. And at the outskirts of this ancient village a high wall on either side of the road. Beyond which beeches towered and the deep green leaves of rhododendrons shined in the sun. The two motor cars turning left into an entrance.

"Hey where are we going."

"We're here Schultz."

"Hey that's what I thought, back there I noticed a hotel, The Lord Nectarine, is that you."

"Schultz you do have sharp eyes don't you."

"You bet I do. Those were some kind of gate lodges we passed there."

"They were Schultz."

"Jesus they're big enough to live in. Hey Jesus look at that. Cattle. Cows. Sheep. Horses. Hey this is beautiful. Christ a river. What are those your Lordship. Those big hill tops of trees."

"Ah Schultz your curiosity is insatiable. Binky do tell Schultz, you know so much more about these things than I."

"Those my dear insatiable Schultz are the park arrangements. Set out in such fashion by a chap Capability Brown who had rather a flair for that sort of thing. Placing trees, hills and various vistas so that they would be agreeable to the eye and bewitching by moonlight to the ladies."

"Jesus you guys. As if you didn't have enough bewitchingly agreeable already, now you got to have a guy shifting the whole landscape and countryside around so you get your rocks off if you even look sideways. Hey where's this cottage. We've gone a couple of miles. There's a church. And a cemetery. Don't tell me you have your own church and cemetery too."

"I'm just counting these cows Schultz. Binky I'm sure will explain."

"Ah Schultz unlike you brash rushing Americans we Brits do like to equip ourselves for life. One must upon occasion be seen to pray you know. And even, in due course get buried. One does however attempt to delay that event by pursuing one's comfortable habits as long as possible."

"What's that Binky. Up on top of that hill."

"The ruin of the old cottage Schultz."

"Cottage. That's an old castle."

"Now Schultz if you wait but a moment, you will see just as we cross this little bridge and rise up this hill, the new cottage. Ah. There."

"Jesus christ almighty, your Lordship, that's not where you fucking well live is it."

"Survive is a better word Schultz."

"But it's fucking massive. What has it got a thousand rooms or something. Jesus look at the turrets and towers. And all them windows. Hey wait, it's gone out of sight now."

"Be back in view in just a minute Schultz."

"Jesus I hope so, I want to see that again."

"Just as we get up this little hill now. And just around by this clump of trees."

"Wow. Look at that. It's like out of a fairy tale or something. What the hell do you do in there all by yourself for fucks sake."

"Ah Schultz you have asked a most marvellously pertinent question. Which of course I think I can answer. In one word. Cower."

"Jesus cower. I wouldn't cower. I'd go fill the place up with pieces of fucking ass and screw my brains out."

"Of course Schultz being already familiar with your personal habits, we both fervently believe you."

"Hey some guy's running up a flag on that turret. This place is fucking incredible. What a film set. I mean Jesus, for porno films, your Lordship. You'd make a million."

"Ah Schultz I knew the time would finally come when you would provide me with a solution to my life."

Crossing a moat, the motor's wheels rumbling over a drawbridge. The cars swinging around on pebble stones to draw to a halt in front of a great oaken door. The castle's long shadows spread out beyond its dikes across sweeping lawns and pasture and reaching up to a forest edge of trees. Where two great birds, their vast black shiny wings flapping gave deep cries as they flew swooping out over the parkland.

"Christ your Lordship you got a team of fucking retinue waiting."

A tall austere butler his grey hair parted in the middle and combed flat back on his head stood flanked by two footmen in livery. The shortest of whom stepped forward, opened the car door and bowed to his Lordship alighting. The butler's chin rising as he tweezed a fingertip of one hand with the fingertips of his other, intoning into the moist soft late afternoon air.

"Welcome home my Lord, I trust your journey was pleasant."

"Yes thank you Batters. Schultz this is Batters. Mr. Schultz. And of course Batters you know Mr. Sunningdale."

"Mr. Schultz, sir. And Mr. Sunningdale, so good to have you back with us again."

Schultz led to his room by a young footman in dark green livery. Toting Schultz's bag between two brass cannons and across the stone paved floor of the enormous pillared hall. Up the Jacobean staircase. A mullioned window looking down on the moat and out over more parkland. Massive gilt framed portraits. Some folk in their ermine and scarlet robes staring dolefully down. Along an arched corridor to a doorway entrance which went through six feet of masonry from the hall. Inside the outside door an inner door covered in a soft green damask silk opening on this pine scented perfumed high ceilinged room.

"Thank you, here's a half a crown buy yourself a drink."

"I'm sorry sir but his Lordship does not permit the acceptance of gratuities."

"Holy shit, kid, you should go on strike, that's unjust. Don't let his Lordship push you around."

"Yes sir, thank you sir."

Schultz standing at the tall window. Turning a handle and pushing it open. Staring out across the twilight parkland. Vast haunted lonely landscape shut away from the whole world. Towering oaks, elms and pines. His Lordship's church steeple in the distance. Evening birds chirping and singing. A bat crisscrossing the air. A beast mooing. Fresh moist cool breeze blowing in the open window. The great grey granite still cold to the touch.

"Jesus christ, his Lordship while he goes around London with holes in his socks, has a whole fucking personal kingdom here."

Schultz washing his face in the big bathroom. Full of scented soaps and glass trays of bath salts. Towels stacked warmly over a large chromium heating rail. Aiming his piss down on the flowers decorating the toilet bowl. Changing his corduroy suit to ivy league grey flannel trousers and popping on a yellow silk shirt, brown knit tie and a fawn tweed jacket to descend the wide carpeted oak stairs. Feet pounding below as his out of breath shirt sleeved Royal Grace raced upwards.

"Hey what's the hurry your Lordship."

"Schultz there is always a hurry concerning a dangerous disaster of some kind in this place. The chimney sweep is stuck up the chimney of the music room with his feet kicking down bucketfuls of soot. And I may have left my bath running."

"So what's so dangerous about that."

"Well for a start some silly young fellow from the kitchens lit the fire under the sweep and then pulled off the dust sheets from the furniture in such a manner as to succeed in breaking considerable crockery."

"Jesus your Lordship take it easy for christ's sake. Your jugular vein is standing right out from your throat. What's a few dishes. Or a bit of overflowing water. You're going to bust a blood vessel. This is a swell fucking place. Relax, enjoy it."

"Ah Schultz you are inspiring. But I'd rather a few dishes did not happen to be irreplaceable Meissen. And that the chimney sweep's socks weren't scorched off him up the music room smoke hole. The staff in this place do compete in their efforts to make life easy for me but they only succeed in fucking up everything in sight."

"Hey with all servants around you want to watch your language your Lordship. Where do I go, I'll turn off your bath."

"O god Schultz. I'd be grateful if you would. Just up to your left

169

then left then right and it's the last door on your right. And let me advise you, never take up residence in a large house."

His Lordship jumping back down the stairs. Schultz not quite following directions, promptly getting lost plus hysterical as he opened doors, pounded on locked ones and ran back and forth in hallways and finally shouting blue murder. Until meeting two footmen with blackened faces who led him rushing to one last door. All three in feverish haste through the book lined study, bedroom and dressing room and bath. To happily confront a chambermaid, the same rosy cheeked buxom stunningly beautiful young girl Schultz had caught sight of in the local village.

"Thanks guys, I think I can handle this little problem for his Lordship now."

"Very good sir."

The footmen withdrawing. The chambermaid putting her finishing polishing touches on glass shelves and stacking towels. As Schultz nosed around his Lordship's private apartments. Silk dressing gowns. Eight pairs of slippers. One gold embroidered with crossed shotguns. Dinner clothes neatly laid out in his dressing room. Piles of architect's drawings on the massive desk in the study and a strange convoluted contraption that appeared to be a telephone. Paintings and statuary in the bedroom hall. A gilt coronet above the canopy of his Lordship's bed. And awfully good looking well dressed people in silver framed photographs on a high dresser in his bedroom.

"These are nice little rooms his Lordship's got."

"Yes sir."

"Is this your station."

"Excuse me sir but I do not know what you mean sir."

"I mean do you work here in his Lordship's rooms."

"Well it's me who tidies out and does his Lordship's bathroom sir."

"What's your name honey."

"Roxana sir."

"Are you satisfied with this kind of life here. A good looking girl like you."

"I am sir."

"Girl with your looks, you could be up in London."

"Oooo I wouldn't want to be living in an awful big city sir. I wouldn't know what to do with myself."

"No problem. None. And tell you what honey, just in case you are ever up in town, here's my phone number, you just give me a little tinkle. How about that."

"Well sir that's extremely kind of you but I don't have cause to go up to London."

"Give it time, honey. Just give it time. Domestic slavery is going out of fashion. And you just give me a tinkle. Be seeing you around."

"Yes sir."

Schultz went out in the evening light strolling around the cobbled courtyards and reconnoitering beyond the moat in the castle gardens. And even to the staff's astonishment nosing about the basements. Later bathing and changing his once rather ripped tuxedo now miraculously repaired and freshly pressed and laid out on his bed.

"Shit. The god damn rich sure do get the pleasure. And Jesus the poor sure do get the pain."

Schultz, following a session walking about admiring his erection in his various bedroom mirrors, presented himself at eight for sherry in the library. His Lordship in the large panelled room playing a madrigal on his gramophone as they sipped their fortified wine. Until Batters announced to these three gentlemen.

"My Lord, dinner is served."

Schultz on his Lordship's right sitting back expansively in the candlelight of the pillared dining room. Digesting his dinner of freshly caught salmon with reisling and followed by slabs of tender rare roast beef, Yorkshire pudding, broccoli and fat dark burgundy ferried in by Batters and two footmen.

"Holy shit, your Lordship, what the fuck are you doing spending your time in London. This is paradise. The furnishing fabrics alone, they're gorgeous and priceless. The gardens out there, the birds, the flowers. Flocks of deer grazing down the hillside. Being

171

here like this makes me feel like two and a half million bucks."

Over port and cigars, Schultz sucking back deeply both smoke and liquid. His silk cuffed wrist extended on the mahogany and his fingers twirling the deep purple glass of wine. Binky pushing a gold toothpick between lower teeth and blowing his smoke out over the decanter.

"Ah don't you think Schultz is, your Royal Grace, the stuff of which country gentlemen are made. Indeed the expression, like a duck to water, is, I think appropriate."

"Of course that's true Binky, but while Schultz is advising me to abandon London he is at the same time advising certain members of my household to go there and to strike for higher wages here."

"Holy shit your Lordship I never said anything of the fucking kind. Who told you that. All I was saying was the middle ages are over. I mean christ, do you know what's going on down there underneath us up here, a whole fucking mob of people working in cellars. It looked to me like they needed fresh air."

"Ah Schultz you do, don't you, take the fucking cake sometimes. I don't suppose it has crossed your mind that all of them are being paid, housed, fed and are without chains. And indeed I should be all but too delighted were they to disappear entirely out of my life."

On the billiard room walls, portraits of fierce looking gentlemen in military uniform. Schultz with dinner jacket off and chalking his cue tip like a master, proceeded to devastate and awe Binky and his Lordship with a magnificent display of bank, carom and full massé shots.

"By god Schultz wherever did you learn to be so marvellous at billiards."

"In my local neighborhood pool hall. And outside of show business it's the first fucking thing I'm able to teach you guys a lesson in."

"Binky and I are suitably impressed. And now Schultz if you'll just press the button behind your elbow, perhaps you might like a palate cleansing champagne."

"Yeah sure, why not. This life with you two eccentric guys is beginning to really suit me."

They repaired to the music room. A long shadowy ornate gallery with white gold embellished organ pipes at one end and a black gleaming concert grand piano and two ancient harps at the other. A wood fire now blazing and crackling where the chimney sweep had his socks scorched. Tall windows looking down from battlements over the moonlit deer park. Batters entering with an ice bucket of champagne. Followed by the young footman whose hand trembled as he proffered his tray to Schultz.

"But now Schultz I think you will admit when you hear Binky's little recital that he might teach you a lesson or two as an instrumentalist."

Binky sitting in his smilingly affable manner at the organ and boomingly playing a medley of tunes ending with a rousing trumpeting march. With Schultz jumping to his feet clapping. Binky modestly nodding and finally, crisply and clearly playing Handel's organ concerto number two in B flat major. As he now stood bowing to Schultz's rousing cheers.

"Shit Binky that was fucking marvellous."

"Ah pleased you enjoyed it Schultz and now having had a most commendable evening with much soul stirring mutual admiration, may I your most humble and obedient servant thank you your Royal Grace and beg your permission to withdraw."

"Of course Binky."

"As you know one must arise before dawn to stalk your deer in your surrounding moorland hills and one's eye must be bright and sharp in order that there be venison. Goodnight Schultz."

Binky departing the music room. His footsteps dying away along the echoing floors of the gallery outside. A wind blowing at the panes of window. The fragrant whiffs of wood smoke as little puffs arose from the chimney piece. The faint hoot of an owl.

"Holy shit your Lordship Binky can do everything and he's so fucking implacably urbane and nonchalant about it."

"Ah an Englishman Schultz although liking to be perfect at his

173

pursuits, always prefers to give the impression of the amateur."

"But Jesus your Lordship, doesn't Binky have any weaknesses."

"Yes I think he does, at least one Schultz."

"Well I'd sure as fuck would like to know what it is."

"Ballet."

"You're kidding. Ballet. A weakness."

"Yes Schultz, Binky would do anything for the ballet. Anything. Even to suffering a court martial. As he did once being absent without leave from his regiment just as they were about to ship out."

"What just to watch the ballet."

"No Schultz, to watch a great ballerina dance. Binky had his Tobias stationed every late afternoon waiting to drive him to London to a performance and then through half the night back to base at.six a.m. in the morning. And this one morning he missed his regiment as they shipped out."

"Holy shit."

"Binky has wrecked cars. Bought outrageous presents for his favourite dancers, showered entire companies with gifts. He even risked arrest in Russia impersonating an impresario with an enormous contract to present it to this ballerina to travel away with him on the same train to the same town just so that he could be in the same city alone with her. Of course his scheme didn't succeed. But he did follow her across Europe wherever she danced. A story of infinite sadness. He simply lived to see her. Always the first in the audience to start clapping. The last to stop. Always on his feet shouting bravo even when she had already stood through as many as thirty curtain calls in cities like Prague, Leningrad, Moscow, Warsaw. There was Binky faithfully on his feet cheering. His flowers for her carried on stage for ten minutes at a time. The blossoms stacked around her like a funeral pyre. And later he would station himself at the stage door. Just for a momentary glimpse of her over the heads of the crowd. Then he would finally stand shivering knee deep in snow across the street from her hotel looking up at her window until her light went out."

"Hey Jesus stop your Lordship. Shit I'm crying."

"I'm sorry Schultz if I've upset you."

"Jesus that kind of hits me where I feel it. I always thought Binky was just one of those rich pukka public school boys who just liked being near the porno shows in Soho. I have a new respect for the guy."

"Of course later back in London he did finally impersonate a reporter of a daily newspaper and presented himself to the ballerina who was kind enough to receive him and he spent half an hour of her valuable time mumbling hardly able to speak and staring at her in abject awe until she gracefully relieved him of his misery when he confessed to being only a worshipping fan. And when he was leaving she accidentally touched him on the sleeve. And to this day Binky has never removed the jacket from its special place in his closet."

"Jesus I had no idea. I guess with guys like you with everything you got already, that the things you end up wanting are beyond the emotions of ordinary men."

"Ah Schultz I'm afraid that one just does not know what's in any man's heart."

"Fucking greed is in mine, even as much as I love the theatre. But holy shit, your Lordship, you know what I'm thinking. That religion does not teach the only important truth there is, that man saves his soul by money alone and to be rich is right and true and from that derives all beauty and justice."

"By god Schultz, although you are indeed stretching your imagination tonight."

> You
> Have also
> Said
> It all

14

"**Y**OUR Lordship this has been the most blissful fucking time I have ever had in my entire life."

Sitting following tea on a rear stone porch above the shimmering moat. Orange backs of goldfish peeking above the water. Tiers of formal gardens stepping down to pasture stretching in a long valley vista of deerpark. The sun faint pink descending the misty heavens. Balmy breeze, buds bursting forth on shrubberies. Great shiny black winged ravens croaking their cries as they slid and tumbled over the treetops.

"Ah Schultz I see your palate continues to appetize over the grapy green gleam in this wine."

"Shit, I'll say it does."

Batters discreetly coughing as he shuffled out to place another bottle of Moselle in the ice bucket. Touching away the drops with his linen napkin as he replenished glasses.

"Batters, next let us have a trockenbeerenauslese for Mr. Schultz. I think this dying afternoon invites discovery of further, better and perhaps sweeter particulars of the riesling vine."

"Very good my Lord."

"Holy shit your Lordship you're going to get me god damn drunk."

"Ah Schultz, it can't but do your hysteria a world of good."

"Jesus, who's hysterical. I'm floating on a fucking cloud."

"You'll be floating on a fucking bed of watercress in the moat Schultz if you lean back any further on your chair there."

"Holy shit, you're right."

That morning Schultz lay abed. The country champagne fresh air flowing in his window. Breakfast brought tiptoe by the young footman across the red silk persian carpet and placed on a bed table over his lap. On the tray in a milk glass vase, a black fragrant rose. As they sat in the music room the previous evening Batters whisperingly taking his preference.

"What do you suggest I should have Batters."

"Large or small breakfast sir."

"Large. With coffee."

"Then may I suggest half a grapefruit, followed by all bran cereal specially milled for his Lordship. With perhaps a sliced banana. Poached eggs. From our farmyard hens. Sausages. I recommend them. Made from his Lordship's own peach fattened pigs. And do try some of our heather honey from his Lordship's bees on our own toasted wholemeal bread. Our Ayrshire butter and cream is also a real treat sir. And I suggest, to finish sir, fresh figs."

"Hey hold it. What does his Lordship have for breakfast."

"One cup of very black very hot coffee and two cigarettes sir."

"Jesus when you got everything there is to eat. That's what he has."

"Yes sir. Mid morning sir, his Lordship may occasionally have a banana. And we do try to keep a constant supply of his Lordship's perfectly ripe bananas."

Breakfast brimming before him, Schultz watched this suddenly blue liveried servant light the log fire and depart beyond the green door. And sighing Schultz closing his eyes on this dream.

"Holy shit, I could, if I had the fucking sense, end my life right here and now, right after I've had breakfast, a good crap, a nice hot bath and threw a spine electrifying fuck into this Roxana wherever she is. Hey Roxana, you're all I need where the fuck are you."

"I'm here, sir."

"Holy shit, you are. Gee honey you gave me a scare. I'm sorry for my language and what I was saying."

"O that's alright sir, upon occasion his Lordship when exasperated does use similar language."

"He does, no kidding."

"Yes sir."

"Hey how did you get in my bathroom."

"There is a secret servants' entrance sir. I was tidying sir."

"Jesus, so that's what happens. I wondered. I dropped a towel and came back in ten minutes there was a new one."

"Yes sir."

"O god."

"Is there something wrong sir."

"No."

"But sir, are you crying."

"That's right. For joy. Now get out of here honey before I start chasing you around the room."

"O you wouldn't do that sir you're a gentleman."

"I might be for a couple of more minutes but not after I've had this breakfast."

In a stout motor with twelve forward and ten reverse gears, Schultz accompanied his Lordship around his domain. Up hillsides, down vales, rumbling across cattle grates, tearing across fields. Until his Lordship got marvellously stuck in a boggy patch and had a wonderful time shifting through the many gears and sending up spumes of spattering mud high into the sky as Schultz screamed.

"Hey shit your Lordship stop don't do that you're ruining the nice grass."

Later by a pasture Schultz sat awed watching a calf being born. Its mother grunting and with a long groan squeezing her progeny plopping out steaming on the grass. The pink nosed little animal licked clean by its mother's tongue and finally struggling to its feet nudging to find its mother's teat.

"Holy shit look at the fucking thing. Dumped right out on its head. And here it is in two minutes walking and sucking a tit imagine that. When it takes us two years to learn to stand up."

"Schultz I can see you have an enthusiasm for the country life. And unlike me you are made very calm by it."

"Calm, Jesus I'm excited out of my fucking mind by the magic wonder of it all. What the hell are you wasting time fooling around with showbizz in London when you could be here all the time enjoying this."

Schultz wide eyed toured the great walled gardens. With its cherry, apple, plum, pear and damson trees. The vast exotic conservatories and glasshouses. Sultry and full of vines, flowers and plants. Then walking through forests up hillsides where his Lordship had brief nervous words with his various foremen and nodded and smiled to the salutes from his endless staff.

"Holy christ your Lordship, I mean this place is a fucking major production. Not only could you be feeding armies but you must be making money."

"Ah Schultz alas it is lack of that latter item you mention which makes what you see here slowly but surely creak towards a financial abyss. One merely waits for it all to tumble over the precipice into total ruination."

"Let me tell you, boy if I had this set up I'd keep it going and I'd never go out my fucking front gate for the rest of my life."

"But indeed Schultz for the rest of your life, you might instead then go out of your fucking mind."

Binky had with two head shots killed two stags. And following an afternoon nap now appeared in the doorway facing the stone porch terrace. Smilingly resplendent in tweed jacket, cream cricket shirt, pink dotted mauve cravat, chamois gold buttoned waistcoat and bright green socks peeking between his grey flannel cuff and suede shoes.

"Jesus christ Binky that's the only fucking word for you. Urbane. It really is."

"Schultz you flatter me. And by the sentimental gleam in your eye I can tell that his Amazing Grace has recently told you some heart warming sentimental story about me. As I beseat myself, pull up my socks and pull my finger out. And appropriately here the two of you are. A contented picture. His Royal Grace's acres stretching endlessly beyond to the horizon. Indeed Schultz, one might even think you more than just ordinarily handsome in such a setting. Even a man of some spiritual accomplishment. In the nature of which only a few selected Church of England neutered Archbishops may boast."

"Binky I swear I'm completely dazed."

"You Schultz, dazed. Rubbish. I don't believe it."

"At this exact moment I'm not even thinking of where my next piece of ass is coming from."

"Ah Schultz, then you are benumbed and one must assume you are heartily enjoying our nearly last interlude of bachelor peace. Which I think his Amazing Grace especially needs. Did you know Schultz that up until the moment our dear host's engagement was announced, that he was being annoyed, telephoned, besieged, invited, fawned over, and chased. By both mothers and their blushing daughters."

"Binky you forget I always try to read his Lordship's personal mail."

"Ah of course you do Schultz. One forgets. Well then you know they pursue with an ardor which can only be described as manic. Thank god he has chosen a wife and removed himself from the hurly burly of the marriage market. Ending such nuisance pest and bother. Both of us will alas now take up serious family responsibilities. Till old age makes one's weapon finally wither away. But in that context do allow me to refresh one's carnal hopes a moment. My randy old grand uncle. Retired to a villa in the south of France. One four a.m. shouted out to the whole of his household to come quickly. To witness the old sport stark naked in the middle of his bedroom floor. Pointing with pride and delight at the age of ninety one to his erection trembling with a most remarkable rigidity."

"Ah Binky you do encourage one to go on taking the steps in life. My god, join Schultz and I in getting tight on this most bowel stirring of Moselles."

"Hey listen you guys. With all the debutantes after you what the hell are you always looking in the casting books for. From where I sit a Lord on the loose, is to women what catnip is to the cat."

"Ah Schultz, good observation but I think I speak also for his Royal Grace when I say that it is most deflating that still you do not regard his Royal Grace and I as serious theatrical producers."

"How could you be for christ's sake the way you live like this. Even when I'm up on top of some dame screwing the pubic hairs off her I'm all the time thinking of how much sets are going to cost or whether the costumes will be ready in time."

"Or Schultz, how you can get everybody to take a cut in salary."

"That's right too, Binky."

"But Schultz such girls as those gently invited to frequent our humble offices are an entirely different sort from those young ladies one brings home to introduce to one's long admired mommie or to one's nice dear old nanny. This is Schultz our last week on earth as single men."

Twilight descending over the great hollow silence. A castle bell high in the battlements tolling the hour. A breeze flapping the edge of linen table cloth. Rain beginning to fall slantingly across the parkland. Deer with their nervous little steps, lifting and lowering their heads, grazing slowly from the edge of huge shadowy trees, and moving down the hillside. The distant western sky faintly streaked pink. His Lordship's wicker chair squeaking as he leaned back to stretch his corduroy trousered legs. One sock wool and blue, the other silk and black. His long tapering fingers cutting paths in the condensation on the side of his wine glass. His cold blue smiling eyes sparkling and a breeze lifting back a blond lock of hair from his brow.

"Holy shit, I don't want to scare you guys but looking at the two of you, such specimens of beauty. For the third time in my life I realise that given the setting, the encouragement, and the banishment of women from the world, I could become a raving homosexual."

"Well dear me Schultz, how nice of you to interject this most piquant emotional departure. I was only this very second teasing myself with a rather risqué little fantasy of a game I plan to play with my soon to be wife. Perhaps we might make it a threesome."

"Shit. Sure. Why not."

"And of course Schultz, let me further hasten to add, that although his Royal Grace may not be, I distinctly am most excited by your totally unexpected observation. Now if you were a wee bit more, shall we say, willowy. Who knows. What do you think Basil my dear, shall I for a start, begin by calling you Dorothy. For myself I rather like the plain name Jane. And Schultz certainly is every bit attractive enough for us to immediately start calling him Sabrina."

"Binky please do allow me a second to anchor my chair before Schultz jumps on me so near the moat. If you haven't, I at least have had sufficient unencouraged attention in that quarter."

"No panic, your Lordship. But if there were women here, would we be sitting contented like this. Not worried whether Hollywood was calling. Sipping wine. Talking. With the whole fucking world around us in absolute peace."

"Schultz if I may say so it is charming the way you are so easily pleased."

"Sure I am your Lordship. It's the fucking marvellous atmosphere. Gives me a constant erection. Makes you wonder why in the world everyone is fighting, pushing and causing trouble. Jesus, this is why. Because everyone wants to be like this. In all this fucking god damn bliss."

Binky, a long black cigarette holder lifted between his fingers, as his confidentially tempered whisper forced a smile to the corner of his lips.

"Yet Schultz from all this seeming contentment, I understand you are attempting to entice away a member of his Royal Grace's household."

"Jesus how did you know that Binky. Holy shit your Lordship what have you got going, a spy ring. You want to imprison a beautiful girl like that here."

"Schultz I assure you, although we do have our dungeons, shackles and chains and many windows barred, this is not a correctional institution."

"Well can't you transfer her to another castle of yours closer to town. Or let me take her off your hands."

"Good god Schultz. Not on your Nelly."

"But your Lordship that girl could really go places out in the world. Her fucking blue eyes, her tits. Her waist couldn't be more than twenty two inches. Jesus even what I can see of her ankles. She's a real dream. Unspoilt and charming. I want her for the chorus line of the show."

"By god Schultz, you have your nerve. And I suppose she is to be taught her footwork down your town house cellars with all your other teeming screaming au pairs awaiting their turn to be kicked out into the inclemencies of the London streets."

"Holy shit you guys make me out to be some kind of roué or something."

"Ah Schultz of course his Royal Grace does not want to incarcerate a lovely lady. But sometimes I do seriously wonder if we are ever going to succeed in making you understand the difficulties, the frustrations and yes, I dare to say it, the thankless heartbreak of this land owning way of life."

"I understand it, don't worry. I'm right here remember getting a front row view of you guys. In all your rural frustration and heartbreak. Hey Jesus your Lordship, how many places have you got like this."

"Ah Schultz I hope you will not take offense, but on such an agreeable afternoon one prefers not to contemplate such matters."

"Well let me tell you I'll take one of them off your hands anytime."

On this last evening, dinner arrived in four courses. Batters with his tiny hand claps as footmen swept in and out. Asparagus

183

soup and sherry. Trout and Chablis. Partridge and Clos de Tart. Trifle and champagne. Vintage port and cigars. And repairing to the billiard room Schultz got directions to go for a pee.

"Turn right. Turn left. Third door on your right Schultz. You will find my grandfather's reserved water closet. It requires some effort to lift the seat but you will be rewarded by an exquisitely decorated Meissen toilet bowl."

Schultz these seconds later, face white as a sheet, bursting into the room. His prick hanging out of his fly. Cobwebs all over him, head to foot.

"Hey Jesus christ. I opened up the fucking door you told me. And right as I'm going to piss I lift up the fucking seat the light goes off. And down from the ceiling behind me drops a fucking whole human skeleton dangling glowing in the dark."

Binky holding his stomach lurching about tripping over his cue. And his Lordship knocking over a pole screen as he too fell back laughing.

"Hey you guys did this. Deliberately. Just to ruin my peace of mind. Holy shit, look at me and you're just laughing."

"Ah Schultz we are looking and I regret laughing and I do apologise. It's an old joke my grandfather was fond of playing. To jolt guests out of their drunkenness."

"Well I pissed all over myself for christ's sake. I could have had a heart attack. Jesus your Lordship, you know sometimes I think you're highly irresponsible."

Schultz, his nerves calmed, having been personally conducted by his Lordship to another water closet sans skeletons. Now set out in boots and tuxedo for his Lordship's favourite sport, badger watching. The three of them making their way down a hillside through the forest paths to stand silently and motionlessly in a dank vale, chillingly waiting for one of these nightly creatures to come crawling by in the moonlight.

"Holy jumping christ the fucking thing is stepping on me."

"Damn you Schultz don't scream and run. Trust you to ruin what promised to be a most memorable night of badger watching."

"Holy fuck you already have me a nervous wreck scaring the shit out of me in the crapper now you want me to let wild animals maybe bite me."

Departing Londonwards that Tuesday after lunch. A gentle rain out of heavy grey clouds. His Lordship's faithful retinue lined up to say goodbye. Umbrellas held over their heads entering the motor car. Roxana peeking round from an upstairs window. Schultz having deposited five pounds on his dresser with a note.

Dear Roxana,

You gorgeous creature. Now don't forget what I told you. Give me a tinkle as soon as the spirit takes you to flee Alcatraz up to the big smoke.

S. F. Schultz

At some speed the two limousines motored along the winding byways of his Lordship's estate, until the skies clearing, the sun shining, they arrived down a long straight stretch of narrow road lined with lime trees. His Lordship busily leafing through sheafs of catalogues in preparation to attend an auction scheduled for three in Bond Street.

"Hey where the hell are we going Binky."

"To the railway station, Schultz."

"What for."

"The cars Schultz will go by road and we and the stags will proceed by rail."

On the steps of the little station with a sign reading Nectarine Castle, a gold braided station master bowing to his Lordship alighting. Splendidly attired porters rushed to unload the stags. The monstrously long train for London sticking out down the track. Steam pouring out of its throbbing hissing locomotive.

"Hey really what is this all about Binky. Is this his Lordship's own private station."

"This Schultz is. By his Royal Grace's request the London train stops here. And you must be absolutely confidentially quiet about it. Some people of course don't like it one bit. I dare say it's envy. Rather an unpleasant amount of that about these days. But it is after all, his Royal Grace's land the train crosses."

"This is fucking too much. But I love it. Holy shit look at that. A red fucking carpet. I can't wait to get my feet on it."

"Schultz hold fast."

"What for."

"Well as a matter of fact a small ceremony accompanies his Royal Grace's mounting the train."

"Wow. This I got to see."

The station master and porters now lined up as his Lordship with tiny frequent nods of his head proceeded between them on the red carpet. Followed immediately by a widely grinning Schultz who gave all the watching eyes from the train windows his personal Woonsocket hi sign.

A small panelled drawing room inside the train. A side table covered with the day's newspapers. Schultz plopping himself on a sofa chair and staring into space. Binky smoking a cigarette and taking in the passing acres of Nectarine Castle. His Lordship smilingly contemplating Schultz.

"Ah my dear Schultz, you really will now be glad to get back to the familiar comforting ways of the city. Tell me. What's on your mind."

"Well aside from slowly tearing my appetites away from all this privileged bliss and back to attend to the problems of the production, I'm thinking christ you guys. I never know what's going to happen next."

> And nothing
> Sacred or
> Profane
> Would surprise
> Me

15

SCHULTZ, his Gladstone bag toted behind him, popped up his town house steps in Arabesque Street. Pressing his key in his door absolutely restored to its previous undamaged gleaming green condition. In the hall, the smell of fresh paint. The painting of a rural scene back on the wall. Schultz lifting his case up on the newly repaired chair. Standing and listening. And suddenly began to run. Up the stairs. Past a new bust of Justinian back on his plinth again. Towards the sound of bath water pouring into a tub.

"What the fuck are you doing here."

"O darling please don't shout. Where have you been. I've been worried sick here waiting for you. I'm here because I love you. I love you deeply darling."

"You love me. You're worried sick. You're waiting for me. I'll tell you what you're doing. You're suing me. Do you think I'm out of my mind. Letting someone sit using my hot water in my bathtub while they're suing me. I saw you disappear with that big fat fucking black King."

"Darling he wants to invest money in your show."

"What, are you kidding. The closest that big black cunt's ever been to showbizz is a fertility dance."

"I did it for you. Can't you see."

"What did you do for me. Let him shove up his big black prick."

"Darling you're as crude and rude as he was impeccable and charming."

"Impeccable. Charming. The fucker is cutting everybody's balls off except his own all over Africa."

"Well I speak only for myself. And I don't know a thing about his balls. He is one of the most wonderful gentlemen I've ever met. He knows how to treat a woman. To make her feel marvellous. To make her feel wanted, loved, adored."

"Come on honey. You get your fucking teddy bear there sitting on my crapper and you just go back and swing from his big black prick then. Out."

"He's gone. He's gone back to Africa. And darling nothing happened."

"Nothing happened huh. Only that you left me sticking out like a sore thumb nearly getting murdered. While you were eating grapes he peeled. And flashing your ass around dancing your head off with him."

"Darling none of that would happen if we were married. It's not my fault that I'm beautiful. And that men want me. Don't you see that."

"I see plenty. Especially the fucking damage you did in this house."

"Well darling the damage you did to me. Doesn't that occur to you. I've been hours at the dentist. And everything is fixed in the house."

"Only by a fucking miracle. O.K. come on. Out."

"You're staring at my body."

"Cover it up."

"I think you're jealous. And in fact I have a standing invitation to His Imperial Highness's palace."

"You mean to his tree hut in the jungle. With about three

hundred other pieces of ass he's got collected waiting around powdering their fannies behind the foliage."

"You are jealous. Please hand me that towel and avert your eyes. And get out while I dress."

"I'm not getting out of my own bathroom while you throw another fucking coma as soon as my back's turned."

"For your information I won't in future need you or your bathroom. His Imperial Highness's London embassy is available to me any time I wish. And any time I care to go to Africa a private plane will be sent for me. I'll have a palace all to myself. With all the eunuch servants I want."

"Here's the fucking towel. Now while my balls are still intact let me tell you something. You get dried. You get dressed. You get down those stairs. And you. Honey. Get the fuck out. And stay out. And leave the keys to this house behind you. And now stop the crying."

"I won't."

"Where's my mail."

"Your mail is down in the kitchen. I tried to do everything to help you. Don't you see that. In your stubbornness and meanness. And a Mr. Magillacurdy called. He left a whole new script for you he said. And did I do anything. With that opportunity. When he's beautiful handsome and so poetic. No. I didn't."

"Honey I wasn't here. Besides you're such an actress that nobody could tell you weren't fucking your head off all afternoon. Just like you could have been doing with those vine swinging African apes."

"And what would you care anyway if I were."

"I wouldn't."

"For your information those vine swingers as you call them are potentates and all products of England's very best schools. While you're merely from Woonsocket."

"Hey honey, get dressed. And for your information, Woonsocket is the best fucking place to be out of on the face of the earth. Plus don't forget I spent time in Brooklyn."

"How could I forget."

189

"O.K. Duchess, just without a tearful ceremony get out of my life. I'm going to give you ten minutes."

Schultz turning. A long moaning wail erupting as he walked back out into the hall. Reaching the door of his bedroom. My sweating palm turning the crystal nob. Big Ben booming. More sobs rending Belgravia. In spite of everything sensible my mind is telling me. I've got a hard on. Which fucking human nature uses to pole vault me out of old disasters into newer bigger ones. Like already hit my father with my mother. And made his neck go all stringy with tension. My uncle dropped dead of heart attack in the bathroom. My aunt hysterical looking at his inert heap. If this keeps up. Could be me in a few more years. An ambulance came to collect him. The guy with the stretcher says don't worry lady this happens all the time, he's the fourth I collected since lunch. Unbelievable. Half hour after the most wonderful weekend. And I got fucking death all of a sudden on my mind. As well as her luscious bloody tits. Which I would love to fuck off her at the rate of one semi quaver per second. Throw her gorgeous body backwards into the tub. With a splash. Jump right in on top in the suds. Holy Jesus what was that. That was a splash. Or the whole fucking bathroom has fallen through the ceiling.

Schultz running back. His red silk polka dot tie in his hand. The room empty. The carpet soaked again. Jesus where is the bitch. Shit she's under the water. What is she trying to do to me. Isn't it enough she's already given me enemy microbes up my prick. Now eyes closed she wants to let her hands float from her wrists and put bubbles coming up from her nose and mouth. I knew it. I should have stayed in the country. A cowhand on his Lordship's estate. With a life of peace and dignity. Instead of a drowning on my hands.

Schultz tugging and lifting Pricilla. Draping her by the white glistening arms out of her freshly shaved armpits, over the edge of the pink bathtub. Water dripping from the curled long black strands of hair. The phone ringing. Holy shit. Hollywood. It's about nine a.m. out on the coast. The call I missed last time this bitch had my life in turmoil.

Schultz pinching Pricilla hard on her arse. Test her for life. She twitched. She's alive. Playing her usual death scene she does to perfection. Boy should fairness ever sneak back into the world, you madam, had better watch out.

Schultz wiping his hands on a towel, necktie flying, running down the stairs three at a time. And carramba. Crashing headlong into the table at the bottom. The phone bouncing on the floor. Scrambling on his knees to snatch up the instrument to his mouth and ear. Fucking phone. If it's the one last thing I ever do. I'm going to grab you. Jesus before the show is even previewed they could be offering me a hundred grand option for the movie rights. Act like I heard a better offer from New York and be tough from the first syllable. Like Mr. Schultz is busy long distance on the other line but let's hear the deal.

"Yeah."

"Hello. Hello."

"Yeah who is it."

"Hey what's going on. All the banging. Is this you Sigmund. It's Al."

"Holy shit you. I nearly killed myself just now coming to the phone."

"Sigmund I lost my temper the other day. I'm calling you up to apologise. Tried to get you the whole weekend. I mean two old friends. It shouldn't be like that between them. I'm dropping the case."

"Yeah, I'm listening."

"But Sigmund I want to be sincere with you. I want to give you some good advice. The girl loves you."

"Holy shit. Not this subject again."

"Sure this subject. The girl loves you."

"You should tell me she washes my socks and shirts. I'd be impressed."

"Look the girl was seven years old when her father jumped."

"I'm expecting a long distance call from Hollywood Al and you phone to tell me someone jumped. What the hell are you talking about."

"Look Sigmund. I'm telling you this. Because it's serious. He put on his overcoat, his hat. Took his brief case and his umbrella. He ran, Sigmund, across the floor of his office."

"Hey wait a second Al there's a knock on the door."

Schultz peeking out the open crack of door. The sky darkened. And in a gust of rainy wind, two green uniformed delivery gentlemen. Each with a stacked armful of cellophane covered red roses.

"This is Four Arabesque Street, sir."

"That's right. Says so on the door. Hey what's all this."

"Sir there's a whole van load."

"I'm not paying for these. You got the wrong address."

"This is the address. And they're all paid for sir. You want them in the hall."

"Holy christ. I'm on the phone. O.K. put them in the hall. O.K. Al I'm back. Where were we. Before the roses arrived. Good title for a song for the show. O yeah. Pricilla's father. Running across the floor of his office. And yeah I know Al, exactly what's coming next. He took a flying leap right out through the window. Fifteen stories up over Madison Avenue. And killed three innocent people when he landed on them in the street."

"Hey come on, what are you, a soulless evil son of a bitch. Using that tone of voice. Plus it happened from twenty stories up over Lexington Avenue. And he killed only one single person."

"So even in death he was a conservationist. Or maybe vaudeville missed one of its biggest stars. And with the two tons he was married to he could have been a double act."

"Hey Sigmund. One second. Do you mind. Just one second. I'm doing what I'm doing. As a friend. And for both of you. Do you want me to get angry again."

"Sure get angry Al. But you blow hot and cold. One second I'm the biggest son of a bitch going and you're going to sue the shit out of me. Next you're telling me the excuses some bitch has who's dedicated already to destroying my life."

"Don't you understand. The girl wants to get married. She needs the security and protection of matrimony. That's why she does those things."

"Shit she needs protection. I'm standing here getting buried in roses. I need protection."

"So you should get married. At your age too."

"Hold it Al, hold it. I got to stop these fucking roses coming in. Hey you guys. Stop. That's enough. No more. Give the rest of them to your relatives. I'm locking the door. Back to you Al. So now what's fresh."

"Sigmund it was her who pleaded with me we should be friends again."

"Who. You and her."

"No. You and me."

"So why should we be suddenly friends again Al."

"Well I'll be up front. To avoid you dragging her good name through the courts."

"Hey Al. Am I hearing you right. Am I. Dragging her through the courts. I'm the fucking defendant remember. The two of you are suing me. It was your knees nearly ruptured her tits landing on her chest. Remember. And I should get married. Holy mackerel. Thanks for picking the wife for me."

"Not only is she beautiful. She has the most sexy telephone voice in the world."

"So that's wonderful. She should keep in telephone contact. Or am I supposed to now set up an answering service for freaks. Or what. Are you recently Al some kind of pervert. Maybe getting your engorgements on my telephone bill."

"Yeah I was. I admit it. I had an erection."

"You had an erection Al. Will wonders never cease. Maybe in morse code she could give you an orgasm."

"You're such a damn wise guy, aren't you."

"So your telephone erection Al. What's it supposed to do with me. Tell me. I mean it's swell. I mean I hope you get them watching television and listening to the radio too."

"Sigmund this was a friendly communication. But I'm not going to stand for one more second of your shit."

"My shit. You mean your shit. Al relax. Before you have a coronary. If it's any consolation to you she gives me an erection.

Even as she was stark naked draped over the edge of the bathtub upstairs."

"What did you say."

"I said draped over the bathtub."

"What."

"Yeah, I found her under the water Al."

"You found her under the water."

"Here we go again Al. That's right Al. I found her under the water. Bubbles coming up out of her mouth."

"Why you son of a bitch she needs oxygen. You drowned her."

"We're into the routine again Al. Next tell me you're going to kill me. For what I done to her. Which she done to herself. Which if you had any sense you'd get it through your head Al that she is always doing to herself. She's still alive. But I'm reassured she gets all her practice in suicide because it runs in the family."

"If I could get my hands on your bare fucking neck."

"Cut it out Al. I've had enough from the two of you. I'm not going to spend the rest of my natural life like a fucking hospital nurse in a loony bin. What the hell is it with you Al that you're telling me to marry her so much. You talk like you're in love with her."

"I am."

"That's great. So why don't you bring her up the aisle, feed, clothe and house her. Like recently she's talking about palaces."

"Because she's just that little bit too young yet to have the necessary insight to know that somebody mellow and mature like me, with my beautiful mind, wit, sensibility, love of life, and who doesn't want to hurt people, is right for her at my older age."

"Who doesn't want to hurt people, Al. You were around here attempting grievous bodily harm in this hall."

"For her I'd kill."

"Jesus Al. You're having a geriatric breakdown."

"All it is, wise guy is I can't give her as much of my future as she can give me of hers."

"So in the prime of my youth you want to stick me with her with the thousands of gorgeous girls around I haven't fucked yet. Thanks a lot Al."

"Hey by the way shouldn't you go upstairs and see if she's all right."

"No Al I shouldn't. But just think a second how long it took you to ask that question."

"Jesus wise guy you got a lot to answer for you have."

"That's right. But I'll tell you why Al I don't go upstairs if you'd shut up sermonizing me for just one second. So are you listening."

"Yeah for one second."

"The reason I don't go upstairs to see if she's all right is because she is wrapped up in a towel or maybe my dressing gown and is hanging her tits and ears over the bannister at this very moment listening to every fucking word I'm saying on this phone. That's why."

"I don't know what to say to you. I should hang up. I just don't know what to say."

"And Al as soon as I hang up she will rush back into the bathroom, take off the towel and dressing gown, lay herself back into the bath, drape her beautiful tits over the side of the tub and make like she's fucking unconscious again."

"Jesus I really am dumbfounded and speechless. I don't know what to say to you."

"I'll tell you what to say Al. Just say that good old Sigmund Franz Schultz knows what he's talking about for a change. That he's seen plenty of women in his time. And that he knows what they want."

"O.K. Rabbi Schultz. Lecture me. What do they want."

"They want everything Al. Everything. A guy's guts, his balls, his prick, his money, his life insurance. But more than just that they want his imprisoned proximity. To make sure he doesn't have the juice left to fuck anyone else when they're finished with him. And you know what I want Al. You there Al."

"I'm here. And Jesus christ it's a disgrace. That an American, a fellow American should end up talking talk like this. When was the last time you pledged allegiance to the American flag."

195

"I'd talk like this if I was a fucking Eskimo Al. Pledging allegiance to the north pole."

"You tell me then mister snowman. What do you want for a wife."

"I want a woman like my mother. You hear me. My mother."

"I heard you. The first respectable thing you said so far."

"You know why Al. Because she would nag me to eat the good soup she made. She would sew my clothes. Iron my shirts. She would rock me to sleep. Whisper comfort to me in pain and disappointment."

"This is some kind of inverted incest you're talking about. That's what I think."

"That's right Al. I'd fuck my own mother. You got me figured to a T."

"You would wouldn't you if you thought it would get you somewhere."

"No Al. Not because I think it would get me somewhere. Because I would be giving her back the love she gave me. Which has smothered me."

"You lurid motherfucker."

"Go back Al to Ohio."

"Don't slander me please. I'm from Michigan."

"That figures. You've got just the right kind of morals. And Al let me criticize your life for a second. With your heart condition who's fucked more different women than you. Who's kicked more out of his house."

"That's bullshit."

"Four girls. This year alone."

"There were five. But who's counting."

"And you go around clucking like some pious romantic old mother hen. And over a bitch who's opened her white thighs for the biggest black prick in darkest Africa."

"Stop Sigmund stop. For christ's sakes. This is a serious call I'm making back to you. How long have we known each other. Five years. I've remained a friend through each of your flops. Right. Come on. What are you doing tonight."

196

"I'm fucking trying to compose my wits and mentality for the busy day I face tomorrow to avoid another fucking flop."

"So O.K. let me take you two young kids out to dinner. A nice little nosh at the Savoy. How about that. Beluga. All the trimmings."

"I feel I'm getting trapped Al. No shit. I really feel that. That this is some kind of plan. You got stuck in your brain. You love her. I don't."

"Why did you do what you did to her then."

"Do what Al. I didn't do anything to her Al which I wouldn't do to any other gorgeous creature. I can't resist beautiful women Al. That's all."

"So you're different from any other guy in the world."

"That's right. Because unless you change them every five weeks beautiful women are nothing but a pain in the ass."

"Sigmund. O.K. I accept. You're just mister cynic. But the Savoy, O.K. In an hour."

"I ain't even unpacked Al."

"So unpack. Get rid of this paranoia out of your life."

"Let me tell you Al. I just got rid of it. After one of the most blissful few days I've ever spent. I don't want any more hassle. I got enough with the production."

"Hey how is the production."

"The production is swell."

"Good I'm glad to hear it, Sigmund I really am. So come on. A little nosh at the Savoy. If I don't bring you two kids together at least you can be friends. Besides this is my birthday."

"Holy shit Al, why didn't you tell me in the beginning."

"I'm shy. Besides who wants to go counting years."

"Happy eightieth birthday. I'll bring you a few nice red roses. Like a railway car full. Hey wait a second while I run up and see if the subject matter is still there."

Schultz pulling back and forth on his polka dot tie in marvellous anticipation, tiptoeing back up the stairs. At the half closed bathroom door. Pushing it slowly open. Shit if I could only just catch her getting herself back into her coma position. There's the corner of the tub. Just push a little more. Get a good gander at the long curvaceous spine from the end of which hangs that marvellous ass. Just peek in. Jesus where is she.

"Hey honey. Holy shit."

The deluge of cold liquid fresh out of a bucket hit Schultz full in the face. Just as he stepped around the door.

"You scum talk about me like that."

"Jesus hold it you wildcat what am I blinded with."

Schultz grabbing in all directions for a towel. Feeling the wind of something sail past his ear. Wiping his eyes to see. A soap dish. Duck. Get out of the way. And the fucking cover hits me in the head. Followed by her nails. Sinking in. And christ, stinging down my face over my just healed scars. Toes of her slippers kicking my shins. Welcome back from the peaceful countryside. Into a hurricane.

"I'll kill you."

"You insane bitch. That's what you're doing, stop."

Schultz turned, And ran. Along the hall towards his bedroom door. Pricilla grabbing the polka dot tie flying over his shoulder. Like a lassoed calf Schultz's head jerked back nearly off his neck. The world going, going, gone black. A dim light. Somewhere. At the end of a damp long passage. Running miles. Through catacombs. Skulls and bones. My violin teacher. The butcher round the corner. Watched him every afternoon. Charlie. Cutting through his meat. His bald head bent. In my own romantic youth. Hovering over me. Slapping my face. Jesus. Where am I.

"Darling, please, wake up, wake up. I didn't mean it."

Schultz opening eyes. Rolling over on his hands and knees. Lifted to his feet by Pricilla. Hobbling back and forth outside his bedroom door. Dabbing the blood dripping on his face. Shaking his head, rubbing his neck.

"My adam's apple is crushed. And holy shit, I left Al on the phone."

Schultz carefully guiding by the bannister, back down the stairs. Breathing in the perfume. Christ just like my uncle's funeral. When it was stacked with roses.

"Al."

"Hey Sigmund, for christ's sake, what took you so long. I heard like violent noises in the distance."

"Al, you did. Boy let me tell you. The subject matter is still there. I need a fucking bottle of champagne. See you at the Savoy."

"I'll send my limo for you."

"Thanks Al. Believe me, tonight it would be a big help."

Pricilla radiant. Her body clinging moss green low cut dress. Milky breasts ready to squirt at you. Carrying a rose. Turning heads everywhere. Smiling at the commissionaire bowing her out of Al's limousine. Her ass wagging across the pavement under the shiny entrance of this hotel.

"Good evening Mr. Schultz. Good evening Madam."

"Hi."

Schultz following through this pink brown marble evening lobby. Pricilla swirled in as if she owned the place. Sweeping past men hopefully and friendly rising half up out of their seats. The hostile eyes of women looking her every inch up and down. And christ they're even getting to know me. Up these familiar stairs. And through to the bar. Al. Jesus there he is. The son of a bitch. Full of his bonhommie. I think he's trying to get me to keep this filly in my stable feeding her hay and oats and kicking the shit out of me, while he smells around for a way to shaft her in his king sized celebrity bed. But for some fucking reason I can't stop loving him. Maybe it's his bad taste. He's in another one of his semi-rustic evening numbers which might also do on a grouse moor.

"Pricilla, my darling. And Sigmund. Sigmund. Hey what the hell happened."

"A cement truck. Hit me Al."

Al kissing and hugging Pricilla and then taking Schultz's hand in both of his and pumping up and down. And all seated at the table. The champagne corks popping.

"Hey Al, here's to you, happy happy birthday. And this is on me."

"No kids. It's on me."

"O.K. Al you convinced me. At the recent price of this stuff, it's on you."

Al and his party escorted by half the Savoy's staff to his table by the window in the River Room. The Beluga heaped up throne center on its tiers of plates in coffers of ice. With more champagne corks popping. And not ten minutes passed shovelling in these fish eggs when who do you think should sweep in. Accompanied by a tail coated major domo, assisted by two waiters taking up the rear.

"Now Sigmund, stay right where you are. Sit down for christ's sake. Now you're here, lets not ruin this pleasant little party. Pricilla's mother just thought she might drop over. Like for to celebrate my birthday."

"Well pardon me while I rejoice dropping through the fucking floor like I'm going to do."

"Don't you insult my mother like that."

"I'm not insulting your mother. I'm stating a matter of physical fact. And if I don't go through the fucking floor I'm going to go through the fucking roof. Which do you want."

"Come on Sigmund. For your old pal Al. Do this for me. I'm begging you. A whole cake's coming. With my hard earned candles on it. The orchestra is ready to play my own latest hit tune I composed. Make it a happy family."

The recent addition to the happy family polished off in one serving flat, the entire remainder of the caviar. Schultz sat through the music, soup, entree. The cake, the sauterne, with his jaw muscles twitching on a stony face. Ordering ice water while Pricilla's mother ordered everything else from the menu. Her plate empty seconds after her plate was full. And in addition to the food I'm the big subject of interest once more when suddenly the big black King of Boohooland has gone back to his jungle.

"Mr. Schultz I understand your family is in manufacturing textiles. It must be so nice with that business back home to be able to change your interest when your hobby with the theatre gets too dull for you. Of course I hope you will be settling down now with the new event."

"Excuse me, Mrs. Prune I don't understand. What new event."

"O of course you know. I don't have to tell you."

"I don't know. You tell me."

"My daughter."

"Yeah."

"Mr. Schultz. Surely you know she's pregnant."

"Pregnant."

"Aren't you my dear. The blessed event is expected, November ninth."

"Well. So November ninth. That's swell. So."

"Well as the proud father aren't you pleased."

"Pleased. Me. The proud father. Holy shit. I can't believe my ears, what is this, some kind of blackmail."

"Sigmund, Sigmund that's no way to talk. Respect what's being said. You go right away flying off the handle. Mrs. Prune here just wants to protect her daughter's interests."

"Yes Mr. Schultz. Since my daughter here is with your child. Her chances with the aristocracy are ruined. Now that it's known all over London. That you're responsible. We can prove it. If you think blood tests are necessary. And unless you know what's good for you we've got lawyers."

A barge hooting out on the river. The clink and clatter of cutlery and dishes. The stillness at Schultz's table. Till a waiter jumping to pick up the chair sent flying backwards, tripped and catapulted into another carrying a massive armful of soups. Schultz ashen faced, managed to stand upright.

"You got lawyers have you. Well I'll tear the fucking bunch of you to ribbons, and spit you out like tobacco juice. And bury the gang of you in those fucking roses."

"Be reasonable Sigmund. For the sake of the one and only god come back. Sit down."

Pricilla's mother, all two tons of her in a shiny scarlet dress rising up from her seat. Her hands supporting her monstrous shoulders and bosoms as she leaned forward over her newly replenished plate and now as she shouted, lifting one arm to point in the direction of the departing Schultz.

"That man leaving, inseminated my daughter."

Schultz making his way out across this familiar room. All its assured sombre plushness. The haunt of ladies and gentlemen. Amazing what new things you notice in old familiar surroundings when the brain has received a shattering shock. The gleaming gold base of the marble pillars holding up the restaurant ceiling. The nearly empty wood panelled lobby. The white frieze high around the wall. Carts, oxen and ladies dancing to flute players. Out under the gleaming canopy of this hotel. Got to look up. A bronze warrior with a shield and spear on the roof. Jesus I should be him. They sounded like the wedding's all set to happen. How did they do this to me. Excoriate me. Convict me. So I should go marching down the aisle. Into the depths of hell. Or up the steps into the chamber of horror of some fucking registry office. Why didn't I put a condom on my prick. You want to feel flesh. And Jesus you end up feeling you're falling into a snake pit. Just when in the incredible bliss of Shangri La I learn from his Lordship what life could be all about. They get together a birthday party. To fuck me. For my whole life.

Outside the revolving doors, Schultz doubled up, hand on his stomach, hobbling back and forth. The doorman calling up Al's limousine. Schultz unable to lift an arm to wave it away. The concerned commissionaire holding the car door open. Waiting as Schultz bent further over. Both hands across his stomach. And the doorman niftily jumping back. As Schultz delivered from his lips. With a heaving groaning roar. His champagne, caviar, vichyssoise and steak tartare. Into the rear blue soft carpeted interior of Al's limousine.

> Jesus
> This is what
> The Jews
> Did
> To Christ

16

THAT night stepping crumpled up from a taxi. Schultz perambulated about the shadowy gardens of Belgrave Square. Until a black cat scampered along the pavement across Schultz's path as he headed up the steps to the perfumed hall of number four. And shivered past the stack of roses. Past the pantry. Down the stairs. To flick the light on in the kitchen and look in the cupboards for some kind of stomach soothing concoction. And wham. Kick and trip over the garbage pail. Strewing contents across the floor.

"Holy shit. I'm distraught. What's all this. On the tiles. My fucking mail. O dear god, my Royal invitation to the palace. Torn into little pieces. And this. Photographs. Ripped up. The bitch must have gone through every one of my drawers and papers I had under lock and key. This is the god damn ruination of beautiful memories. Every girl I ever knew nearly. Or ever tried to seduce when I cast them in a fucking production. Or who might have meant something to me. Including, would you believe it, pictures of my own mother. And Jesus, my Aunt Essie, when they were good looking young women back in the ghetto in Prague. Nothing, fucking nothing is sacred anymore. I could cry. Jesus I am crying. My poor fucking mother and father. When you come to look at it, all the sacrifice they did for me. Marking down lingerie which were already bargains. Just to make a sale. Jesus this is too painfully sentimental. I'm having a fucking breakdown. I need an aspirin. Al calls himself my friend. He's a big fucking mother spider. I'm going to keep out of their web. For the rest of my fucking life. I don't care who hears me all over Belgravia at midnight, I, Sigmund Franz Schultz, am going to sweat, practise and train, and turn myself into the most indomitable muscle bound mountain of resolute unyielding fucking stubborn fortitude who ever avoided marriage. And no woman fat, beautiful or otherwise is ever again going to do to me what was done to me through the recent past. Jesus what's that."

Schultz's shoulders jerking backwards as if shot. And spinning around from his commiseration. Staring towards the larder.

"A noise was made in there. Christ now I got rats or something."

Schultz stepping across to the cream panelled door. Waiting listening. Slowly pushing it open. The kitchen light. Shining in.

"Jesus what the fucking hell are you doing in here."

"Forgive me. Please. I am nowhere to go. I run away. I look. I find nowhere. I come here. Don't make me go. I am Greta."

"Holy shit. I know you're Greta. Honey come out. As if I didn't have enough trouble without you already. Jesus you're all dirty. Where the fuck have you been. Go have a bath."

"Thank you. Thank you."

"But Jesus. You can't stay here."

"I no like it there to go back to Hornchurch."

"Hey baby. Look. I'm telling you. You can't stay here."

"Please, I beg. Please. I no can go back."

"What's wrong."

"The man of the house. He try all the time jump on me to kiss me."

"Jesus tell his wife."

"I cannot. She try all the time jump on me too to kiss me."

"Well Jesus, let them kiss you for christ's sake."

"I have done. And now they fight with knives over me."

"Holy shit kid. You got a problem. O.K. for tonight you can stay."

"O thank you. Thank you."

"Shit no kisses for me tonight. Just make me some Horlicks with some honey and hot milk."

"O yes. Yes."

"Bring it up to the bedroom."

"O yes. Yes."

Schultz staring in darkness. The light from the throbbing diesel of a passing taxi flashing on the bedroom ceiling. A quiet sobbing shaking the mattress as Greta wept. Schultz reaching out to touch this arm and hand which squeezed tight to his own. Suffer little children to come unto me. Heard that somewhere in my life. Probably was some publicity provoking statement made by a grown up Jesus. Feel a welling up just below the lungs. My own tears now are pouring down my face. Christ here we are. This au pair turning now to comfort me. And we're both clinging together, sobbing to sleep. Boy if that don't make sad headlines. In my personal history.

A streak of light waving between the drawn bedroom curtains. Greta snoring beside him. Schultz reaching over across her to turn on his lamp. And catching his wristwatch by the strap to read the time. Christ almighty. Do I have to knock over a glass of water. First move I make waking up is a disaster already. It's twelve o'fucking o'clock. I should have been at the office two hours ago. Now I got all this on my hands. Even with her limited English she must have understood everything I said in my moment of personal collapse last night.

Schultz rushing through into the bathroom. Turning on the shower over the tub. As the nozzle blasts off and hits him in the head. Followed by scalding hot water. And a nearly neck breaking scramble to safety.

"What next. Jesus what next."

Schultz dressed. A last peek in the bedroom. Greta one ankle sticking from under a sheet. And sprawled, her arms and legs flung out like she was being drawn and quartered. Her yellow hair splayed over the green and blue striped pillow. A breast peeking up pink and soft. And the long deep snores as she slept.

"Honey they may be fighting over you with knives but let me tell you it's better than having a bunch of blackmailers at your throat."

On a breezy sunny corner of Belgrave Square Schultz dabbing his face with a hanky and flagging a cab. Cutting himself twice trying to shave around his claw marks. And now jumping out of the elevator nearly catching and amputating four fingers as he slammed the expanding door closed. Rushing past Rebecca who followed behind him with a handful of letters, into the chairman's office where a cavalry twill attired Binky sat with the newspaper, his open coat displaying a pink blue striped shirt, and a light blue polka dot tie.

"Ah Schultz I have been just trying to ring you. And was as usual answered in the customary fractured English. Those vague unhelpful expressions one expects at your end of the line. He gone no here."

"Jesus Binky come on, I got work to do."

"Schultz I should say you have. Everyone's been on the phone nonstop to get you. Your property developing industrialist investor friend especially. Trying to get a personal urgent message to you."

"He just can't wait to put more money into the show, that's all."

"Agents are ringing about unsigned contracts for clients. And my god, Schultz. What. More scratches on the face. What ever do you do with yourself on your quiet London evenings. O and by the way your composing team residing at the Dorchester want a larger sitting room."

"Jesus christ what else can fucking well go wrong with my life."

His Lordship entering the office stepping out tiptoe from behind Rebecca.

"Good morning Schultz. I'll tell you what else can go wrong.

And it's with my life. There's been an absolute outcry to discontinue trains stopping at Nectarine Castle station. Several prominent members of the local county council who happened to be on that train we took claim that a member of my party gave them a sign signifiying the word fuck you or sentiments distinctly similar."

"Holy shit your Lordship. Hold it. One problem at a time. Let's take the city problems first."

"I'm sorry Schultz if I distress you."

"Your Lordship you don't distress me one bit. If everyone in this world did for me what you've so far done. My life would be one big fucking paradise believe me. Sorry Rebecca about the language."

"That's quite alright sir. But I have I'm afraid further difficult news."

"What."

"Mr. Magillacurdy's Agent rang to say that Mr. Magillacurdy has received an offer from Hollywood to which he cannot say no."

"Jesus. This really is my lucky day. The fucker. Says he has no agent. Now he's got one. Who starts right off trying to shake me down."

"Ah Schultz, there is another matter."

"Yeah Binky, just tell me don't do dramatics with that up and down on the toes stuff."

"I speak this most disturbing news flat footed I assure you. Our dear old chap Mr. Gayboy has, it appears, on this momentarily very sunny day, rented your theatre to another production."

"He's what."

"Another production, Schultz, is booked in."

"What. Just say that once more."

"Another production is booked in."

"I'll kill the fucking cunt. I'll fucking well kill him. Jesus christ, get out of my fucking way. I'm going right over there this fucking second and I'm going to kick his ass all over the West End of London."

"Steady, my dear Schultz, steady. Gayboy will have you arrested. You may be sure everything he does is vetted by his numerous lawyers."

"Lawyers. That fucker is going to need numerous undertakers."

Schultz storming out the door. Down the hall. Into a secretary bearing two hot cups of coffee for her tall blond charming employers.

"Excuse me honey but I'm in a fucking hurry."

Schultz in the soft mist capturing a taxi. Sitting upon the edge of his seat undoing his collar and tie. Leicester Square. Piccadilly Circus. Look at all these people thronging the West End with nothing better to do than buy tickets and go to my show. Maybe fucking Gayboy is a friend of Al's and this could be a conspiracy.

Schultz jumping out of the taxi. Slapping a note in the driver's hand.

"Keep the change."

"Thanks Gov."

Schultz stepping towards the curb. Holy canine shit, something soft under foot. Wipe some of it off as I go flying up these usefully carpeted stairs. Same sourpuss secretary reading the same novel she was reading last time. That's right honey, take off your eyeglasses and jump to your feet as Schultz goes zooming by.

"Can I help you."

"I'm going right the fuck in there."

"Mr. Gayboy's auditioning light is illuminated."

"It's going to be devastated when I'm fucking finished with him."

Schultz striding along the hall to the door marked Private. Pushing, banging and finally pounding.

"Open this fucking thing."

"Who is that."

"It's Sigmund Franz Schultz. That's who."

"Just one minute please."

"You better be just one minute."

Two minutes later. The door opening. Schultz charging in. Stopping center carpet, and hunched forward, raising a shaking fist. Gayboy behind his desk reaching for a cigar. A bosomy brunette in a finishing school pose with a script open across her lap, clearing her throat, brushing her hair back loose at her temple, an embroidered piece of white petticoat hanging lopsided down one curvaceously muscular leg.

"What's the fucking idea you smug son of a bitch renting the theatre to another production."

"By your abusive and threatening language Mr. Schultz, are you giving me cause to call the Police or my lawyers."

"Call whomever you like, we had a deal and you're going to fucking well stick to it."

"At most we had a very informal gentleman's understanding, my dear chap. And do mind your language."

"I'm going to mind you boy and sue the shit out of you."

"Mr. Schultz I do admire your nerve. Channelled in a proper direction it one day might get you somewhere but as it is, you are giving me and this young lady here offense. Now why don't you just calm yourself down a moment. I have not, as it happens, rented to another production. But due to an unforseen large overhead recently incurred there's been a thirty three and a third increase in the rent I shall require plus a commensurate improvement in the share of the gross."

"Hey what is this, you not only want more fucking rent but you also want to hack an additional major weekly slice off my balls."

"Well I wouldn't use your precise imagery and adjectives Mr. Schultz, but that is about the summation of it. Two other productions at this moment want this theatre. They have no objections to the increase. Now it isn't that I let money corrode the principles I most deeply cherish but."

"You limey bastards can't be trusted an inch."

"Tell me Mr. Schultz, are you personally at war with England. Or is this the usual manner in which you conduct your business."

"Both."

"Well it's not going to get you far. Let me tell you that."

"Well let me tell you how far it's going to get you. Right through every court in this town. Up to the House of Lords if necessary."

"O dear me. O dear."

"I'll give you ten per cent increase in rent."

"Dear O dear. Now let me see. Here. Do. Yes do. Come on. Have a cigar. And sit down. Go on. Take it. Best Havana."

"But no increase in the share of the gross."

"Ah Mr. Schultz you're not as untutored in our English ways as I thought. I see you use the penknife to make the Churchill cut on the slant. A good cigar gets more oxygen. Let me light you up. Now you know Mr. Schultz, although you exhibit behaviour totally alien to the true spirit of the theatre, I don't think you're such a bad sort. In view of the circumstances I'm being generous with you. I see your associates are shortly entering wedlock."

"That's right."

"I assume you've not taken that step yet."

"That's right."

"Plenty of time for a young man like you. Now I rather like some of these latter lyrics of your show. Hear rather encouraging things of the production. Mr. Magillacurdy a performer of whom it's widely said that he will achieve the heights."

"That's right. Signed up."

"Wouldn't it be fairer to say Mr. Schultz that you hope to sign him."

"He's going to be signed don't worry."

"Now. In our little preliminary misunderstanding I haven't had a chance to introduce Miss Sphincter."

"How do you do Mr. Schultz."

"Hi ya."

"Miss Sphincter was recently runner up as Miss West Midlands. Talented singer and dancer. And as it happens, reading the script of your show."

"Fifteen per increase in the rent, no increase in the share of the gross."

"Perhaps you might consider auditioning Miss Sphincter."

"Sure I'll do better. Honey if you don't fall on your face every two seconds I'll guarantee a prominent position in the chorus."

"Ah Mr. Schultz, that's so sweet of you not to be averse to one's little artistic contribution. Then let's not argue, twenty per cent on rent, plus five on gross."

"Argue. That's highway robbery. Fifteen per cent on rent and two on gross. Take it or leave it."

"I think unfortunately I shall leave it."

"Goodbye."

"Now wait a moment Mr. Schultz. Come back. Sit down. Why not be reasonable about this."

"Sure, why not. Fifteen per cent on rent and two on gross."

"You're being most singularly stubborn."

"That's right."

"I must say if it weren't for Miss Sphincter here having an opportunity one would dismiss your counter proposal out of hand."

"What. Holy Jesus christ almighty. The rent already and your cut of the gross is a fucking holdup."

Schultz sweeping out with his clutched sheets of contract as the door closed on a pleased Miss West Midlands and Mr. Gayboy's strangely smiling face. Guiding down the bannister to avoid tripping on the stairs. In a fresh smelling brand new taxi to diesel throb back through the late lunchtime street. Wiped my feet on his carpets. Like I was wiping them on his face. Poor son of a bitch had me by the balls and didn't know it just as I kicked his.

Aromatic mouth watering smells in the door of Sperm Productions. The Italian chef and his assistant scurrying around his Lordship and Binky seated at table. Binky lifting a glass of wine to his lips.

"Ah, Schultz, just the man we want to see. Take a pew. Help us knock back a little late lunch. Mario's speciality, oeuf mollet au ragout fin. His Royal Grace and I are engaged in a last minute discussion of honeymoon plans and how one might avoid those traditionally embarrassing bed chamber wretched first moments of laying hand to one's dear brand new little wife trembling so with her schoolgirl modesty. Mario, do pop down another place for our loyal fellow director, Mr. Schultz."

"Of course sir."

"I got calls to make."

"Dear me, always business Schultz. Never a moment to relax."

"Jesus we were all just relaxing. A whole weekend nonstop."

"Ah but do tell us how did your little meeting with Gayboy go, Schultz."

"That fucking cunt. Wanted thirty three and a third per cent increase in rent and five in gross. But naturellement I'm tough. I want my price. It was a battle of nerves. He was having a shit fit screaming and squirming as I stood right up and walked out. And he calls me back. Like the nice guy I suddenly decided to be I agreed to let him make a little artistic contribution to the show and to cast his gorgeous girl friend in the chorus. And in the end all he got was fifteen extra per cent on the rent and two on the gross."

"Schultz."

"And what can I do for you your Lordship."

"Schultz, my god."

"What's the matter."

"You've been had Schultz."

"What the fuck do you mean."

"Schultz, while you've been gone we have learned that as recently as three o'clock yesterday afternoon Gayboy who didn't think you had any money, was offering another production a third reduction in rent and no gross at all."

"I don't believe it. Is that true Binky. This is another joke. I had Gayboy on his knees begging for mercy. Beaten. Hey sit down your Lordship, don't go laughing around the room like that."

"O my god Schultz, O my god, you take the fucking cake, you really do."

"Hey Binky stop him, he's going to hurt his stomach."

"O dear, Schultz while his Royal Grace is indisposed with laughter, you ought to pay attention to the more gastronomic matters at hand."

Mario's assistant nearly toppling a tray as his hunched over Lordship lurched helplessly holding his belly, to struggle to stand straight again as Rebecca stood at the door, her neat shapely fist knocking.

"Mr. Schultz there's an urgent call for you on Lord Nectarine's private line."

"And Schultz, how many times have I told you. Not to use my line."

"You guys tie up this joint, what am I supposed to do. Your weddings, appointments with tailors, shooting parties, races. Jesus christ excuse me."

"Schultz, I want to fervently urge you not to be long. Or you'll miss Mario's triumphant soufflé aux fruits de la passion."

"I shouldn't miss a deal. That's what I shouldn't miss."

Schultz rushing into the hall. With a crash. Tripping over two shotgun cases parked against the wall. A renewed roar of his Lordship's laughter. Rebecca helping Schultz up, and holding open his Lordship's door, her hand lowering suddenly to stay Mr. Schultz on the arm."

"Mr. Schultz, be prepared, I think it's rather bad news."

"What, I could have bad news. That'll be a big novelty all of a sudden. But thanks. I appreciate your warning."

Mario the chef pouring brandy and cutting cigars, his assistant brewing coffee. A moment of golden sunlight in the windows fading. Sky darkening and a roll of thunder. Schultz slowly entering the chairman's office. His head shaking back and forth. Binky holding out his cigar between his lips as Mario flourishes a flame to it.

"Schultz, whatever is the trouble, you're wearing your most quizzical frown."

"You won't believe it. I don't believe it. I simply don't believe it."

"What don't you believe Schultz."

"It's like suddenly there's nothing anymore you can have faith in. Like England. Something solid. Hear that. Just listen. The newspaper guys down in the street are shouting it out. One of the most prestigious firms in this country. Suddenly. Has gone bust. And my biggest investor involved with them is pulling every penny he's got out of the show. I feel sick."

"Pour Mr. Schultz a large brandy Mario."

"Everything was coming together. And now. In a fraction of a second all that was rosy, promising and wonderful suddenly becomes insane, disastrous and horrifying. I got to pay wages at the end of the week. Astronomical bills at the Dorchester. Where on top of their laundry, long distance phone calls and dry cleaning, they want sitting rooms. Jesus. And what a mistake I'm making telling you guys. Look at you. You're grinning. Like vultures who are going to descend any second on what's left of my bones."

"Schultz you always accuse one with that unflattering description."

"Sure I do. You've got me at your mercy. Haven't you. You're going to squeeze me out. You're going to ruin me."

"But of course we are, Schultz. Whatever did you expect. Don't you want us to finance you one hundred per cent."

"And make me just an employee. Hey your Lordship you wouldn't when my defences are down do this to me would you."

"Ah Schultz, my dear Schultz, in mitigation it must be admitted you have for a long time now made the best of bad situations. Which however has always made them worse."

"Hey come on. You got to leave me with control of the show your Lordship. A few unpredicted circumstances out of the fucking wild blue yonder have tripped me up for a moment when usually I'm ready for anything that can happen."

"Schultz if I may say so, having just heard you trample my shotguns, I've come to the conclusion that you are so meticulous at being absolutely ready for anything that when the obvious happens, as it invariably does, that you're not ready. And what's that you're mumbling Schultz."

"Your Lordship I'm mumbling a sentimental little poem."

> Do not shit
> While you're
> Shitting
> Do not go blind
> While you're going
> Blind

17

ABelgravia morning sky bright breezy blue outside. Greta brushing Schultz's shoulders down
as he stood morning suited in front of the mirror adjusting his
formal grey tie in the front hall of number four Arabesque Street.
And popping on and off his distinctly flattering grey topper. The
phone ringing.

"Hello."

"Jesus you're a fine one."

"It's not you Al."

"Yeah. Me. Al."

"Holy christ not now, Al, not now. I'm this second about to go
out my door to his Lordship's wedding."

"It should be your wedding."

"Al for christ's sake, here I am, the day's sunny, I'm all dressed
up in a hurry to take a few minutes off to go to do something that
might be a nice experience for a change."

"So you want a nice experience. Thanks for the one I stepped
into where you puked over the whole back of the car and me and

my guests had to use a taxi. But never mind that it took a three hundred quid new upholstery job to get rid of the smell."

"It's your capitalist way of life, Al, a socialist wouldn't have to worry about such things."

"Wise guy you wouldn't find it so politically funny if it was your automobile."

"Look Al I'm sorry. Who could control a dinner in my stomach after what I was confronted with in that trap."

"It was my birthday party."

"O.K. so let me wish you once more. Happy ninetieth."

"So help me god Sigmund. They've taken Counsel's opinion. It's going to be front page paternity proceedings with blood tests. Save anguish. Marry."

"Save anguish Al. Are you kidding."

"Sigmund don't you realize you could end up in a few months being the father of a human being."

"Al I'm just easing up one inch from last week's catastrophes to take a peek out of the deepest fucking abyss of my whole life. Sixty thousand pounds I got to find before Tuesday. I'm at everybody's mercy. Looking for money at this last minute is impossible. Nobody wants to know. I got a theatre now and I ain't got no show."

"What do you mean no show."

"The show is in a shambles. Equity could close me down. Unofficially I'm in rehearsals. While Magillacurdy's Agent is asking an astronomical salary against a straight ten per cent of the gross, like his client recently sleeping between gravestones, is a West End Hollywood Broadway star already, instead of a discovery."

"So he's got a good Agent whom I happen to know."

"That ain't all, Al. Everyone hates everybody. Magillacurdy bodily threw the director off the stage into the third row stall seats and broke his collar bone."

"So. He has an artistic temperament."

"I'm being sued."

"So what's recently new about that."

"I'll tell you what's recently new. The director is the lowest kind of creep, demanding body guards and threatening to slander the show to the newspapers."

"Why didn't you ring me when you got these troubles Sigmund."

"Al I don't ring you because you bring me more trouble that's why I don't ring you."

"Tell me. What else is bothering you Sigmund."

"You don't think that's enough, which yet is only a fraction."

"Take it easy. Just tell me."

"You want to hear about what they did to me over the sets, the costumes, and the designer who thinks he's El Greco."

"O.K. O.K. Don't get hysterical. Look. I'll tell you. Sigmund do you want to zing mit der dick dick."

"What the fuck is that Al."

"It's like everything going your way."

"For that at this moment I'll zing with any fucking dick dick."

"Then promise to sit down like a civilized person without jumping up to puke over everything."

"Hey Al I don't jump up to puke over everything. It's something like the horrorsville you sucked me into that makes me puke."

"O.K. O.K. calm down. If you talk to Pricilla I guarantee you Magillacurdy is signed for a nice medium round salary and maybe a per cent or so of the gross."

"Al it's got to be less than a medium round salary and no per cent of the gross."

"What, you expect to get a genius for nothing."

"No Al. But I'm paying exorbitant rent for the theatre."

"O.K. you meet Pricilla and it's no per cent of the gross."

"Will you guarantee Al that that two ton tarantula is miles away in her fucking web gorging caviar someone else is paying for."

"You have my word, you won't see her. Plus I'll get you sixty thousand."

"Al don't joke."

"I'm not joking. Since when have I ever joked over something I said I was going to do. Tell me."

"O.K. Al I believe you."

"So three thirty today alright. Let's say the lounge of the Dorchester Hotel."

"Jesus not there Al. Except for the price that place is costing me I still try to go there for peace of mind."

"The Ritz then, the palm court, under the gold embellishments. Have a nice tea."

"Thanks a whole bunch. On second thoughts, make it at the Dorchester. I need the peace of mind. So long Al."

"Wait a second Sigmund."

"What."

"I got news."

"What news."

"I'm in love."

"Holy jesus another pair of balls for the guillotine."

"Don't say a thing like that. I'm in love. With the most wonderful, the most serene and beautiful creature I have ever met. You will love her too."

"Al, that's great, you fuck her for me but meanwhile I'm missing my sunglasses and my chauffeur's waiting. Goodbye."

Greta smiling by the door in her yellow gingham dress, a flower in her hair, Schultz's sunglasses in her outstretched hand as he puts fingers forth petting her under the chin.

"Honey, you know you've been a real great help to me. You really have. But soon like tomorrow or the next day you got to find somewhere else to stay. You're a nice sweet girl. You're going to meet some nice guy someday to settle down with. Jesus don't start crying."

"You no love me just a little bit."

"Sure. But if you got ears can't you see what my life is like. Somebody maybe could come again trying to throw you out on the street."

"Don't throw me out. No don't."

"Jesus kid, stop the tears will you. Here take this. Now you go buy yourself something and see a movie."

"I love you."

"Calm down now. That's a good kid. You shouldn't get a fixation on just one guy."

"What is fixation."

"O Jesus, fixation is, hey I'll tell you later. I'm gone now."

Schultz catching a flash reflection of himself in the window of the limousine door. The hired chauffeur pulling it open with a salute and bow.

"Good morning sir, looking very spruce."

"Well when you don't feel that way that's the way to look."

"I agree sir."

The door closing a gentle click on Schultz. Sitting back in the sweet soft perfumed unpuked upon upholstery. And holy shit. The Ambassador on his stoop. Dressed for a wedding. And waving grinning out of his black mind at me. Hi ya. Jesus Your Excellency where do you get such constant happiness all over your face from.

By the palace wall and the park, the limousine purring down Constitution Hill. Beneath the mid morning shade of trees. Into the Mall full of sunshine. The town humming. Like everyone who is anyone is heading for his Lordship's nuptials. And holy shit in the sudden gorgeous few moments rolling along like this, I nearly completely forgot. My invitation to go to the palace. Torn up by that bitch.

Schultz's car slowing down to a standstill in a long queue. Sound of a loud speaker in the distance.

"Holy christ, driver what's the hold up."

"There has to be a clearway left for the Sovereign sir. All traffic is stopped."

"I'm late, honk your horn."

"Sir I'm sorry I just can't do that."

"Hey isn't this a democracy."

"Sir with all due respect, if you'd just look at the people in these cars I think aristocracy would be a better word."

"Christ, it's the one guy in the world I really like. I'm not going to miss him getting married. I'm walking. Pick me up on the church stoop later."

219

Police on the pavement holding back the crowd watching the resplendent wedding guests in their carloads popping out into a blaze of flash bulbs. Film and television crews adjusting lights and cameras. Oohs and aahs at the arrival of the bride. Schultz shoving his way through onlookers caught suddenly in the surge forward of reporters.

"Jesus christ you guys watch who you're pushing."

Ladies clutching hats in the breeze. Police locking arms and holding their backs against the crowd. Schultz buffeted pitching forward to his hands and knees. Grey topper flying off his head and kicked by several feet till a photographer's foot squashed it. An appreciative chuckle as Schultz shouted.

"Hey Jesus don't ruin the rented clothes."

Helped up by hands of wedding guests, Schultz led to safety inside the church door. In the calmer cool Schultz punching his desecrated top hat back into lopsided shape. As a familiar handsome smiling face stepped out of the shadows.

"Schultz, not a pair of shotguns to be seen and still you manage to fall flat on your face."

"I know Binky, I know. And this topper is the first fucking hat I ever really looked good in."

"I must say I did at the commotion nip back into the shadows here in case someone thought I knew you."

"They were trying to stop me coming in, my invitation got torn up in the turmoil of my life."

"How ever did you get in through the strict security Schultz."

"You saw me. The guests took me through by the armpits."

"Schultz, you do amaze me. Here. For your buttonhole. This specially hued carnation from his Royal Graces's conservatory will identify you as a special friend of the groom's. But my, but for your little tumble, and your squashed topper, you do look quite splendid."

"I got blinded by a flash bulb and pushed. The publicity, holy christ, why didn't you tell me. Some of these people here are legendary. I could have told our publicist to come. The show could use this publicity."

"It has rather brought a lot of folk crawling out of Debrett and the pages of history but I hardly think Schultz that many of them care to hit showbizz headlines before they crawl back in again."

"What a fucking waste. Jesus look at this. Not a profile, not a countenance out of place. Except yours truly. Jesus, who's that, who's that. What a handsome distinguished looking guy."

"That is his Royal Grace's former university tutor."

"Who's that. Who's that."

"That is a former Conservative Prime Minister."

"He's got such impeccable dignity. Hey what are you doing hanging around here at the door. And I thought you and his Lordship were having a joint wedding."

"In answer to your first question Schultz an armoured security vehicle should appear any moment with the ring and other assorted baubles which I'm ashamed to say as best man and after a rather hectic night, I forgot to bring for his Royal Grace. In answer to your second. Alas my little Lady's pa the Duke and especially her ma the Duchess, are, at the second thought of my being their son in law, to use one of your own nice little phrases, having kittens and due to their daughter's tummy now risen quite noticeably we're to be married in the Duke's private chapel hidden behind some rhododendrons in their garden."

"Pregnancy. Don't remind me. But his Lordship's bride. She's a real knockout."

"Good heavens Schultz, but of course. You didn't expect his Royal Grace, after his exhausting years of searching, to move an unlikely filly into his stables. She is also Schultz, along with her stunning eyes, lilting voice, and creamy complexion, a vivacious conversationalist."

"I can't wait to talk to her."

"And when you do Schultz, you will find her witty, compassionate and understanding."

"What else for christ's sake."

"Good bone, strong quarters, nice shoulder, perfect gaskins. In short an ample but thoroughbred figure. Works on behalf of many charities and is dedicated to a multitude of good causes. She is often to be seen serene at public functions and ceremonies. She has been to his Royal Grace a ministering angel in his recent dark hours suffering from swollen tonsils and toothache. She can illuminate hope in any man's blackest despair. She has wisdom and poise. She bears tragedy with an iron constancy."

"Holy shit stop Binky. Before I collapse in envy. Tell me something wrong with her."

"In one of her occasional but violent bursts of temper, she pushed his Royal Grace fully clothed into a chilled tub of bath water while expressing one of her strongly held opinions which his Royal Grace was at the time disputing."

"God you fuckers, you end up with everything I'm dying to find in a woman, like consideration instead of cunning, discretion instead of deceit, like backbone instead of bitching."

"Ah Schultz, you're such a romantic, but you must now excuse me as I see his Royal Grace's baubles have arrived."

Amid the marble statues and memorials, grey coated ushers in a rush at the appearance of two foreign reigning sovereigns. Escorting them between the phalanxes of dignitaries from Church and State, from the military and industry. Vestments of Bishops and Archbishops on the altar. Red, blues and greens glowing high in the stained glass windows. The nearby massive booming bell of Big Ben. Throbbing chords of organ music. Voices of the choir. The Abbey echoing. Ladies heads turning with their hats of yellows, purples, pinks and creams. Perfumes, incense, rustling dresses. Jesus the elegance is crippling. Everywhere you look. Why wasn't I born with relations and friends like this all so fucking polite and good looking. Wearing clothes and high quality leather goods you couldn't find within ten miles of my parents' store. The diamonds alone would make Uncle Werb have an apoplectic fit of envy that he didn't have the mark up on the gems. What marvellous singing. The whole church shaking. Here they come, gold braid all over her father. Holy christ she's even more gorgeous than Binky says. Giving me, all the way from nowhere, a fucking erection right in this pew. For the first time I know what my mother meant when she said I was too good to play with anybody else on my block.

"Dearly beloved, we are gathered together here in the sight of god, and in the face of this congregation."

Stifled coughs erupting in the hush. A child's voice. I must I must nanny, do wee wee. Holy shit, down to earth human nature has intruded at last. Binky with all these important people around looks like he's up there shaking with laughter or nervousness. Who wouldn't be, watching his Lordship get tied up like this. After all the time they've been wantonly satisfying carnal lusts and appetites like brute beasts in Sperm Productions, they then, just like magic go get spliced to creatures of quality.

"I require and charge you both, as ye will answer at the dreadful day of judgement when the secrets of all hearts shall be disclosed that if either of you know any impediment."

The echoing vowels of the grey headed bishop. The figures before him. Wow is he kidding, I ask you, who could find an impediment. Jesus the difference between people in this world. In the early struggling days of my father's first store a customer came in near closing time after a whole day of hardly any turnover and between my mother and father tearing her to bits between them reducing the price to sell her something the woman could hardly escape she was having so many bargains pushed in her face.

"Basil, Andrew, George, Albert wilt thou have this woman to thy wedded wife."

The voice resonating in all this ancient history. A child whimpering. Jesus. I love the words. Wilt thou obey, serve, love, honor, keep him in sickness and in health and forsaking all others, keep thee only unto him. Just like having a stray au pair at your mercy. His Lordship real close now. Wilt thou, Violet, Elizabeth, Alexandra, Felicia take thee, Basil, Andrew, George, Albert, to thy wedded husband, for good times and better times, for richer or millions, for healthier holidays, castles and estates. Any second now. With this ring I thee wed. And it's curtains. With all my endless goods I thee smother. In the name of his Lordship's forests,

223

railroads, ranches, mines, distilleries, amen. Jesus what women won't do to get up that fucking aisle. They'll even sacrifice the man they love.

"Those whom God hath joined together let no man put asunder."

The organ thundering. The choir in full voice bellowing. This moment I can't forget for the rest of my life. It's just too beautiful. Makes me want to cry. The new radiant Countess beaming. Coming along the aisle. Marching out on his Lordship's arm. Whispering nodding little hellos to the smiling faces in the rows of pews.

Schultz on the aisle. Giving the pale as a ghost bridegroom the Woonsocket hi sign and then promptly tripping over an armorial emblazoned kneeling pad to stumble out of the pew altogether. Bumping into a naval suited disembarking reigning foreign sovereign. Who politely sidestepped as an immediate small commotion was triggered off among security personnel at the back of the Abbey. Binky's face slightly blue with bottled up laughter turning to look back.

In the sunlight and blaze of cameras the newlyweds stood on the Abbey step. The bride ecstatic and the groom stretching his neck in his collar frowning at requests from photographers to smile.

In a snug courtyard environ of St. James's another cavalcade of cars disgorging. Schultz ducking out of his limousine, hopped up the steps to jerk thumbs at his carnation as the major domo stepped to intervene.

"Invitation sir."

"It was destroyed. My carnation is the password."

"Sorry sir."

"Hey I got a right to go in there."

"Sorry sir. Other guests are waiting. Step aside please."

"Like hell I will."

Schultz striding forth into the massive marble interior festooned with flowers. The gleamingly smooth staircase balustrade ahead between which guests slowly ascend. Schultz bounding up

three steps at a time towards the din of voices. The blue uniformed beribboned commissionaire above on the landing. Jesus
my name is going to be announced.

"Excuse me fella, you don't mind if I just squeeze by incognito."

"Sorry sir. I must announce you."

"Whisper will you. Sigmund Schultz is the name."

"I know who you are sir."

"You do."

"You're Mr. Schultz, the well known impresario."

With a gentle ushering by the elbow and friendly nod from the
commissionaire, Schultz steered into the receiving line. Waiting
behind a monocled Field Marshal who looked around once like I
was trying to steal a decoration off his chest. Jesus but what a
relief somebody at last knows who the fuck I am out of this fucking collection of big shots. No sign of his Lordship. Gloved hands
held out. One lemony smile after another. The bride's highly
fuckable mother with a lorgnette, yet. And her lemony smile.

"How do you do Mr. Schultz."

"Hi."

"So glad you could come."

Into the crescendo beneath this vast gold embellished ceiling.
Wandering past the talkative little groups. Massive portraits
around the walls. Whiffs of perfume. Clink of glass. Cutlery
clonking on plates. High pitched vowels everywhere. Eyes looking
down their noses. And Jesus christ right now the side view of my
face is more than ever out of place. With not a single soul I can
talk to. My god. Except that.

Schultz stopping stunned and transfixed. Through a gap between two naval uniforms, stood an awe inspiring tall tanned
silken limbed ash blond female. Her fruity body engloved in a raw
silk orange dress. Holy cow, now that is exactly what I've been
looking for all my life.

Schultz giving his lapels a quick brush down with his fingers,
straightening his shoulders and moving towards the lady. Just as
four dark suited security men increased their speed and quietly
closed in behind him with a tap on the shoulder.

225

"Sir if you wouldn't mind coming with us."

"Holy shit when is somebody going to leave me alone for christ's sake."

"Now come along quietly now please sir."

Schultz, flanked by two broad shouldered gentlemen, was led by another and nudged from the rear by a fourth gent and guided through the babbling assembly towards a distant door in a distant wall.

"Hey come on, don't for christ's sake exasperate me."

"Quietly now please sir, we must warn you. One false move and you will be shot."

"Shot. Hey come on. This is a joke."

"Quietly sir. No joke. This way now."

"What, are you trying to throw me out. Look at the colour of my carnation for christ's sake."

"I'm afraid sir, the colour of your carnation is a deeply suspicious shade. And we would appreciate your helping us, sir, with the making of our further enquiries."

"Enquire for christ's sake right here, I'm not moving another fucking inch."

The bride in white silk, her veil held under a diamond and pearl tiara, stood a mere ten paces away, her hand to lips, as Schultz, wrenching his arm free from one dark suited detective, bolted. Knocking a high ranking clergyman's champagne splashing on his black toggery, as a security guard made a grab. Only to rip open Schultz's tailcoat seam down the back as he spun around loose in a move practised from previous unwanted apprehensions.

"I say there, stop sir, stop."

Schultz sailing through a group of pages and bridesmaids and across an open space on the parquet. Chased by the detective who'd taken up the rear of the proceedings and who now flung himself in a horizontal rugby tackle to hit Schultz from behind just below the knees. Both engripped bodies flying face first across the polished floor amid the oooing and ahhhing of the rapidly space making guests. Schultz's head coming to rest face up between the feet of a tall languid pink Chantilly lace encrusted lady lifting her lorgnette and eyebrows, staring down.

"Dear me, the incredible cheek of gatecrashers these days. It does make one yearn. Doesn't it. For previous and more decent times."

Madam
I couldn't
Agree with you
Fucking more

18

A T the commotion on that fatal mid day, Binky had in an ante room excused himself from his Lordship's presence, being as his Royal Grace was more than surrounded by two of London's leading dentists both trying to get a good look with pencil torches into his Lordship's mouth as well as a throat specialist peeking into his Lordship's trachea where it was believed a toothbrush bristle lay lodged.

Binky spying the altercation just a mere thirty yards away near the room's main vast rose marble chimneypiece, hurriedly made his way through the nearly hysterically animated assemblage, while bracing himself to dispense suitable vowels to quell whatever disquiet had arisen. Until catching sight of the starring participant. Binky's striped trousered knees buckling, his elbows gathering tightly into his ribs as his sides helplessly split with a silently cataclysmic laughter.

An apprehended red faced Schultz nailed to the floor by several knees. A detective's hand over his mouth, an arm across his throat, feet shaken out of his shoes, one toe twitching whitely out of a considerable hole in his black sock. Binky's pained face, eyebrows contorted to erase the glee, his hands help limp and helpless as he struggled walking backwards further and further away from the pinioned Schultz who at last managed to sink his teeth into one of the detective's fingers as both of them howled out loud.

"Binky, Binky, for christ's sake this isn't funny, get them off, they're trying to castrate me."

Binky, mirth exploding through his teeth, taking a deep lungful of air and finally rigidly straightening his back to slowly march, chin raised with parade ground splendour, towards the pinioned Schultz. To stand tiptoe over him.

"My dear chap I have never seen you before in my life."

"I swear Binky I'll never forgive you for this."

"Take the wretch away."

"You son of a bitch, Binky."

"And I must say to you gentlemen of our Metropolitan Police Force, such a splendid job you've done at downing this imposter."

"Only doing our duty sir."

The monocles and lorgnettes up over eyes looking distinctly the other way. A wide space opening wider around the red faced Schultz. Detectives lifting him by the armpits to his stockinged feet. As Binky feigned a presto pronto wide eyed surprise.

"O my goodness gentlemen. O dear me. But I do think there may be some misunderstanding here. Upon my word, it's the well known Impresario, Mr. Sigmund Franz Schultz. I simply did not recognise him in his floored horizontal position. You must not bring him to the tower for execution as he is, I fear, a very special guest and an acquaintance of some duration of Lord Nectarine's."

"Boy, Binky thanks a lot, you really know how to ruin friends and influence people, don't you."

Faces flushed and ties askew. Schultz sticking his foot back into his one shoe as security men with a litany of murmured apologies brushed and patted him and went searching for the other of his missing footwear. Binky, a hand on his strained stomach muscles now making a space for Schultz through the newly collected circle of interested folk. Pushing past a moustachioed eagle nosed chap with the conspicuously low rank of major who not only was assuming an instant vigilante posture but who also cleared his throat to loudly boom.

"A good bang with the broadside of a sword across the backside is what some of these wretched wogs need these days."

"Ah Schultz, did you hear that. What on earth are we going to do with you. First nearly causing an international incident stumbling out at passing royalty in the Abbey. And now dear me here you are tail coat in tatters, shoe missing, with hysterical security men thinking you a terrorist assassin. One even overheard a thoroughly alarmed relative of the bride ask if you were related to the groom."

"Christ Binky, I went the fuck out my door this morning to this wedding with a song in my heart."

"When in fact Schultz as his Royal Grace might say, you should have gone out with a built in steel jock strap over your balls."

"It's all the result of what that bitch you made me visit in the hospital did to me, ripping up all my mail, my photographs, my invitations. So now I don't know what the fuck I'm doing. Jesus don't they have any drink here."

"Schultz, can't you hear. Champagne corks going off like shotguns at the shoot. Ah waiter. Allow us to lighten your tray."

"And you fucker. I saw you when you saw me when I was down. Look at this carnation you gave me. Everytime someone sees it I get suddenly jumped on by secret police."

"Ah Schultz perhaps the hue is a little dark. But we do love you. We really do. You must never, even in your own most worst stricken abyss, think that we don't. You're the only man I know who can reduce dull reality to the sublimely ridiculous in a trice. One understands now why you're sent Royal invitations to the palace."

"For the confidence bolstering thanks a lot Binky. Boy do I need this drink. But before all this violence, the solemnity of that whole church ceremony really got me. No shit. I was nearly in tears. A nice guy like his Lordship tied up for life. Thank God I'm still married to the theatre. And nothing else."

"And dear Schultz although you do sometimes sound like a colonel in a dud regiment, one does so admire your resolve and especially the way you so easily combine your social, emotional and theatrical activities."

"Activities. You mean tragedies. Jesus where's his Lordship so I can say something nice to him."

"His Royal Grace, poor old devil, is at this very moment being attended upon in an ante room by a bevy of specialist chaps."

"Holy shit he's not clapped up or something."

"And well you might Schultz, think such a dire thought. But an impacted molar is I believe the difficulty. And some little trouble in the trachea. One does I suppose so hate to see him sail off into what may be sometimes questionably referred to as wedded bliss. But then such disruptive things do befall one in life. Nevertheless let me propose a toast Schultz. To that stunningly inspired batsman and bowler, one of Oxford's and England's most revered cricketers, that dear dear old skin, his Amazing Grace Master of Foxhounds."

"Sure, to his Lordship."

"And Schultz to you. To finding your other shoe. And to victory. Both in showbizz and in matrimony."

"Holy shit leave the matrimony out will you."

Schultz downing two glasses of champagne one after the other, and watching over the rim of his tilted glass the dazzlingly handsome grey swallow tailed figure of Binky now followed by several ladies' eyes as well as those of a rather slack wristed gaitered clergyman, as he strode away out across the polished parquet under the gilt and multi hued ceilings of this vast room. His quietly pleasant countenance smiling. His assuring fingers firmly shaking the outstretched hands. His lips dispensing his softly spoken whimsicalities, as he passed leaving these loud haughty echoing voices in his wake. Admirals, Bishops and holy cow his Excellency the Ambassador from across the street. Who's got one of his Lordship's gorgeous married sisters in deep conversation. And what perfume is this at my shoulder. And christ this orange fabric of real raw silk.

"Your shoe sir."

"O hey gee thanks."

"I hope you will forgive my amusement but you know you did really give a rather good account of yourself."

"I rather to hell I didn't if you want to rather know the truth. But if someone like you turns up with my shoe, holy christ, I wouldn't mind losing both feet."

"You're much too flattering sir. But from your expression standing here alone just now, one would have thought the whole world had fallen in on you."

"Do I look that bad."

"Well perhaps not quite that bad."

Schultz bending to tie his shoelace. And at the same time taking an eye straining gander at this creature's splendid gaskins.

"Hey who are you."

"I'm Basil's sister."

"What another sister. I thought I met all his Lordship's sisters."

"I'm the sister about whom little is said."

"Well let me tell you straight off the bat I'd say plenty about you. You're absolutely gorgeous. What's your telephone number."

"Mr. Schultz, you are rather quick off the mark."

"Sure I am, where have you been all my life."

"Well for the last awfully dull six months I've been sitting lonely abandoned in Monte Carlo watching the yachts come and go."

"Well Jesus honey, thank god you got back. I got to have your phone number."

"Are you Mr. Schultz meaning to have me over to that notorious town house of yours. Where ladies are seen by dawn's early light running for their lives out the door."

"Hey who said that. Notorious. Not a thing happens there. Hey don't go. I'm in love with you."

"Ha ha, I must Mr. Schultz, ha ha. I must."

"Hey I beg of you give me your phone number."

232

"Ha Ha, Mr. Schultz, ha ha."

Schultz watching her silken shimmering hair, her small waist swelling to splendid hips, as this aloof twinkling eyed lady departed. And suddenly feeling a hearty lung contusing clap on the back. Schultz's mouthful of champagne sputtering out over the floor as the rotund figure of his ever present neighbour the Ambassador parked elbow close, his ebony face ablaze in his usual smile.

"Ah my dear gladiator. I see you have successfully once more weathered yet another contretemps."

"Holy mackerel it's you Your Excellency. Yeah I weathered it by a shoe and a whisker."

"And where is your so so beautiful companion today. Ah but then while I am with one of Lord Nectarine's divine sisters, I see you were with another, the so marvellously elegantly curvaceous Lady Lullabyebaby."

"Jesus Your Excellency do you know her phone number."

"My dear boy, she is married, mistress of a great estate, you must play fair and not touch."

"Jesus marriage is ruining my relationships everywhere. I got to get to know her."

"Ah my friend I detect a note of real urgency."

"You bet you do. I speak not only from the bottom of my heart but from the bottom of my balls."

"Ah but dear chap, while I assure you I am not spying, one does still see an awe inspiring selection of ladies calling upon you. I am especially interested in the blond lady with the attaché case on the red bicycle."

"You mean that obsessed lesbian with the whips."

"Ah exactement and precisely monsieur."

"Your Excellency feel free next time you spot that kraut knocking on my door to invite her over to your house will you."

"Ah that is kind of you. And of course I shall. And please do understand that I appreciate more than anyone the difficulties the companionship of beautiful ladies sometimes presents to you."

233

"Thanks. And you know Your Excellency you really are a pal."

"Well we Belgravians must stick together Mr. Schultz, we really must you know."

On the entrance steps of this great old town house two tipsy hours later, Schultz with his torn tail coat fluttering and his address book one name fuller, stood taking a breath of sweetened breeze just blown in from the cotton ball trees of Green Park. The London afternoon touched with a magic sun goldened splendour. His limousine door opening and his chauffeur saluting to admit him to the great upholstered peace of this motorised interior. Taking him purring up the late lunch time clubby hill of St. James's. Feet propped up on the folded jump seat, to turn left on Piccadilly and right up Down Street and in and about the narrow lanes of southern Mayfair to pop him best foot forward on the front steps of the Dorchester Hotel. The doorman in his long green coat and brass bright buttons, saluting Schultz with a touch to his emerald gold braided top hat. And in the soft soothing perfumed shadows Schultz dreamily ascending blissfully by lift upwards four floors. To tread the soft swirling red, green, blue and grey carpet down the long mellow lit hall. To knock. And try to kill about five birds with no stones at all.

"O hey gee hi, Mr. Schultz, come in. Hey you're all dressed up."

"Messed up would be a better word. Sorry I'm late."

"Well boy are we really glad to see you. Come on in. Having this suite is so much better for us. We got such a nice view of the park. Sit down."

"What's the new problem."

This diminutive dark eyed brunette attired in thigh and arse clinging grey flannel trousers. Tight red cashmere sweater over her pneumatic bosoms. Between which rested a gold six cornered star suspended on a gold chain. As she stood perfume close to look up into this tall black curly haired producer's pleasantly green eyes. Smiling her mouthful of large white gleaming teeth.

"It's the old problem. The director is just not able to impose control Mr. Schultz."

"So what else is the problem."

"Well, if you want us to be frank."

"Be my guest."

"Well we think the designer's statement in the sets is getting in the way of the lyrics. Again being frank, so is Magillacurdy. He's in the way of everything. He's trying to write, compose, act, sing and direct the whole show. We don't know who he thinks he is. The whole cast is frightened to death of him. And he threw."

"Yeah I know, the director."

"Like a discus or something. Right out over the orchestra pit."

"Yeah I know. Into the third row of the stalls."

"He was unconcious for so long we thought he was dead."

"Well kids he's living and suing, so relax. Now what about the music for the second act. To start with it's too adagio."

"Mr. Schultz, we're making good progress with a faster beat. Hey can we offer you something from room service. It really is a good room service."

"No thanks. I know the room service is good."

"We're so wonderfully, wonderfully comfortable here now. It's so nice with a real fireplace and everything."

"So I see."

A chiming tinkle of two bells from a silver dialed brass carriage clock on the mantelpiece. Sylvia prayerfully joining the tips of her fingers. Her crimson manicured toes curling down against the dark leather edge of her sandals. Her thighs flexing as she did a slight knee bending curtsey.

"O gee Mr. Schultz. Gosh this is kind of embarrassing. But it's like an unbroken rule with us for really a long time and we expected you at one o'clock. Gee I don't know how sort of to put it."

"Put it. I'm listening."

"Well. Gosh I can't say it. You say it Herbie."

"Hey, what's wrong Sylvia, you got a voice."

"O all right, I'll say it. Well Mr. Schultz it's like this. Two o'clock every day Herbie and I like to go to have a few minutes in private."

"No problem."

Schultz levering himself up from the blue and pink flowered

upholstered armchair. The sun sending yellowing beams in the window. And below, the steady moan of traffic up and down Park Lane.

"O no. Stay. We just go in the bedroom. Gosh this is crazy. But you wouldn't mind waiting would you. We'll only maybe be fifteen minutes. At the outside twenty."

"No problem."

"After we'd like you to hear the couple of new songs we're trying out for the second act."

"No problem. I'm here to listen."

"Gee Mr. Schultz that's real understanding of you. There's all the newspapers, and some magazines. Won't be long. Meanwhile, really help yourself to room service."

"Well since I'm paying for it, maybe I will."

Schultz ordering two bottles of Alsatian beer and a plate of smoked salmon. Herbie with a sheepish wag of the head and Sylvia with a coy little smile and crooked little wave of her fingers, disappearing after Herbie in their bedroom door. Curtains billowing with a breeze blowing in from the park. I'm really having a full day. As Binky says mixing social, emotional, theatrical and now somebody else's meditation all together. And Jesus last night in a dream someone asked me to remove out of her grave the body of an old girl friend of mine died young. Had to carry her wasted body wrapped in brown wrapping paper up a hillside to another grave. It woke me up and I had my hand squeezing on Greta's tit and her hand on top of mine and both of us crying again. This beer, this bread is good. My hardworking father always used to say you can't eat your inventory. So what a nice situation that I can sit here gorging salmon fumé on production expenses.

Schultz halfway down his second bottle of beer and staring out into other childhood memories as the bedroom door comes ajar. The wavy brown curly top of Sylvia's head peeking out.

"Gee you alright Mr. Schultz, you're not getting bored out there."

"No. I'm fine."

"Well gee we just thought, I mean this is entirely up to you. I mean if waiting is irksome. And if you don't mind, we don't mind, then you could come in here. Like maybe it would we hope be less boring."

"You mean come in the bedroom."

"Yeah, sure, Herbie and I don't mind. I mean gee, that is, if you don't mind."

"Sure O.K. a little company helps keep the mind off big troubles."

"Well come on in then. Bring your food."

Schultz with his plate of smoked salmon, and sliced buttered brown bread in one hand and the neck of his beer bottle in the other. Pushing open the bedroom door with his knuckles and stopping in and momentarily reversing his tracks as an almighty involuntary fart erupted.

"O hey. Excuse me. And excuse me twice."

"O no, it's all right Mr. Schultz. Come right back on in. You're really welcome. Come in. Close the door."

"Well if you say so. I guess you just made me an invitation it would be a shame to refuse."

Schultz tiptoe heading for the furthest sofa by the curtained window. Putting his victuals on a side table, lowering himself into this ringside seat. And to make sure he was still in London, leaning to peek out through a parting in the gauze at the towering cotton ball trees of the park. The endless stream of cars and red tops of buses and black throbbing taxis roaring by below.

"Come on Herbie. Don't suddenly pretend you're all bashful. And gee please, we don't mind Mr. Schultz if you want to watch. And help yourself to fruit in the basket there."

Schultz settling back in the sky blue satin covered chair. Crossing his morning suited legs as he took out and put on his sunglasses. Choosing a pear with one hand, lifting his beer bottle to his lips with the other. A small bare arsed pert titted Sylvia, climbing up on top of chunky hairy Herbie and slowly lowering her arse astride his stumpy thick prick. Sylvie two hands behind her, fingers flickering, squeezing and flapping Herbie's balls. And with a slowly increasing tempo, gyrating and wagging her shoulders. Till suddenly her head flung back, and her arse and thighs erupting into corkscrew paroxysms, she emitted breathless grunts, moans and groans.

"O gee Herbie, it's bending."

"Sylvia, take it easy."

Sylvia falling forward on top of Herbie. The sound of flesh slapping flesh as Schultz administered squeezed lemon drops to the remaining pink slivers of smoked salmon. Forking a piece up on to a corner of brown buttered bread and pushing it between his lips. With a swig of beer washing the orange fleshed fish down one's throat. While now hearing whispers coming from the bed.

"Jesus christ Sylvia just because you have an audience, don't go try and break it."

Schultz loosening his tie. From his breast coat pocket, pulling forth his beige silk hanky monogrammed with three large interwoven S's. Wiping beads of sweat from his brow. The bottom of the beer bottle tapping uncontrollably on the table as Schultz lowered it in a trembling hand. Removing his sunglasses to quickly polish them and place them back over his eyes. Tints the scene nicely. These days you don't know which people's personal ethics are on holiday. Really thought they were meditating in here instead of screwing their heads off. Shows what my recent problems have done to my brain. Real democracy must include the right to throw a fuck into somebody and to be seen doing it. While my prick is going to explode. The way she uses her magical ass she must sense there are already enough people on the globe that you've got to find something else beautiful to do with your libido than produce babies. Shows you have to keep going out into the world to see where the fuck it has morally advanced without you. Leapfrogging into lewdness on his Lordship's wedding day. If only I could find some long term, daily two o'clock, peaceful low cost fucking. Without blackmail. Without a wedding. Without having my house ruined. Without ambulances calling. Now even a sparrow has landed chirping outside on the window sill to watch.

238

Sylvia's no great shakes in the face but, wow, the rest of her being like that, who needs a face. Which she has turned around now and is looking at me. Holy cow, after her performance, maybe I should be clapping for an encore.

"Mr. Schultz, gee, you're kind of left there. Out in the cold."

"No problem, kids."

"Hey what's that. All that clip clop clattering."

"I'll take a look. It's the horse guards. On their way down to the palace."

"O gee isn't London so kind of excitingly historic. And Mr. Schultz, you don't have to just go on keeping sitting there like that."

"No problem, I'm fine."

"Well gee maybe wouldn't you like to join us or something."

"You mean come over there and join you."

"Sure."

"In bed."

"Sure. While Herbie takes a rest. Or is that kind of a problem."

"No problem. I guess like I said previously it's an invitation it would be a shame to refuse."

"Well come on then."

"If you say so."

"I say so Mr. Schultz. But hey hold it. I mean don't you want to take off your clothes."

"You mean like take them off."

"Yeah why not, unless like it embarrasses you."

"No problem."

Schultz, struggling to get his grey tail coat off, ripping the seam further down the back. Garment now hanging attached in two halves by its collar. The waistcoat with a footprint of a detective still on it. I'm telling you. Don't ruin the rented clothes is the understatement of the year. Tie stained, buttons missing on my shirt. Shoot these braces off my shoulders. Holy cow, look at her. What a beautiful rippling belly. Propped up by her double jointed arms. Leaning back on the bed like she's waiting for me. Her for

239

sure double jointed spine arched like a bow. With her mesmerizing cross eyed pair of bouncing tits blazing. And pear shaped Herbie with his big hairy arse rolled over like a collapsed walrus.

"Gee I like the nice bright colour of your suspenders Mr. Schultz."

"Well they keep the trousers up I guess."

"And my gosh. Gee wow. O boy Mr. Schultz. Gee wow. When you drop them, that's really big. It really is. O Herbie. Look at what Mr. Schultz has, something out of the record books."

"Sylvia swell, but don't bother me a minute to take the nap I need."

"Gee Mr. Schultz, it's wonderful. And what two nice balls. Take off your shoes and socks why don't you."

"Holy christ honey with the way surprises are exploding around me, I forgot they were still on."

Schultz yanking shoelaces undone, and digging the heel of one shoe in the instep of the other and ripping out his foot.

"Hey leave the socks on, the sunglasses too Mr. Schultz it kind of gives me a kick."

"No problem."

Sylvia reaching out with undulating inviting fingers to welcome Schultz's record breaking pudenda advancing across the light green carpet. Jesus christ, suddenly this expensive suite is beginning to pay dividends. One second I'm being embarrassed out of my mind prostrate at the feet of dignitaries and next in that good old American let's make friends tradition, my pulse is pounding with the prospect of doing what comes naturally.

"Wow. O Wow. Look what's sprouting out of those black curly locks you got."

"Honey you're not so bad either."

"Mr. Schultz O my god. You have no idea. I swear you don't. Of what this is doing to me. No kidding. Hey just stand a fraction back. So I can really view."

"No problem."

"Mr. Schultz it is beautiful, beautiful. O hey wow, stand in profile."

"Fantastic, fantastic, Mr. Schultz. Herbie, the camera, get the camera."

"Honey, the flattery is appreciated but please no god damn pictures, Jesus christ."

"O. Not even one."

"Not even one, honey. And is it all you want me to do is just make me just stand here."

"O gee, gosh, I'm sorry. Step right over."

Schultz approaching in his best bedside manner. Down in the street fire apparatus bells clanging. A snore erupting from Herbie. Sylvia running her fingertips up and down the underside of Schultz's erection.

"Mr. Schultz, no kidding it should be cast in bronze for posterity."

"Never mind casting, keep touching honey. You got magic fingers."

"A perfect prick deserves perfect petting."

"And how, honey. And how."

"Gee we should waste not a second Mr. Schultz, let's get going. Fuck me."

"No problem."

Two bodies clapping together. Schultz's sunglasses hanging off caught on an ear. Sylvia heading backwards towards the pillow, two legs shooting out into the air locking in a scissor grip around Schultz. Who broadjumped upwards from the woolly carpet. To plunge into these soft entwining arms and squeezing strong legs. Another snore from Herbie. Sylvia's mouth biting, her hips squirming and turning and tossing Schultz over crashing into Herbie who went arse thumping out of bed on the floor.

"Hey christ Sylvia, watch what you're doing."

Schultz and Sylvia, limbs still clutching in each other's paroxysms. Herbie standing surveying the wild flailing bodies as he brushed off his arse. Schultz's sunglasses landing at his feet. Herbie picking them up, and with his eyebrows raised, putting them on to survey the bodies on the bed. To turn away scratching his head, flat footing it over to the dressing table mirror. Where he

241

made several contorted faces before lifting his lip and prising loose with a fingernail a particle of food lodged between his incisors. Shouts from Sylvia. Herbie turning to look. The bodies reflected in the mirror pounding up and down.

"Fuck me, fuck me inside out."

"No problem."

Herbie emitting a long belch. Clearing his throat as he took a hair brush to the upstanding strands on his balding scalp. Now standing to dab Vaseline on his private part and pat eau de cologne on his neck, armpits and in his pubic hair. Herbie turning. And facing the bed with a brand new erection. Schultz's arse ramming away again on top of an open mouthed crying out loud Sylvia.

"Mr. Schultz, shoot. Shoot."

"I nearly am honey."

"Shoot. Shoot. Shoot."

"Holy shit I'm coming, coming."

"O my god Mr. Schultz, O my god. You've shot. You've shot. You've shot."

"Honey when you said shoot I just had to go bang, bang, bang."

Schultz's perspiring head hung in the nape of Sylvia's neck. Her gold chain caught across his mouth. The feel of her hair softly on the ear. Musky aroma of her skin. Like a so faint, so faint taste of truffles, so sweet, so sweet.

"Jesus Mr. Schultz someone somewhere must be a lucky woman. Still waters flow deep. O God it feels so good. Still way up in me. Still so hard in there. You're a surprise I'm never going to get over."

"Should I give your husband his turn maybe."

"Don't move, don't get off. Herbie can wait. Can't you Herbie."

"I can wait. Like what am I. Just the husband."

On the wide white expanse of sheet, Schultz slowly grinding away once more. Sylvia's eyes closing. Purring out little long groans. Her lips curled back from her teeth. Jesus I look up and the Dorchester clock has gone backwards. Somewhere in the back of my mind hidden by all my troubles, I remember the first second I saw her, what a glint she had in her eye. Juicy girl. A genius. Has my cock in there working like it was part of her. Plus she's backed up by one of the best little arses I've ever known. Which alone is worth the price of admission. All women I fuck from now on will be measured against her. Imagine such bliss as this. Without spending a penny of my own personal money. Without jam flung all over the walls. Or busted antiques and floods. Without a geriatric old hen like Al trying to corral me up the fucking aisle. Holy Jesus. Even that. Wow. Her finger. Pressing down on my ass. And Jesus, going right in. Right at the right time. Shows you looks don't matter a damn. Sylvia and Herbie's faces could win contests for designs for the back of a bus. And even I wasn't always as handsome as I am now. My buck teeth growing up were knocking over all the girls on the block. Till Uncle Werb paid to have them fixed. My own father saying leave them. So what if they stick out, they make him noticed, it could help his personality. Thanks a bunch dad. Holy Jesus is it two fingers she's sticking in. Or three knuckles. Jesus that star on a chain flipping all over her chest. Like she could be she's stamped approved kosher by my whole family. Aunt Essie, Uncle Werb. Sigmund why don't you find a nice girl and settle down in the diamond business. Because Uncle Werb, this is only my first arse thrilling fuck I've got out of this production. But holy jeeze at first with one finger or two it was wonderful but now it's all her fingers or her whole fist going up my ass What's this kneeling. Now right over me. With hairy arms. And a chronometer watch on the wrist.

"Hey for christ's sakes what's going on."

"Let him, Mr. Schultz, let him."

"Let him. Like hell I will."

Schultz grabbed from in front by Sylvia. Herbie crashing down from behind. Schultz struggling between the compressed bodies.

"Stop stop."

"Let him Mr. Schultz, it only hurts in the beginning. No problem."

"No problem like hell, you pair of fucking rapists. Get your prick out of my ass."

> It's
> Some problem
> Hurting me
> In
> The end

19

TWELVE minutes to four by the clock above the hotel revolving doors. As Schultz with his grey battered top hat in hand came out of the elevator looking twice behind over his shoulder. Walking between the deep green sofas and settees full of people. And spotting Pricilla sitting by a black marble pillar in a mauve taffeta dress, mauve high heeled shoes and a blue spotted green scarf tied around her waist. Just like she's come fresh from selecting a dozen creations at a mannequin parade at Fortnum's who are going to send me the bill.

"Hi ya baby. Sorry I'm a little late."

"Late. You're more than late. How dare you come to meet me dressed like that. Where have you been."

"Look honey I've really had a long day. And I'm glad you're here already. Let me go see my car's alright. I'll be a second."

"Look at you, is that supposed to be a morning suit. Your coat is torn in two."

"I know it's torn in two for christ's sake."

"Your shirt is open and your tie looks like someone was trying to hang you."

"Honey they were, they were."

"Who were."

"Nobody was, it's a figure of speech."

"I've been waiting eighteen minutes with men ogling me. And this is how you show up. Everyone staring at you. And laughing."

"O christ, hey Jesus, let me sit down. And get the fuck out of sight, then."

Three swarthy gentlemen encouched nearby licking their lips. Staring at Pricilla, then at Schultz and then at each other. China tea with lemon served by a tail coated solicitous waiter as Schultz put his own tail coated back snugly out of sight into the cushions. Pricilla selecting a watercress and cucumber sandwich followed by one of smoked salmon and then two pastries surmounted with whipped cream and stuffed with jams.

"O.K. honey. Now how do we solve this."

"Solve, what do you mean solve."

"I mean you know, solve."

"I'm not a crossword puzzle."

"O Jesus, look, come on, all I'm looking for is a sensible solution."

"That's your problem."

"Well, would you like to, say go to stay in Monte Carlo or something. I mean take three weeks or a month. I can get in touch with medical treatment here in London. Then you could convalesce, like I say, in Monte Carlo. Even bring your mother. Watch the yachts come and go in the harbour."

"What are you suggesting."

"Nothing. I'm just saying. Everything could be taken care of. At my expense. I'll pay."

"You'll pay."

"Sure I'll pay, no problem."

"What are you going to pay for."

"Come on honey, you know what I'm talking about for christ's sake."

"I do not know what you're talking about."

"Come on, don't make me say it, I got too much on my mind already."

"Well you're going to get more on your mind. More than you ever dreamed was possible."

"Hey Jesus, it's a simple operation."

"What is."

"To terminate. To terminate a pregnancy."

"So that's it. You want me to kill my baby."

"Jesus, keep your voice down for christ's sake. People can hear."

"Kill my baby. Is that what you're telling me to do."

"I'm not telling you to do anything. I'm merely mentioning. Holy cow. Out of the frying pan and right smack into fucking burning embers."

"What do you mean by that."

"Nothing honey. It's just that I recently escaped out of a horrendously difficult business conference and my mind's not calmed down yet enough to think straight."

"Your mind had better start thinking straight in a quick damn hurry I'm telling you."

"Jesus and I'm telling you not so loud will you, they know me in this place."

"That's tough."

"What the fuck do you want out of me. Jesus I'm bulging out at the temples with troubles."

"My stomach is bulging."

"Holy shit don't start with the tears now too on top of everything. I'm only just emerging from horrorsville. A simple operation that's all. It would clear everything up. O Jesus come on honey, have mercy will you. Have mercy."

The tea cup, spoon and saucer in Pricilla's hand fell splashing into her lap as her head fell backwards and her mouth opened with a groan. The three swarthy gentlemen straightening up in their seats as Schultz leaned forward trying to straighten up this fainted lady.

"Honey, please, please, don't do this."

247

Nearby conversation stilled. Folk turning to look. The three swarthy gentlemen to their feet. Their gold adorned wrists and diamond ringed fingers reaching to assist this lady in distress.

"No help needed. Come on, don't make a big thing of this. Don't touch her."

"As gentlemen we must be of assistance to the lady. We think sir that you have insulted her."

"Mind your own god damn business will you. Before you get your jaws broken."

Schultz standing, two fists knotted at his sides. The solicitous expert waiter propping Pricilla's head up and putting a glass of water to her lips. Her eyes opening wide.

"Where am I. Where am I."

"At the Dorchester, Madam."

"Yeah, you're right here, honey. You're right here."

Schultz made his way leading a weeping Pricilla by the elbow across a blazingly colorful carpet. Stopping while a helpful passing concierge picked up his dropped battered top hat from the black and white tiles of the lobby floor. To hand it back to Schultz entering the revolving door. The doorman waving for Schultz's car parked up on the curb alongside the triangular little garden and lawns with their goldfish pools. Schultz stepping forward on the hotel's top step, and suddenly yanked back in his tracks. Half his tail coat pulled off down his arm. The other end caught jammed behind in the revolving door. A fur encased fat American lady stuck screaming and fist pounding the other side of the glass.

"Let me out, let me out."

"What next, christ almighty, what next. There's some kind of world fucking conspiracy after me. Holy shit, stop lady stop trying to move the doors, will you. You're dragging me back in."

"I want out. I want out."

A detachment of porters rushing to the rescue. The revolving doors reversed and Schultz's coattail released. A chair was brought to the furry fat American lady for her arse and a glass of water for her nerves. Schultz draping half of his collar attached tail coat over his shirt sleeved arm. The doorman holding open the car door. And Schultz as he bent his head to enter looked up. Pricilla her long curvaceous legs crossed, safely ensconced. A smile now instead of tears on her face.

"That's what makes you really happy isn't it honey, anything that makes me look ridiculous."

The limousine, its tyres whirring around Speakers Corner. Black man up on a ladder slapping his fist on a sign haranging down at a little crowd. Always somebody somewhere complaining.

"Why wasn't I invited to the wedding."

"Because honey, it's just me who is the guy's friend. And honey for the third time I'm telling you we can't go to Arabesque Street."

"Why."

"Because we can't that's why."

"Because you have some floozie installed, is that why."

"No honey, because from the times you've been there, the fights, the ambulances, and the damage you done, I'm being sued already for eviction by the landlords trying to make a case out of moral turpitude."

"I'm not going to damage anything."

"Holy mackerel. I got a dozen phone calls to make upon which my life depends. Don't be unreasonable. For just tonight. Let me take you home."

The blocks of flats, the tall terraces of once upon a time town houses and cream walled hotels facing the park along Bayswater Road. A pub with outdoor tables. A church so peaceful with its tall steeple sitting in a little square. Nothing like a Protestant house of worship in which to take a few minutes' private sanctuary. I ought to go disappear somewhere in this part of town. Just have a little room. A pot to cook in, one to piss in and a hole maybe in a brass monkey to fuck in.

"My mother's so right about you. That you're like a child thinking only of itself. And what you've done to me. The cruelty."

"Done, what for christ's sake. Cruelty. What are you talking about."

249

"Yes. Cruelty. You're going to drag my name through the Courts."

"Holy Jesus honey, don't you get it. If you do something like suing me I'm the defendant. I'm the one with the name dragged through the Courts."

"And you'll deserve it."

"Honey goodbye. Here's your house."

"I love you. Don't you understand that. I love you."

"You call it love to tear up every god damn thing precious to me. Like photographs, valuable invitations."

"Yes I do. Because I love you."

"Holy shit. O.K. you love me. O.K. fucking show it to me just once. Just once, that's all. By being some kind of help to me and stop the tears again. I'll phone you. Tonight. O god please, stop the sobbing. I mean shit people are stopping to look at us. Would it make you happy honey if I went home and shot out my brains."

"No."

"What would make you happy."

"To get married."

"Goodbye. I'll call you."

Shadows falling, tints of pink on the bottoms of clouds. The limousine saluted as it turned left down the private tree lined road of great embassy houses standing behind their hedges and fences. Curtains drawn on confidential windows. That's what I need. Diplomatic immunity. Jesus you give a little bit of yourself to a woman and they keep wanting more till they got all of you and then they think you are theirs to kick in the fucking balls. If their foot hasn't something better to do.

The black Daimler limo pulling up in Arabesque Street. Schultz pressing the switch to lower the glass division between passenger and chauffeur and reaching for his wallet. Digging in the inside pocket of his morning coat draped over his lap. Now shoving his hands into his trouser pockets. And jumping up from the seat and looking around behind him on the upholstery.

"Is something wrong sir."

"Jesus yeah. I've lost my wallet. I was going to give you a tip."

"Another time sir, no problem."

"Jesus don't say those words no problem. All they mean today is some problem."

"I quite understand sir. I can see you've had a full day. If I come across the wallet sir, I'll see they are right on to you with it."

"Thanks. Thanks."

Gathering his tatters together Schultz alighting. The Ambassador's car parked across the street. Jesus I have a good mind to go over there, ring the bell and beg to become a citizen of Zumzimzamgazi.

Schultz crossing the pavement. And looking up to see a sky blue coated comely figure turning around from knocking on his door. Schultz rushing up the steps. Hurriedly taking a key out of his still intact trouser pocket.

"Jesus."

"Mr. Schultz."

"Roxana. What are you doing here."

"I am in London."

"I can see that."

"For his Lordship's wedding. And the staff party. I took the liberty of thinking what harm would there be to call on you as you suggested."

"O boy."

"I hope I am not a problem arriving at an inconvenient time. But of course I will go. I did ring but the phone just kept clicking off. I'll come and see you another time."

"No don't go. Stay. Come on, come in."

"Thank you. But I hope you're not just being polite. I just have been walking. I knocked earlier but no answer."

"Well as you can see, I'm a little messed up. Jesus come in. So I can close the door."

"I really think perhaps I am disturbing you."

"No problem. I mean, no difficulty, really come in."

Roxana shyly entering, standing aside as Schultz quietly closed and bolted the door. The telephone ringing. The door at the end of the hall opening. A honey blond head peeking out.

251

"Hey Roxana just go sit in there a second. And be right with you. Thanks. Thanks a lot. I'll just close the door."

Schultz taking up the talking instrument and with his hand over the speaker turning to Greta.

"Greta, hey just go back down the kitchen will you, be right with you. I mean it. I'll be just a second."

The sullen face of Greta disappearing. Schultz listening to her steps down the stairs and to the kitchen door shaking the house as it was slammed closed and tinkled the crystal chandelier above his head. Jesus if I could only charm this instrument to bring me some good news and tidings. It's got to be, it's just got to be once that Hollywood is ringing one of these days.

"Hello."

"Sigmund."

"Not you Al."

"What do you mean not me. I'll hang up if that's what you got to say."

"Sorry Al, but I've just been through a day to remember."

"Well I got something else will make you remember today."

"Jesus don't tell me Al. I think I'm getting ulcers or something."

"How did the meeting go."

"It went O.K. It had its low moments too."

"What answer is that."

"You know Al, I mean it was fine."

"Let me talk to her."

"I took her home, Al she was tired."

"You took her home."

"Yeah Al, what's so strange about that."

"She could rest in your place with someone concerned to look after her. The beginning of pregnancy is tiring."

"I'm glad you told me that Al."

"I can tell by the tone of your voice you don't mean one damn word you're saying."

"Come on Al, Jesus come on. It's a miracle after today I even have a tone of voice."

"Well you listen to my voice a second. I got you sixty thousand plus overcall."

"Come on Al. Don't shit me. How could you get sixty thousand like that in twenty four hours."

"You want it or not."

"Jesus Al, of course I want it."

"So don't ask me how. Just agree I got it."

"Hey Jesus Al you're now talking about a life and death matter, I don't need kidding."

"It's no kidding. And tomorrow by two o'clock I guarantee Magillacurdy, maybe a little bit more expensive than I promised, but on a straight salary. Now. You tell me something. When is the wedding day."

"That's fucking blackmail Al, that's fucking blackmail."

"I'm going to ask you once more, nice and quiet and calm. When is the wedding day."

"Don't do this to me Al don't do it. What are you. A marriage broker or something bringing people together by torture."

"I'm a humanitarian who believes in brotherly love. And so for the third and for the very last time, when is the wedding day."

"I wouldn't do this kind of thing to my worst enemy. Jesus christ Al. This is human beings' lives you're talking about. What the fuck do you want to do a criminal thing like this to me for."

"Because sometimes Sigmund you're a real shit of the lowest kind."

"I'm a real shit, Al. Holy shit could it ever be Al, that maybe it's you who is the real shit. I think you want to make her your mistress later, with me meanwhile minding her for you in an unhappy marriage."

"Goodbye."

"Wait."

"For why should I wait."

"For me to think a second, that's why. You call up. You put a gun to my head trying to blast me into the biggest mistake of my life."

253

"You call sixty thousand pounds a gun blasting."

"I do Al when it could be what ends my life."

"Settling down into marriage will begin your life and do you a lot of good."

"Why Al, why."

"Because it's a natural condition in a stable society."

"You should know shouldn't you Al, after three divorces."

"I loved and was happy with all my former wives. Who still remain dear friends."

"Well the wife you're picking out for me is already an enemy, suing, harassing and embarrassing. She's the type of woman who after two weeks living with her will bore the shit out of me. What do I talk to her about in my old age. We have nothing in common."

"What are you. Some kind of special big profound thinker or something. That kid is as smart as she is beautiful and will give you a lesson in brains anytime."

"She's given me a lesson Al. In fucking brain damage."

"Which by the way is getting more noticeable with you every day, Sigmund. Learn to play checkers together in your old age if you're so worried about conversation. Also think of yourself someday decrepit in a lonely house with your balls shrivelled, and no one like a young beautiful woman to look after you."

"I grow old Al and she stays young and beautiful."

"That's right."

"Thanks for the nice arrangement. But at the moment I'm not yet with both feet in the grave and my balls are not shrivelled and I am not living in a lonely house."

"What you got somebody there."

"No Al, it just so happens I haven't."

"Well you heard me. Sixty thousand is yours. The moment you sign the marriage register or whatever they do over here in England to make it legally final. Now goodbye."

Schultz replacing the receiver. Right down smack on a bundle of money the other end of the wire. What the fuck. I could marry something worse than her incredible body and good looks. But

Jesus I see a ring go silently on her finger and I hear a deafening clank of chains in my brain. I need a sedative.

Schultz halfway up the stairs to the bathroom. Stopping in his tracks and slapping his palm against his brow. Holy shit. His Lordship's chambermaid down in the living room. I completely forgot. Not surprising after a day with a pair of sex maniacs trying to bugger me.

Schultz turning on the landing. Give a pat on the head to Justinian and tiptoe back down into the hall. To push open the door. Roxana demurely seated, a magazine featuring nude ladies held open across her lap. Which she closed as she stood up.

"Jesus, don't stand, this isn't his Lordship's here. I'm just going to change my clothes O.K."

"Can I be of any help, sir. I mean Mr. Schultz."

"Sigmund, honey, call me Sigmund."

"His Lordship would be aggrieved to hear me address his friends by the familiarity of their christian names."

"You leave his Lordship to me. This is a changing god damn society. People are getting more equal by the minute. You got to get rid of his Lordship's primitive ideas."

Schultz in a light blue checked shirt, navy blue sweater and green corduroy trousers heading down into the oven warmed kitchen. Greta, sleeves pushed up her tan arms, pressing a fork around the edge of a pie crust as she turned it in a circle on the kitchen table. She's wearing one of my shirts, one of my sweaters and even a pair of my trousers. And all of them look ten times better on her than they do on me.

"Hi ya Greta."

"Who is that girl."

"Hey calm down honey. You know his Lordship. Well that's his niece."

"What is niece."

"A relative, like uncle or aunt. She came all the way up from the country to the wedding. Like I'm doing his Lordship a favour. She's just at a momentary loose end in town. Hey gee that smells like apple pie."

"I bake one for you because you say it is your favourite."

"Well blueberry is. But that's really swell. Apple pie is great."

"What lucky girl she is who married his Lordship. He is so kind. So handsome."

"He's fucking rich beyond the dreams of avarice too."

"What is this avarice."

"Jesus honey, it's just a common disease we all got. And hey while I take his Lordship's niece for a drink could you get a little snack together just for the two of us."

"O yes I cook ravioli."

"Swell. Make a salad. Leave out onions. And I got a great idea. A quiet evening at home. How about that. Hey now what's the matter."

"But now you go out. I would like to go out too. Again I am left. I am lonely."

"Sure. No problem, I mean don't worry, soon as I get rid of her I'll be back. Gee I just notice. In this light what a nice few freckles you got."

"I am more than just the freckles."

"I know that honey. I know."

Roxana walking sedately at Schultz's side down the street. Telling little stories about his Lordship. Of how he wore two different shoes to the wedding. And for that previous entire week had dined only on bananas.

"His Lordship is also fond of draining his ponds. Taking the mud from the bottom and removing it to his vegetable gardens. He so dislikes wasting anything."

"Jesus is that the only problem he has."

"O no, sir."

"Sigmund, for christ's sake."

"Very well, Sigmund. His Lordship also has found that somehow a nasty pike has got into the moat and has eaten nearly all his goldfish."

"Holy Jeeze that is tough."

"Yes he is most upset. And now every one of the castle staff is nervous awaiting her Ladyship's arrival in residence."

Turning under an archway into a mews. Opening the door to this crowded smoky interior. With this healthy cheeked blue big eyed girl in tow. Led into this den of high pitched voices. A sprinkling of debutantes oooing and aahing. Their boy friends talking of motor cars. The viscosity of oils, speeds of acceleration, smoothness of transmissions, and the safety of tyres. Even a champagne cork popping. As Schultz and Roxana took seats on this bottoms polished oak bench in this cubbyhole.

"Jesus. You can have something more than a glass of bitter beer."

"O no, that's exactly what I want. And also I want to tell you something."

"Sure."

"You remember when you were having breakfast. And what you said."

"Where. What. What did I say."

"At Nectarine Castle that morning in your bed. You said you wanted to fuck me."

Schultz in the middle of a sip of beer lurching forward in his seat. As the mouthful swallowed the wrong way. Choking and sputtering, Schultz spat out back into his glass. Roxana clapping him on the back.

"Christ excuse me. But you believe in direct language honey."

"Yes."

"Jesus. Just give me a second or two. I got to think."

"I have said the wrong thing, haven't I. Exactly what you weren't expecting."

"No no. I mean I wasn't expecting. But it was beautiful the way you said that. Wow."

"Were you thinking you were going to have to chase me, tear my clothes off, throw me down on my back and prise open my legs."

"Honey. Jesus not so fast. It's just that at this moment I am in the middle of a lot of deep thoughts that are hanging over the crossroads of my life."

"I should not have called upon you."

257

"No, no, it's absolutely perfect you did. But christ, what kind of environment are you living in down there at his Lordship's."

Schultz lighting a cigar, put aside his beer and popped back a brandy. Taking Roxana by the hand. Her fingers tightening in a reassuring squeeze. Prick painfully swollen caught the wrong way in the underwear. The day darkening. This girl's cunt I can read in her face. Just like lips pouting soft, like half a bite of a ripe sweet black cherry. Holy god what's happening to me. I don't want to totter into old age with a bitch and her mother setting me up as a machine to provide them with the lifelong comfort of caviar."

"Honey I think I need some fresh air."

Schultz and Roxana walking arm in arm in the shadows of branches along this fence of Belgrave Square. All the shrubbery and trees in there. Never even noticed this jungle growing right in front of my nose. And this should happen to me right now. A doll. Long brown soft gorgeous hair. Ladies treat each piece of ass they hand out as an investment in their future. I'm already laden down carrying portfolios. And if I put it up this mouth watering unspoiled country girl his Lordship will be trying to knock the shit out of me with a cricket bat.

"Gee honey."

"Yes."

"That's all I can say. You really have got me with such a hard on I'm speechless."

Schultz tiptoeing behind Roxana up the front steps of Four Arabesque Street. His finger over his lips for silence. Slipping the keys in, the bottom one, now the top one quietly one at a time. Eyes staring into my back. From the Ambassador's windows. Get Roxana up the stairs and quietly into the bedroom. If only I could screw with the peace of mind that I had the kitchen door locked.

Schultz sniffing the ravioli scented air as he and this latest country fresh morsel softly, slowly tread along the hall and up the stairs. Jesus I could also be down feasting around the kitchen table. With both ladies jumping up in turn to serve the courses.

Ended with apricot brandy from the bottle in the library. While I supply laughter doing a post prandial jig around the floor followed by a partial strip tease and my own special erection war dance.

In the semi dark of Schultz's bedroom. Roxana sitting on the side of the bed. The rustling sound of her taking off clothes. A streak of light coming through the curtain. Eight thirty p.m. by Big Ben. Roxana standing. Putting her hands behind her back, and undoing a clasp. A naked Schultz lying on the bed. His erection twitching and pointing all over the ceiling. And holy shit. Here they come. Loose into my personal view. A pair of luscious tits. Nipples sticking out engorged for sucking. My palms itching. My god, her pubic hair. Shape of a black heart. A mole on her belly. Perfect soft and fluffy heftiness in the thighs.

"Now Sigmund. Now, you can throw a spine electrifying fuck into me. Because here I am."

"Jesus you sure are kid."

Schultz reaching up to take this Roxana softly on top of him in bed. Roll her over. The smell of her. Musk. The feel of her satiny silk. Christ her fingers. She's playing a magic symphony over my shoulders, my back, my arse. Jesus my motto used to be don't waste time with women you're not fucking. And here's this gift of the gods arrived because I wasted a minute showing her some attention.

The door of the bedroom opening inch by inch. And stopping. The eye of a human head peeking in. Watching. Schultz, all hands and lips all over this creature. The door coming further ajar. A long fingered hand holding it. A slim wrist disappearing upwards into a blue sweater. Schultz's head between Roxana's legs and her hands gripped in his black curls. As a right shoulder comes round the door and a left hand closes it behind. The entire slender honey blond Greta tiptoeing into the room. Moving step by step closer. Schultz feeling Roxana's thighs stiffening tight around his ears. Her hands dug in pulling his head by the hair.

"Hey, honey, what's the matter am I hurting you."

259

Wide blue eyed Roxana. Her speechless mouth wide open. Her one eyebrow raised hysterically higher than the other. And her voice finally squeaking out in fear.

"Behind you."

"Please, O please, do not mind. It is just me Greta. I only watch."

"Holy cow."

Roxana biting her lips turning her head away. Schultz looking backwards over his shoulder. Roxana's breath drawing in. Jesus when god is suddenly giving me everything I want, what the hell do I ask him for now. An extra prick.

"It's O.K. Roxana. It's O.K. No problem. Roxana, it's alright. This is just Greta."

"Please do not mind I come in by mistake. And it is so beautiful. I did not want to frighten you."

"Jesus Greta, this is kind of private."

"Please. I am do no harm."

Schultz kneeling up now over his eyelash fluttering chambermaid. Her two front teeth just ever so slightly bucked. Her eyes even more wide open, looking over Schultz's shoulder and staring at the new arrival limelit in the curtain slit of light. Who my god is taking off my sweater. Letting out her own masterful pair of tits. Which could get her burning through steel right into the bullion fortress of Fort Knox. Holy shit, even in the fucking lingerie business you never see anything like this all in one day. What a surfeit. As well as a heart stopping memorable lesson in comparative anatomy. She's taking down my trousers. And, would you believe it, even wearing a pair of my shorts. Her belly button in the shape of a question mark. Right in the shaft of light. Which don't worry. I'm not asking why stunningly naked she's heading right towards this bed.

"I come closer. I am do no harm."

Greta's long honey blond hair falling around her shoulders. Strands parting around her nipples. Half smile on her lips. Long slender, athletic body. Muscles on her stomach. Hands held out from her sides and now slowly placed back on her hips as she sensuously slowly twists and sways. Holy christ again I don't have to ask what she's doing. Fucking well trying to seduce us. And succeeding. And now she's putting her hands all over my piece of ass. Fucking hell. When she could go back to Hornchurch where she learned these bad habits and kid around with her employers who not only both try to kiss her but pay her as well.

"I am do no harm."

Greta climbing further up on the bed. Running one hand softly up Roxana's leg, and momentarily squeezing Schultz's prick with the other. And suddenly throwing herself on top of Roxana. Who welcomed her with open arms. Schultz in the melee, his fingers here, feet there trying to press between the so recently met young entwined ladies. Holy shit, not nobody even noticed the size of my prick, one third bigger than it is usually. With the way their tongues are kissing down the other's throats. Hands and fingers stroking each other between the legs. Wagging breasts against each other's breasts. In one day. Holy christ. The things you don't plan for. Happen right in front of your face.

> Hey Jesus
> Girls
> What about
> Me
>
> I am
> Do no
> Harm
> Either

20

BRIGHT with the occasional shower said the early morning wireless forecast. But the day remained windswept and pouring with rain. Big Al Duke in a tweed fishing hat smiled as if he were the father of the bride, pressing a bouquet of orchids into Pricilla's hand and kissing her on both cheeks. A photographer outside the registry office with his flash bulbs popping off. Al beaming, his arms about the newlyweds.

"Come on, once more, the happy couple and all of us together. What's a few rain drops on this unforgettable day."

Schultz shivering in his thin grey flannel ivy league suit. Rubbing his eyes after each picture as if he did not know what hit him. Bumped into as he was once or twice by Pricilla's mother. And having for the first time learned the rest of Pricilla's christian names, Prunella and Prudence. And ushered by a back slapping Al into this long limousine.

"Come on kids, let's all go for our little nosh I got ready for you at the Savoy."

The suspension of the vast motor lowering as Pricilla's mother got on board. Schultz at the sight of this familiar interior had his hand on his stomach and then across his lips as particles of a bacon and toast breakfast came up his throat to sourly taste in the mouth. Wedged in by a wife on one side and a mother in law smothering everybody in her perfume, insisting to be on the other. Al taking up a jump seat alongside surprise of surprises. Agnes. An equally beautiful equally creamy skinned tall softly blond closest girl friend of Pricilla's. Who flew all the way from Argentina to be at her best friend's wedding. And who, as she gazed admiringly at Al during his tourist commentary, also made Schultz's prick tingle into erection.

"Agnes, even in this inclemency isn't our wonderful London still beautiful."

The rain speckled vehicle majestically purring through Chelsea down a traffic jammed King's Road. Passing around the fountain in Sloane Square. Speeding up through Cliveden Place. The greenery beyond Eaton Gate. Here's where they keep freshly painting the houses every week. Got my hair cut only a hundred yards away right over there. In these streets where once I wandered free. Now a whole roll of Pricilla's mother's fat is pushing under my elbow like the arm rest of a chair. Jesus when will it ever be when I'm getting annoyed by nothing. Never be another night like that one. With Roxana and Greta. Screwed what must be one of the most beautiful holes in Europe. After half an hour's trying. Managing to steal up on Roxana from behind. As Greta was otherwise engaging her from the front. That privileged fucker his Lordship. Doesn't even know what's hanging around just one of his fucking castles. And now. Just when I'm meeting one after another, exactly the kind of women I need supplied in my life. This happens to me. A coffin lid slammed. Catching my fingers, my prick, my neck, my balls. With two tons live weight of a mother in law sitting on top crushing it closed. Eight new grey hairs this week I pulled out of my head. All I can do is holler and sceam bloody fucking murder way down in the abyss of my guts. And Al, holy shit, can he be appropriate. Choosing flowers related to those that trap and eat god damn flies.

In a green damask walled private drawing room over looking the tops of the trees and the tugs and barges on a rain swept Thames River, the wedding repast was had. Tail coated waiters deftly in attendance. Schultz his black hair framing his ashen face, eyes glazed staring at the table cloth. Pricilla wearing her Queen of Sheba smile. Then a grimace as Schultz dug out a piece of wedding cake which toppled off the knife to fall on the floor. While Big Al, his eyes glistening, his glass of champagne raised, stood at one end of the table, and reflected in the many mirrors, made his little speech and proposed a toast.

"It is sad that Sigmund's own parents couldn't be here to witness this, this wonderful moment, the marriage of their one and only child. But on such short notice they were caught busy opening up yet another of their large textile factories on the East Coast. And it is my own little unhappiness on this wonderful occasion that my own dearly beloved is not here. Being as she is so charmingly just too shy. But nevertheless Agnes is here. This beautiful flower we welcome from the Argentine. And together with the new bride's beautiful mother we wish happiness for the both of you two good young kids. To Mr. and Mrs. Schultz."

Big Al Duke the day previously having got investor's contracts from Sigmund Franz Schultz now let this recently married impresario examine these four slips of certified variously coloured and water marked paper. Which were produced in the gleaming marble and polished wood panelling surrounds of the men's room of the Savoy.

"Here you are Sigmund, mit mazel and broche."

"Holy shit, Al. I don't need that kind of sentimental yiddish shit just now."

"Sentimental, like hell, since when can especially you do without luck and blessing."

"O.K. Al, O.K. You win."

Schultz in his pale faced daze did manage to be intrigued by the three legged emblem on a cheque drawn on the Isle of Man Bank, as he folded these amounts of twenty thousand from one investor, thirteen from another, twenty five from a third and two from Big Al himself. Putting them one into the other and shoving them into his side jacket pocket.

"Jesus, Sigmund, don't just stuff away sixty thousand pounds like it was a hat check."

"What do you want me to do."

"Put them safe in your wallet."

"I lost it."

"Hey that's what I'm saying. You could lose them. Don't be careless. Sometimes I think I must be crazy the way I help you out of jams."

"Out of jams. Into jams. What the fuck are you telling everybody my mother and father are opening big factories for. When all they opened is a back street cut price lingerie store. They already think I'm made of money. When all the fuck I'm made of is overheads. And it's ruining me."

"Sigmund, come on. I like to make you sound good. That something is backing you up. Like who doesn't know the theatre is treacherous. But from now on, you're going to zing mit der dick dick. Right. At the beginning of what is to be for you lifelong happiness. Right."

"Al. Wrong. Stop. Just for a second. And I'll tell you something. Holy shit I feel sick. Jesus, just for a second the whole room began to spin."

"Here. My car's not nearby. So puke in the basin."

"Fuck you, I'm not going to puke Al. And you know what it is that I want to tell you."

"No what."

"I want to tell you Al. Thanks from the bottom of my heart for some things. But Jesus christ almighty."

> No thanks
> For others
> From the bottom
> Of my soul

265

21

SCHULTZ's two day honeymoon was spent in
Brighton. Deposited at a begrimed grim Vic-
toria Station in Big Al's limousine. And with his face buried in five
different daily newspapers, reading in the train swaying through
the Surrey and Sussex countryside. The sky clearing approaching
the coast. The big massive hotel's wind shivering windows overlooked the cold slate grey waters of the English Channel.

"You would wouldn't you, book us into a morgue like this."

"Honey, what the fuck's wrong. Look it's got palm plants all
over the lobby."

Taking a taxi through a night opened wide with stars, there was
a candlelit dinner in a famed fish restaurant where Schultz sat
over his plate of sole meunière staring into oblivion. As Pricilla
glowered and waited for doors to be opened, her wine to be
poured and for her momentarily culturally orientated questions
to be answered.

"Never, never will I ever go out and sit with you in a restaurant again with you behaving like that. And people thinking that we have nothing to talk to each other about."

"We don't honey, we don't."

Schultz taking a lonely midnight stroll on the shore. Ships out to sea. A liner, her decks aflood with light. Binky says good fortune makes one belch and fart and misfortune makes one think and worry. And holy shit, I've just wet my only pair of shoes and filled them with sand. With this fucking wave washing in.

"What a foolish childish thing to do. Imagine at your age getting your feet wet."

"Shut the fuck up."

"Don't you dare speak to me like that."

"Shut the fuck up."

Schultz shoving his feet down deep between cold sheets. The sounds of a wife climbing in her own bed two feet away. A night of nightmare. Dreaming of living in a doss house. Full of apprenticing whores. A dingy smoky bar. Drunken lurching figures. Where the inmates were hoping to hatch a revolution. Then a slap on the face. Pricilla in her flimsy negligee looming over him.

"How dare you fall asleep without making love to me."

"Honey, I'm exhausted. Not only in mind and body but in spirit."

"At least my father was a man. You're a mouse."

"Jesus what are you saying that for."

"Because it's true."

Early morning Schultz walking on the promenade. Hands dug in pockets. Cold in a rumpled flannel suit. A sour gnawing in an empty stomach. Passing by pasty faced oldsters. Thin hollow cheeked husbands and fat wives. Some who sat hunched up in deck chairs reading newspapers in the momentary sun. And Schultz took a taxi up to the high cliff tops overlooking the sea. Swooping dive bombing seagulls. Waves pounding down below on the rocky shore. Jesus, if the show didn't have to go on, maybe I should jump like Pricilla's father. Only my mind's full of Roxana. And heaven would never have such an incredible cunt without a thousand angels' pricks trying to get in it all at once. Her unforgettable wares. Jesus the way she exhibited them. Greta and I even fighting to take turns with her. Safely behind the changed locks on the front and basement doors of Four Arabesque Street. Jesus what narrow escapes I was having. Till I got trapped in this big trap. Pricilla twice turns up trying to turn her own keys and ends up kicking and banging. With the Ambassador's Third Secretary and Financial Attaché coming over. The three of them standing on my front stoop. In a conflab I could hear up in the bedroom. All of them thinking that's where I was. Inside. Which I was. Teetering on the edge of an orgasm.

His Lordship was rumoured to have left a considerable fortune at the gaming tables during his honeymoon in Monte Carlo. And upon his return to England went directly to deer stalk at one of his northerly castles on a bereft windswept western peninsula in Scotland. From where he took a helicopter to be best man at Binky's wedding held in the Duke's private chapel in a rhododendron shrouded corner of their walled garden. His Lordship now repairing with the new Countess to his favourite Castle Nectarine. And on the way spending a day or two at his highly confidential and secretive town house in London to attend the first night opening of the show and to let the new Lady Nectarine consult decorators concerning her extensive plans to refurbish the southerly situated of his Lordship's residences.

"Holy jeeze your Lordship you already got paint and wall paper on your walls."

And now in the surprisingly calm splendour of the chairman's office of Sperm Productions where Binky made a point of keeping all feverish activity to a minimum, his Amazing Angry Grace accosted Schultz.

"Don't lie to me Schultz."

"I'm not lying."

"You are."

"I'm a married fucking man now."

"You weren't when Roxana disappeared."

"The girl dropped in innocently for tea I'm telling you. I don't know where she was after that. Christ there were fresh scones, I had delivered by taxi from Fortnum's, all that kind of thing."

"You'll have sledgehammers and all that kind of thing delivered by hand on your head Schultz."

"Hey your Lordship I mean, Jesus, you want to keep tabs on a free human being like that."

"No Schultz I do not. But her father, her three brothers and two of her irate uncles, all of whom are stone masons and possess arms which could break you in two, want to keep tabs on her."

"Hey come on, your Lordship, it's nearly opening night, I'm crushed already with problems. Everything gets blamed on me like I'm some kind of sex maniac. Can't you tell them what I'm telling you. She must have stayed at a hotel somewhere wanting to see London in private. I never touched a hair on her body."

Ten minutes later, his Lordship waving an envelope sailed back into the chairman's office and for once tripped over his own shotgun cases.

"Schultz I found this on my desk."

"Yeah what is it."

"It's addressed to me. The Earl of Eel Brook Common, secretary to Mr. Sigmund Franz Schultz."

"Holy shit, why do you have to find such things right this very minute."

"Because this very minute it was staring me in the face on top of my mail on my desk."

"Your Lordship I need to see what that letter says. I was just having to look good to somebody for a second. Don't you understand, you English are ga ga over titles."

"It would seem Schultz that you are ga ga over titles. And do this once more and you will be ga ga ga forever."

Magillacurdy was signed. Exactly as he absolutely insisted. Standing in the central avenue of Brompton Cemetery near the mausoleum where he'd recently slept. His signature on the contracts held under an umbrella while surrounded by Al, Schultz, the Agent, plus two lawyers.

"It's done me boyos. It's done. I can tell by all your astonished faces you thought I'd be gone to the big money in Hollywood."

Magillacurdy departing in his own limousine back to Claridge's Hotel. To later that afternoon arrive in the street below Sperm Productions' windows, attired in a sandwich board advertising the show and with a street band in tow to sing aria after aria. Binky throwing rose petals out the window to him. Magillacurdy catching each one and eating it and throwing back a kiss. Till the police came to remove the obstruction.

The broken collar boned director was replaced. Instantly giving a press conference to slander the show. His picture in the evening newspapers with his arm in a sling. And suing to have his name removed overnight from all posters and advertising all over town. Schultz on the phone to Al.

"Be thankful Sigmund, his name wasn't up in lights. At this last minute don't worry. You could be director of the show."

"Al I hate directors. I wouldn't be one of those creeps for all the gross on Broadway. Better make that off Broadway. Yeah."

"O.K. Sigmund give me a couple of hours."

Schultz on the pavement outside the theatre overseeing the repainting of signs. And now handed a note by the ever endlessly helpful efficient Rebecca, recently so subdued and saddened by the weddings of Binky and Basil.

At Home
Sylvia and Herbie
Two p.m., Dressing Room Five

Schultz just on the verge of heading back stage. When Al produced out of his limousine a new director. Black leather jacketed, balding in glasses and beard who sported similar suede chukka booted feet to the old one. And smoothly maintained that he had the nerve, courage and sheer insane guts to give Magillacurdy some last minute pointing up of his performance. As even Al warned him to duck deeply when Magillacurdy's fist whistled over his head. As it invariably would when any director made what the

270

massive Irishman considered a slander. Instead of the suggestion that was meant.

"O.K. fine. O.K. get in there in the ring. I got to rush to an urgent meeting backstage where I don't want to be disturbed."

Half an hour later with the second director shaking like jelly, Magillacurdy was equally shaking with rage. The chorus line and Debutant co star cowering behind the scenery through which Magillacurdy's Welsh mining boot had twice been sent on the end of his foot. And he was now just on the verge of busting the director in the kisser.

"Begorra I'll kill the ignorant pretentious fucker."

Schultz in dressing room five on top of Sylvia, having to constantly look over his shoulder at Herbie who was still not averse to attempt a mounting of Schultz by the rear. The drama unfolding on the stage came blaring over the sound monitor. And Sylvia shouting.

"I want all of it, Sigmund, all of it. Shoot. Shoot."

Schultz listening a second in the blaze of noise. A bloodcurdling scream over the monitor. Letting go of Sylvia. Pulling up his trousers. Jumping in his shoes. Falling over a chair. Getting up and jacket flying rushing out on stage. Fists knotted at his sides as Schultz threw himself between the stagemanager and Magillacurdy who held the stagemanager's throat in one hand as he shook his other in a fist across the footlights at the director rearranging his misplaced long strands of hair over his bald spot as he stood atop the grand piano in the orchestra pit having leaped there off the stage in his hasty retreat.

"For christ's sake easy Terence, easy. Before you kill somebody."

The cast and stage hands slowly showing themselves again from behind the scenery and props. To watch this latest director trembling on the piano.

"Mr. Schultz I absolutely refuse to work with Mr. Magillacurdy unless he takes my direction."

"Your direction is wrong sonny boy, I got fucking ears. I was listening in on the monitor. I know how that bar should be sung.

271

Just like Magillacurdy is already singing it and my composers want it sung."

"Mr. Schultz I admire you as a producer but certainly not as a human being who knows anything about musical comedy."

"Who says it's musical comedy."

"Well if it isn't then you can be sure it's a musical tragedy. And I refuse to conduct my profession in this violent and grossly obscene environment and I resign."

"So resign and get the fuck out of this theatre."

The director stepping down on the keyboard, striking a discordant chord with his foot as Magillacurdy advanced on Schultz his hand held out.

"Ah me old son, you're a man of principle like meself, to hell with the mediocre."

Magillacurdy suddenly stopping pointing at Schultz with a finger wagging at the end of his outstretched muscular arm.

"Now that me boyo I'm telling you is by no means mediocre."

Schultz looking down. His prick hanging loose full length flapping out between the flies of his trouser. Which as he quickly handled it back in, brought an ovation from the entire cast, chorus, musicians and stage hands and a cheer roaring from Magillacurdy.

Begorra
I've seen
The origin
Of the
Species

22

J UST as Big Al was at two o'clock that day, forever the patcher up of production problems
and the begetter of new ones, he was at four o'clock also forever
the doting marriage broker eager to learn how his handiwork was
proceeding. Ringing Schultz again at Sperm Productions where
he'd retreated for a breather from his recent exposure and new
popularity at the theatre. Binky placidly sitting puffing a cheroot
his foot up on his gout stool, and handing the phone to Schultz.

"Hi Al."

"Sigmund. I just heard about the director. That he resigned.
That you came rushing out on stage at him with your prick out."

"Jesus christ Al. That director was a creep. And who told you
that load of shit."

"O yeah, there are people saw you. And their agents, including
their lawyers are ringing me. Was your prick out or not."

"It was out Al. I was taking a pee when I heard a scream on the
monitor. How could I remember my prick in such a panic."

"Reliable witnesses said it was engorged."

"Holy shit Al, haven't you heard, I just happen to have through no fucking fault of mine, inherited from my Prague grandfather, a big prick."

"And you're not circumcised."

"Holy shit Al. What are you anyway a kosher fucking Hebrew medical inspector on my trail."

"It's sacrilegious you're not circumcised."

"Look Al I'm going in two minutes to rush out right now and get circumcised. If it will make you feel any better."

"Sigmund I just rang case I don't see you before curtain time. That's all. To wish you lots of luck for tonight."

"Thanks Al, we're going to need it."

"But Sigmund. Don't let the constant crisis of show business blind you to the rest of your responsibilities. I'm getting messages from your beautiful wife's mother. She is unhappy that her daughter seems to need her now and she wants to be near her."

"Al. Never. Never is she, that two ton bitch going to move into my house. It's final."

"She loves her daughter Sigmund."

"Shit. Stop. Not now. Enough. Al. No more. Don't meddle in my life. Please."

"Sigmund I'm trying to help."

"You're not helping. That two ton whale is never going to crush her weight down on one of my dining room chairs and fill her face with my groceries. Especially while I'm sex starved by her daughter already."

"That's the first decent thing that I've heard happen to you in years."

"Well I'll tell you what else happened. Besides clap, hemorrhoids and horrors. She threw water on an electric fire, and fused the lights. In the dark I grabbed my tube of athelete's foot paste to brush my teeth with and nearly died of poison."

"Ha ha ha. A hercules like you should put it on your erections too."

"O yeah Al you think that's funny do you."

"Come on enjoy a laugh don't be a big cry baby Sigmund."

"With the show opening tonight. And everything else that's been happening. You want me to laugh Al."

"Sure."

"At this moment I am ready to get permanently hysterical. The sixteen clackers I've hired to beat their fucking palms together and bring the house down with bravos are holding me to ransom for double the pay we agreed. Let me tell you the show could fall on its face."

"Sigmund, nothing fatal can go wrong for a genius impresario like you."

"Al, you can make all kinds of remarks to me but Jesus, don't right now give me sarcasm. In front of me I got a lawyer's letter delivered by hand two minutes ago. Claiming his client, who would you believe it, sings about fifteen lines in the whole show, has been grievously libeled in the program. With his name misspelled sounding like a four letter dirty word. And that he is married and the father of five kids."

"That's not libelous for christ's sake, that's an olympic qualification these days."

"O yeah Al, well if it's not libelous it's god damn dangerous then. The guy happens to be a real genuine bachelor. At dress rehearsal last night he brought his nice Jewish prospective mother and father in law to the show, who, even before the curtain went up left their seats out front and attacked him physically backstage over what they read in the program. And what this news did to their daughter."

"Sigmund, it's minor, minor. You should worry about the major."

"Don't worry this is major. I don't need broken sound equipment into which we both smashed when he was trying to sock me after his prospective in laws left in a huff. Shit Al, I'm already way over budget. I would have swatted the fucker through the wall only I can't find a replacement in time. His lawyer now wants all the billing and the page in the program reprinted in four hours."

"Sigmund. Give me the lawyer's number. All right. And you

forget all about it. Don't worry about a thing. See you at the theatre. I'm bringing my very own wonderful beloved with me."

"I thought she was shy."

"I'm pulling her there by the hair. You've got my deepest sincerest best wishes for a real all time smash hit."

"Sure Al. I know I have. Because you got your own two thousand in it."

"Goodbye, Mr. Cynic."

Binky loftily raising his eyebrows from his book. Shifting his foot on his gout stool and frowning as he turned to stare out at the cloud gathering sky.

"Ah Schultz. One feels that theatrical history is being made on this sombre London afternoon. I couldn't help overhearing your little chat. And especially your statement concerning your lack of what one takes to be satisfaction in sexual matters."

"Binky it's opening night. Is that all the thoughts you can come up with."

"Ah Schultz, you do don't you, demand such unrelenting devotion to duty. And yet here we are. Such momentous change wrought in our lives. All three of us snugly cosily married. And for you to say at such an early stage that you are sex starved."

"I am."

"Dear me then. You must learn to sublimate Schultz."

"You just tell me how, Binky."

"Well there are so many things. Anti blood sports for a start. Take this little tome I have here, The Moral Justification of Foxhunting, written by a dear old uncle of mine. Who felt rather strongly on the subject. You could vigorously oppose the pursuit and killing of the fox. Attend meetings. Fire off letters to the press. Considering our three positions one must think of preparing a good clean sportsmanlike world for the next generation coming."

"What three positions."

"Haven't you heard, the new Countess of Nectarine is rumoured to be with child. Therefore the future concerns all three of us deeply. Even the subject of the child bearing role of women in society."

"Holy shit, his Lordship is going to have a baby, that's great. He must have put it up before the wedding."

"Well Schultz, you know how his R. G. is not past a little playfulness now and again. With all due respect of course to his most marvellous dear wife."

"Holy shit Binky. I'm getting the fuck out of here back to the theatre. Jesus you can sit wasting hours."

"Ah business, business, always business, not a moment for tackling the mysteries of life. Just as tea is coming. Why don't you have a cup, Schultz."

"How can you stay so calm about the show Binky."

"Simply Schultz, because I have such absolute faith in you."

"Christ maybe I will sit down. Jesus we haven't seen each other for a while. And you know, you can do my confidence wonders sometimes."

"I'm glad Schultz. And I do so miss our little chats. We must not let our marriages come between us. Ah Rebecca, what a very splendid yummy sight, thank you my dear, put the tray there so Mr. Schultz has no trouble reaching. And stop all calls please. This poor man does slave so that we must try to provide him with a quiet moment or two of diverting reverie. Tea weak or strong Schultz."

"I'll take it any fucking way you do, Binky."

"Ah, weak then. And do, please select a gateaux Schultz. Take that one, for starters, a light airy lemon roll fresh in from Fortnum's. Now Schultz. Do sit there a moment, so that I may smile at you. Dear me. Penis out in front of the cast. Understandable of course. In view of your starved state. But good gracious me, is wedlock cramping your style."

"You heard, a fucking colossus mother in law trying to move in on me."

"Ah Schultz you should spread out your life a little."

"Like how. Tell me. With that solid two tons blocking my way."

"Most normal people keep a discreet flat in London as well as a town house. Then together with a country house perhaps in southerly Sussex and a grouse moor with suitable accommodation in northerly Scotland, bob is your rud."

"That's normal huh. Well I've already gone abnormal trying to keep up with the one place I got and may not even have much longer where instead of bob being my rud, electricity is nearly my executioner."

"O dear. We must somehow help you Schultz we must."

"Now you tell me Binky if wedlock has cramped your style."

"Ah Schultz. I'm rather glad you ask me that. Indeed it has rather cramped mine. As you know most normal Englishmen do have their little fetishes. I mean, if only his Royal Grace didn't keep his personal life so private I'm sure we'd find that even he has his. But by the way Schultz, surely you have had a wee tiny taste of the whip."

"What. With all the blows landing on me already."

"But hasn't there been a nice muscular blond lady with her chastisement case knocking on your door. Haven't you let her in. She gives the most marvellous lessons in deportment."

"Why you dirty son of a bitch, Binky. It's you who's been sending that kraut around."

"Ah Schultz, ha, ha, yes. I thought it would serve as a little mortification for you in view of some of the shoddier treatment ladies have received at your hands."

"Shit why don't you take some mortification."

"Ah but I have, marrying as I have one of these higher ups in the aristocracy. They do have a way of making one feel lower down. Even when I suggested one of my just slightly deviate filthier frolics to my spouse, I was told, go do that sort of thing with your fille de joie in Soho. I acquiesce of course in such dilemmas. But my dear little creature of such a delicate constitution, with her belly quite popped out now, has suffered much morning sickness. Our setting up house has been rather a hectic time. Difficult getting staff. Had to take on an Irish butler who while he demonstrated to me his expertise in disemboweling a chicken in the kitchen was, while flicking parts of the entrails about, also sending particles of guts landing in the cream jug to be used for that night's pudding. Most discomforting. Do Schultz have another gateaux."

"Holy christ your butler I hope has never worked in Fortnum's."

"To be sure Schultz, he hasn't. He claims however to have held quite grand posts in various Irish midland situations. Ah but then, our brand new cook who wasn't at all bad at baking cakes, had to be dismissed. Secreting rashers of bacon as she was from our larders and shoving them out through the bars of our cellar windows. Plus all other sorts of nice tasting things. Her boyfriend waiting on a motorbike fitted with the appropriate receptacle alongside our house to roar off with them. My dear wife's old nanny who had witnessed the thefts has now been put to cooking as best she can."

"Christ you can replace groceries. Don't lose a good cook."

"Good point. Yes very high marks you get for that observation Schultz. But you don't understand. Lurking in the psyche of the British upper classes is a strong desire to discipline the lower classes. Plus the barren feeling of unhappiness it gives one as a member of the increasingly apologetic lower middle aristocratic class, to think there she is, one's cook on her day off, with her boyfriend in a Pimlico maisonette sizzling one's bacon for their own Sunday morning nourishment while we, the dispossessed, stare at our empty plates. Dear me servants these days do have it all their own way don't they. But Schultz do have another spot of tea, there is worse to tell I fear."

"Shit, I must say Binky sitting here like this listening to your marvellous troubles for a change, is a moment of fucking bliss."

"Ah that word bliss. With or without the fucking, is often applied to honeymoons isn't it. And on mine Schultz, secreted away in an inn by a waterfall up a valley all belonging to my father in law, I had that first night, a most erotic dream about the Sovereign. Whose beauty has, I must confess, always managed to arouse the beast in me. Had me turning and tossing in bed the entire night. My little woman notwithstanding. I woke acutely embarrassed, being as I was in the dream trying to storm the gates of the palace. And as I was entirely nude I was being quite properly repulsed by guardsmen. However as a former captain in the Grenadiers I barked out a few parade ground commands which made the chaps in my nightmare quite sympathetic to my temporary insanity. O but dear me there I was newlywed, sitting up in bed under this ancient beamed ceiling, shouting out rifle drill. Little flecks of foam at the corner of my lips and my dear little one frozen in fear and trying to keep me from toppling from our bridal couch. It was all quite nearly as bad as my. arrest when I had once on an undergraduate dare, strolled naked with my bowler and brolly under the sky lighted pink ceilinged roof of the Burlington Arcade over there in Piccadilly."

"Jesus Binky why weren't you with your genius at bullshitting, a fucking actor."

"Of course upon occasion I do fuck. But as to being an actor, alas my shyness Schultz, my shyness. But do let me relate an even more woeful and recent event which befell me. Which of course you may think entirely unremarkable. Ah, you are, aren't you Schultz, enjoying your tea."

"Binky it's a life saving ceremony you English have invented."

"And note Schultz how appropriately it has begun to rain outside. Pitter patter of drops striking the window. But now I must tell you. How my view of the citizens of London has wretchedly changed. Having taken up residence in my old grandad's town house to begin practice of my marriage vows. I spent many hours overseeing certain exterior improvements to grandpapa's paint peeled victorian pile so that neighbors might feel we were doing our little bit in keeping up appearances. And I must confess I was feeling quite proud of my handiwork. When suddenly on a quiet sunny Saturday my engagement book blank, I remained snugly ensconced at home. My new little wife pottering off to look for her little bargains in baby clothes in an area of Bayswater to which, I admit openly, I am not attracted. Having breakfasted morning long over the newspapers and had a nice further nap plus the enjoyment of a self administered bed chamber diversion, I then, upon completing my ablutions, found myself facing the pleasantly empty afternoon with the household staff departed. I happily descended downstairs and throughout the early afternoon played Chopin with shutters closed and curtains drawn in a candlelit and incense perfumed music room. And well you know how one does, Schultz, get a sudden feeling, if not a desperate need, to go out of doors. I thought dash it all, with the seemliness of the weather, I would have tea in the garden. So with a mildly sheepish guilt over my solitary selfish self indulgence, I flurried about as one does trying to make the setting reasonably comfy for myself. Ah you smile Schultz. Well damn it, I do confess to obtaining a certain spiritual nourishment from an agreeable milieu. Despite the dearth of London garden bird life, sparing as some naughty cats may have made it. So with a cushion for my chair, my granny's best silver, I deposited a cake table centre. One of those gateaux which as yet uncut looks so nice just sitting there. Well, dear me, all was in readiness. My lemon neatly sliced. A suitable scandalous news item in the paper selected to peruse. And back I went into the house to pour the kettle in granny's tea pot. And when I returned. My cake, Schultz, was gone. I looked here, I looked there, I looked everywhere. Well I just couldn't believe it. This most awful ill fortune. Then suddenly I saw. Just over the wall. The neighbors' wretched dog licking its cream flecked chops. Having totally devoured it. Well I don't need to tell you I was more than somewhat annoyed Schultz. I thought damn it. I want some satisfaction. I promptly popped out to the street and rang their front bell. After waiting two of the most irritating minutes of my life, their cook answered. I said, your dog ate my cake. Well she looked at me in a tone and manner as if I were something the cat dragged in. I nearly stamped my foot. Indeed in fact I did. And repeated my demand for some satisfaction. Well off the creature went. Presumably to her employer. She was gone another highly irritating three minutes. And when she came back she handed me two shillings. I mean Schultz I was thunderstruck. Two shillings. The wretched cake had cost at least something like twelve shillings at Harrods. I looked at her incredulously. She was about to shut the door. I said it was a brand new cake. Indeed a marvellous cake. Two layers thick with jam filling and with three cherries on top. Well do you know she went away again. This time for an exasperating four minutes. And she came back and handed me a further coin. A threepenny bit. She then closed the door in my face. Standing there Schultz, those two cold clammy coins in my hot little disappointed hand, I realised that something had changed most grievously in our English way of life."

"Jesus."

Schultz wiping his lips with one of his Lordship's coronet embroidered napkins and staring at Binky. The rain now splattering the windows. In the greying afternoon, lights across the street flashing on.

"Holy shit Binky, sue for christ's sake, sue."

"Ah Schultz thank god you agree I was aggrieved. Yes indeed I thought of that. A battery of Q.C.'s righteously mouthing their way up into the House of Lords. But instead, clutching my coins I went lonely back up my steps. In through my hall and into the pitch blackness of my music room. I put my fingers down on the ivory keys of my little piano. In diminuendo I played Land of Hope and Glory. And I wept."

Schultz rising from the chaise longue tucking the long end of his black knit tie into his belt. Then looking down and feeling to see if his flies were firmly shut. He headed out through the half open door. Banging straight into Rebecca standing in the hall, tears coursing down her face.

"Holy shit, kid, what's the matter."

Rebecca rushing off down the passageway. Closing the door as she disappeared into his Lordship's private office. Schultz following, stepping slowly in. Rebecca across the room by the window. In her grey sweater and skirt. Her head turned away and her shoulder pressing against the wall. Her long slender fingers up against her cheek. As she heaved in sobs.

"Hey please, please, tell me what's the matter Rebecca."
"I love him. I love him so."
"Who, honey. Who."

    Binky
    Binky

23

LIGHTS blazing outside the theatre. Pedestrians lining the pavement. Cars bumper to bumper jamming the street. Police on foot and horseback. Flash bulbs popping. London's glittering people pouring out of taxis and limousines in one orgasm of celebrity after another. Two fanatic fans holding up a sign.

MAGILLACURDY
FOR
PRIME MINISTER

Big Al in a black velvet dinner jacket. Pricilla and her mother both in blazing red. Arriving out of Al's limo, their faces beaming at the cameras and waltzing like royalty into the thronged lobby. With a sprinkling of first nighters from Hornchurch, Bromley, and Golders Green. Voices babbling. Matches striking, cigarettes lighting. Eyes flickering here. Eyes flickering there. Eyes flickering everywhere.

Schultz that late rainy afternoon, comforting Rebecca in his Lordship's office. Then taking her to a snug Chinese restaurant up a narrow little Soho alley. Where this saddened creature poured out her heart over the sweet and sour pork.

"Jesus kid no man is worth your marvellous kind of love. Plenty of guys are dying to adore a wonderful girl like you, marry and settle down and have kids. But if you have to love somebody, love some guy who needs it. Like me for instance. See, you laugh. So now you're going to start feeling all better."

Schultz, at ten minutes till curtain time, coming down the lobby stairs from his private balcony box, where the previous half hour he sat subdued screened away in darkness. Without answering the deputy stagemanager's knocks concerning a screaming tooth and nail female fight in a chorus dressing room. As other words of Binky's echoed around between his ears.

"My dear little one Schultz, spent the entire second night of our honeymoon weeping and sobbing in my arms, saying among other things, that she had trapped me by her being with child and that any time I wanted I could abandon her. Cast her out cold and naked on the moors. Alas owned by her father fifteen miles in each direction. But I mean of course, we were overwrought, the nearby waterfall thundering in our ears with a recent heavy rainfall. By dawn I simply loved her. Loved her truly. My dear sweet cherished poppet, my petkins."

Schultz tearing himself out of his solitary reverie. Went towards the lobby. Stood on the staircase, his hand on the gleaming brass rail. Looking back into the grey sad eyes of Rebecca. And her beautiful hands manipulating her chopsticks. Putting her fingers touching mine, when she said thanks for comforting me. We went back out on the London streets under the encouraging clearing skies. Our lonely taken Chinese meal in both our bellies. Her honesty, her shyness, her warmth. Now the perfumes of these fucking people. Who look like they don't have a care in the world. Except bored curiosity to see if this is a smash hit or a dismal flop and whether tomorrow I should be smiled at or shown an ice cold shoulder. Fuck you, you cunts all of you, I'll show you. Jesus, even some tiaras, and more than half of the audience are in evening dress. While I'm in physical and mental incarceration. Give a little bit of yourself to a woman, and they keep wanting more. Till they got all of you. Till they think you're some fucking ornament they wear in their lives. Thank god a production shuts out the entire rest of the world. But tonight it lets them all back in again. Everybody, Jesus everybody down there in that lobby thinks they're such hot shit. Not a trace of humility anywhere. Except that girl in a nice sombre black suit. No staggering beauty but what a serene nice face. Holy fuck, could that be Al's new girl friend. Jesus, I know her from somewhere, that soft nice lovely brown hair. O god what new complication is this in my life. In the kind of recent erotic escapes I'm having, I could have maybe even fucked her in a blind hurry without even knowing it. On top of all the other crazy things that are happening to me recently in the dark. Still taste that god damn athelete's foot paste, it's going to be in my mouth for the rest of my life.

Schultz sneaking along the wall across the jammed lobby. Stopping behind a pillar to drink in this delicious sight of people lined up at the box office and snaking all the way out into the street. If only business would be like this every night. The phones jangling. Wallets opening and peeling out the cash. My god, Lady Lullabyebaby. Over there. On her aristocratic treetop. With that big gawking guy who may be her husband. The marvellous imperious way she sweeps her head. And sticks that cigarette holder in her mouth. Not giving a fuck about anyone in sight. Blinding everybody with a necklace of diamonds and emeralds. What a doll. And Agnes. Wow look at her. She must think this is a bathing beauty contest. Tits popping out of the top of her dress. Some kind of chinless hawknosed stockbroker she's got in tow flashing his teeth and eyes in all directions especially at Agnes's gorgeous creamy cleavage. And shit and shinola, the fucking Ambassador turning up out of the woodwork. Stealing the show with that wild looking towering ebony absolutely bald beautiful creature he must have flown in fresh out of the steaming jungle and twice as black and tall as he is. God, his Lordship right next to them. Killing himself as usual to be inconspicuous while everyone is breaking their necks turning to look at him and the radiantly beautiful Countess. Christ I'm shaking. Jesus I've missed the real emotional boat in life. Why can't I have someone unbiased out of the blue love and adore me like Rebecca loves and worships Binky.

"Why won't you sit with us."

"Because I can't honey. I got to be ready to jump backstage for any catastrophe."

Pricilla stalking off. Schultz repairing alone back to his box. The buzzer going. Take your seats please my Lords, Ladies and Gentlemen. Safety curtain lifting. Lights going down. Strike up the band. Whoopsie doodle. This is it. Curtain up. The moment of Chinese torture. Come on now, you fucking overpaid clackers, clap clap. For the sets. Jesus at least we got over that one. Christ the fucking chorus is off key. And now latecomers. The smug cunts. For months you string your guts out and these fuckers come barging in right at a magic fucking time looking for their god damn seats. Christ Magillacurdy is shaking his fist at them. Jesus Magillacurdy don't overdo it. Just let's get through this number. Sometimes I ask myself are actors the lowest form of life on this earth with only actresses lower.

Schultz wiping the sweat from his brow. As the clapping outlasted even the paid clackers at the interval. With two boos and a few whistles and someone slamming a door storming out of the theatre. Followed by the harassed theatre manager knocking with news of a problem in row E of the stalls. Schultz peering cautiously out from behind his screen down into the interval emptied seats. With one on the aisle still absolutely full. Of Pricilla's mother. Who, with two usherettes tugging at her by the arms, could not be budged.

"How dare you sit up here laughing at my mother who could have a heart attack down there. I'll kill you."

"Shit honey. Don't make my life complex as usual. Please."

At the second interval, Al trying to direct the rescue operation. Pricilla ashen faced, her mother beet red huffing and puffing. With the assistant master carpenter and the chief engineer attempting unsuccessfully to dismantle the seat from around this mass of imprisoned flesh. And only succeeding in stabbing the fat occupant with a screwdriver. Her screams fortunately drowning out Schultz's hysterical guffaw.

"Holy Jesus christ, this really is one for the fucking books."

A photographer coming down the aisle to take pictures. Pricilla's mother heaving a spare box of chocolates at him. Jesus this behemoth bitch while she's making my laughing muscles sore is also stealing the whole show. I hope the fuck they never get the seat off and shift her with it still attached so she can sit in god damn exile somewhere.

The salvage undertaking interrupted again by the returning audience. Who shushed the protesting prisoner. Lady Audrey and Lady Emeline and husbands sitting viewing just two rows back. And the concerned Ambassador two rows in front turning around to watch with his entire black party. Holy shit, what have I done to myself in the middle of my fast expiring youth to have a hippopotamus anchoring me in a sea of nightmares. With a wife demanding to be loved and then wrecking things all over the house. And speaking of nightmares there's one from the past, my Doc, from Harley Street. Sour faced Herbie laughed for the first time when the engineer's screwdriver dug deep into my mother in law. Sylvia going around now whispering insults under her breath. Expects me to leave my prick behind in her when I had to run out on stage to stop a murder. Got to accept people for what they are, dirty rats. While I'm busy in the thankless task of catapulting a gang of unknowns into celebrity orbit. That incredible hulk Magillacurdy going head first. Each potential massive disaster on stage he turns into a mini holocaust which flames up around him in all his burning glory. Only every five minutes now he bothers me to compare the length of pricks.

"Ah now me boyo take out that yoke I know you've got there and show it to your regimental sergeant major again. Sure I served two years in the Irish Guards and never did I till now see an organ the likes of which at a stretch might compare with me own."

Magillacurdy's finest moment came in the last act in an angry aria, wrecking a table set for tea. With a swipe from the back of his hand sending the china pot smashing into smithereens. And throwing a bottle across the stage at a mirror. The bottle missing and bouncing off the scenery. The mirror two long seconds later, breaking. At the same time a bag of flour plummeted from the flies landing bursting on Magillacurdy's head. Smilingly he blew the white clouds off his face, bowed and brought the house down with laughter, cheers and applause.

At the final curtain amid the bravos, and shaking fists, two fights broke out. Al flailing his arms in the aisle and creaming someone in his tracks who had punched him in the ear. And as he symbolically wiped his hands in victory, he stepped straight into his girl friend's open box of chocolates knocked to the floor, tripped, fell and lay on the carpet both hands clutching at his weak heart.

Pricilla's mother's dress ripped as she was lifted in her seat by six stage hands out into the aisle. Safely reclining on a couch in a dressing room, a seamstress sewing her up trying to stitch the fabric back together over the roll of fat bursting through. While Mrs. Prune polished off a box of dried figs.

"I'm going to sue the theatre, the management and last but I'm telling you not least, I'm suing the producer."

After all the horror Schultz reenacting every dance and replaying every note of the show in his head and sneaking to the corner of the stall bar for a quick double scotch and soda. And just as he felt to see if his flies were undone there was a nudge on the elbow. The blond flowing haired bejeweled sparkling eyed Lady Lullabyebaby handing him his wallet.

"Holy jeeze."

"I'm sorry to be so late in returning this. You lost it at the wedding along with your shoe."

"Hey wait you look gorgeous, don't go, Jesus I've got to talk to you."

"Sorry, I must I must."

Lady Lullabyebaby turned to look back from the door and gave a little smile over her shoulder. Schultz opening his wallet thumbing through the notes. Christ my four different currencies, still ready in case I got to leave at a moment's notice for a foreign land. And everything else intact. Jesus how honest can somebody be. And a card. White and pristine. Holy cow it's her phone number. Knightsbridge 1234. At last, something in my love life looks like it's ready to go right for me.

Schultz turning from the bar to go backstage. Pushing halfway through the smoky crowd. A figure blocking his way.

"You're Schultz."

"That's right."

"You want to sell this show, kid. I'll give you a good price right now tonight before the reviews come out in the morning and I'll take it straight to Broadway."

"No deal."

"What's the matter. I'll give you more than the show's worth. It could be worth nothing tomorrow."

"It's worth a fortune tonight and it will be priceless in the morning."

"You know who I am don't you."

"Yeah I know who you are. Joe Jewels."

"Well what's the matter kid, you like taking risks or something."

"That's right."

Schultz turning away and heading straight into the ever smiling resplendent Ambassador with his towering black lady looming behind him.

"Ah my dear gladiator. A truly magnificent evening. I am so happy to see that all the hard work you do casting and auditioning at your house has produced such marvellous results."

"You're too kind, Your Excellency."

"Ah let me introduce you to my friend."

"How do you do honey."

Schultz shaking hands with this long ebony armed amazon as she answered in an unfamiliar drum beat rhythmic tongue.

"Zeek geek goo bug ding doo."

"And the same to you, honey you've said it all."

Like as if the pair of them had nothing whatever to do with the show, Binky and wife slipped silently away as did his Lordship and his Countess who were catching a train to the country.

"Ah a splendid evening maestro which both I, my dear wife and his and her Royal Graces enjoyed thoroughly."

"Jesus, Binky you fuckers you're completely abandoning me."

"Ah I wouldn't put it quite as subtly as that Schultz. It's simply that domesticity calls."

Al with four tables booked at the Savoy. And with marzipan and crushed rum truffles adhering to the soles of his shoes and his heart beating again as usual, he went backslapping and shepherding his party of show backers growing larger by the second out to his and their limousines.

"Sigmund, put it there, a great show. See you at the Savoy."

"Thanks Al."

Schultz from dressing room to dressing room squeezing between the backstage visitors, his head popping in the doors. At least tonight unlike some other nights, it's not like a morgue backstage. Maybe I stopped the curtain calls too soon. Fuck it. Four should be enough for anybody. Some people don't know when to stop milking the adulation. It's like I got to be a father to a bunch of children. Wiping noses. Shaking hands. Waving. Thumbs up.

"You were great. Just great. Keep up the good work kids. I love you all."

At the Debutant's dressing room. Schultz calling out over the heads of her bubbling bevy of admirers. The Debutant making her way through to Schultz. Between all these smart assed smoothie men about town.

"O Mr. Schultz was I alright really."

"You were sensational, honey believe me. Sensational."

The Debutant kissing Schultz on the cheeks as his hand headed straight down to cup around her arse, one of the most magnificent ever to go waltzing spotlighted on a London stage. And she, dear girl, threw her pelvis forward to concuss this producer upon his now famous and instantly tingling cock. Schultz at this split second of appropriate moments urgently whispering in her musky aromatic ear.

"Honey, maybe after the matinee on a pouring rainy afternoon we could together just have a little food sent in and talk about your future here in your dressing room."

"Maybe we could, Mr. Schultz."

"Jesus sweetie pie I could listen forever to your melodious voice."

"I'll bet you say that to all the girls."

Declining all lifts and invitations in the direction of various parties, Schultz making his way back up the private stair past his box and along the shadowy passage towards the lobby. Stopping to look at a photograph of a fabled female previous star on the wall. Jesus nobody ever puts up a picture or a statue to a producer. Fuckers won't even let me into Who's Who.

"How dare you be just standing here, hiding. Deserting us and my mother like that. After she's had such a terrible shock and ordeal. We've been waiting out front of the theatre for seventeen minutes."

"Honey don't you know I got to go backstage to congratulate the stars. What are you crazy or something, you don't know about that."

"I'm hungry. My mother's hungry. And we want to go and eat. Now."

"Eat. Go eat. Eat. Go get the fuck out now. Right out that way is the door. Go eat. With the hippo. I'll order two tons of hay sent to the Savoy for her."

"I could scratch your face. You're hysterical and rude."

"That's right. Fucking right I am. After I've been sweating my balls off for months to see this night happen. All you and that whale can think of is to fucking eat. Then go and fucking eat."

"I will scratch your face."

"Like fuck you will honey."

Pricilla lunging out. Schultz side stepping back as the claws whistled down past his cheeks. And the open palm of his left hand hooked upwards in a resounding slap on Pricilla's face. She stands glaring. Groans. And as usual topples. And lays in a heap at my feet. Christ while there's a distant sound of happy voices and glasses clinking in the bar. Holy shit. Blood. Trickling out of her nose. I did it now. Killed her. What the fuck did I have to go and do this for. Jesus to last in this business you got to speak with a languid voice. If somebody sees us. It will end me up again in exactly the wrong kind of publicity for the show.

Schultz dragging Pricilla by the arms along the carpet and into his private box and closing the door. This is just like a murder. How do you dispose of a body in such a blazing red dress.

"Honey if you can hear me, don't move while I get a bucket of fresh water to throw on you."

Schultz rushing backstage down his own little empty cul de sac corridor to his cubbyhole dressing room. Filling a fire bucket with a glass ladling water out of the basin. Stopping to examine his face in front of the mirror. In this silence. His Lordship says he has aunts living quietly in the country who have the art of slowing their lives down till they are just ticking over so that nothing ever distresses them. And me with the fuses blown in Arabesque Street, pissing and missing the toilet bowl. Drenched my box of paper handkerchiefs on the floor. That I later go to blow my nose with. And get a face full of urine. Holy christ when is there going to be a trace of contentment in my life. When this could be my moment of triumph. Of dancing on the waves. A big deal for two seconds before I'm swallowed up in the deep. Sometimes you wonder why you do it all. You know it's because people want to always reach out and touch something that seems glamourously beyond their own lives. When they turn and maybe see you. Debonair, calm as a glacier. Gee that guy in the expensive sunglasses, he did all this. Gave us a real glittering alive magic. Yeah that's right you fuckers. I did. Against all god damn odds let me tell you. While everybody else was just twiddling their thumbs wondering if they should fart or belch or something. I've been playing sudden death roulette dialling telephones. Every moment ten seconds away from disaster. Funny now how finally you don't care if

293

people want to come touch you on the arm for your magic. Not until they stop wanting to. Then, Jesus, all over again you want them to. Especially beautiful women. Sure, touch me. Go ahead. But unless you're gorgeous don't smudge the fabric. Of Sigmund Franz Schultz. Impresario par excellence. Major fucking domo of the West End. Holy jeeze I'm going loco. Looking like this at myself in the mirror. Shaking a fist and talking to myself. With a pregnant wife laid out on her arse.

Schultz abandoning his bucket and rushing back to his box with a glass of water. Cleaners now picking up the cellophane wrapping and paper cups in the empty theatre. Pricilla's mother's dismantled seat still sitting out in the middle of the aisle. Sound of people still drinking in the bars. Jesus, who's this in the passage way ahead. Might have already discovered the corpse. It's the fireman on duty.

"Well Mr. Schultz. It's going to be a hit. I can always tell. By the quality of the clapping."

"You really think so."

"No doubt about it."

The box deserted. Schultz drinking his glass of water. Where's that bitch gone. Probably screaming to her mother I murdered her. O Jesus I was just beginning to feel a glow of hope. In this great theatre. The luxurious brocaded fabric on the walls. Where I could be ensconced for years doing nothing but screwing the Debutant and counting the gross. The nice embellished figures decorating the ceiling. The last of the perfume smell left by an applauding audience. The fireman says the quality of the clapping indicates a smasheroo. When Jesus I nearly hired half of it. Uncle Werb used to say, what's cheaper than doing it yourself. Getting somebody else to do it for less. Binky and his Lordship without a single emotion just come and go. Like they're disowning me. Before we hardly said hello. As if it were their duty to vanish. Al at least saved me from the lawyers again. While at the same time trying to dump on my doorstep the whale who nearly stopped the show. The libeled member of the cast now is with a brand new Jewish girl friend with her brand new Jewish family flurrying about them. In this world it doesn't take people two seconds to replace each other. There always comes a time in everybody's life when you sit on the street curb weeping because of what someone recently indecently did to you.

Schultz stepping out into the evening air. Crossing the street in front of the theatre. Looking up at the lights and signs. There it all is. Come on all you suburban cunts, come to the show. Jesus and what's this coming. A squad car. Bell clanging roaring down the street. Screeching to a stop. Four constables jumping out slamming doors rushing into the theatre. Jesus she did it. Called the Police. The fuckers are after me already.

Schultz retreating back into the shadows of the pub doorway. Lights of the theatre switching off. Limousine coming around the corner. Chased by fans. Magillacurdy. He's got the Debutant. Stealing her right from under my nose. And she's not shouting out the window she's being kidnapped. Holy christ I got to slip away down around the corner. Like a pursued culprit. Right at the moment when I just might have a success. My mind goes wild at the thought of it. A fucking armoured yacht on the Riviera. In Monte Carlo. Have on board Lady Lullabyebaby. Provisions stacked down the hold. Escape to sea without a wife and her mother dragging me down sinking. Greta, Roxana and a few other of your naked chested things could be cook and crew. Sylvia and Herbie could wait on table. Serve me just like Sylvia suggests Herbie and I could make a meat sandwich of her. White slices from the front. Dark from the rear. While between courses, Lady Lullabyebaby and I could screw into eternity amidships.

Schultz heading south towards the river. Taxis and the odd limousine ferrying away the last of the theatre traffic. What a relief to be alone by myself. Without having to want to scream to everybody, hey for crying out loud will you just shut your ass for two seconds. Click of my heels on the cement. Telling me with each step through the fresh breezy air. That shit, this town could be mine. Mine. To wake up to in the morning. Having breathed in this London night. An intoxication nothing like it anywhere. Clapping still ringing in my ears. Even my own bravos I was shouting.

I can't hardly fucking well wait. All we need is fourteen rave reviews. The critics, Jesus they can't just be that dumb to pan us.

Schultz cutting through the narrow familiar streets of Covent Garden. The soft sweet smell of vegetables and fruit. Trucks and lorries halted on the shiny cobblestone. Porters drinking tea and chomping on sandwiches at the kiosk in front of the great pillars holding up the church. In there they have plaques on the wall commemorating theatrical immortals. And holy shit all I can suddenly think of is those showbizz friends who are never heard of again. Vanished. Replaced by a whole new set of smart alec shits scurrying on the scene. Jesus even a poor son of a bitch director who was a theatrical household name. Saw him one freezing New York night shambling along Eighth Avenue. Shabby, stooped and old. While I was a few steps away leaving a Broadway show, glad handing under the marquee lights. And there he was, so cold, so lonely and abandoned. Like a leper you couldn't go and touch. Even ghosts staying to the other side of the street, flapping their big aprons of death in the dust and grime all whorled up by a bitter icy wind. Jesus I swear I couldn't speak. Couldn't get myself to go to him. He was already so dead. That I just wanted to get the fuck out of there quick in a hurry. Even now it makes me walk faster by these bags of onions and sprouts. Down a dark Southampton Street. Into the gloomy nearly empty Strand.

Schultz turning right. The silvered front and green shining lights of the Savoy entrance. Stepping through the glass doors. Everything is prepared for privilege. Every little kid who's growing up in America at least knows he can be President one day. In this fucking country you don't get to be Prime Minister unless your father was.

Schultz halfway across the restaurant floor. As Al comes rushing forward. And a group of folk suddenly standing at their tables. Clapping. Schultz turning to look back over his shoulder. Faces grinning at him from other tables. Schultz stopping alarmed in his tracks. Jesus they're clapping at me.

"Hey what are you Sigmund, the reluctant hero. Come on. Meet everybody."

"Al what's all the fuss."

"Sigmund. We've all been waiting for you. Where's your beautiful wife."

"I don't know I thought she was with you."

"No she went to find you. Well anyway Sigmund. This is an important night. That we all want as investors to fondly remember."

"Al, unless they make a profit, people forget historically touching moments. And there's no proof yet of a profit."

"Mr. Cynic once more."

"All this is ever going to be to me, Al, is a nostalgic explosion down memory lane. Which I hope has left my balls still between my legs."

"O.K. well if it's not too much trouble then, drag your testicles over and come and sit down."

"Jesus Al, it's hard enough to get myself to come here in the first place, I don't want to meet these fucking people. You got to keep investors at a distance."

"Come on, don't embarrass me. Have nice manners."

"Al, they're getting such a good deal I don't need to give no nice manners as well on top."

"Sigmund out of respect for me then, show courtesy at least. You're going to meet my lovely wonderful companion, who with god willing is going to be the next Mrs. Al Duke."

"Al at your age don't be so crazy. Don't do to yourself what you made me get done to me. Believe it or not in spite of the things I can't forgive you for, I also like you."

"Sigmund I'm going to be honest with you. You're sometimes just such an enigma I can't believe I know you personally."

"Well I'm by nature a private introspective type of guy."

"Champagne, caviar, filet mignon, Clos de Tart. For christ's sake. What could be more introspective than that. Come meet the folks."

Schultz shepherded by Al to one table after another. Nodding his black curly head to the grins. Shaking hands and smiling as Al made his quips.

"Here's the guy, ladies and gents, who wears the laurel wreath tonight."

Al crossing to his own table stopping to wait as his girl friend returning from the powder room approached. This darkly tailored tranquil lady, a strand of pearls at her pale throat.

"Sigmund let me introduce you now to the most wonderful loveliest creature in London. Louella this is the one and only Sigmund Franz Schultz. And Sigmund this is Louella the greatest girl you're ever going to meet in your life."

Schultz stopping in his tracks. Looking at this friendly forthright face. Long brown hair parted in the middle gleaming amber in the light. The soft kindly eyes.

"Hi Louella how do you do."

"Hello."

"But don't I know you from somewhere."

A white pallor bleaching Al's face. As he looks from Schultz back to his girl friend now wreathed in a smile of recognition.

"Yes you do Mr. Schultz."

Al slumping at the knees. His trouser lengthening over and covering the diamond studded gold buckles of his evening slippers.

"Hey what is this. You two know each other."

"Hey I just thought I did, Al. I'm sure it's a mistake."

Louella shyly smiling at Schultz. As she squeezed her fingers against a black beaded handbag in her hand and touched the silver initials above its clasp.

"Don't you remember Mr. Schultz."

Al's jaw dropping a further forty miles on his alabaster face. His eyes bowls of horror as he turned to stare at Schultz wracking his brain.

"Yeah I do I guess. It's just somewhere on the tip of my head. Hey are you alright Al. Jesus you've gone completely white. Let me give you some water."

"Never mind giving. Let me ask. Point blank if you don't mind. Do you know each other or not. I want an immediate explanation."

"Al christ you need medical attention with such a color change on your face."

"I don't need nothing but an explanation in black and white and I want it right this second."

Louella putting her hand up to her cheek. Her lower teeth pressing out biting her upper lip. And a tiny catch in her breath.

"I met Mr. Schultz on the floor."

"You met this philanderer where. On the floor."

"Yes. He fell down the stairs."

"Where were you and he so that he fell down the stairs."

"Al, my darling, please, it was only in an office building."

"Sure Al. Relax. I just remembered, This sweet girl and I met late one night in a hotel hallway when I helped her get her key in her door. And I was so overcome by her charm I then fell down the stairs."

"I don't want to hear any more, you hear me."

"Hey Al, it's a joke. I'm joking. All it was. We met for a split second when this really sweet girl picked me up when I fell down the stairs of an office building. She dropped her whole file of papers to assist me. I even have her telephone number."

"You what."

"Relax again Al. I got her number so I could sue and have a witness. Al you really are jumpy."

Al placing Schultz to sit between two investors' wives. As he himself sat readjusting his bowtie and licking his lips between taking in big lungfuls of air. Just as a waiter leaned over him and said he was urgently wanted on the phone. Al popping a pill into his mouth, slowly making his way past his guests and out into the hall. Schultz reaching to ferry a grapy delicious champagne to his lips as one of the investors' wives pressed her big tit into his elbow. And then leaned close to whisper breathingly upon his neck.

"Mr. Schultz where ever did you find such a magnificent singer like Mr. Magillacurdy. He's so utterly wonderful."

"In a cemetery."

"I see. You're hinting you do not want to continue this conversation."

"Madam believe me. That's where I found him."

"O very well then I can see you can't talk seriously."

Al returning into the room. And now puce faced and fuming. Reaching behind his dinner jacket as if to hike up his trousers. Signalling with an angrily beckoning finger for Schultz to leave the table.

"So Al, so now what's wrong."

"So I ask where is your wife. And you say you don't know or maybe you just don't care."

"How should I know Al. She vanished."

"Well I just come from talking to her on the phone."

"So where is she."

"She is at your house attended by doctors."

"Doctors."

"Yes doctors. With her mother also having to recuperate after her shock tonight in the theatre."

"That fucking walrus."

"Never mind the name calling. I just can't believe it. You attacked a woman again who is your wife now. Up to your old tricks hitting defenceless women."

"Defenceless. She tried to scratch my eyes out."

"What kind of excuse is that. You could run."

"What you don't know Al is that you have teamed me up with a ferocious tiger. And now her mother. Right in my house now. Which like the seat in the theatre it would take two bulldozers to shove her out."

"Mrs. Prune in her present nervous condition couldn't climb all those flights of stairs up to her flat."

"So she goes climbing the steps up into my house. Jesus Al think of my nervous condition once in a while will you. And I'm going back to sit down and eat in peace if you don't mind."

Schultz about to slice through a big thick juicy filet mignon arrived in its chive and butter melted yumminess. Surrounded by creamed spinach and mushrooms. The soul soothing Clos de Tart

300

tasting on his palate. As two dark suited gentlemen entered the restaurant and approached the table. One tapping Schultz on the shoulder who turned with his mouth full chewing, looking up.

"Mr. Schultz I'm afraid I must ask you to accompany me please."

"What for."

"It's a private matter sir you may prefer to discuss elsewhere."

Schultz sitting in the upstairs of a police station beside a desk. A shirt sleeved constable at a typewriter.

"Well sir it happens in the best of families. But it is an assault occasioning actual bodily harm committed upon your wife Mrs. Schultz and accordingly you've been charged."

"I was protecting myself. It was only a love tap I gave her on the cheek."

"Well sir, I understand. But you admit you did hit her."

"Shit I wish to hell now I broke her fucking ass permanently forever."

Schultz handing over his valuables and led to a cell. The door clanging closed. The tan tiled walls. A shelf to lie on. On opening night of all nights. Who would believe it. Jesus even my first production. Which I thought had it's bad moments with mayhem galore. Didn't end up in incarceration. Even when all living hell broke loose way before the final curtain. With hissing, booing and catcalling. And there I was sitting in the audience so terrified by the unified, unanimous response raging around me that I became the most audible of the demonstrators. Even shouting and shaking my fist at the scared shitless actors on the stage. The courageous author with such volcanic discourtesy erupting, had already beat it back to Fulham somewhere with his prick trembling between his legs. Shit I thought if they hate it that much, why not attract the international press and start a wholesale riot. Which Jesus was already started. And attracted the flinging of anything that wasn't screwed down including a few of the looser seats. With people even jumping up on stage to wreck the scenery, busting everything. I had to accept that the whole audience had stood up to humiliate me so why not join in. I jammed ice cream down a lady's back who was trying to steal a prop off the stage. You think that if you apprentice through such moments like that, that never never again could anything be worse. But now here I am on a night like this. Arrested. My teeth dragged out of the most delicious filet mignon I've had for years. To go sit on a bare mattress. In a cell. Locked behind bars.

When
In my last
Emotional
Energy crisis
I was a
Burning symbol
Happy and free

24

SCHULTZ rubbing his eyes walking along a lamplit Charing Cross Road. Past the closed shops of this desolate deserted street. A chill rainy mist falling. Released from jail, and now getting wet. And in six bloody hours I've got to be in Court. When I should be planning every last ditch emergency strategy for the show.

Schultz sending a shrieking whistle out between his lips. A taxi stopping two blocks away, turning and coming back. Thank god. At least I can still pipe out a long distance signal for a cab.

"Welcome aboard Gov, where to."

Schultz alighting at number four Arabesque. Tiptoeing silently in. So far she hasn't changed the locks on the door and stationed a policeman on the stoop to protect her life. But christ one can't avoid bitterness after what that bitch has done. Holy jeeze where the fuck will she or her mother be sleeping. And that outsize walrus busting springs in some bed.

Schultz up the first flight of stairs. And up the next. Pressing the light switch. Fucking lights still out. Go into this bedroom at the top back of the house. For peace and quiet. What a night. My head is swimming. About six hours sleep in the last two days.

Schultz wearily taking off his jacket in the dark. Holy shit sounds like there's a cat loose or something in here. I'm getting jumpy. Like Al nearly went out of his skin when he thought I knew his girl friend. A sweet fucking charmer that she is. I should have rung her. But for my unending adversity I would have done. And met her before that greying geriatric strips a gear in his organs trying to fuck her.

Schultz undoing his shirt, stopping listening again. I heard something, Jesus christ, fucking well move. Dear god I beg you, don't after what you've already done to me make me be in the bedroom of the behemoth. Holy jeeze. There really is something fucking well in here breathing.

Schultz with shoelaces untied, trousers dropped to his ankles. Touching and feeling around him. Shit now if I move I'll fall over. Or a skeleton will drop out behind me like it did with me getting drenched pissing all over myself in his Lordship's castle. Christ I haven't even yet recovered from that heart stopping shock. And Jesus I really do feel like I'm going to shit. My nerves are shattered. I'm just not going to last the course. Escape back to America. The land of the free. The home of the brave. Uncle Werb. Here I am. I want to go into the diamond business. Ah Sigmund what a good boy. Welcome to the reality of practical sense. Here, two million dollars worth of stones, take them over to Izzy my old pal on the top floor. They're his for three million. You keep ten per cent of the profit for yourself and like a sensible boy go buy a good raincoat and galoshes, in case next time I have to send you out with diamonds to bring to Amsterdam when it's raining. Holy jeeze. I'd do it. I'd really do it. I'd sell diamonds stark naked in the snow. Even for five per cent commission. And I could be fucking Dutch girls like Greta all over Holland.

Schultz touching his way across the room. Where's the fucking bed I remember was right here. No Jesus, this is the wardrobe. Ah, my knees are touching the mattress. At last I'm going to be warm. Blankets on the bed.

"Holy shit."

Schultz jumping backwards. A rustle of bedclothes. A gasping intake of breath. A female voice.

"Who's that."

"Jesus christ who the fuck is this."

"Who are you."

"I live here. Who are you."

"Get out of here."

"Like fucking hell I will."

"I'll scream."

"Holy shit, is it you Agnes."

"Who are you."

"It's me Sigmund."

"Get out of here Mr. Schultz. What are you doing here."

"I was trying to go to bed."

"Not with me you're not."

"No. I know. I'm sorry. I just got home. I didn't know anybody was here."

"Well now you know. And I hope you'll go. Right away."

"Jesus hold it will you. My clothes are everywhere."

"Go this second. Someone could hear you. And I hope you could explain then what you were doing."

"I'm going to fucking bed in my own house that's what I'm doing. How the hell was I to know you're here sleeping."

"Well I am. Pricilla said I could."

"O.K. honey. O.K. don't panic. Give me a second will you to figure this out. Where I'm going to go and sleep. I only just got out of jail. I'm cold, tired and hungry."

"And if you don't mind my saying, you also appear to be without any clothes."

"O hey gee I'm sorry. Boy what eyesight you got to be able to see in the dark. Momma meeo, a fond du mots by goom de bots."

"What are you saying."

"Nothing, it's just an expression I used as a kid when every god damn thing was going wrong. Holy fuck, pardon my French but I'm dropping everything I can't find."

305

"How can you drop it if you can't find it."

"Honey you'd be surprised what I can do."

"Yes, punching Pricilla."

"Hey why the fuck does everybody see everything from her side."

"Because she's a lovely person."

"Wow. You women stick together."

"Of course we do if a man behaves like a beast."

"Jesus honey, one sock and shoe is missing I got to find to get out of here. Which believe me I want to do in the quickest possible hurry."

"I thought the show was lovely."

"You did."

"Yes. I did. Magillacurdy I thought was magnificent. Such incredible animal magnetism. A lady sitting next to me was jumping out of her seat in delirium over him."

"You don't know how much you're doing my crushed soul a lot of good with those words honey."

"Well I honestly did love the whole production."

"That's the most pleasantly hopeful thing I've heard, no kidding, all night. Even though I haven't had hardly a second to talk to anybody. This is nearly the first moment I'm suddenly come to rest after spinning like a top for weeks."

"I imagine it must be such an awful lot of work to put a whole production together like that. Finding and choosing all the people. I really admire you for it."

"Honey if by any chance that great eyesight of yours can see my face in this obscurity you'll see I'm smiling a beatific smile."

"Are you."

"Yes I am."

"You're rather a funny person, aren't you. So much more introspective and serious than when one just meets you superficially."

"Agnes honey, you're a girl of impressive sensibilities."

"I'm just an ordinary girl. All I've done is just ride horses all my life."

"Honey I'm a little cold."

"O."

"And I'm a little tired."

"O."

"And I've got to be in Court in six hours. Jesus would it be asking too much just to chat and get warmed up in bed for a while."

"Pricilla's my best and oldest friend."

"I know that honey, I know that."

"We grew up together. Her father's ranch was beside my father's ranch before they lost all their money and moved to New York."

"I know that honey, I know that."

"And she's right downstairs and her mother's right downstairs."

"I know honey. But I'm right here freezing."

"Someone could suddenly come."

"Key's in the door. I'll lock it. Please honey. No shit. I really need to be saved at this moment. If you really are a friend of Pricilla's here's a time you could really help her by helping her husband, who needs it. What about it. Come on. You're a girl of impeccable theatrical taste."

"Wow. You can lay it on thick can't you. I just know I shouldn't be doing this."

"Christ Eskimos do this all the time and nobody gets upset."

"I don't have any clothes on."

"That's O.K. honey, I won't in a second have any on either."

"Please, you mustn't. Please don't. She's my only real close friend."

"Honey, easy. Don't worry. Just lift up the blanket like this. Look. See how easy and harmless it is."

"O god."

"See, I just slip in. Jesus, you have no idea what this is doing for me at this moment."

"For me at this moment, it's giving me goose pimples. I'm terrified. Don't you understand. Pricilla and I were at convent school together."

"Honey. Just close your mind to the past for awhile. See, lots of room. Not even touching. I just lie here. Hurting nobody."

"We were confirmed together. Went to our first dances together. Rode together. Took holidays together. Shared our secrets."

"Well here's a secret you won't have to share. It'll make a change."

"Don't you know how close as friends two girls can be."

"Sure. And as the husband of one of you, I could cement you two even closer. Jesus you looked good tonight."

"Did you see me."

"Sure I drank you in. In long ecstatic swallows. Stunning dress."

"Did you really see me."

"Sure. Your dress was a gorgeous satiny green. Who's the guy with you."

"O him. Just a stockbroker who's been dating me."

"Say no more honey. I heard how you've been chased ragged all over town by all those English creeps."

"Some of them are extremely nice."

"What's that."

"What honey."

"There."

"Just my knee. Is it bothering you."

"No. Not yet anyway."

"You know Agnes. I've never so suddenly ever felt better in my life. Usually as I'm lying here like this the ceiling or something has already fallen on me."

"You're a funny person aren't you. I never thought Pricilla would ever in a million years marry anyone like you."

"Hey what's wrong with me."

"Can I be truthful."

"Sure honey. What's wrong with me."

"Well everything if I'm being honest. I nearly died when I saw you. Her description of you in her letters. As if you were this golden haired knight mounted on this white charger slaying dragons. Then when I met you I nearly burst out laughing. Pricilla has had the pick of men all her life, anybody she wanted.

You'll never believe this but her mother was once one of the most beautiful women in Argentina. And Pricilla just like her, has had only to flick her eyelashes and men were grovelling at her feet. Handsome polo players, Italian princes, tycoons. That's why I flew all the way here. I thought, my god, Pricilla must have found the most fantastic man of all time. I even, I must confess on the way, hoped you'd break up or something, so I'd have a chance. Then when, there you were. I could see, that love, is absolutely blind. Sorry if I make you seem like such a disappointment. I don't mean it that way at all. I mean you must have much deeper qualities that aren't apparent. It's not that you're a phoney. O dear. I'm saying too much. Now you're silent. I've hurt your feelings."

"No honey you numbed them a little. It'll be a help when I'm standing in front of a judge in a few hours. But between now and then I hope the fucking christ I hear something from somebody that can make me feel I justify my god damn existence."

"O dear. You're angry."

"Honey I'll tell you one thing that I really am. Right now lying here listening to you. I'm so horny and so dying to fuck you into the next century and centuries beyond, that anything you say only makes me want to fuck you even more."

"O god."

"What's the matter, honey."

"I don't know."

"You want me to get out."

"No."

"What do you want me to do."

"Lock the door."

"No problem."

Schultz twisting the key. Returning to bed. Only slightly spraining one ankle stepping on the one lost shoe. Snaking in between the sheets. Rolling over into the arms of this armful. What a change of scenery grabbing these cornucopious bosoms. Locked sweet and delicious mouth to mouth. Honey this golden knight may not be golden and may not be slaying dragons. But he is going to fuck you with such compassion you didn't know existed. And honey, by the way you're squirming around like a live Prague Christmas carp, you're going to do the same. My god. My Czech grandfather. Thanks for the big prick you bequeathed me. To plant in this joy toy. Who is everything I need at this moment. Her spine bones are just the most perfect keyboard for playing diminuendo crescendo of the nervous chord. Wish I could have seen with my bare eyes the gorgeous arse of this creature. With two handfuls already, my fingers are crying out for an extra helping. Just when I was suddenly feeling like an old dog who is petted no more, mangy and kicked in the teeth, here I am climbing up to go to sleep drowsily on a cloud. After a good fuck first. When ten minutes ago I thought I would have to end up letting my curls and whiskers grow. Go black hatted in a long black coat along a jammed packed Forty Seventh Street. Wearing ten pairs of eye glasses to see gems I'm blinded by all day long. Uncle Werb trying to teach me fucking Yiddish and Czech like my grandfather spoke in Prague. And now Jesus with a nectar flowing cunt, this is suddenly the garden of Eden after Adam and Eve have left. I got to taste this unforbidden fruit. Gripped right around my finger. A fucking miracle down there. Demanding insatiable investigation by all the senses. If only screwing women did not result later in my getting fucked in so many other disastrous ways. Nearly ruining my appetite for evermore. Except wow. To kiss, lips smacking, this real honey. Seeping from soft silky thighs spread wide. Conjuring hope to arise from the forlorn vistas of my life. This sure is an opening night at last. Just like no time is the perfect time for a production. Everytime is the right time to fuck. Keeps me sane in this theatrical life which is too sparsely filled with infrequent peaks of ecstatic joy popping up isolated in a vast sea of tortuous uncertainty. But honey. This is one of the peaks. From which the prick of yours truly will salvo. Into this body you got which ought to go touring on stage in my private life. God, please don't make the show a flop. Let's settle between us for a soft hit. In London anyway, no one will speak to you if you're too successful. In New York no one will speak to you if you're not. Honey you cunt. You

miraculous cunt. You love it. Don't you. Heaving in rapture. The
state of unhappiness can become so familiar that you don't dare
embrace any moments of delight. Then you fucking well dare.
Holy shit she fucks like a horse cantering on her pampas. Who
designed her. To sprout out of those vast treeless plains. That was
the only thing I ever learned about Argentina in high school. And
honey since you come off those grasslands. I'm going there in a
hurry for further education. Showbizz makes you when you're
happy very happy. And when you're sad you're suicidal. But this
is catapulting straight into heaven in one nice easy plunge. The
wealthiest guys in the world say that no matter how rich you get,
you've got only one mouth to fill and one asshole to empty. But
what they forgot to say is that Jesus you can have more than one
cunt to eat. This is it. What women are really good for. To transport you in two seconds. On their soothing bed of flesh. From a
bed of deep piercing cold nails. Into a whole new world of perfect
comfort. Holy mackerel. She's pulling me off by the hair. Away
from her delicious pulsating snatch. Jesus don't moan fuck me so
loud. And honey don't rush me. In a ten second count down I'm
going to slam it in all way to the moon. Kiss me goodbye. Kiss me
hello when we both weightless get there. Momma meeo. Her
teeth sinking sucking in my neck. The green green eyes you got I
kept looking at when I was undertaken to the Savoy for the post
funeral celebration after the disaster of my wedding. This is the
first thing good now that's come out of it. With your hand around
my balls. Tugging and squeezing away. And you'll get every
ounce, honey. You firecracker. You just explode my amazement.
Maybe my indelible motto I was for a second thinking of abandoning, should remain absolutely the same. Don't waste time with
women you're not fucking. Unless later that was exactly what all
the wasted time was for in the beginning. Honey don't squeeze
and pull too hard. They'll hear my balls ringing. With the bitch
down there who eats like a cement mixer listening. Uncle Werb
says there are over two thousand categories of diamonds. And for
him I've got news. Uncle Werb believe me when I tell you, there
are twice as many categories of cunts. And my prick is in one of

the most delightful examples. Which Jesus is now going to make me come like Niagara Falls after a deluge. Momma meeo. Something fatal is happening. I'm coming. All over the world. How am I honey, ever ever going to do without you. After this I could happily drift into senile paralysed old age like Al. Who should at his time of life be leaving young girls to the young guys like me. To screw without having a heart valve blow out. Like I think mine nearly just did.

Schultz reaching up a hand to feel if the top of his head was still on and to brush back Agnes's silkily soft hair stuck in the beads of perspiration of his brow. Sounds out on the London night. And all's quiet on the Arabesque front. Agnes half an inch away. Nice fresh air coming in the window from the back garden. Big Ben tolling a quarter to five. Holy Jesus I must have for a minute fell asleep. In a dream I was on my way from Woonsocket to Boston on the train. Lost my luggage. In the big shadowy gloomy station. Then found myself not knowing where to go out in the twisted streets. Kept asking everybody directions to the Ritz Carlton Hotel. They kept saying you go left, you go right, then through a door of an old office building and down a long tiled hall. And out another door. I'd get there. End up standing around hearing doors slamming. And ask and get the same direction from somebody else all over again. I kept saying it's by the Public Gardens. And Agnes suddenly was there, magically opening up every orifice. And Jesus I found my way. Right up into a Ritz bedroom having sausages and buckwheat cakes drowned in maple syrup. Blueberry muffins and melted butter. And quaffing coffee. Reading the newspapers. Watching the television. Happy on top of the world.

"You've got to get out of here."

"Holy cow take it easy, don't push."

"I thought I heard a sound."

"Could be a cat in the garden."

"I've just betrayed my best friend."

"No you didn't honey, you just did her a big favour."

"I'm in her house. Her guest."

"You're in my house. You're my guest too honey."

"You sound like a cat who just got the cream."

"Honey you just saved my life."

"That's nice for you. But I'm not in the life saving business. O dear, what's that."

"Nothing honey."

"It is. Someone's coming up the stairs."

"Holy shit, there is. Agnes don't panic, door's locked."

"O god what are we going to do."

"Lie low. I'll get under the bed just in case."

"Get your clothes."

"No problem. Holy shit. What am I saying again. It could be some problem."

"Shush."

Schultz on hands and knees, grabbing around on the floor in the dark. Dragging his clothes after him squeezing face up in under the bed. A creak of floor boards in the hall. A long long listening silence. Another creak. And a knock on the door.

"Agnes. Are you alright in there."

"Yes."

"Are you sure. My mother thought she heard someone screaming."

"I had a bad dream. I'm alright now."

"Can I come in."

"The door's locked."

"Why have you locked it."

"I just locked it. I always lock my door in a big city."

"I do think you had better let me in. Open the door. Please. Oh the door is open. I thought you said it was locked."

Schultz squirming further under the bed. Holy jeeze, how the fuck did that happen. Too much on my mind for too long and mistakes are happening all over the fucking place. They teach you day and night in the Coast Guard. Check and then double check everything. Now with the way my life has become, if I don't fall head first downstairs, I leave doors open, my fly open, and even my prick out. Which would you believe it, is at this moment pushing a hole up into the bedsprings.

A candle glow coming into the room. Followed by Pricilla. In a purple satin nightdress, with transparent crimson lace over the bosoms guaranteed to turn tired husbands on fire.

"Now are you sure you're alright Agnes."

Agnes shifting down in the bed. Schultz pulling his armful of clothes in tight around him. Foot entangled around the lamp cord. Holy Jesus christ. There's a break in my favour. No electricity to electrocute me. One more inch lower and I could never even with my prick bent back double, fit under this fucking thing in the first place. Look at the bitch. The hem of a brand new purple fucking outfit to go to bed in. And she's wearing my god damn hand sewn custom made slippers. If my heart pounds any louder she'll hear it. Come on Agnes. Time to be as cool as a cucumber in the September rain. Keep up the performance. Act like you were masturbating and blew your lid in a paroxysm. Don't give the game away with nervousness. Like I'm beginning to do with hysteria. Jesus this is just like once instead of hiding under it, I had to lie in full view in the bed. With a Mafia gunman four feet away pointing a god damn Smith and Wesson thirty eight calibre revolver right at me between the eyes. When I had two minutes before been forty two miles up his luscious chorus girl mistress fucking the tits off her all afternoon. When the banging on the door came just as I was banging her for the seventh ecstatic but unlucky time. Her jaw dropped and her eyes nearly fell out while she nearly ripped my prick off jumping into a kimono. The guy was hammering the apartment door down while I said should I hide under the bed. She said no. He'll kill you soon as he finds you there. Just go to sleep and look like you got pneumonia. I'll tell him you're my nephew from Albany who's visiting town and got sick. I got sick in a second like I had malaria, double pneumonia, clap and leprosy. The fever I threw made me so red all over the face I nearly exploded. Like I thought the end of the revolver barrel was going to do any second. With his bodyguard just behind him, he kept standing there. In a black fedora, chesterfield overcoat and black skin tight gloves. Holding the gun on me. Looking. Saying. If this fucking kid's been up to any monkey business I'll blow first his head away and then yours. She kept saying can't you see he's just an innocent kid Al. Imagine this gangster called Al. He was also called hairy ape because he didn't have a hair on his body. Never before did I try to look so young, innocent and vulnerable. Only time I ever truly changed character in my life. It was a tour de force. Even to fluttering my eyelids to look effeminate. So help me fucking god I swear that was what must have convinced him. I was a pansy. He locked the bedroom door. As he was leaving he socked her breaking her nose. Shoved his knee in her stomach and made her vomit. Then threw her crashing back through the bedroom door where I was to my own astonishment getting up to protect her. Fortunately he was gone. And holy shit I left this god damn bedroom door open. But Jesus instead of Pricilla, give me the Mafia anytime. She could be giving evidence against me this morning in Court. Christ I already hear her sniffing.

"Agnes. I smell something, like tomcat or something."

"I don't smell anything."

"Well I do."

"A cat might have got in during the night. In the window."

"How could a cat climb up three floors up the side of the building."

"The drain pipe."

"What's this."

"What's what."

"This Agnes."

"That."

"Yes."

"I don't think it's anything is it."

"It's a man's sock. And this is a shoe. I think I am entitled to an explanation. Well."

"Honestly, really honestly, Pricilla, I just woke up."

Holy Jesus, my whole life is passing in front of my eyes, come on honey make it sound more convincing. Or else this could be the third situation of major mayhem in this house. Just like the psalm singing girl I invited in off the street. There she was playing in the band, pink skinned wearing glasses early one Sunday morning. In her little dark green straw bonnet with its big bow. Singing that old rugged cross. Coloured ribbons on her tambourine. Watching her through the curtain, every time she opened her mouth I wanted to shove my prick between her beautiful teeth. Then shit ten minutes later when I thought they were gone, the bell rang. And there she was standing in front of me at the door collecting donations. I said step in. Don't mind my kimono. A big flower on her collar and purple epaulettes. After giving her two ten shilling notes one after the other I listened for five minutes to her shit trying to convert me. Praise my soul the king of heaven. She made her decision to consecrate herself. To god who is wonderful. I have promised to serve him to the end. Under my breath I said for Jesus' sake honey serve me a piece of ass. She said she'd found peace. Plus plenty tranquility and rich fellowship through the blessing of the Lord Jesus Christ. Jesus I don't know how I did it. And I don't think she knew what I was doing. But I said take my mace, honey. In the name of the father, the son and the holy ghost. I had her on her back, drawers down, green dress up, legs open fucking her right there on the carpet downstairs in the front hall. With her tambourine and collecting tin lying next to her. When a bunch of the fucking rest of the choir came all at once looking for her right to my door. Jesus what a battle that was. In and out the hall, up and down on my stoop. In the middle of screwing she said divine and human nature is combined in god, the governor of all things. Blood and fire she said. Crossed swords. Snakes around our cross. Every word she said, now I believe. And only hope her religion will forgive me.

"Where is he."

"Where's who."

"My husband, this is his shoe."

"How can you be sure, Pricilla."

"It's his shoe. That's how I can be sure."

"Honestly I don't know where your husband is Pricilla. It must have just got left here somehow."

"That's not all that's just got left here. His smell is here. The smell of his sperm."

"That's the candle you're smelling."

"This is a beeswax candle. I know what my husband's sperm smells like."

"Well I'm sure that you do, Pricilla. But I don't. And I wouldn't want to know. Please Pricilla, can't you just go back to bed. You're making a mountain out of a mole hill."

"Don't tell me what to do in my house."

"Pricilla, god, I'm not telling you."

"And what's this. Over here. Look at this. This is his tie, he wore tonight to the opening."

"It couldn't be. It's my boyfriend's."

"You liar you came here to escape your boyfriend. And I let you into my house. This is his tie clip. Initials S.F.S. Is this your boyfriend's. Is it. You fucking betraying treacherous bitch."

Pricilla rushing forward. The candle on the dresser toppling over and falling to the floor. Two bodies bouncing on the mattress over Schultz's head. Screams and scratching. Holy jeeze. Here we go folks. I wish the fuck this didn't have to happen. Thank god the candles just gone out. With what's going to happen now, any darkness is merciful.

"I'll kill you, you slut."

"Get off me."

"I'll kill you."

Dust and debris dropping down into Schultz's face. Jeeze. I'm choked. This fucking house. I once called a home. I lived in decently and civilized as a respectable occupant once. Holy god. Pricilla's going to ruin that beautiful piece of ass. Christ, who knows maybe this should be flattering to my ego.

"I'll tear your tits off you cunt. You cunt."

Schultz pulled his shirt over his face as more dust puffed down. They're murdering each other. Fond du mots. Grunting, thumping, screaming and groaning. Am I a dumb bastard. Momma meeo. What a dumb bastard I am. What the fuck is it I can't do things in the right sequence. If ever guidance and flexuosity was needed in my life, it's now. Greta and Roxana's fight turned into the greatest bout of screwing. But these two are never ever going to love each other again.

"Pricilla, stop, stop. O god. My face. My face."

"Teach you a lesson you dirty slut."

Grunts, groans, and curses turning to choking croaks. O Jesus one of them is giving out last gasps. Somebody's hands are around somebody's throat. Got to make an appearance now. Even stark fucking naked. To save lives. God gives me for every little sprinkle of pleasure, a deluge of horror. Never did I know how well off I was two hours ago behind bars in jail.

Schultz squirming out. Crawling on hands and knees, entangled in a piece of underwear torn pulling it on. An arm through where it should have been a leg. And a leg wound in the lamp cord. A crash of white pottery. There goes another light out forever. Just rip everything off. Jesus where am I. I've been hit already. I wish I was miles away.

"There he is you bitch, the fucking bastard. Hiding under the bed. You hussy."

Pricilla kneeling astride Agnes. Her hand pressed down squeezed around her throat. Holy shit, got to hold this tiger. Who came into my life like she wouldn't hurt a moth.

"Let go of her. You're killing her. Let go for christ's sake."

"Shut up you."

Schultz tearing at the fingers. Shit suddenly she's got the fucking strength of a stevedore. When at any other time she could have fainted, now she's wide awake alive like a maniac. When here's something for her to faint about. When it would make everybody happy. Instead she erupts like an insane volcano.

"You're killing her for christ's sake. Let go."

Schultz hauling back and releasing a left hook slapping Pricilla's jaw. Holy jeeze. Like hitting fucking granite wall all of a sudden. Hey what's this.

Light coming in the door. O no. Please Jesus. Not that. Not the

318

fucking walrus behemoth whale. Tits heaving like ocean waves. Three candles blazing on her ice breaking bow.

"What's going on in here."

Mrs. Prune in a black satin nightdress pushing her plate of candles on the dresser. Three flames flickering in the mirror. Shadows on the wall. The imitation crystal ceiling chandelier tinkling as the weight of the behemoth vibrated the floor and window panes.

"It's you again. Striking my daughter. You beast. Being arrested doesn't teach you a lesson."

"Fuck you madam, there's a killing going on here."

"I'll kill you, that's who I'll kill."

"Get your fucking fat hands off me, you tub of lard."

Mrs. Prune pounding forward. Her arms grabbing around the stark naked Schultz. As his one free hand grabbed out clutching at her hair. Which holy shit. No. My god. The whole fucking thing is coming off her completely bald head. This is the end of my life. If only I could get to the window to jump. Like her husband did. Out away from this Arab Israeli war to end all wars.

"Give me back my hair."

"Let fucking go of me."

Schultz shaking loose. Pricilla arms flailing. Agnes, arms up shielding her face, still gasping for air. Schultz throwing punches. Landing sinking in these bottomless bosoms. O god. I can't look. The sight makes me sick. She looks like a man. Except for her mountainous tits. Fucking hell the behemoth is going to hit me with the rest of the broken lamp.

"Put that down you bitch."

"My daughter. You're trying to make her miscarry."

"Shit, stop, stop everybody."

"Look at you. Look at you. Disgusting pervert. With your penis erected. I'm going to smash that prick and balls with this lamp."

The bald headed behemoth stalking him. Schultz circling backing away. Sounds of sobbing. Agnes hands up to her face. Pricilla at the bedside, fists clenched, snarling down.

"That's what you deserve you sneaky slut."

319

"You've hurt me, my neck, you've hurt me."

"Next time it will be your brains I'll knock out. And you get out of this house. And I never want to set eyes on or speak to you again. Who do you think you are."

"I am your best friend. He came in. He had nowhere to go."

"Except up you, is that right."

"No no. Nothing. Not a thing happened. He said he was cold and hungry."

"For a piece of ass as he always is."

"We did nothing. And you've scratched my face."

"I smell his sperm."

"Please, Pricilla. Leave me alone. Leave me alone."

Schultz cornered between the dresser and the window. One of the landlords ersatz antique chairs held legs up jabbing at Mrs. Prune. By the dawn's early light. Cold draught of air on my arse. The behemoth standing, her eyes wide eyed. Staring transfixed. Catching her breath. Holy Jesus the most horrible obscene sight of my existence. They say you get a hard on at a hanging. She's mesmerized. Can't take her eyes off it. Give it a twitch. For once in my life my stiff prick is saving me from a broken arse. With an erection you could use as a high diving board. Giving such signals. And making in this situation my prick go wagging up and down pointing at the bald behemoth. Still got her jet black wig in my hand. Just watch me. I'm going to god damn well put it on. Top of my head.

And go
Fucking
Gay

25

DING a ling a ling. Jesus what's that. Ringing. I fell asleep again. Dreaming I was walking bare arsed across the desert in the setting sun towards the Grand Canyon. Dragging tattered clothes behind me. Mumbling to myself that the only thing left to do was die and forget. Then suddenly I'm running. When who should come chasing two miles behind me. His stiff prick out two miles six inches long. Nudging me in the ass. Fucking Herbie. Sylvia's twat was the canyon ahead. No escaping nightmares. Break my arm reaching for this telephone.

"Hello."

"So that's where you are."

"Where am I. Who's this."

"This is Al. So now you're at the Dorchester."

"Holy Jesus Al, I've had a night."

"You're telling me you had a night. Other people had one too."

"Al what time is it."

"Don't ask me the time. My god you're a skunk."

"Al I had to check into this place at five a.m. with a shoe and sock missing off one foot. Shirt torn."

"So what's new about that. Last time I heard you were there wearing the vertical half of a morning suit and jamming up the doors of the hotel with the other half."

"Holy christ Al. Be a friend for a second. What time is it. I got to be in Court this morning and I lost my watch and I can't turn my neck to look at the clock on the wall because I was nearly strangled last night."

"Tell me if it is correct that you're married already."

"Yes Al it's correct. Unfortunately."

"So I'm asking you just one question. I want to know why do you do it. Why."

"Why do I do what, Al."

"Try to fuck every woman you come across."

"The production's at stake. And you ask that."

"Yes, why. I want to know why."

"Al. When I tell you, you're not going to believe me."

"You just tell me that's all."

"I'm looking for true love, Al."

Schultz holding the telephone to his ear with his shoulder. Reaching for a glass of water. Ferrying it up from the bedside table. Silence and breathing the other end of the line. Jesus Al mustn't have been ready for that one. So convinced is he that there are no finer feelings in me.

"Hello, Al. You still there."

"I'm still here."

"Well Al, that's why I have to fuck all these women."

"Jesus, you would even demean love, wouldn't you."

"Shit Al, I mean it. I'm looking for a girl I can love."

"You don't know what love is. You know what rape is. That's what you know. Like you did last night. Is that how you look for love."

"Al. Rape. Who did I rape now. Who."

"You raped Agnes. Then attempted rape on Pricilla's mother."

322

"Raped Agnes. Holy shit. Fuck a duck. Now look what you made me do. Spill my fucking water all over me in bed."

"Good."

"Al I already got to go to Court. In a borrowed pair of shoes and socks from the hotel. Don't abuse me this time of the day. I've got to be at action stations over the show. Have you seen the reviews. Can you imagine what my life's been like I haven't even seen them yet."

"Yeah I saw. They stink."

"Holy shit. All of them."

"Every one but two. One written by an imbecile. And the other by a guy thought he was writing about some other show."

"Al, I'll ring you back. I got to take an awful crap."

"You crap. That's all you're good for. Don't bother to call me back. Because this is just to say on behalf of your investors to close the show immediately and cut losses."

"The investors can go fuck themselves Al. I'll close when I decide to close."

"That's exactly the constant kind of irresponsible stupid behaviour I've come to expect from you."

"O come on, Al. Do you always have to be like the way you always are. It's only a little more money we could lose."

"It's not your money you're losing."

"Al don't be a geriatric grandmother. What are you going to do leave me friendless now."

"You son of a bitch. Pricilla's mother is under intensive psychiatric care as a result of you. You pulled her wig off. Traumatized her."

"Please don't make me feel sick Al. Please. Not before I even have breakfast with the waiter knocking at the door this second. Come in. How was I to know she had a wig jumping out of the dark at me in my own fucking house which is now like a circus where I live that I have to move into a hotel."

"You tried to rape her too. Your own mother in law and right in front of your wife."

"Al. Are you crazy. Touch that hell hag ogre. I couldn't under pain of death put my prick in that. I'd rather put it in a mincer. You just don't understand."

"I understand. After you pulled her wig off you charged at her with your upraised prick. Which plus your balls should be put into a mincer."

"Waiter just push the table between the beds. That's fine. Thank's a lot. O.K. Al. Please. Listen a second. I didn't charge anybody. I admit I had a giant hard on. I don't know all there is to know about physiology. But I think it was petrified fear that gave the erection."

"A female bee flying by would give you an erection."

"Hey will you listen Al. I'm telling you I was as surprised as anybody when I saw it myself believe me. It was some kind of involuntary medical aberration."

"It was your crazed sexual appetite. Which needs compulsory medical treatment. Meanwhile you should be committed to a zoo."

"Al goodbye. I love you. But I just don't have time this moment to submit to your usual avalanche of criticism. I'll talk to you later."

Schultz shaved, showered and dressed. Waiting in the cloistered peace of the hall landing and looking out this window down on to a little roof garden below planted with blossomed flowers between the white wings of this soul soothing hotel. The elevator door opening. A slender perfumed lady inside with an alligator bag. Beige tweed suit. Blond soft hair. Jesus she could be a grandmother. But I'd go to bed with her at the drop of her big ochre felt hat. If only I had a few more hours' sleep and didn't nearly get killed, maimed and driven out of my own fucking house last night. Christ the show. O my god. Just opened. Meanwhile a lifetime of horror has happened since. Got to keep the show going. Fuck all the dumbbell critics. Paper the house every night to capacity. Supply transport and give free tickets to mental institutions all over Balham, Tooting and Streatham if necessary. This lady looks like the sort who'd still say yes to a thrill in her life.

"Excuse me madam. But do you like attending the theatre."

"I beg your pardon."

"Would you like to see a wonderful show I recommend. Kiss it. Don't hold it. It's too hot. Free with my compliments."

"How dare you."

"Holy christ madam, don't get excited, it's really the name of the show, ask the concierge in the lobby. I'm sorry please. Here's the ground floor."

The morning sunny and cool. Schultz jumping into a taxi with a smiling salute from the doorman. Down Park Lane and left along Piccadilly. O my god. Thank god for the discretion they got at that hotel. I go in and out looking like I come from a holocaust. And they keep showering me with courteous attention. I'm going to need it. Standing up in Court. With drunks and thieves. Haven't even returned the morning suit that got ripped to pieces off my back.

Schultz pacing the floor in the smoky noisy Court corridor. Amid the solicitors, clients and culprits. As what fucking choice do I have. But to listen to the advice of these detectives.

"Sir you can get it all over with now. By pleading guilty. And avoid a big Court case later."

Schultz in the dock. The distinguished judge, the son of a famous actor staring down over his spectacles. Frowning slightly as the evidence was read. Clearing his throat in some disbelief. Then with a deep breath looking leniently upon Schultz. As Mrs. Prune stood giving her heated evidence.

"But were you there madam."

"He struck my daughter. I came here to Court by ambulance from under psychiatric care."

"But were you present madam when your daughter was struck."

"I was there when that bastard pulled my wig off."

The judge pushing up his spectacles looking at the charge sheet. Lifting his chin to look out across the courtroom as the behemoth got up as if she were heading to Ascot.

325

"But that's not what Mr. Schultz is charged with. Please stand down madam if you weren't a witness to the charge. Now Mr. Schultz. I'm quite sure a man in your position momentarily lost control. So I'm not going to have you bound over to keep the peace. Fined ten pounds."

Schultz nearly saluting from the dock. This pleasantly commanding figure calling for the next case. As Schultz ducking away, now ran rushing out into Bow Street and diving into a taxi. My god all this happening right across the road from the Royal Opera House where tonight they're performing the ballet.

"Taxi. Stop. I'll only be a second."

Schultz emerging from the Opera House with tickets. Popped back in the taxi catching his breath. Till he charged in the door and along the shadowy hall of this familiar office of Sperm Productions. The door opened into the smoky chairman's office. Rebecca cutting out reviews from a stack of newspapers. Binky with a cigar held out in one hand and pressing down with the other a whole page spread of newsprint. A massive picture of Magillacurdy and the Debutant.

"Ah my dear Schultz, you have arrived."

"Yeah I have arrived. I want to see these reviews. Where's his Lordship."

"His Royal Grace Schultz is in his knickerbockers as you Americans risqué́ly call them, and is I believe with the little wife going for a tramp up in his heather."

"Holy shit. He should be here."

"Ah. But we have chatted. At length. By telephone. And decided on the proper course. Be seated, Schultz. While we map out the funeral route. Pop right down there then on our trustworthy chaise longue."

"I'm standing. And what the fuck do you mean funeral."

"Pray tell, these, Schultz, the orations. Here for all to see. And this. Especially this. Perhaps the most devastating review ever written about any show in the history of London theatre. Headlined across three columns. Take a look yourself."

MISS IT, DON'T SEE IT, IT'S TOO AWFUL

Last night saw what this reviewer must regard as the greatest
load of rubbish ever disported on a London stage. In attending the opening of a show entitled "Kiss It, Don't Hold It, It's
Too Hot," one was of course forewarned. But the ensuing
pyrotechnics consisting of lyrics grossly insulting to the in-
telligence, music so vulgar and brash crashing upon the ears,
plus garish costuming and sets, the latter which trembled or
ripped at a breath, made for an evening of headache inspiring proportions.

The chorus were frequently off key singing, as they were
out of step dancing and who, en masse, seem to have been
rounded up from some housewifely amateur group from Sid-
cup or Surbiton. However, they did at least, by their appalling display, help distract from other terrible matters. Only
that a member of the audience became stuck in her seat
which gave one the release of laughter at the intervals made
the evening tolerable. It was little wonder that one noticed a
player's name changed and the director's name blacked out in
the program.

However there was one exception, embodied in the two
star players, who handled such horror with grace, dignity and
poise. Genius is a word one uses sparingly but it would have
to be applied in the case of Mr. Magillacurdy whose powerful
yet sweet voice charmed and at times profoundly awed and
moved his listeners. The rendering of his final aria was a
tour de force. And indeed this hardened reviewer admits to a
tear in the eye and a lump in the throat. He and his spectacularly beautiful co star, whose shimmering, exquisite balletic
limbs and dulcet voice equally captivated the audience, did by
their performances redeem what would have been an otherwise theatrically totally ruinous event.

To those of you who are still reading this, unless you feel
you want to witness a little stage history being made by the

debut of two young splendidly promising stars, my advice is a repeat of my sentiments heading this column. Miss It, Don't See It, It's Too Awful.

"Well Schultz. The other reviews are no better. No clearer case has there ever been for one to throw in the towel. Wipe our hands clean of the embarrassing matter. His Royal Grace on the phone, agrees."

Schultz with a left hand holding up the newspaper suddenly sending his fist whistling through the air and crashing through the review like a pane of glass.

"My goodness Schultz whatever did you do that for to a perfectly good newspaper."

"Because never never is that show going to close. Over my dead body."

"I do believe his Royal Grace can find room for you in one of his cemeteries Schultz. Even in those most strange shoes. A grace and favour grave so to speak. And as a respected director of this firm, Sperm Productions will gladly accord you a most dignified funeral and foot the bill."

Schultz pacing the floor shaking a clenched fist up and down. Rebecca leaving the room with a folder full of clippings instructed to check on the stars to see if there were any suicides. Schultz suddenly tripping on the carpet. An instant smile on Binky's face. Schultz turning and leaning forward over the chairman's desk.

"I don't give a shit what the reviewers say. I'm going to beat the fuckers. That show has got balls."

"Dear me Schultz you are in a tizzy."

"That's right."

"Well in spite of such testicular hope Schultz, the box office phones have been practically dead all morning. There is simply no advance booking. The reviews are unanimous that the show is atrocious. That little newspaper you've just put your fist through is read by about five million people."

"I don't care how many read it. They can wipe their asses with it, piss in it, but that show stays on."

"And Schultz we understand from Mr. Gayboy, to whom I must confess I sold half my share of the show, that you could have sold the whole production to one of Broadway's biggest producers last night where it would be ensured to find a suitably gauche audience."

"That's right."

"And you didn't."

"That's right."

"You didn't even entertain the thought."

"No I didn't Binky."

"Ah because you thought it would be so nice to keep your sterling reputation intact as a producer of resounding flops in which you have consistently guaranteed that the entire investment is always lost."

"Fuck you Binky. You thought even before it opened it was going to be a flop. Selling half your share. Well I'm not selling anything and I'm not closing this show."

Rebecca quietly stepping in. Solemn faced whispering to Schultz that Magillacurdy was not at Claridge's all last night. And handing over the afternoon editions of the evening newspapers. Two more panning reviews. A headline next to one of them.

SOCK HER DON'T KISS HER SHE'S YOUR WIFE

Sigmund Franz Schultz the impresario, and producer of "Kiss It, Don't Hold It, It's Too Hot," was fined ten pounds this morning at Bow Street Magistrates Court for causing actual bodily harm to his wife whom he punched following last night's performance at the Regent Theatre.

"O dear Schultz, here we go again. Same old headline. Sperm Productions, that innocent company dragged yet again into another Schultz intempestivity. With Gayboy already in a state. Raging that the show is giving the theatre such a bad name that it could ruin business for years to come. And dear me this little news item will promptly blow his hemorrhoids clean out of his backside. Forgive me Rebecca."

329

"Bullshit. That's a fucking headline everybody's going to read. Mentioning the show, the theatre. I know in my bones this fucking thing is going to work. Shit, months, months of my life are not going to be buried suddenly by a fucking bunch of nincompoops who don't know their ass from their elbows. You heard the laughing and cheering."

"Yes I did Schultz. Under the booing and jeering. But most distinctly of all I recognised your clapping. Or were you applauding your rather large incarcerated mother in law."

"Binky that audience for real were being genuinely entertained. Three quarters of them loved it."

"Ah Schultz permit me, to leaven your heartfelt words with those of sobriety. I have not yet had his Royal Grace check with his laser beam financial eye all the figures but having myself peeked under items marked hotels, lodgings, transport and especially items miscellaneous, I would say you have the overcall already spent. And my dear young man does it not occur to you that you may live to fight another day. That this is just another little flop that people will quite quickly forget in three or four years. But to persist in the present agony is only merely prolonging the future ignominy."

Schultz taking up the torn newspaper from the floor. Hold up the perforated review. Piecing it together.

"Rebecca, you read what that fucking critic said. Well let me quote to both of you. Genius. Shimmering grace. Spectacularly beautiful. Captivated the audience. Stage history being made. Those fucking words are going to be emblazoned all over this town. And give me a cigar Binky."

"Schultz have you no ethics. You can't possibly print what you've just blatantly quoted entirely out of context."

"Can't I, just watch me. These fucking critics have such egos trying to bust out of their half assed guts that when that son of a sour bitch sees his name plastered all over he won't even murmur a sigh of protest. Rebecca."

"Yes Mr. Schultz."

"Take this down. A tour de force. Vulgar, brash, garish, grossly insulting, and stage history is being made. Genius is a word one uses sparingly but it would have to be applied in the case of Mr. Magillacurdy and his stunning co star whose shimmering, exquisite balletic beauty captivated the audience. See it, don't miss it, it's too wonderful. Got that Rebecca."

"Yes Mr. Schultz."

"O.K. Rebecca put it into respectable grammatical order and slam all that into the classified ads. Use caps on the see it, don't miss it, it's too wonderful. And I want big spreads in the Sunday papers using the same thing under the picture of the two stars. And Rebecca on that phone get me this Knightsbridge number."

"Ah my dear Schultz sometimes I do really detect a flavour of the naval man in you, albeit one, who has cast his moral principles overboard."

"That's right. Just excuse me a second. Hello. Hey. Hi. It's me. Sigmund Schultz. Yeah Sigmund Franz Schultz. Come to the ballet tonight. You got to. Why not. That's no reason. This is life and death O.K. I'll pick you up at seven. See you."

"Schultz I couldn't help overhearing. The ballet."

"That's right. Taking a box at Covent Garden. Just for one evening to catch my breath. To put some grace and beauty back into my life."

"Schultz. I'm impressed with you. Yes. Very much so. You are truly remarkable. You're not with your tail anywhere near between your legs. I think perhaps I may even decide to lose my shirt with yours."

"You mean half your shirt."

"Ah yes, half. But old Gayboy will only be too relieved to sell back his share. Dear me in a business which is nothing but risk, I don't know why I'm so cautious sometimes. You know many foolish and misguided things happen in the name of friendship. And when one has assumed the responsible position of Chairman as I have, there are times when one must take decisions on an empirical rather than emotional basis. It was from a very skinflint ancestor that I've inherited what may be thought by some to be an unflattering tendency to, how does one put it, to hedge one's bets."

"You're a shrewd hard cunning son of a bitch Binky."

"Thank you Schultz, thank you. But at least you've found in me, at this moment, a trusted ally."

"Christ that's the last thing I need now is people I can trust. Because from now on, nobody, including you is to be trusted."

"Ah that's a bit of a blow to one's team spirit Schultz. Is not even his Royal Grace to be trusted."

"Well I might trust him. I must confess he owns so fucking much of this world that all he has to do is look out for crooks."

Schultz brushing down his clothes. Straightening his borrowed tie. The phone ringing. Binky picking it up. Putting his hand over the speaker.

"Now Schultz, this is an historic moment. The first phone call of the afternoon. Sperm Productions here. Ah how rude but nice of you to say so, Mr. Magillacurdy. Your embattled producer is right here and I shall put you on to him. Schultz."

Schultz, both hands raised outstretched in a flying leap across the floor grabbing the phone.

"Hello."

"It's Magillacurdy me boyo."

"Christ Magillacurdy where are you. I've just been having heart attacks. They said you weren't in last night at Claridge's. Where were you."

"I'm at Claridge's now me boyo."

"Where were you all last night."

"Ah me boyo. It was a vow I made one awful desperate night in despair. A vow that had to be kept. I promised the poor fucker resting in peace next to me whose mausoleum I was squatting in that I'd be back sleeping next to him if ever I opened on a West End stage."

"Jesus Terence, you could get fucking pneumonia doing that."

"Ah now me boyo, you don't think I'd abandon me old pal laid in rest back in Brompton Cemetery. I slept alongside of all these months chatting to just because I was a West End sensation. Now what kind of thankless indifferent behaviour would that be now."

"Jesus just promise me Magillacurdy, you won't do such things without warning me. And I could heat the place for you."

"Ah a bit of hardship harms no one. But I see we've been slated in the press. Rumors abound the show is closing."

"Nothing is fucking closing. And that's from the horse's mouth."

"Ah glad to hear it. Just give me my cues and a soapbox and I'll perform on stage or off stage. I'll sing this show on top of a fragment of Nelson's Pillar that they blew down in Dublin if necessary."

"Jesus Magillacurdy at last."

"What do you mean at last."

"At last there's someone with some fucking guts who doesn't have to be persuaded to fight alongside me."

"I'll fight beside you and break any arse of any man who opposes us."

"Just keep breaking the hearts of all the women, that's all I ask."

"Well said me darling boyo. Depend on me."

"I am depending on you Terence. To save the goose that lays the golden eggs."

"Ah me boyo, be careful. Kicking the shit out of the goose that lays the golden egg is a great Irish custom. Goodbye now. And good luck."

Schultz putting down the phone. And a hand up to his brow. Shaking his head. Shaking his shoulders. Clenching his hands and firing his fists around him shadow boxing in the smoky air.

"Ah well Schultz, the enemy is engaged. I suppose it behooves one to see in your fighting spirit a cause for optimism, however one must in caution also remain amply armed with pessimism. But there is yet another slight little matter. Over which I regret to say his Royal Grace is alarmed."

"Holy jeeze what did I do now."

"Schultz you wrote an anti blood sports letter to the Times newspaper."

333

"Christ I clean forgot. Hey, they printed it. That's great."

"They did Schultz. And as it happens, his Royal Grace being a well known Master of Foxhounds. And does not think it's great."

"Shit it was you you son of a bitch who told me to write it for christ's sake."

"My dear, it was suggested in the most jokingly off handed manner to divert you amusingly for a moment."

"I really enjoyed writing that letter. Why the fuck do people want to go killing poor foxes for. But meanwhile. I'm getting the fuck out of here. Before you start dragging me out into the philosophical depths again."

Schultz in the hall pecking Rebecca on the cheek. Down in the street heading towards the theatre. Stopping nearby on the corner. The lobby lit and empty. Jesus business looks bad. Just a woman coming along. Good. She's slowing. Come on, stop. Look at the posters. Shit she is. Good. Turn in you bitch. Christ. That's it. She's going in. A customer. Hope yet.

Schultz entering the theatre. Crossing the luxurious cozy lobby. Approaching the pleasant grey haired lady in the box office.

"Hey. Hi."

"Good evening Mr. Schultz."

"Hey what happened to that woman did she buy a ticket."

"No sir. She's the manageress of the stall bar."

"Holy jeeze."

"Booking sir, has increased a tiny bit since the afternoon papers have come out. But I'm afraid it's been an awfully slow morning."

"How about tonight."

"We'll be lucky if we're a fifth full. Business could improve at the doors later. But it's not going to be a good week sir."

Schultz stopping into his favourite amusement emporium. Shoving sixpences in the pinball machine. Warming up and winning free games. Then racking up one record score after another. A group gathered to watch this master at work. With his delicate tilting, bumping and massé shots. Only thing left besides fucking I'm really good at.

Schultz walking back through Mayfair to the Dorchester along

Curzon Street. Heading past a hairdresser's, book shop, wine merchant. If I have a future left, I could get a flat around here. Everything one needs. Even a good selection of whores. Patrolling on this moist pavement. Jesus I got to start fucking them. So much cheaper than ruining my life screwing women that make you pay not only with all your assets but with blood.

Schultz passing some black railings. Fronting a velvet green lawn spreading towards a gleaming cream town house. A drunken gent swaying on the sidewalk ahead. Blocking Schultz with his upraised arm.

"Ah now sir, have you the right time."

"Sorry I've lost my watch."

"Ah you've lost the time. Lost it. Ah but I can see you can afford it. And now what a time it is for me to be wasting your time when you don't be having the time. It's light enough to carry if you only want to know what time it is. But believe me it's an awful weight when it accumulates. Ah Jesus the weight of time."

"Here, here's a couple of tickets to the theatre tonight."

"Ah well now imagine, manna falls into me hand when least you'd expect. Would you have a price of a drink for the interval."

"Sure. Here."

"You're a gentleman, a gentleman."

"Promise to clap your head off at the final curtain. Cheer. Do anything that sounds like you enjoyed it."

"Ah I'll do that. Be glad to. They'll be bravos. Now pray tell me who have I the privilege of talking to. Are you yourself by any chance a man of the theatre."

"You might say that."

"Well I'm a man of erudition. But latterly of the streets. And a bridge player of championship standards. Down a little bit on me luck at the moment. But I was a great man for attending the theatre in me day."

"Come see me at this address tomorrow. I might have a job for you."

"Ah I'm not a great man for working. But if you have something to challenge the intellect I'm your man."

Schultz opening the door into the quiet peace of his suite. Turn on a lamp. Ring room service for tea. Get a wake up call in three hours. Throw myself on this bed. Toes of my borrowed shoes pointing to the ceiling. Jesus I could go down a flight and along the hall and slam a quick fuck into Sylvia. Before they get their walking papers out of this place. No. Stop. Don't. Be smart for once for christ's sake. Besides. After all these marvellous foreign women, an American girl's voice sounds like noise. I got to review my whole life. Where the fuck I took the wrong turning. Only I'm too exhausted. Can hardly stay awake. I'm fucked. I'm finished. And broke. The show's a shambles. Nothing will resurrect that fucking thing. With every shit who can string two words together, slaming it. The Sunday reviews will crucify us. Binky. Jesus, the son of a bitch knows there's no money left. And I'll never be on a yacht on the Riviera. Dispossessed of a whole fucking house. My private personal papers strewn all over. There they were. The behemoth and a fucking wife. Throwing me out of my own home. Out of which. Shit. I tell you. I needed no encouragement to go. Imagine at dawn. Me on my own doorstep. Them shouting to get out. Jesus these fucking women. Think it's so god damn easy to make money. Go step out there yourself you bitch. Go ahead. Where the financial guns are blazing and you make some money. Otherwise, instead of bitching sitting back there in the comfort of free room and board, shut your fucking ass. Shut it you cunt. Holy Jesus. I'm shouting. I'm delirious after all these nonstop horrendous days. Don't know which are worse. The day horrors or the night horrors. But nothing, nothing could be worse than back working for my father. Or Uncle Werb. O Jesus. It's only diamonds or erotic ladies' lingerie left. I don't think Binky and I are good for each other. Too many of the same kind of showbizz disasters have befallen us. We both shove the same crutches at each other for support. I need them and he doesn't. My last hope. My only hope. Is his Lordship. Got to get him somehow to open up his coffers and save the show. He's got to have some fucking humanity left I'm sure. He's really an understanding guy. When I asked him, Jesus your Lordship why don't you stop using your titles altogether if it causes you so much anguish. Ah Schultz, that would deprive people of their so clearly enjoyed pleasure of addressing me for what I am. Holy shit. I've got to stop fucking women. Before they kill me. When you're just looking for a nighttime of thrill they're looking for a lifetime of bliss. Only Rebecca is still absolutely loyal. The other secretaries skulking about. Shifty eyed. Cleaning their fingernails. Sneaking out of the office to fuck off every chance they get. Holy jeeze. This is the time. Of utter utter treachery. Everywhere. If I live through this I'm going to make a pilgrimage to Prague. Discover the beginning of my origins. At least see that before the end. In the beautiful mother of cities. Growing up I was happy. Never knew then what the horrors meant. Except trying to practice my violin after school with frozen fingers. These could be my last fucking hours. Born in Woonsocket. Sigmund Franz Isadore Schultz. A special a instead of the i in Isadore. For is adorable Schultz. Following four flops, he died in London. Fuck him, don't help him, he's too dead. At least during my life I had a beautiful name. I'm going to be a father. A kid born with no daddy to look after it. The behemoth could be raising my own flesh and blood. That monster fucking woman trying to tell me how to behave in my own fucking private house, in my own fucking private moments conducting my own fucking private body with my own fucking private desires. I couldn't stand it. I got to win. Jesus I've already lost. Bills cascading from every direction especially this hotel. Even owe Binky rent on the coffin space I got my desk in, squeezed into an office for a midget. In the most polite and friendly kind of way, I know the flint hearted fucker will kick me out. But Jesus there were times of joy I had up there sometimes. Whenever those two fuckers weren't plotting something against me. Just sitting around and bullshitting for hours. In those moments I really could have relaxed in utter happiness if I only knew I had already made millions. Or else was totally flat on my arse in failure. Once the trade reviews get out, it will ruin and smash my career. Those commercial minded cunts will revile the show. Boy have they got the jargon to do it. They love seeing you go down the drain for a

337

fortune. My previous flops were too small to notice. They vanished like a saint's fart. Now I have to bomb with a bang heard all over showbizz. Uncle Werb says, Sigmund, diamonds don't evaporate. A fucking production sure does, the second the closing notice gets posted. Uncle Werb used to come up from Brooklyn to Rhode Island to build me snowmen in the snow. Put a yarmulka on the snowman's head. Jesus I'm already crying tears for the unborn. I could have a son or a daughter. How can I support them. When my parents had me. They sold fire damaged ladies' underwear from an outdoor stall in a market. Holy shit, how near the bottom can you start. Ten years it took of saving to get them just one lingerie store. We moved from the worst apartment house to the best apartment house on the block. Uncle Werb kept saying why don't you go to the suburbs out of the slum. Make a social milestone in the family's history. By that time Uncle Werb had a big suite in the St. George Hotel in Brooklyn. Holy cow, how did such a sweet nice guy like him make all that money. Jesus, simple, he stayed a bachelor. Retained the peace of mind to overcome disasters. As I keep reminding myself, expect the worst and that's what you'll get, only it will be much worse. I'm shaking. A cold sweat. Hold tight on the sides of the bed. This is an emotional emergency. And let me tell you. At today's prices emotional satisfaction is not available to mankind. It's a lure to keep you looking for it. Happiness is not money. The biggest asshole remark of the century. Holy jeeze how content I would be to wallow in a big bank account. Al. O god Al. You geriatric motherfucker. Taught me so many of the ropes. You helped. Did favours. And momma meeo. Why did you then have to finally suffocate me. The day you sent Pricilla over, everything in my life was like eating bagels, bananas and coconuts in the sun. Since that moment. How could I put on a decent production with all the pressures. Flesh bone and blood, that's all women are, and Jesus what they can fucking well do to you. Now Al it's you who is in love. Victimized. But come to think of it Louella was the only serene pleasant thing I saw all of opening night. Louella. Christ what a beautiful name. Maybe what I would like is one of those gorgeous intelligent half bitches who really understands sweat, men and money. Who loves to hear all the nuances of the kill. Wipes your brow after every business transaction and pats your hand as you reach over to feel her thigh. Who tells you that the fucker deserved what you did to him in that deal. Instead here I am landed with the complete bitch. Who after she's corroded my guts away will grow old after I'm buried, hanging jewels on herself to compensate for every line and sag she's got. As a kid I was known as Guts Dutch Schultz. I slapped girls all over the place. When I was a little child in my high chair eating a bowl of spinach, Uncle Werb said to my father, Milton I'm telling you he would make a good diamond merchant because he will grow up into a genius. My suspicious father who thought for a long time I was pretty stupid, looks at him. Says nearly hysterically, hey Werb how can you tell. Ah, of course Milton, I can tell. It's you who doesn't bother to look. See. If the bowl is more than an inch away from his fingertips, instead of reaching, he throws a screaming fit at the inconvenience. Let me tell you Milton. Such impatience over a detail makes a brilliant diamond merchant. My father told me the story every time Uncle Werb wanted me down learning merchandising gems on Forty Seventh Street. Why did I ever come to England. Jesus I know why. As a tiny tot still crapping in a potty, I heard London's Big Ben ring nine o'clock one night on the American radio at the abdication of an English King. It sounded profound like nothing had ever sounded to me before. Imagine. That same fucking bell now is measuring off the time in the longest and maybe last chapter of my life. And Uncle Werb before he hit the big time, lived in deepest Brooklyn. Would you believe it, in an area called Kensington just off Coney Island Avenue. With streets named Westminister, Rugby, Buckingham and Marlborough. When Uncle Werb's whole stock in trade was just one diamond wrapped in tissue paper carried in the shell of a vest pocket watch, when he stood dealing in the snow and rain on the Bowery. Jesus here I am with a date now with Lady Lullabyebaby. His Lordship's sister. As high up as you can get in the aristocracy without being annoyingly conspicuous wearing a crown. Nearly

339

said to her on the phone. To bring her down a peg. Hi ya baby. How about a cocktail, ballet, dinner and fuck, not necessarily in that order. I must be getting old thinking such shit. The way I feel right now, it won't be long before I'm popping down pills and timing my heart with a stopwatch like Al. Jesus am I over the hill. Like two of the most stunning women I ever knew. When they were only a few years older than Roxana and Greta and ripe and beautiful in their prime. Went to see them when I hadn't seen them in ten years. Cramped up in an attic, furniture jammed everywhere. There they were, unable to move in the proximity. One of them trying to get me to screw her for old time's sake. The other dying. Lungs black and cancer riddled from cigarettes. My god her hair was falling out. Her back was burned from exposure to X rays. And she wasn't going to live long enough to sue the hospital. Holy shit, back that night I could hardly take it. Threw my cigarettes down a sewer. Nearly had to drag myself through the streets and there as I looked at these two women who were once both so fucking beautiful, all three of us those years ago screwing away in the same bed howling out orgasms and now one of them in tears at death's last trap door. The other like an American matron. All the hell I wanted to do was get the fuck fast out of there. And thought Jesus, that's why women behave as they do. They got to make it while their beauty lasts because shit they're going to end up on the scrap heap. And only that I'm so crucified by a fucking female at the moment, I'd nearly admit they deserve a tear of sympathy. Christ right this minute I'm in the middle of my own doom. Maybe it's my compassion that has stymied me. Once when I was being a nuisance saying to Uncle Werb, don't get anxious, he suddenly got angry and shouted. Anxiety is a Jewish characteristic for christ's sake, with good fucking reason. Now it's me who's anxious. And I only wish I could feel more fucking Jewish. If I suffer like this now. What will it be like at four or five in the morning when the pre dawn ghosts are hooting and howling up my arse. Momma meeo. Stop. I got to stop. What the fuck is all this foolishness. Wasting valuable time trying to dig a hopeful omen out of my soul and only finding more horror. Fight you son of a bitch. Fight. Up. Off the fucking bed. Fight. Jesus look at me. My fucking tie, shirt, jacket, pants, shoes. Are all looking like two generations behind the times. I got to get in style again.

Schultz stripping off his clothes. Running along his little hall into the bathroom. Popping in under the shower. Fight, team, fight. Splash chill water on prick and balls. Revive them. To fuck another day. Wrap up in the big warm white bath towels heaped on the towel rail. Cotton tips to dry in the ears. Comb hair in the mirror. Lean in closer. O no. One. Two. Three. Four. Christ. Five. Jesus. Six. Fucking new grey hairs.

Schultz draped in towels as the waiter brought tea. Setting it up in the sitting room's bow shaped window. Gaze out through the branches of the trees at the backs of Mayfair town houses. Christ, although I'm still feeling I'm still dying, at least a cup of china tea with lemon, smoked salmon and brown bread and a piece of pineapple pastry will take the edge off my appetite till I get to heaven.

"The evening papers sir, were outside your door."

"Thanks. I've seen them."

"Terrible isn't it, this massacre in Africa."

"Yeah."

"Is there anything else sir."

"No this is swell thanks."

Schultz shaking a fist at the newspapers on the side table. Suddenly focusing an eye at a new emblazoned headline.

COUP IN ZUMZIMZAMGAZI

The Zumzimzamgazi army assisted by invading troops of His Royal Imperial Majesty, Field Marshal King Buggybooiamcheesetoo, overthrew the government of Zumzimzamgazi in a sudden coup last night. His Imperial Majesty vehemently denies giving any aid to the new military regime.

Schultz putting down his tea cup. Picking it up again. And putting it down. My hands trembling. Jesus the behemoth and wife at dawn this morning were threatening to go live in royal cheesy buggyboo's palace. Take my unborn child with them. To be raised by a fucking bunch of blacks killing each other fighting over snake infested jungles. Like hell they will. Abduct part of my flesh and blood back into primitive society. Fucking around with that big charcoal sambo joke in Africa.

But holy Jesus this. O no. The Ambassador. Holy christ. The poor fucker must have got it in the neck. I never even this morning turned to look up at his windows where he was usually watching when I'm having a disturbance of the peace on my steps. He was becoming one of the last comforts and true friends I had in my life. This is really curtain time. Holy shit. I can't cry now. In the middle of tea. Got to make rules. Rule one. Keep going Jackson. Rule two. Don't read newspapers no more. Rule three. Put one foot in front of the other. Four. Fuck the cost. Get on the phone and get a limousine. Five. Get outside into living life. Rule five and a half. Don't fucking trip on carpets or get garments caught in revolving doors. And even though I was a child prodigy with my prick.

> Rule six
> Don't screw
> Horror and sex
> Don't mix

26

I̲N a misty soft drizzle of rain Schultz's limousine purring past the street lamps on The Carriage Road alongside Hyde Park. The big evening lit dining rooms of the hotel. Turning down Sloane Street and left right between the red brick buildings of Knightsbridge.

Lady Lullabyebaby stepping into the lobby from the lift of this sedate block of flats as Schultz came in. Sweeping forward in a long blue dress past the doorman rushing before her to open the doors.

"Ah now milady, you have a good time tonight."

"Thank you Alfredo."

"Ah milady this is your gentleman, right."

"Yes, Alfredo. This is my gentleman."

Schultz's chauffeur smilingly opening the limousine door. Lady Lullabyebaby ensconcing herself far back in the upholstery, taking in a deep breath and exhaling a great sigh.

"Well honey, you're on time to the split second."

"I abhor lateness, Mr. Schultz."

Speeding along Piccadilly. Past the clubs. By the luggage and food emporiums. Around the circus. Across Leicester Square. The lights. The buskers. People everywhere. Buying tickets at box offices. And Lady Lullabyebaby lighting up a cigarette in a long ivory holder.

"Well Mr. Schultz, I'll say one thing for you. You do know how to appear out of the blue."

Ascending the soft carpeted steps. An usherette unlocking the door to their box. Schultz ordering champagne for the interval. As the curtain rose and the dancers pirouetted and arabesqued. And Schultz fell promptly asleep. His head hung over on his shoulder as he snored. To be shoved awake by her Ladyship.

"My god Mr. Schultz, sleep, but please don't snore."

"Holy christ honey, sorry. Went out like a light. The beauty of the dancing and music just carried me straight off to dreamland."

"Mr. Schultz, I don't think, do you, that we should remain present at the ballet."

"I'll be alright honey. I'm wide awake now."

Schultz through the crescendoes, leaps and slides falling promptly to sleep once more. His elbow sliding off the arm rest as he slumped in his chair. Lady Lullabyebaby, knuckles sharp, punching him awake again in the ribs. At the interval Schultz taking a walk down to the lobby.

"Honey I'm sorry, I really am. I haven't slept for days. You stay I'll go home."

"No. We'll both go."

Schultz on the sidewalk looking for his chauffeur and car. Beginning to slam the heel of his hand against his forehead, as Lady Lullabyebaby pointed with her finger.

"No doubt you'll find him over there. In that pub with a pint of beer playing darts. If you wait here. I'll fetch him. You might fall asleep crossing the road."

Lady Lullabyebaby sending the chauffeur back in, insisting to bring away the bottle of champagne and commandeering the car back to Knightsbridge. The bottle between her feet and now cradled in her arm as she leaned forward, the chauffeur holding open the door.

"Well you poor man. You need your nice comfortable bed for the night. But if you've the strength to take my lift up four floors. I'll give you a drink of this very good champagne that it would be a shame to waste."

Alfredo in the lobby asleep on a chair by the elevator. Startled awake and looking at his watch.

"Ah milady. Back already. What, you not see the whole ballet. What a disgrace."

Schultz putting his head back on the blue swansdown cushioned sofa. Sinking deep. Christ, the peace. What a place she's got. Each room dressed to kill. My god, the antiques. Everywhere you look. A museum. Everything perfect. Polished into a sheen.

"Let me Mr. Schultz pour for you."

"Jesus not for me. Apple or orange juice if you got it please. And can I use your phone."

"Certainly, please do. Right over there."

Schultz crossing the room on this silk carpet. Blue taffeta curtains drawn on the windows. Shut out London. But now I got to phone the box office. Dial. Hear what the damage is. Numbers that's all it is. Fatal numbers. O god, I've got to hold my breath. Even if there's any hope at all. It's only the beginning of the Chinese torture.

"Hello."

"Sorry booking closed."

"I'm not booking. Mr. Schultz here."

"O hello sir. Well sir, we've just finished tabulating this moment. I'm sorry but the figures are much worse than we feared. Hardly any business at all on the doors. Ninety one pounds, eighteen shillings."

"Holy christ ninety one pounds."

"I'm sorry sir."

"O.K. thanks, goodnight."

Schultz turning away from the phone. Blowing breath slowly out of his lungs. Cross back again to where I was sitting. Before I

345

faint. So now this is really it. The end of the line. Not even ten rows sold in the whole place. When I need at least a hundred sold just to hold out hope. To stop the cast from committing suicide in dressing rooms. Or god forbid right on the stage in the cold clammy death that an empty theatre collects. I should have been there. But if I was I'd be sunk in a coma of depression. As it is I'm in a coma of despair. Or maybe just a coma. O god I'm so fucking weary and tired. Blue. Everything is blue in this room. Or am I seeing things. Demon possessed. O god everything now. Rides on his blue blooded Lordship. That fucking Master of Foxhounds, cricketer, crack shot and prince. Who doesn't give a fuck if I live or die. And if he finds me with his sister. After I turned one of his staff into a lesbian. Holy fuck. That will really spell disaster. With his temper he's already flung me around a room at the end of a telephone. Asking people for money is the utmost in humiliation. The guy who can invent an unhumiliating way of asking, is going to make a million. But the real humiliation comes when you don't get it. Here I am all these months dreaming of finally dipping my toes into a nice steady cash flow. Now I look down into a snake pit. After all the deals. All the cut and thrust. The outwitting, the out manoeuvring. The constant in between face slapping you get. So severe it can be ball shattering. And each slap if you don't watch out, it can be a knockout. Lords address each other in the House of Lords as noble. What could I say to his Lordship that will melt down his noble resistance. The son of a bitch has an accountant's mind. Snow him with figures. And he doesn't miss a fucking trick. His eyes flash down a ledger. And motherfucker if he doesn't put his finger right on what you don't want him to know even ever existed. What do I do. Plead to him. On my bended knees, kneeling on top of all the stacks of unpaid bills. In this world Judas is Jesus and Jesus is Judas. Binky says his Lordship can't find his own foot in his own shoe. That his Lordship has never used the word marvellous in his life. That he abhors skiing on water or snow. Constantly loses cuff links. Because he takes off his shirt and shakes it to get his prize Arab horses to strut. Wears his underwear back to front and frequently inside out. And Jesus once he said to me. Schultz, have you ever chosen to disadvantage yourself by doing the noble thing. That really hurt. Only for a second. Because at the time he was signing me a cheque. That really helped. I could cable Uncle Werb as a last resort. He was like a father to me better than my own father. He has the midas touch in big business. While my father has the minus touch in his two bit operations. His Lordship could be anti American underneath it all. Told me once his nanny taught him to whistle the American national anthem over his bowl of raspberries to get rid of any wasps lurking in the fruit. This is still what the fucker does. And once his nanny got irritated at him whistling over the raspberries as she taught him to. She said stop that you naughty little lord. And his naughty little Lordship said it would make the wasps fly out of his raspberries. And just as his nanny was reaching over to slap him. A wasp flew out of his raspberries. Holy fuck. He's a stubborn bastard. But I know he's got one weakness. His noble rich Lordship, the cunt, is really an impressionable romantic. Thank god. Because once I saw real big tears in his eyes. When he told the story of how his grandfather throughout the remainder of his life, in a locked chamber called the Titanic Room in one of his castles, had that ship's last meal served on the anniversary day of the sinking. In memory of a young lady lost on the Titanic with whom he had been in love. Jesus it even gives me tears. And how his Lordship's grandmother in high dudgeon would entrain for London where she would stay at Claridge's till the mournful ritual was over. The Grandfather had pictures of the ship on the walls. And his letters in a glass case written to her awaiting her arrival in New York. And his Lordship had tears falling down his cheeks when he said, but Schultz saddest of all, when my grandfather was a young man, she was a dairy maid banished from the estate, and she'd gone steerage on the *Titanic* to the new world. But my grandfather celebrated his remembrance of her, not from the steerage menu but from the menu served in the Titanic's first class dining room.

"Mr. Schultz, dear me. Are you asleep again."
"Sorry christ."

347

"Well you are a surprise. Stretched out somnambulant on the sofa. The aggressive go getting producer."

"I was just thinking about your brother. Trying to figure him out."

"O god. Don't waste your time. Sets of encyclopaedias about him wouldn't help you figure him out."

"Jesus don't say that. And I shouldn't even be telling you this. But I got to figure him out by next Friday."

"Why. Of course I ask why, full well knowing why. You're going to ask him for money."

"Holy shit, you know."

"But of course. That's all anybody asks him for."

"Well you're right. But I'm asking for money for a good cause. And I got to know exactly where his sentimentality ends and his financial caution begins."

"And I may as well tell you. The latter begins long before the former ends. But for heaven's sake when asking him for money, don't beat around the bush looking for ways of doing so. It won't help."

"I could get him mellowed over a few glasses of wine maybe."

"And you will find my brother then infinitely more mysterious, difficult and astute than he is unmellowed. However, you can be sure of one thing. He is totally, utterly and absolutely unpredictable drunk or sober."

"Thanks for the reassurance."

"Now, do you or don't you want to bang me."

"Holy shit."

"Dear me. Your language is a constant stream of shit, fuck, holy christ and Jesus. But what a quaint expression. You, I take it, mean religiously holy shit."

"Hey Lady Lullabyebaby, the term bang. You ain't exactly not using quaint expressions yourself."

"Well isn't that what you invited me to the ballet for. To bang me afterwards. But I won't be awfully insulted if you didn't. I was in fact on my way to the country this evening. To spend the night with my husband, and to exercise my horses in the morning. And indeed right now I'm ready to heat myself some honey and milk and read myself to sleep."

"Wow."

"Why wow."

"I'm floored. I don't know what to say."

"From stories one hears, you usually have quite a lot to say to women."

"Let me take a big deep breath will you. Can I admit something to you."

"Yes, provided it's not baring your soul. I detest men who get gushy and mushy."

"I don't think I could bang you. Not tonight. Not the way someone like you deserves to be banged."

"Ha ha ha, Mr. Schultz, you're priceless. You're marvellous, in fact. Although I don't do so, I prefer to demand rather than deserve. The woman who deserves anything is the woman who will be last to get it."

"Well I went out of my hotel room to see you this evening reciting rule six of new rules I got. Don't screw, horror and sex don't mix."

"Are you trying to put me in my place or something."

"No no. It's me. I'm in horror. Which is piled up all around me. Christ I'm letting my hair down."

"Let it down. Do please. I'm enchanted."

"I'll tell you something, I've never been able to speak to a woman like this before."

"O. Now I'm the trusted confidante."

"Christ don't say it like that. Christ. I'll go home. I shouldn't have ever come out in the first place. I'm sorry. This reminds me of a night standing in the theatre when a fucking god damn Catholic nun saw me lurking in the aisle. She must have been looking at my nose, when she said that the Jews had been condemned by God to forever wander the face of the earth."

"O dear. And what did you say. Nothing."

"I said fuck you sister, Israel is born."

"Ah Mr. Schultz. Good for you. Full of surprises you are."

349

"Yeah. Too many. And I'm still fucking wandering. It won't surprise me if the first thing I do tomorrow morning when I get up is to sit down and cry."

"Well I don't mind women who do, but I dislike men who weep. And since you're not going to bang me. I think I shall go to bed. Or else I shall start feeling like my old granny who had it put in her will that she was to be cremated and her ashes sprinkled on her faithful dog's food."

"Christ you're fucking eccentric like your brother."

"Am I. I hadn't noticed."

"Jesus I don't even know your first name. And we've even gone without eating this evening."

"Mr. Schultz, it appears that we are going to go without fuck all this evening, if I may use the expression."

"Christ here you are. Married. You got a husband."

"Yes I have. If that worries you. And he is a twisted, perverted, despicably cruel monster. And my christian name is Lulu."

"Holy christ Lulu honey you couch your words carefully. Like you stand there in the middle of the floor like a battleship blasting out salvoes at me. Hey do you mind telling me what your social rank is."

"Not at all. I'm the daughter of an earl and married to an earl. Which to date has not once stopped me from behaving as a commoner when I choose."

"Wow. I don't know what the English upper classes are all about but looking at you I don't know what I should expect next now."

"My tiara is in a safe in that room there. Shall I wear that and nothing else. It may help to explain me better. It's not an awfully good tiara. I'm my brother's wayward sister. And have been left the dregs of what family jewels were doled out. Although I must confess Basil did secretly offer me the pick. Even a woven bracelet of my great grandmother's hair. But I can see, nothing is going to arouse you to bang me."

"Honey I'm busting my brains here, thinking. You're the most fucking."

"The most fucking what."

"I don't know."

"Well provided I'm not entirely unfuckable it may help to let me explain myself. I pretend to believe in Christ. And do devoutly believe in reincarnation. I can be a very smartly got up gentlewoman when I please. And despite my many men friends I masturbate frequently. I also go on solitary continental travels for kicks, cocks and gigolos. And in search of groaning moaning orgasms. And is it any wonder. And of course you're married Mr. Schultz."

"Yes I am."

'And how would you sum that up."

"In a nutshell. You mean."

"Sum it up in a codpiece if you prefer."

"Well in a codpiece. She gave me maybe three months of wonderful fucking and gave herself enough time to get her clutches deep enough into me to start to begin to give me maybe thirty future years of fucking misery."

"Par for the course my dear. And you know, such wives are out by night and day all over London with wire cutters, screwdrivers, matches, petrol and hammers with the intent to damage the property, and the body and soul if possible, of their husband's mistresses. And perhaps it's time I peeked out the window."

"What about your husband, coming back here."

"This is my own private private flat, my dear. To which he is not privy."

"Jesus your doorman, who's he."

"He is a very special favourite of mine. He has nine children. Everyone in the building thinks he's too outspoken for a doorman, and would like him sacked. But although no one knows it, I own the building, and therefore he stays."

"Jesus you own the building."

"Yes, I saved up my little pennies and bought it."

"Hey let me ask you something. Are you really under all this strong exterior just a lost little creature."

"Let me ask you something Mr. Schultz. Are you just someone who's repeatedly gone the way of all flesh and suddenly after a kick in the teeth is now trying to go the way of all sensitive souls."

"Shit you hit below the belt."

"Gentlemen feel it much better there. In their spiritual solar plexus."

"You're fucking tough."

"Out of my misplaced regard for females pretending otherwise, I won't comment on that."

"I'll drink my apple juice. And beat it."

"Please don't hurry. You know, all most women want Mr. Schultz, is just six kids and a farm in the country with horses, hens and a house cow."

"Thanks for telling me. I'm learning everything tonight. And boy I'm learning less and less about you."

"I must then tell you more. Did you know that I keep extremely fit. I do a naked standing run at the open window every morning."

"You mean here."

"Yes."

"Holy christ, the neighbors."

"Well yes, unless it's dark or extremely before dawn it does attract considerable male binocular neighborly attention. But I also own the building opposite."

"Boy you're a real Lulu."

"Shall I tell you more about me."

"Shoot honey, shoot. I'm listening. You're driving all the worries in truck loads right out of my mind."

"I have an extremely wide circle of extremely mixed friends. I'm given to moods and angers. I huff and I puff. And I will sometimes quite literally scream the house down if I don't get what I want."

"Yes. That figures."

"But Mr. Schultz. I make up for it all. By occasionally being a riot of laughs. By being a good cook, a good lay and compassionate when sufficient tragedy requires."

"Ah honey. You're looking at it. A sufficient tragedy. I've had my worst day yet. Everything is a shambles. We've just had a nice long strained pained evening together. But one mistake I'm not making. Is asking you for one ounce of compassion. All I'm thinking of just now. Is how do I get up from this sofa and as unmiserably as possible, go out your fucking door and crawl home to Park Lane."

"I hope upon leaving you will at least give me a token peck on the cheek."

"I'll give you a token peck on the cheek as I leave."

Lady Lullabyebaby shifting her stance. A knee and strong thigh showing through her pale blue dress. A glass of champagne in her left hand, the veins swollen blue across the back of her right. A chime tinkling the half hour in a domed golden clock on the chimney piece. Schultz pulling himself forward. Pushing himself up. Halfway there and falling back again.

"Look at that. Can't get the fucking hell to my feet. Whew. Well there. Now I'm up. Honey it was sure swell knowing you. Like running a mile barefoot over upturned razor blades. I should in my best English be saying, madam allow me to present my compliments and to abide your preference as to whether I should linger longer. But I know when I should no longer linger."

"And Mr. Schultz, what on earth are you going to do back in a lonely hotel. Where I presume you're going."

"Countess. I'll tell you. Exactly. Now when I get back there. And if I had them, which I don't have, which is my red polka dot silk dressing gown, and my custom made slippers. But if I did have them I'd put them on. Switch on the television. Put my feet up on the foot rest. And wait till my favourite meal in all the world was wheeled in from room service. Vichyssoise soup. Mixed salad with extra onions and a garlic dressing. Shish kebab with brown rice. Whole meal rolls and unsalted butter. And an ice cold bottle of Prague Pilsner beer. So goodnight. O and I forgot to mention, at two p.m. sharp I always have ordered a big plate of strawberry ice cream. Well upon that gastronomic note I leave you."

Lady Lullabyebaby following Schultz along the blue carpeted hall of marble topped gilt side tables and mirrors. Crossing this large arched entryway. Schultz turning the latch on the door.

"And now here's your peck on the cheek, honey."

Lady Lullabyebaby reaching up her arm and putting her hand on Schultz's shoulder. Her soft soft eyes, tiny little lines crinkling at the corners as they nearly but never smile. And her lips. So soft too. Quietly speaking.

"Hey come on."

> Come back
> Into bed

27

As the nail biting week went by. Business at the box office creeping up in amounts agonizing in the extreme. The returns slipped in a white envelope under Schultz's hotel suite door each morning. And holy shit which I should avoid reading till after breakfast. Even knowing already the figures inside. I leap on the envelope, ripping it open like an animal into a carcass.

And this the fatal morning. Following the appointment with the chiropodist. Who comes ministrating, nail cutting and my corns excised. Leaving me after a foot massage, like I was walking on a cloud. Stare out between the curtains of my peaceful sitting room windows. It's worse dying like this. Enjoying luxury you want to cling to. If I had something to lead up to it. Like months of terrible boarding house rooms. From which death is an escape. It wouldn't be so bad. Like a guy I saw in New York. Fat Jewish and ugly. Wearing suede shoes and searching trash cans at Fifty Ninth Street and Fifth Avenue. I thought what a disgrace or compliment to the race, whichever way you want to look at it. Plus now I've met the most exasperating woman of my life. Lady Lulu Lullabyebaby. She said I fucked her to a standstill. Then said I looked as smug as a corpse. Momma meeo. She is the most open, the most closed, the coldest, the warmest, the most incredibly generous and the most hugely selfish female I have ever met. And what's a million times worse. I could after she's driven me crazy, be in love with her.

Schultz heading this noonday east on foot across Mayfair. Birds singing up in the big plane trees they say grow so well from the bodies of plague victims buried here in Berkeley Square. To this meeting Al so urgently arranged. Christ with this barracuda Joe Jewels, god's gift to the theatre. Who would bite your legs off to the knees over fifty cents. Al with his little get together planned to convene in the pre lunch time cocktail lounge of a brand new hotel. Got to give the guy at least an E for effort. Which would get hidden by the big D he gets for being dumb sometimes.

Schultz checking the shows ads in the newspaper's classifieds as Al came through the door.

"Holy shit Al, what the hell's happened. Jesus, not now you too. A toupee. My god."

"What's the matter don't you like it."

"Jesus no, throw it away, it makes you look like something they're getting rid of out the back door of a funeral parlour."

"Throw it away are you crazy. It's specially matched to the color and texture of my own natural hair. It cost me a fortune, it's made out of the best most expensive tresses, curls and ringlets in the world."

"Al has she seen you in it."

"Who."

"Louella."

"No. Not yet. Today I'm just taking it out on a test flight."

"Well for me Al, you just crash landed."

Joe Jewels entering in a black vicuna coat. Crossing the cocktail lounge to Schultz and Al. Where he fell back into a chair and slammed his feet up on the cocktail table, rattling the ashtrays.

Schultz puce faced. And Al chewing his cigar, blood pressure up, face lathered, half conciliatory, half angry. Beads of sweat on his brow below his new hair line. Jewels waving away the smoke with his hand.

"O.K. kid, just give me a figure."

"Joe please don't straight off ask Mr. Schultz here for a figure. We should discuss this a little philosophically further as gentlemen."

"As long Al, as my name is Joe Jewels I can't operate without figures. I need figures. What figures kid, have you got in mind."

"The show's not for sale."

"Look kid, don't waste my time. And don't be stupid, I'm offering you a deal. Who else is going to take the show off your hands. When I could be telling you to go find someone else to buy into the flop you've already got. Come on give me a figure."

"Joe don't ask him, please. Let's talk artistic standards first."

"I'm only asking for a figure Al. Artistic standards can come later. O.K. kid. Give me the number of figures you got in mind. Three figures. No. Then it's four figures. What. No. Hey kid you're nuts."

"I told you Joe. Please. Don't ask him. I'm telling you please don't ask him money at this stage. It's too volatile."

"Al keep your shirt on. Mr. Schultz, Al, don't worry, he's got a price. And the number of figures in the price is all I'm asking."

"And Joe I'm begging don't ask him the number of figures right now."

"Kid, O.K. what is it. You don't sit there and tell me you're trying to go above four figures in dollars on this."

"It's five figures. And it's in pounds sterling."

"You see, Joe. Didn't I tell you. I told you, I told you, didn't I, not to ask him. And you had to ask."

"So now Al, we got near a figure. It's five figures. So we know at the low end of the scale that means at least ten thousand pounds. So Mr. Schultz, you tell me, is it ten thousand pounds you want."

"It's fifty Mr. Jewels."

"So sonny boy, let me tell you what you can do with the numeral five that is followed by four zeros. You can, in pounds, shove them. One zero at a time right up your ass. I'm not interested. What are you, Mr. Schultz, some kind of maniac that you go around asking for that kind of money with a show dying on your hands."

"That's right. But you wouldn't be here if it was dead. With two of the biggest star discoveries in recent theatrical history."

"Well goodbye Mr. Schultz, it takes me a phone call to a publicity agent to create all the star discoveries the public can stomach in any one week. Nobody with fifty thousand is stupid enough to buy at your price."

Joe Jewels shrugging and squaring his shoulders. The corners of his mouth turning down in a nose dive as he stood up. Departing in his black vicuna coat. His black silk socks in his black patent leather· loafers sliding forward on his tiny feet. Al turning on Schultz. A fist made which he shakes.

"You son of a bitch. Now he's gone. You stupid son of a bitch. You blew it. Blew it. What the fuck's wrong with you. Asking like that for a ransom. If the show dies now it's dead for always."

"Jesus Al, you are the one that's stupid. He'll be back. With his tongue hanging out."

"Stupid. Huh. Look you fucking son of a bitch, if your cock should be out right now I would choke your stupid mouth with it. I went through the embarrassment of my life getting that guy even to sit down with you again. Now you've fucked this up like you have done everything else. You're dead. Believe me. You're dead."

"Hey Al your toupee is slipping."

"Never mind my fucking toupee. I got a mirror right here anytime I need to straighten it."

"Jesus Al, not in public like this. You're not turning into a narcissistic creep are you."

"Never mind what I'm turning into. You've turned into an asshole. Who should be covered up in bandages. I had in the dining room there for lunch already reserved the best white wines of this century."

"Jesus everybody gets to hate me for doing what I think is right."

"With good reason because it's wrong. What is it with you Sigmund that you cause in me always guilt, always anger. Always shame."

"Hey shit Al stop it. All this about guilt, anger and shame. How about innocence, joy and pride too that I cause."

"Ha, ha, I'm laughing. You, you bum, you should go in search of yourself with an analyst. Showing you the direction. You're so lost."

"I'm right here having my grapefruit juice, Al, that's all I need to know."

"You use people. That's what you do."

"Jump off a cliff will you Al. Please."

"Not only are you a business disaster but your sense of beauty and love is destroyed."

"What are you trying to be a fucking humourist Al."

"I'm at least functioning as a human being. While your ego has taken you on a balloon ride miles out of reality."

Al standing. His open hands shaking at his sides. Taking a long last look at Schultz. And turning and storming out of the soft blue hued cocktail room. Bumping into a table on the way. Knocking over four empty glasses. His voice shouting as he pushed through the plate glass door.

"That's the ungrateful thanks you get. For helping a schlemiel."

Schultz dumping back his grapefruit juice. Paying the bill and passing the waiter picking up the broken glass left by Al. Jesus christ, maybe I fucking well did make a shambles. When I see a shit like Jewels so fucking smooth. So fucking sure of himself. It makes me see red.

Schultz out of the hotel popping into a taxi. Through the familiar streets of Belgravia. A moving van parked in front of the Ambassador's. The windows shuttered. And the Zumzimzamgazi flag at half mast as Pricilla stood shouting out the open door of number four Arabesque Street, with Schultz hopping away down the steps. Taking another cab back into the West End. Approaching a counter with his big battered box. The assistant opening it. And frowning deeply as he slowly handled the garments.

"I fear sir, that not only is this morning suit and top hat and accessories long overdue but I'm afraid they are also a total write off."

"Hey what's wrong, a few little rips and dents, can't you sew and clean them up."

"I regret not sir, our clientele simply would not want to wear these after this extent of damage has happened to them."

"What's happened, nothing. I was raised in the garment business. I know fabric. A little tear down the back of the coat, simple to fix, the threads must have been weak in the first place."

"Considerable force, sir, would be necessary to part this garment in this manner. This hat sir is in an absolute state of destruction."

"Just knocked around a little bit, that's all."

"Sir I suggest you keep these and have them repaired yourself."

"What do I want with them, I'm never going to go to another damn wedding in my life."

"Well sir that's entirely your affair. Our affair is to keep our customers satisfied."

"I'm a customer. I've also been hiring clothes and costumes from costumiers all my life. Satisfy me. Fix them up and rent them out again who's going to know."

"Sir this firm is long proud of its reputation and we simply won't do such a thing."

"Wipe your fucking ass with them then."

"I beg your pardon sir. I think I had better call the manager."

"You call him."

"I shall. And meanwhile here you are sir, in return for your cheque which I shall be happy to accept in the amount of one hundred and fifty guineas, they're yours to keep."

The assistant pushing the clothes back at Schultz across the counter. Schultz picking up the trousers and held by their braces, swinging them across the assistant's face.

"I told you once, I don't want them."

The assistant stunned. Staring at Schultz in horror. Schultz two handed taking the grey top hat and clamping it down over the startled assistant's ears. Who pulled the hat off and threw back the trousers across the counter into Schultz's arms. The battle on. A crash of glass as Schultz lashed out with a fist. And kicked a plaster cast morning suited mannequin in the balls. Clothes flying in all directions. As other assistants' shouts brought the manager running.

"I say what is the difficulty here."

Schultz proffering his cheque in the manager's office. Outraged sensibilities soothed and ruffled feathers smoothed. One hundred and fifty guineas. For the writing off of the wedding regalia. One hundred and sixty five guineas for the damage to three male display mannequins and the busting of a display case containing silk handkerchiefs now sprinkled with broken glass. Because a fucking customer could get a bloody nose if he blows with one. Holy living shit. Why do I have to go cause damage in a place charging in guineas. Which means three hundred and twenty five pounds and ten shillings down the drain. How much longer can I stand it.

Schultz stepping out on the street. With more packages now than when he went in. And enough silk handkerchiefs to last two lifetimes. A man standing obstructing his way.

"Sir, do please excuse me stopping you like this. But I should like to firmly and warmly shake your hand. I've been wanting for years to do what you've just done in there. I simply never had the courage. Thank you."

> Rule seven
> Always
> Thank god
> For admirers
>
> Thank
> You
> God

28

HIS Lordship returned to town. This noonday, Binky in the chairman's office with his gout stool nearby ready to take up his seat on the side lines. His hair gleamingly brushed and himself attired in a camel hair suit, suede waistcoat with gold fox head buttons, cricket shirt and orange tweed tie. As he stood behind the desk, his back bathed in sunlight from the window. Schultz rushing in.

"Hey where the fuck is his Lordship."

"Ah good afternoon Schultz. May I just pause here for a moment and look at you. With your packages under your arm. Yes indeed. Certain words in an under rehearsed manner come immediately to mind of a biblical bent, albeit, to wit, lay not up for yourself treasure upon earth where moth and dust doth corrupt and where thieves break through and steal. But lay up for yourself treasure in heaven where neither moth nor rust doth corrupt and where thieves, Schultz, do not break through and steal."

"Come on you bastard, don't do this to me. There's not even seconds to lose."

"Read that awe inspiring quote in this morning's newspaper. Heading the agony column it was. I was most touched. And right underneath it Schultz, in the same column was another insertion, instantly reminding me of you Which read, St. Jude help me, please never let it happen again."

"Binky come on, I'm begging you. Don't fuck around. I got the figures here. We can just buy enough seats to bring the gross up to keep the theatre. I got everybody ready to go start buying. Why don't you kick off, put up a thousand."

"Schultz I do appreciate the splendid effort you're making. But I do think it would do my miserly blood awful insult to lose one further penny."

"Who's talking about losing. You could make."

"Having already sentimentally and foolishly bought back, at a substantial discount of course, the piece of the show I so wisely sold to Gayboy, I could Schultz, like you, be far away up shit's creek. Without, as you say, an outboard engine. Now why don't you Schultz very softly and briefly just bounce a cheque."

"I'm not going to bounce a cheque, you fucker. I couldn't if I wanted to. Everybody is demanding cash paid for everything. I'm telling you, Binky. The show's building. Believe me. You can see yourself. We did triple the business on a Wednesday night that we did on last Saturday."

"And of course Schultz, we did fuck all on last Saturday."

"Hey what are you Binky, a saboteur. Here, some silk handkerchiefs for you. Of all fucking varieties."

"Ah I must say, how nice Schultz. My aren't they nice. And may I select."

"Select, sure. Anything you want. Here have this one too."

"I've already taken four, Schultz."

"You've taken five, but who's counting."

"Ah Schultz, to be sure, I have. How mistaken of me. This is indeed the age of misgiving. Schultz such nice things as these could have brought joy to the Pygmies in the days when one was on safari there. As indeed these will now do so nicely as a spot of color to enliven the tableau of a shooting party knocking the woodcock out of the sky."

"Shit. Stop. Fuck the haberdashery. Let's go. Let's go. Fuck misgiving. Fuck tableaus. This is the moment of life and death with no god damn room left for giving or misgiving."

"Yes Schultz I do see your point. I believe Gayboy is desperately trying to get the theatre back to give to another show."

"The son of a bitch is never going to get me out of there."

"Now Schultz as one father to be, to another, let me invite you to a little seance this afternoon to relax you."

"I'll be hysterical till the banks close at three o'clock and I don't get the money to keep this production open."

"Ah at four then. A little tea will be served. It's rather in the way of a small intimate at home by myself away from home that I'm having."

His Lordship appearing in the doorway. In a crumpled blue suit. His jacket open, tie loose at his collar. Flecks of mud on his shoes. Soup stains on his lapels, and blond hairy hairs curling on his belly exposed by two missing shirt buttons.

"Holy shit, at fucking long last. Jesus your Lordship, what's wrong with talking to me on the phone. What took you so long away all these days. With me having kittens."

"Schultz. If you must know. I've been buying cattle. And you. Never mind kittens, with all those hankies. Stand right where you are. Don't come an inch further near me."

"Why, what's wrong. Have I got the oriental clap plague again."

"You may have but I am more concerned with something much worse indicated by the look you are wearing."

"What look."

"Schultz you have the look of a man looking for money."

"Holy shit. What gives you this idea."

"The idea is given to me Schultz by the unmistakable expression on your face. And the overwhelming aura of desperation."

"I'm not desperate."

"You should be. As I think Schultz that shortly, if you are not extremely careful, you will take a slide down a very nasty slope indeed. Roxana has still not been found."

"Holy jeeze, don't look at me, your Lordship."

"Don't feign innocence Schultz. I prefer you looking desperate."

"O.K. I am. I'm desperate. On my ass down the slope. Anything you say."

"And what I say Schultz is close the production."

"O Jesus, you don't understand, there's just a fraction of a gap left to reach the gross to keep the theatre."

"Schultz that's nonsense. The production account is at this moment overdrawn by six thousand seven hundred and eighty four pounds eighteen shillings and nine pence. By this time tomorrow it will be overdrawn by another thousand. Plus another fifty or sixty pounds while you, my dear Schultz, are living at the Dorchester."

"Everybody else I guarantee, is now kicked out of there. But Jesus I got to live in dignity somewhere. It's money, just money, you talk like it was flesh and blood or something."

"I talk Schultz as the guarantor to the bank."

"O.K. O.K. That's what I mean. Everybody is already going to lose. And that's exactly certain what's going to happen if we close. Look what I've done already. Advance booking has quadrupled. Daily business has tripled, and building every second. From nothing, from disaster."

"Schultz stop eating your fingers off. And wearing the carpet out. And also writing your anti blood sports letters."

"Your Lordship my lips are sealed forever. I'm behind foxhunting one hundred per cent from now on. I'll even go further. You put up enough money to buy enough seats to cover the show and I swear I'll get myself rigged out on a fucking horse and go foxhunting with you."

"Done."

"Holy shit, your Lordship, what are you saying."

"I said done."

"You really fucking mean it."

"Schultz you are a circus."

"I'm anything you say your Lordship. But please. No jokes. Jesus you mean it."

"Schultz I said, done. For the third time."

"O.K. O.K. I'm on my way right now to get riding lessons and have a pink coat made. Hot diggity dog, Jesus you bastard I could kiss you."

"Schultz please don't. And for the time being it will have to be a black coat you must wear hunting. And if you would wipe that hot diggity dog look off your face, someone is not only going to have to go to the bank with a satchel but someone is also going to have to go and buy tickets."

"I've got him. His name's Padio O'Kelly and he's waiting right in the next room."

"Schultz you really are a flying circus aren't you."

"Holy cow, now begins what I hope is the last horror."

"Yes Schultz, because if you get caught doing this, it's fraud."

"What's fraud about buying complimentary seats and keeping the theatre alive and kicking and actors, musicians and dancers in jobs."

"It could be construed Schultz that it is a conspiracy to breach a contract."

Binky lighting up a cigar. His chin raised and eye lashes fluttering, beaming one of his best smiles.

"Ah my lords and esquires. Do permit me as chairman to suggest blaming it all on the author. Or is there one who wrote the wretched silly book in the first place."

"Binky no one's getting blame, except me. Only I'm going to deny it."

"Ah Schultz once more, you rekindle in me my admiration for the forthright human spirit embodied in you."

"That's right Binky, I'm never again pleading guilty to anything to be clapped in jail."

His Lordship scribbling out a cheque. Handing it across to Schultz whose trembling fingers held the watermark up to the light.

"Ah Schultz, you're wondering if it will bounce, are you."

"No your Lordship. I'm wondering about just one little magic word Nectarine. Written at the bottom of this little piece of paper. Which can mean so much in the saving of my entire life."

Schultz and Binky striding at this strange precise time of two p.m. when little is happening along Piccadilly. The rear taken up by a newly jaunty confident Padio O'Kelly. This rotund faced gent met in Curzon Street. Following Schultz and Binky into this Byzantine interior. Domed ceiling, deep rose pillars. A table with newspapers and elegant chairs.

"Holy christ what a bank."

"Yes Schultz long patronized by his R.C. One may sit there reading while they, the chaps go fuss about his Lordship's little business. Rather nice. I keep a modest little account here myself. The concierge there when requested keeps out awful people who might have been following one. Note how quickly he enquired of your Mr. O'Kelly's business."

The teller stacking notes, pushing them out to Binky who laid them in the attaché case. The threesome hurriedly heading back to the office of Sperm Productions.

"Come on gang. Let's go. Fight. Fight."

"Do shut up Schultz. This costly business is bad enough without your thinking you're in the middle of an American football game."

His Lordship sitting like a paymaster behind the chairman's desk. The sun shining on the stacks and stacks of bank notes. Rebecca, Schultz and Padio, heading out in relays, buying batches of tickets at the box office and booking agencies. Schultz as the last pounds had gone, standing looking at his Lordship in his shirt sleeves.

"And Schultz now what is on that scheming mind of yours."

"Your Lordship you have turned into a fucking gem. Jesus you son of a bitch, you really are a fucking fighter once you fight.

Christ it went just like a military operation. You even caught that bastard barrow boy trying to screw us out of three hundred quid. God bless the aristocracy. I take everything back I ever thought against them."

"I'm sure Schultz, the aristocracy will be extremely pleased to hear that."

Binky at the door. Peeking in on tiptoe. Tapping his finger tips together. A pink carnation in his buttonhole.

"Ah what a nice calm little scene. And Schultz, I've come to collect you my dear, Tobias with my car is waiting."

"And you Binky, where the fuck were you, why didn't you help us."

"Dear me, I must keep up standards Schultz. The Chairman of this charming firm must not ever be seen doing the dirty. And looking at my watch Schultz, soon time now for our little seance with my fortune teller, we shall be late if you don't join me immediately. I shouldn't like to, as my old uncle did Schultz, who horrified by the imperfection in one of his gilt ormolu sixteenth century clocks which was four minutes slow, took his afternoon walking stick to it."

The hallway ministrations of Rebecca as she brushed the back of Binky's black cape. Straightening his tie, refixing his carnation and handing him his brolly and bowler. Jesus it's fucking pleasant for a change to see that women can be a help sometimes. At least that girl is making steady progress into Binky's life. And I wish her every bit of luck, with all the odds against her. A girl you could depend on if your ass got permanently smashed.

Sun behind clouds. Darkening grey sky. Drops of rain sparkling on the limousine as Schultz and Binky motored in the direction of deepest Mayfair. Binky frowningly listening, now stuck in a Brewer Street traffic jam, to Schultz's latest recriminations against womankind.

"You really should Schultz try homosexuality. It would I'm sure keep you from these awful complications in your life. O dear, London citizens do, don't they, get in such a tizzy for taxis when it rains, jamming up the roadway. And making an awful nuisance of themselves."

"Hey Binky why the fuck don't you or your Lordship try a little poofta life."

"Ah Schultz my tastes have already taken me in other directions. And his Royal Grace has a rather strong but I think ill founded antipathy towards queers. I do think they supremely and much annoyed him as a beautiful young man. Indeed when he played cricket for the university side there were a whole section of them collected chanting and cheering each time his Royal Grace knocked it for six. Lord Nectarine is supreme, is what they shouted as a matter of fact. Some of the more blatantly cheeky devils even held up signs. We love Basil. The legend Lord Nectarine is a homosexual was chalked up on many a college wall. The latter alas done by my own hand. I rather enjoyed to see his expression of annoyance as we strolled the college quads together."

Stopping and alighting on this Mayfair pavement. Black railings along by these red brick town houses. Binky waited till his car had departed. Walking a few paces and turning through a gate. Out into a little spot of greenery. Crossing this tiny park and stepping over the street and turning the corner into a cul de sac.

"You see Schultz one must be discreet about certain locations in one's life."

Schultz following Binky in a door. Up three flights of stairs to a cozy sumptuous flat. Through a hall into a large room with fur covered sofas, pillows piled everywhere. Curtains drawn on the windows. Smell of incense.

"Ah now Schultz we're a little late but now do beseat yourself comfortably."

Binky pressing a button. The wall at one end of this large drawing room parting in sliding doors, revealing a small proscenium stage.

"Holy shit, Binky."

"Now Schultz, never mind holy shit. You did in your anti blood sports letter neglect to say that foxes are part of a national heritage and not the preserve of a minority. Of course as a foxhunting man myself. One would naturally reply that do anti blood sport bods also claim so in respect of the earthworms in their gardens. Please, Schultz, don't stand up like a sore thumb, sit down. One would think you'd never been in a theatre before. Try over there on a nice chinchilla sofa. Tea will presently be served by nanny. And shortly the show will begin."

Schultz sitting down. Binky tinkering at a camera on a tripod. A smiling grey haired uniformed elderly lady entering with tea. As she exited, a buzzer sounding. Lights of room dimming. And a splash of illumination on stage. Sound of a Viennese waltz. The scenery, a thatched country cottage. Clouds passing overhead and smoke coming from the chimney. A field of clover in the foreground. Two masked young ladies in pinafores carrying milk buckets entering on stage. Gamboling playfully back and forth. Raising a spot of dust. Schultz sneezing into one of his silk handkerchiefs. The young ladies putting down their pails and slowly tantalisingly undressing each other. Till they fell naked to the floor, writhing in passionate ecstasy. Schultz sneezing again. Binky abandoning his tea cup and saucer. Standing at a tripod clicking a camera. Frowning as he manoeuvred to get the more difficult shots. Schultz at the final curtain standing to applaud.

"Jesus christ Binky, bravo what a show."

"Of course for the sake of frolicsome jollies, one is at certain miserable times an occasional pervert, Schultz. That is not to say that one's life is a shambles of debauchery. And it gives some of our lazier London girls something to do in the afternoons. Had I known Schultz that you were as deeply interested as you are in viewing the female in rapture. I should have invited you long before."

"Binky I'm flabbergasted. This is really high quality this little set up of yours. Real clouds. Real god damn smoke coming out of the chimney."

"Do you really think so Schultz. This is what I like to call my little theatre in the home."

"Jesus the fucking lighting and sound is god damn magic."

"Do you really think so. Ah Schultz you are a charmer you know, just when one's spirit needs a lift you come suddenly to the rescue. I was so worried about the standard of lighting. Especially dealing with black and white contrasts. I occasionally have had big black men come to perform with the girls. Alas the former developed the bad habit of stealing backstage valuables."

"Christ you fucker, you have everything, everything at your feet."

"Not quite Schultz, the stage is at knee level. But Schultz it's fun to have a little spare money. Of course there are those who simply don't know what to do with it, when indeed it can be so useful to onc who has, by a lifelong training been taught how and how not to spend it."

"The sumptuous luxury, the scones, the cake."

"Ah Schultz happily along with his Royal Grace, one does also try to avoid that dastardly English habit to entertain on the cheap."

"Where did you get that girl in the mask."

"Ah Schultz her breasts are a little perhaps on the large side."

"They may be but this is one guy in the audience who is going wild over them."

"Yes Schultz, I think we must settle for the word delicious for her."

"Jesus I feel I almost know a fucking girl who nearly has a body as beautiful just like that. Only all I could do was just fccl it, I never saw it. Holy shit, what have I said. All the while I'm watching I'm wracking my brains. That's fucking Agnes. Agnes for christ's sake."

"Schultz, are you alright."

"Holy christ what's going on here in London. I got to go see her."

"Strict rule we have Schultz, the audience is not permitted backstage."

Binky touring Schultz in and about the various erotica on tables and on walls and encased in vellum. Schultz now instead of being relaxed, was hopping, skipping and jumping all over the place. And now strolling with Binky through Mayfair on the way to the Dorchester, Schultz was slapping his forehead again and again.

"Where the fuck did you get that girl Binky."

"Ah the one you call Agnes who has given you apoplexy. Well as a matter of fact I have a rather elegant little Greek friend who does my casting. One doesn't normally enquire too closely into such things. But she I believe, Schultz, was found at one of those dinner parties at which, if one is not careful at introduction time, one might miss all the prime ministers and heads of state."

"Jesus Binky that was my wife's best friend."

"You don't say. But how nice Schultz. Perhaps the little wife Schultz. Surely she too might fancy a little spare time activity. Top prices paid you know."

"Binky, you know, you guys really do take the cake. The marvellous god damn way you got life arranged. To think I missed all this kind of culture growing up in a backward place like America. Jesus, again, why wasn't I born with such good fortune like you guys."

"Ah you Americans Schultz, are sometimes so full of shit. You really are. Wanting the way you do to contribute something to the benefit of mankind, instead of, as we British do, donning our straw boaters and popping off at mid morning to Henley to watch the chaps do their very best stroking their oars over the water but you're forgetting Schultz, that a dog once ate my cake."

"O christ, yeah, forgive me, Jesus I forgot the tragedies you have to put up with."

"And Schultz as we stroll along this civilized Mayfair Avenue, let me tell you I had one yesterday. My chauffeur Tobias was attending a relative's funeral, as he often does every couple of weeks. And I actually decided to descend into the underground thinking I might take the tube from Green Park to Knightsbridge. There I was, a hundred feet down in the murky neon lit shadows. On a bench minding my own saucy business of watching the better legs passing. When this chap in a blue overall and pail of glue

372

and brush came by putting up posters. One which he proceeded to affix right over my shoulder without so much as a by your leave. The blessed glue was dripping and flicking from his brush as he took out one of his folded posters. Believe it or not, it was for Kiss It, Don't Hold It, It's Too Hot. I was most impressed. Stunned in fact. A train was just pulling in. Yet I just sat. Couldn't wait to see it resplendent there on the underground tunnel wall. Well upon my word, there this chap was, carelessly splashing and slapping it up over another poster. I said most politely, please do mind your sloppy brushstrokes and drips my good man. Well he absolutely ignored me and continued. I glared at him. He dipped his brush rather deeply I thought, back into his pail of glue. And I sat there waiting for his apology, the train now just ready to pull out of the station, the chap wielded his brush as if he had a fish by the tail. Immersing me across the countenance in a single brushstroke. He then jumped on the train just as the doors were closing."

"Holy shit Binky I can't walk another inch."

"Schultz this is the first laughter one has heard from you in a long time. I knew my little story would make you happy. Dear me, Schultz one must suppose that a successful life is one in which one's enemies who enjoyed laughing at one's misfortune, have all proceeded one to the grave leaving one with no such enemies left to take their place. But I did stand and look at the poster. And Schultz I thought of you. The splendid battle you were fighting. And especially the brazen billing. Sigmund Franz Schultz in large letters followed by our firm's title in a print size one could hardly read. But Schultz, before you scream it was a printer's error, let me tell you what happened to me when I got off the train. Rising upwards on the escalator I was feeling quite miserable. Stinking of glue. Wondering how one would tell such a tale to the little wife. Then stepping back out onto a Knightsbridge street, thinking well, at least in this respectable part of town one is safe from further insult. Then there, just yards away, was a chap. Standing right on the border between Brompton and Belgravia and the

373

chap suspiciously looking like a barrister in cutaway coat and striped trousers. He was stamping the end of his brolly on the pavement, with his bowler listing on his head. Shouting at the top of his lungs. That what a bloody diabolical outrage it was, going on in this country, no one giving a damn, an absolutely bloody disgrace, country in a bloody mess. Naturally in the aggrieved state I was in, these were words that I stopped immediately to hear. I really don't know what overcame me. I'm usually most shy of others, especially just having had my face slapped with a paint brush full of glue. But summoning up my courage I went straight up to this chap and offered to shake his hand. Just to let him know how awfully good his sentiments sounded. Well he, without even taking my proffered paw said, well what sir, are you doing about it. Dear me I must confess I was utterly speechless. The only thing that crossed my mind was my small improvement program recently introduced to the household to raise the standard of butlering. Somehow I knew if I had mentioned this to the chap, that he might have considered it most lightweight. Plus I think my face was slightly glue frozen in an expression of amazed horror. Then he shouted and stamped his brolly once more. And my goodness so many people had stopped to watch across the street. As he shouted directly at me. Grave matters sir, are being perpetrated in the Houses of Parliament with the aquiescence of silly nits like you. Silly nit he called me. I fear I rather withdrew. Of course had I said that good butlers were hard to get these days, it would I'm sure have led to instant further ridicule of me."

The two figures stopping on the corner of Deanery and South Audley Street. Binky bowing his head. His eyes cast down on the evening pavement. Taxis throbbing by. Under a cooler and clearing sky.

"Holy shit, Binky, you're not serious, you're crying."

"Yes I am Schultz."

"Jesus not about that, are you, that's nothing to cry about."

"Schultz, I'm afraid it is. Something to cry about. I was extremely hurt. I would never let England go down the drain. And I shall now use one of your silk handkerchiefs. So kindly given."

To wipe
Away
The tears
I shall
Cry when
It does

29

SCHULTZ, hands plunged in pockets, strolling up Park Lane. Whores whispering hello dearie. On this cool Saturday evening. Through the revolving doors. Collecting his key. Get a paper. All the sweat. And in the end. The one who gains anything out of it. Is the telephone company.

Schultz standing in his silent hotel sitting room. Touching the petals of a vase of flowers. Going to stare out the windows. Jesus this is one Saturday when I'm all alone by myself. Woke this morning putting my wrist watch on, and found it felt heavy on my arm. Rule eight. Don't sink any deeper when each day something brand new and horrible happens. After such an anxious afternoon in a deserted office. But christ his Lordship, fighting like a trooper after everybody else had left. Even went to buy a batch of tickets himself. The son of a bitch has guts for an army. Sitting there in his shirt sleeves calculating the gross.

"Schultz by my calculations and estimations, should another twenty four seats be bought we should make it with eighteen or so pounds to spare."

"Jesus your Lordship christ we can't risk it. We got to buy more tickets."

"Schultz enough suspicion has already been aroused which could mean all this money and heartache has been in vain. Gayboy and his acolytes are already on the alert for any misdeed."

"Gayboy's a stupid ass. Who can't read the fucking clause of a contract."

"My dear Schultz many a stupid ass has gone to a smart lawyer. We must just gently nudge the gross over."

"O Jesus. I can't stand it. We could be a quid, a mere quid under."

Schultz now on this green hotel carpet. Pacing back and forth. Shaking clenched fists up and down. Biting his knuckles. Staring at the passing floor. Shit I need distraction. Need to refresh the force which used to be in me. This is like the hours before being taken to the electric chair. Walking my last mile in this room. I got to do something. Jesus it's like there's nobody left to reject me. If only I could get a rolling head start I could escape this spiritual agony. Farting is such foul sorrow. Maybe that's what I did wrong. Last time I left her.

Schultz dialling on the telephone. This now familiar Knightsbridge number. And listening to Lulu's abrupt cold words.

"No. I'm sorry, I'm busy."

"Hey honey, what's the matter, you've been busy, busy, night after god damn night."

"That's correct I have."

"Well what's the matter don't you want to see me."

"Perhaps one afternoon for tea as an acquaintance, yes. At the moment as a lover, no."

"Hey what's suddenly the matter."

"I simply like a change of man. That's all. I don't want to hurt your feelings. But you know you must easily be the most unglamorous person who has ever lived."

"Honey that's one characteristic I don't mind having."

"Well, at the moment I prefer a man who is all brawn and no brain. Who beats me. You have no idea how dull even the most

interesting men get. Like a lump of pudding. Especially when
they lie around luxuriating in one's life. Besides, I think you're
looking for a mother. But you should go home and dominate
your wife."

"Well fuck you honey."

· Schultz slamming down the phone. Jesus what did I do now.
That fucking bitch has problems they haven't even invented yet.
She's viciously ambitious only I don't know what the fuck for. Her
principles last for an entire three hours. She's a moral acrobat.
She wants to be a faithful loving girl friend one minute, and a
nutty nymph beat with whips the next. Dragging big brawny oafs
off building sites by the hair. And bringing me a plate of ouefs en
gelee in bed. Then kicking me in the teeth, by throwing the whole
tray over me. Saying I'm so sorry I simply had to do that. Holy
shit. She just thinks it funny ruining all the bed clothes. Well fuck
her. Spoiled god damn aristocratic women. Nearly as bad as my
own fucking wife. His Lordship says I should apply the statute of
limitations on people's misdeeds. Forgive them after a six year
period. Jesus I'd make it sixty. And if ever after today I'm sailing
again on easy street. No bitch I promise you is going to give me
any lip. God, my balls are exploding. I could have really screwed
her Venus de Milo body tonight. When all this time I'm feeling
the only thing left to do is die and forget. When I go into bankruptcy. I want to go smothered in a big cloud of Rolls-Royce petrol fumes. Or escape to Jerusalem. Suffer my last agony in the
garden of Gethsemane. Or on the frozen tundra with icy winds of
loneliness wailing around you. Holy shit. Al. Maybe I at least
should go see the guy. There's nothing anyway better to do. Take
the flowers there out of the vase. Buy some chocolates. Christ
Binky has me still shook up. I never know when that fucker is
serious or playacting. A minute and five yards later further on
down the street, he was saying.

"Schultz you do not understand England do you, in spite of our
having lost our Empire we do still hold our heads up with a mea-
sure of dignity if not pride."

378

Schultz with a towel drying off the stems of the flowers. Wrapping them up in the morning's newspaper. Now comb my hair. Before I start crying myself right now in this lonely room. Rule nine. I don't know what the fuck it should be. I'll think about it. Maybe it should be don't ring people up. If I call Al now, he'll slam the phone down.

Schultz through the evening gowned stirrings. Popping on foot out the door of the Dorchester. Lugging a box of chocolates and bouquet of flowers. Strolling an hour aimlessly through the streets. Past two whores tearing each other's hair out. One kicking the other in tits when she was down. And a pimp rushing up to save his merchandise. Everybody's got problems. But fucking suddenly I got no one. I could go back to the theatre and give these to the Debutant. Only I just couldn't stand the box office tension of tonight.

Schultz in an unfamiliar street by a post office. Flagging a taxi and throbbing back across the town. Alighting near this tall block of flats. Count two three floors down from the top. On the twenty second floor. Lights on. Al's in. That high living fucker. Up there in tax dodgers towers.

Schultz heading down an incline to the garage. Spying the concierge up in through the window behind a large counter. Got to get in without being announced. Through this car park basement door. Give Al a big surprise. Before he has a chance to say drop dead. Jesus, we both come from a consumer society. Encapsulated on wheels. Daily fanned by propaganda. To buy buy. To keep the whole heap glowing. And the tyres rolling and rolling. And that's what I got to keep doing.

Schultz ascending to the ground entrance floor. Elevator door opening. The grey carpets, beige walls in the lobby of this palm festooned building. Swarthy guy and a dazzling girl get in. The lift gliding upwards in the sky. Christ that son of a bitch has just farted. And holy shit Al could punch me in the god damn face right at the door. Duck as I reach out to shake his hand. And shout to remind him how he always wants people to love each other. Can never understand how such a nice guy can be such a stupid ass. What a place to be coming. On this most crucial fatal evening.

Schultz emerging on this landing. Four directions to go. Al's door is southeast. Where he likes to look down his big long celebrity nose over the best part of London. Get my foot ready to stick in the door when he tries to slam it in my face. Jesus he can be such an inadvertent fucking show off. Last time we came out of this building together, his chauffeur brought up from the garage his great big long black seven passenger limousine. Al looking down from the front steps annoyed. Saying, no, not that car, the other one. The chauffeur returning a minute later in his sky blue convertible Rolls-Royce. And Al, now getting up his phony blood pressure shouting, no, no, not that car, the Aston, the Aston.

Schultz in the foyer pressing the bell. A smell of cooking. Christ mushrooms. Jesus maybe now I'm busting in on a dinner party. Couldn't be. There's a scent of garlic in the air. Sends Al always hysterical. About how his breath could smell. At his age he should instead be hysterical about how his prick could stay limp. If he doesn't eat wheat germ. Feet approaching. Better now step back. Let the first roundhouse right fly harmlessly over my head.

The click of the lock turning. Which stops turning. A female voice. A tremor of caution.

"Who is it please."

"A friend, open up."

Door coming ajar a fraction. The side of a face and a kindly soft eye peeking out. The door opening wide.

"O goodness it's you, Mr. Schultz."

"Yeah me, how are you."

"I'm fine. How are you."

"Can I come in."

"O sorry, yes of course, it's simply that I wasn't expecting anybody."

"I'm sorry, I'm just calling out of the blue."

"Please, do come in."

In this white walled hallway. Schultz smilingly handing over his flowers and box of chocolates.

"These are for you. I only just popped by to see Al a second. I was in the district."

"What beautiful flowers. And chocolates. Well dear me, how nice. These are lovely. Thank you."

"Hey is Al still sore at me. And by the way, nothing is good enough for you honey."

"Al isn't here."

"When will he be back."

"I don't know."

"Holy shit honey, put your foot down, don't let the guy go out and not know when he's coming back."

"He's in New Orleans. He left yesterday."

"Holy shit. New Orleans. The son of a bitch never told me. Sorry that's just my friendly term for Al. What was he angry."

"Well that wasn't the reason he went to New Orleans. He's giving a concert. Please, won't you come in. And sit down. A minute."

"Well honey, I'd like to stay for hours but this is a little awkward, Al and I left each other on kind of bad terms, maybe you heard."

"He did say, he thought you were being difficult."

"Holy shit honey he must have said more than that."

"He did. Yes."

"Well I'm hearing from everywhere all over this town what a shit I am. How touchy, how impossible. Nobody can deal with me. People threatening to sue. But I get the productions on. And so help me god this one's closing over my dead body."

"Please, just excuse me for a moment. I've got something on the stove."

Louella turning out the door. Schultz getting to his feet and crossing the long green carpeted drawing room. Full of musical instruments, record players, speakers. A black baby grand piano. In an arched foyer the walls covered with photographs of Al with celebrity after celebrity. Singers, actresses, presidents and kings. Schultz looking out the large picture windows southwesterly over London. The lights sparkling in a great magic carpet of roofs and buildings. An aircraft slowly wheeling in over the West End, lights flashing, and long beams cutting through the sky from its wings. The streams of traffic pouring along the boulevards around the park. Rear lights red in one direction and approaching white in the other. Christ I could be happy up here like this. Looking out all over London. All those shrill emotional shrieks you hear. Are just cries about money. That a place like this costs.

"Can I get you a drink, Mr. Schultz."

"Jesus, I better not really stay, no kidding. Al with his penchant for paranoia would get the wrong fucking idea I'm telling you."

"Well it's entirely up to you. I have some very marvellous sherry. Awfully nutty and rich as well as being medium dry."

"You suddenly convinced me honey. I'll have a sherry."

Louella going to a cabinet along the wall. Opening up the polished walnut doors. A whole bar. Bottles reflected in the mirrors. A stainless steel sink. Al's every modern fucking convenience laid on. Like this wonderful girl. In her same quiet clothes. Her flat heeled shoes. Brown tweed skirt and green cashmere sweater. Her legs could be better. Tiny bit heavy about the hips. Jesus everything about her could be improved. But then you look at her. And Jesus, it's magic. She smiles for one second and you think, holy christ that's just the way that girl ought to be.

"Jesus honey, I'm no alcoholic. That's a big sherry."

"Well I have heard of all your troubles you know. That you've been having over your show."

"Yeah. Cliff hanging."

"Which by the way I thought was one of the most entertaining I've ever seen."

"Honey. Thanks. And let me tell you in the absolute silence up here in this, what do you call them eyrie or something, where eagles get to, way up on inaccessible mountain cliff sides, safe from predators. Well let me tell you that this sherry and just you sitting there really hits the spot. Hey what do you do, just here all by yourself up here like this."

"O I read, sew, cook, clean and polish. Watch television. Write letters. Listen to music, eat, drink."

"And wait."

"Yes."

"Till Al gets back."

"Yes."

"Jesus honey, old as he is, he's absolutely in love with you."

"I don't consider Al old. He's extremely young in mind and vigorous in spirit."

"Sure. Sure. Right. Al's a bombshell. But shit, you know, this is the first time I've ever really been in close contact with you. I see what he means. I wasn't believing all his recent guff he's been spouting about love. But Al, I can see has finally made it. With obviously one wonderful girl."

"O please. You're exaggerating. I'd better put on some music."

"Honey you're blushing."

"Of course I am. What sort of music would you like to hear."

"Hey why not play Al's Palm Beach Concerto."

Schultz stretching out on the couch. Head deep in a pillow. Sipping his sherry with a bent elbow. Louella serving squares of toast, pâté, olives and fresh celery.

"Hey Jesus I don't want to delve into personal histories but how did you and Al ever meet."

"Well as a matter of fact right in the next building to where you fell. He came to the office where I was working to see my boss. Looking for money for you and the prosecution, O dear I mean production."

"Honey. Prosecution it could have been."

"I was the receptionist."

"Holy cow."

"He did rather make an entrance but he was so absolutely charming."

"But Jesus, honey, a young girl like you. I mean Al. He's even too old to be your grandfather. You should be settling down with some guy your own age. What good is Al to you in a few years pushing him around in an oxygen tent over a wheelchair when he could blow himself up lighting a cigar."

"That's mean. Al is quite robust. He does have to be careful but he's one of the sweetest kindest and most thoughtful people I have ever met. He's always been perfectly honest. He said all he could offer me was the rest of his life, for just a few years of mine."

"And honey, a beautiful place to live."

"Yes that's true. And everything I wanted. That I would meet everyone or anyone I wanted to meet. That I would be at the center of the arts."

"Holy cow the son of a bitch, he gave you that snow job. Wow."

"That's not a snow job. Are you attacking him. Because of what's happened."

"I'd never attack Al. I love him for christ's sake. That's why I'm here. I really love him. He is. He's one of the most wonderful people in the world. I'm the first to admit it. He's saved my life a hundred times. And ruined it completely just once. But you. You're a flower. Just blossomed."

"Al's been as good as a father to me."

"He's been a father to me too honey. But Jesus I don't wrap up my life in his. He's got hundreds of women. Real hustler types. Who just go along for the ride. That a nice quality girl like you is up here all lonely by yourself, just waiting for Al to croak, that's crazy."

"I'm not waiting for him to croak. That makes me really angry. You know Mr. Schultz."

"Sigmund for christ's sake, call me."

"Well at this point I think it had better be Mr. Schultz. You know I really don't understand you. From the impression I get, you must dislike and perhaps even despise women."

"What. Who told you that. Al."

"Not in so many words. But one did get that overall impression. And here you are now trying to advise me, a female, of supposed

384

harm I may come to at the hands of someone I'm deeply and terribly attached to."

"Attached. So you admit you don't love him."

"Mr. Schultz. I hardly think this conversation is appropriate.
How on earth did we get on to it."

"You're right. Christ. I'm I guess hysterical over any subject
especially Al these days."

"And how are things faring for you at the theatre."

"Tonight's business tells all. It could be the end. Or the beginning. I'm just waiting. I'll know about nine forty five."

"Please. Why don't you stay. And have dinner. It's nearly ready.
If you like garlic and mushrooms. And steak. Salad. And Al, I'm
sure won't mind if I open up one of his burgundys. You know
how he absolutely adores wine. He's got this Bonnes Mares which
he absolutely insists is one of the great wines of the last thirty
years. That's another thing he's taught me. Wines, I've learned so
much from him."

"We all learn from Al, honey and I'm listening like I'm hearing
for the first time in life something I want to hear."

"Then you'll stay."

"With the utmost pleasure. But Jesus don't ever, whatever you
do, ever tell Al, for christ's sake. I think his paranoia is already
dangerously near the edge."

"Mr. Schultz honestly. I really don't know what you're talking
about, Al is no more paranoiac than anyone. And I'm free absolutely to do whatever I want, when I want and how I want. On
Al's insistence. Al has never once shown any sign of the slightest
concern."

"O no, you watch. Don't kid yourself honey. We all admit for
the hundredth time that Al's completely wonderful, understanding, all those things. But that fucker is not above trying to
drag something like you right into the grave with him."

"I do think it's time we really did change the subject. And I
get you another drink. And I go get things off the stove to the
table."

"Let me help honey."

385

"No. You just sit happily, I just hand things through the hatchway."

At a long teak table. Set with sparkling glasses and looking out over all of London. The wine fragrant soft and delicate. The filet mignon tender and blood sweet rare. The garlic scented mushrooms aromatic. The salad crisp and fresh. Wholemeal bread, brie and camembert. A bowl of fresh sliced peaches, muffins and whipped cream. And an ancient crème de tête, whole god damn tarnished gold, ice chilled bottle of Al's Chateau d'Yquem.

Schultz sitting staring down the table's gleaming woodgrain. Candlelight sparkling on the glass and reflecting in the windows. This warm pleasant marvellous soul soothing creature. Jesus I keep wanting just to go down the other end of the table and touch her.

"My god honey, this is the best god damn meal I've had in centuries. So this is how Al privately lives."

"You do have Al on the brain don't you."

"I have his Chateau d'Yquem on the brain, honey. Never in all my fucking life have I ever, ever tasted anything like this. It makes even Al's Palm Beach Concerto sound good. And Al's new toupee look good."

"God you can be cruel, can't you."

"Hey I'm just joyously kidding. Honest. But Al, he's going to have a fit. This bottle of Chateau d'Yquem is one of the best years of all time. Imagine the grapes ripened for this twelve years before I was even born. Momma meeo. You drinking it, is one thing. But Jesus, me drinking it. With you up here alone. Wow. That's another."

"O please, can't we talk of something else."

"I'm sorry honey I can't get off the subject. But shit sure, fuck Al, and maybe I'll try one of Al's best Havana cigars. What the hell, like you said, you're a free agent. What time is it. My god. I got to ring the theatre. Can you imagine. Here I am sitting here feeling so god damn wonderful that I completely forgot. For five minutes that is. O Jesus honey. This is the phone call. To end all phone calls. Christ I don't know if I've even got the nerve, maybe I should leave it till tomorrow. But if I do that, I could never sleep a wink. Which I don't do anyway."

"Do it now."

"You really think so. I should."

"Yes. I do."

"O.K. I'll do it, just for you. I'll do it. Spin the cylinder and put the gun right up to my head."

Schultz taking a swig of d'Yquem. And sucking in air between his lips. Folding his napkin. Pushing back his chair. Crossing silently on the soft deep carpet and picking up the gold plated telephone.

"Mr. Schultz here."

"Good evening, Mr. Schultz. I'm afraid it's bad news."

"O christ."

"We've just completed tabulation. And are rechecking. And it's been so close."

"How close."

"Well, we'll know exactly how close in just a minute. I'm really sorry. I really am. It deserved to keep the theatre. Tonight's audience just loved it."

"Thanks."

The phone dropping out of Schultz's fist. His knees buckling. A groaning great sigh as he reached out to put his hand supporting on the wall and began to stumble backwards. Louella rushing up from the table. Grabbing his arm by the elbow. Putting her hand up supporting his back as he collapsed slowly on the couch.

"Dear Mr. Schultz. You poor darling, you poor darling, are you alright. I'm so sorry it's bad news. I really am."

"I'm O.K. I'm O.K. You'd think after all these years I'd get used to it. But it gets harder and harder to take."

"Let me get something cool for your head."

Louella passing and reaching for the suspended phone, swinging back and forth hanging down from the table. Lifting it to put it back in its cradle sitting on the side of the polished work bench festooned with electronics. Louella holding up the telephone to her ear. A voice sound coming out.

"Mr. Schultz, Mr. Schultz, are you there. Are you there."

"Yes he's here."

"Would you put him back on please."

Schultz closing his eyes, shaking his head back and forth, and feebly waving his hand.

"I'm sorry but Mr. Schultz, can't at this moment."

"Well this is the Regent box office and would you tell him please that he made it. By exactly eighteen pounds, thirteen shillings."

Louella putting her hand over the speaker, turning to Schultz, a smile on her face.

"Sigmund, they say you've made it."

Schultz's ears twitching and straightening. Eyes opening, lids crashing up into the eyebrows. Blood pouring back into the arms. Schultz catapulting himself up off the couch. His feet taking a flying leap across the floor. Grabbing the phone from Louella.

"Hello."

"Mr. Schultz."

"Yes."

"You've made it."

"Holy cow. Holy cow. Holy fucking cow. Sorry about the language. Thanks a lot."

"I'm sorry Mr. Schultz we were nearly finished and I thought the figure would surely be under. But we've just this moment finished double checking. And you have made it. And the advance is excellent."

"Thanks. Jesus thanks. From the bottom of my heart."

Schultz hanging up the phone. Holding his arms out wide. Louella hesitating. And then stepping forth in a smile. Putting her head on his shoulder. Schultz hugging her.

"Honey, no shit. I swear. I've just crawled up on the beach. And you're standing here. And I don't know what the fuck I'm ever going to do without you. Not being with me for the rest of my fucking life. Because. So help me god. I love you."

And it's
Goodbye
To diamonds
And lingerie

And hello
To enjoying
Life
To the fucking
Full

30

"Y fucking god. So this is serenity."

Schultz lying propped up by the linen swansdown pillows. In the potentate sized bed. A breakfast tray across his belly. Staring out into the passing clouds and heavens. Soft guitar music. The sound of water pouring in the tub in the mirrored walled bathroom beyond the door. The distant steady roaring hum of the city below. Blue and white Meissen plate of sausages, pancakes and maple syrup. Jams and honey. Butter, hot rolls and croissants. A jug of coffee. All the morning's newspapers. And Louella. There standing looking down. In her dressing gown. After thirteen hours of sleeping. With bouts of solid insane fucking in between.

"Are you alright, can I get you anything else Sigmund."

"Alright, are you kidding. I'm wonderful. Fucking wonderful. I'm just borrowing these sunglasses of Al's."

"I'm just running my bath."

"Hey just open that dressing gown. O christ close it. My tray is going upwards on a hydraulic lift."

Louella stepping in the bathroom. Steam coming out the white door just ajar. A shelf full of model replicas of Al's cars. Beyond sliding doors, Al's three hundred suits and hundred and fifty pairs of shoes. If only they weren't all in such bad taste I could get outfitted while Al's away. Jesus this is really waking up to living. To a whole new ball game. After striking out for eight innings. And in the ninth. Whamo bammo. I belt a fucking home run over the bleachers with bases loaded. Or said like his Lordship might say. Ah, an agreeable sup, sucking snipe brains out of their skulls, after a long fatiguing journey, don't you think. The British are always saying don't you think. But I love the sound of his Lordship's voice when I asked for a beer at his club. Schultz I deeply regret to say that it is insufferably improper to look for beer at one's better clubs. Christ now I can walk up Fifth Avenue in ecstasy looking for beer anywhere. And no longer looking for ass everywhere. Last night nearly died with only seconds to spare before I got the good news. One thing I don't remember how to do anymore, is to die gracefully. Lulu staring at me when we were last in bed. After a fuck. Telling me I was smug and patronizing and looked like a corpse. Well fuck you honey. Because, here I am. Anything but. Sigmund Franz Isadorable Schultz. No longer not all alone and ignored, having thoroughly lost the race for prestige and success. There he is folks limping but alive crossing over the finish line. A fucking god damn winner. The only thing that can ever ruin me now is my next six flops. But always in bliss, something happens. You get cheated, short changed and reminded again of the world. Once love is over it conveniently turns to hate. Holy shit. Al maybe he won't take it like a man. At his age he's desperate enough to come looking for me with a gun. With everything around here in his personal life showing symptoms of him being super stupid rich. Christ I'd do it. I'd murder Al with my bare hands. She's the first woman I've ever met worth killing for. In a day or two. I'm going to be in Prague. Give her time to unload Al. I knew the moment I clapped eyes on her on opening night. This girl and I. Meant for each other. There she was. Just standing there in all that blaring vulgar fuss, totally serene. Christ, when it happens. When it hits you. You fall in love like a ton of bricks. And don't know or care how. Everything about her. All her little physical faults are the most precious beautiful things. That you want to kiss and pour your love all over them. Church bells ringing. Today Sunday. Where I would be meandering down into the lobby of the Dorchester. Sitting all alone. Like I did last week. Staring at the fan of grey and white marble in the floor. Rugs green and orange. The gleam of limousines glinting in the glass of the revolving doors. The pampered women passing who want to be told how perfect they are. And always looking at the displays of gems. Like if I was the jewel, I'd feel in there, like a mouse with a cobra the other side of the glass, ready to strike. And then these rich dolls walk out. To wait for the green, gold braided doormen patrolling over their terrain, to open their big limousine doors. To take them in their own kind of self worship contentment to beauty appointments all over town. Tomorrow I'm going to go get a hair cut. Whatever this marvellous girl suggests. After Al, my black curly head must feel to her like an entire Canadian forest. God the whole body spills itself into somebody that you love. Why. Why did it have to be Al, I'm doing this to. Jesus the way these sausages and pancakes taste. Jars of honey I never even heard the name of before. The fucker is nothing else but a geriatric pleasure seeker. I could call him my most very best friend I ever had. And when you find a friend who is good and true fuck him before he fucks you. That's what us guys always said in the Coast Guard. Or maybe I read that in an unexpurgated etiquette book somewhere. Saturday leaving the office, his Lordship said, Schultz, you'll be exquisitely careful won't you. As if something terrible was going to happen to me. Instead of the best thing that's ever happened in my life. Jesus christ, his Lordship might be someone sorry to see me die. He's a guy who could run a whole god damn kingdom. If only socialism would let him. A fucking shame the qualities he's got went out of style years ago. Yet he's so practical. I'm sure the son of a bitch's ancestor must have been the inventor of the pitched roof. Binky once said to me, when I asked about all this English fucking reserve. Ah my dear Schultz an Englishman does not step out of his private soul in case someone would behave to him in a shitty manner. What am I doing. I'm talking now in my unexpected happiness, like I love those pair of exasperating guys. Who used my balls for billiards and made me piss all over myself dropping down skeletons behind my back for laughs. Maybe I just don't know when people love or hate me.

Louella passing across the room. In that marvellous flowing silk fabric. My father would try to give it a name like The Princess Breakfast Dress. Then add twelve dollars, ninety nine cents to the price. Poor kid looks a little bit sad. Guess you don't kick somebody's teeth out that you're fond of without a little remorse.

"Jesus Louella. Stop. Just there. Open that beautiful kimono. O baby. Jesus. Soon as you do that. Only that these sausages and pancakes are so fucking necessary to get my strength back I'd eat you instead."

A faint smile from Louella. Sweeping her gown closed. God she's wonderful. Not even a day gone by. And I know she's the one for a lifetime. My fucking wife. Demanding champagne to celebrate our first month of misery. I saw stars when the cork of the bottle exploded out, hit me in the eye and sent me reeling around the room knocking over a vase. You'd think she'd worry I was hurt. Instead she shouts, stop you're ruining the house you fucking bastard. Jesus thank god recent events have given me a welcome partial amnesia to all the other horrors at her hands. At last. The way I feel now. Streaking across the stage. Like the ballet dancer I saw the night I fell asleep in the theatre with Lulu. Only when the world invents something faster than light, only then will I need a head start. My life suddenly going again. Somebody like Al is just in everything for the money. Contracts and deals I saw stacked up in every drawer of his desk. Jesus, I got to get this innocent girl out of this lousy commercial atmosphere. Up here with him. Young and vibrant. Imagine, the woman I love. Forced to suck his decrepit wrinkled old prick. Jesus I don't think I can even face the past history of it. A second ago Al should have been here listening. To the radio discussion on hair, baldness, greyness and drying of the scalp. O god. I mustn't knock him, the poor shit. I ought to hope his concert last night was a wonderful sell out. And as beautiful sounding as the sky is looking this moment out there. Christ over these last months the patches of bad luck were getting wider and wider. You nearly couldn't leap across. Till the abyss I finally jumped last night. Fantastic. His Lordship only miscalculated by thirteen shillings. The man would be a genius at any bank. From now on I'm unstoppable.

"Hi honey, you look absolutely gorgeous."

"Do I."

"Jesus no words could do you justice. I swear."

Louella standing naked at the open bathroom door. Steam steaming out behind her, misting over the windows. The casual London Sunday sounds. Drums beating. A parade somewhere. O god. Already I've got another fucking hard on. It comes up like a jack in the box. Her eyes. Not even moving. Like the most magnificent statue standing there. My hands dying to grab her. Her eyes and my eyes. Right while I keep on chewing. We're bathing each other in the juice of each others souls. Jesus, even every noise is beautiful. That sounded like a crash down on the street. And she quivered and her nipples just shivered that fraction. This girl is going to give my life the finished touch. Not like what my mother wanted to give me. Those Jewish girls. Who whenever their mouths opened in a smile you could see the sneer. There she is mom. Just what you would advise against, even worse than my wife. My Louella. There standing framed stark naked in the bathroom door. Screwed each other in every direction. Tongues up each others asses. That's how deep love can get. Holy shit. What's wrong. Her jaw just dropped and she gasped ashen faced. Hey what's the matter.

Schultz turning to look. Where Louella's eyes were looking. In spellbound horror. At another figure. An unidentified flying object. Lifesize at the bedroom door. Except for the toupee, looking like fifty thousand Arabs. Converging on a single Jew taking a crap next to the wailing wall. A time now for every flea all over the face of the earth to fart. And try and make a sound in all this silence.

"You cunt, you schlemiel, you cunt."

"I can explain Al, what happened."

Schultz catching his breath. Al disappearing. Feet pounding down the hall. Christ, the crazy train I'm on is moving again. Good morning folks, welcome to Horrorsville, you have just left Happytown Junction three thousand miles behind.

Louella now with a towel, transfixed, dazed and watching. Schultz heaving over the breakfast tray. Dishes, bottles, jam, butter, maple syrup, honey and the jug of coffee crashing on the floor. Schultz hop skipping and jumping. For his clothes. And life. One foot in the honey, the other in the jam. And a heel crushing a lens of Al's sunglasses. Who's at the door again. His toupee off. Brandishing a breadknife.

"Stay where you are. Don't either of you move."

"Al don't be crazy. I thought you were in New Orleans."

"Yeah. You thought. And now think again. Because you don't think, do you. That your own wife has you followed. You didn't think of that smart guy, did you. That she would phone me. That I would get a plane so fast back here. To catch you. You never figured that wise guy, did you. That your balls are coming off."

Louella holding her towel up. Wish the color wasn't so blood red. O god if it was white it could be me imprinted on that, like the image of Jesus Christ on the shroud. And that poor kid is trembling and pleading.

"O please, Al, please. It's all my fault."

"Louella, you keep quiet. I still love you. No matter what happens. But him. I hate. I despise. I loathe. Up here. Wearing my sunglasses. With my wine, my woman. He had all this planned."

"Never Al, I swear. Don't be crazy Al. It just happened to us."

"Well now this is going to happen to you."

"Christ Al no. Please I'm begging. For your sake more than mine. Spending the last years of your life in prison. Or your last seconds on the end of a rope. Al I can explain everything."

Al stepping forward a step. Schultz backing away. The foot in the jam now into the honey. And the other foot in the honey, now in the jam. Because holy shit, jelly don't shake or feel like that. What thoughts come into your mind at the end of your life. They were irresponsible to abolish capital punishment.

"I came here with flowers, for you Al, I swear."

"And for you, you lousy rat, your grave is going to get the flowers."

Al taking another step forward. Schultz pushing back against the bed. Christ my fucking nerves are making me shake looking like I'm scared shitless. Jesus I am. With Al's breadknife held out like his prick should be if only he ever could get a hard on. Poor Louella, clutching the towel over her face. Her sobs. And plaintive cries. The poor kid.

"O Al, Al please no, don't. Please."

"This is what happens behind my back. You trespassing rapist. In my own home. My dining room table in there, still with the wine glasses. My bed, defiled. My food, feeding him. My girl, used. By this sneaking cunt."

"Al I'm telling you. Let's talk it out. You could be hung. If the death penalty comes back. Put the knife down. I'm in love with Louella. We love each other."

"You love that thing hanging between your legs. That's all you love. And I'm going to cut it off."

"For fucks sake Al."

"Your own wife, your own wife has to go to Court to take possession of the matrimonial home. That's right. She has a court order. The locks changed on the doors. With a policeman there to protect her life. And the twins she's pregnant with. From the likes of you. Cowering there."

"Twins. Holy mackerel. And I'm not cowering Al. You put down that knife and I'll knock the fucking shit out of you."

"You will huh, will you."

"Come on, Al. Face truth. She loves me. Don't you love me Louella. Tell him. To his face."

Louella her head hung down. Like the wet strands of her hair. Legs quivering. Her hands trembling the towel. Al turning to her.

"Louella. Now I'm asking you. And I want you to tell me the truth. Choose between us. This sneaky cunt is not worth killing. So choose. Is it me or is it him."

Louella, her whole body shaking. Her lips moving, as she tries to make a sound. Holy Jesus, this is all this fucker can do. Force her to choose at the point of a breadknife. The quality of the American people is declining like hell. Here is a prime example. The son of a bitch has said things for which he is going to be sorry for later. If I got that knife I'd shift it up through his fucking belly, rip his guts out, sprinkle them with rat poison, and stuff his mouth shut forever with entrails. O Jesus, amazing how even the most satisfying thoughts can find fertile ground in a desperate mind. I'd also tear that I'm king of the apes expression right off his face. Tell him Louella. Come on kid, tell him. That tonight he's not taking you down to the East End like he usually does on Sundays to eat jellied eels and then stuff salt beef, bagels and pickles down his gullet. His Lordship asked me once if I had ever noticed how people who have not had much luck in life are always out of breath. I feel as if I haven't had oxygen in two years. If I could scare Al backwards. Grab something to throw at him. Maybe words are better at this time. With the size of that foot long knife. His Lordship said I should be more English about my remonstrations. Don't say I could kill you. The proper expression is Schultz, sir I assure you I shall shatter your stumps and make mugwump of what remains. Holy christ I knew it. Knew what. Know that guys stop whistling at a certain time in a woman's age and she doesn't know when till it's happened. Also I know. That I don't want to be around for my wife's menopause. And maybe there's nothing else I know. Except that something else could happen. Like it has. When yesterday in a Piccadilly churchyard. A few minutes resting. A bird shat on my shoulder. That was good luck. That I didn't want to press too far. I got up and changed my seat. And another bird shat on my sleeve. And that was bad. But you'd think I wouldn't be so dumb as not to take the warning. When the god damn bird crapped again right down on my chest over my heart. I should have gone back to the hotel last night. And happily without life threatening complications, jerked off. And been followed and watched, would you believe it, by a private eye.

Louella's head bent down, still shaking all over. Her ankles are a little heavy but Jesus she has a nice curve to her calf. Come on. Honey. Tell the fucker. Do it. Before his heart trouble needs an ambulance to the hospital.

"I want to stay with you Al."

Al wheeling around. Crouched moving towards Schultz. Who backing away, knees buckling, sat down onto a stainless steel four pronged fork on the bed. Schultz jumping up. One hand clutching his arse. Al holding forward the knife. Schultz sticking his arms up over his head. Louella screaming.

"Don't Al. Please. Let him go."

"I'm letting him go alright. Unless he makes another false move. Come on you. You just gather up what you can get of your clothes in two seconds flat. And you get the fuck out of here. And don't ever let me see sight of you again as long as you live."

Schultz grabbing in all directions. Hands sticky with honey, fingers encrusted in jam. Clutching undervest, undershorts. Tripping over his shirt tails. O motherfucker my shoes I took off in the next room. And my pants I flung over the bronze bust of Al's head. But thank god so far I haven't provoked the fucker with a hard on.

"Al please let me put on something. My pants."

"You get out that front door or this knife will be sticking out your ass."

"Al I got only half my clothes. I'm naked. At least let me call a limousine."

"I'm counting to three. One. Two."

"I'm going, please, can't you let me find my pants, my shoes."

"I'll find them. And throw them out the window. You catch them down in the street. You creep. You'll get the bill for the damage too. Now get out that fucking door. And never set foot through it again."

Schultz taking the service elevator down to the basement. After a scream from a lady occupant of Al's floor collecting in her stack of Sunday newspapers. O god. You'd think that fucker Al's heart couldn't stand it. But it's like his hatred of me has given him a new lease in life. Imagine that fossilized geriatric gloating while I'm now walking barefoot around the world in shirt tails.

Schultz crouching along the wall of the garage driveway and looking up. Shoes. Plummeting down. Schultz ducking away as they bounced. The fuckers throwing them straight at me trying to hit me. Holy cow my trousers floating past all the windows in slow motion. Like it's taking years. Three people's heads already stick out to look. Thank god, the English don't believe in god. And are not all over the streets going to church.

Schultz, his sticky hands pulling on his trousers inside the tower's boiler room. Tins, cans and bottles thundering down a chute and crashing in a big iron cradle. And Jesus the cunt. He's sliced open my shoe laces. Stabbed the zipper out of my fly. I'm down here among the dust bins. With London grime on the windows, sashes and sills. Corroded facings. Bubbling paint. Like I've been thrown out with the garbage.

Schultz heading across the grass and through the trees. Towards the stone mansion civilisation of Park Lane. Shuffling in shoes. Past Speakers Corner. While I walk. I hobble. With O my god, my fucking wallet gone. Son of a bitch blacks up there on crates bellyaching they got troubles. I could tell you troubles. Which would turn your skin white. I should have known a detective was following me. When Pricilla phoned Lulu Lullabyebaby to give her some of that I'm a poor abandoned wife shit. And Lulu who is no slouch when it comes to losing her temper, lashed into her with a vocal ferocity so intense that Pricilla dropped the phone and dared not pick it up again. Here I am. Glad even for the heat of a bus engine enveloping me as it pulls up to a bus stop. Cork tipped cigarette butts in the gutter. Greasy dust. Greasy pavements. This London. This life. This is what I don't understand. I'm sentenced to ignominy. For doing what god and nature ordained. Fucking hell. I'd shout out right here blue bloody murder. Only that his Lordship says that in England it's mildly bad manners to say things that people will listen to.

> Or make
> Them shudder
> When I
> Holler
> Out of
> Lonely pain

31

THIS noonday Thursday pouring rain. Schultz and his Lordship in a last minute hop skip and jump around the office. Bags packed stacked downstairs waiting ready for Hubert to purr them to the airport. To the plane. Across Europe. Out of this unpredictable London. To Prague.

Schultz slamming down one phone and picking up another. Finally throwing a file across the chairman's desk. Give Binky something to think about for a week. While I take my sex drive somewhere, where my fucking ancestors lying in their graves maybe can teach me something. Tell me what the fuck has gone wrong. And where the fuck I can go right. Dreamt I made a pass at my own mother last night. Then this morning as I'm rushing out, ran smack bang right into His Excellency the Ambassador in the lobby of the Dorchester Hotel. We embraced each other in tears. If nothing else it was a fucking welcome change from hugging women.

Binky in a suede safari jacket, holding up an envelope in triumph, fluttering his eyelashes and pursing his lips.

"I do declare Schultz, my dear. As well as breaking the house record at the theatre, you have not got, have you, another invitation to the palace."

"That's right."

Binky pointing to Schultz's paper bag. Rebecca standing close behind his shoulder. Saw her hand touch him on the neck. Maybe she was too pleasant for me ever to fuck. A guy's lucky who can boast there's a girl in the world who loves him. While Binky the bastard is already toying in my brand new hopes and troubles.

"My god Schultz what's that full of."

"Bran flakes, dried figs and raisins."

"Whatever for."

"I got to keep my bowels moving on the Continent."

"How wise my dear Schultz how wise. And I couldn't help seeing these. In your file. Other bowel moving matters. Gayboy's writ. It is simply full of the most amazing legal flourishes and embellishments. And dear me, from your landlords, a veritable dictionary of torts. Astonishingly they could be distant parvenu cousins of mine. Suitably removed of course, from any cloying close connection. And dear me, their statement of claim. A bust of Justinan, smashed. A pair of early bronze figures of centaurs, thirteen inches high, now ten inches high with necks broken. Electrical wiring out of action. Ceilings down. Paintings."

"Stop Binky, stop. I know you love it. But I'm on a fucking holiday. Don't ruin the last vestige of my peace of mind before I even get on the plane."

Schultz's peace of mind. Ruined half way to the airport. By forgetting all his travellers cheques. Leaping up out of his seat and nearly going through his Lordship's limousine ceiling.

"For god's sake Schultz, you defy gravity. I have enough for both of us. Sit down. That's a bump you've put in my roof."

At last on the plane quaffing a beer. Over Belgium and Germany. The mountains, snaking rivers and valleys. And then Schultz with delight watching his Lordship be interrogated and then nearly arrested by Secret Police because of all the titles and strange names on his passport. In the busy lobby of the palatial hotel. Schultz with his guidebook map. Pulling his protesting Lordship by the sleeve.

"Come on, let's get out of here and see something."

"Schultz for god's sake slow down, you're like a caged lion at a Christmas sale of lambchops."

Sun sinking blood red on this late afternoon. Through the medieval lamp lit gloom of streets. Schultz popping into buy toothpaste. His Lordship watching from the street. As Schultz, abandoning his rudimentary Serbo Croat made a brushing motion across his smiling teeth. The lady behind the counter bringing him a toothbrush. Schultz wagging his head no. Then making a series of undulating squeezing motions with his hand. And the lady slapping him across the face. His Lordship outside doubled over.

"That's right laugh. At a genuine misunderstanding. You have a sick sense of humour, your Lordship. She nearly broke my jaw."

"Ah Schultz it's a miracle you haven't yet broken your neck."

This pair of tourists cross the bridge. One black head, one blond. Ladies turning to stare. Church bells. Calmly ringing. This is like a wonderland of the soul. Someone knew what they were talking about when they said this was the mother of cities. Jewel of cities. Wash hung out on lines like a masterpiece. The river. The statues hovering. Big silence in the middle of Europe. Hidden away. A city of thinking. And I'm thinking there are two kinds of women before they all become the same. One who sells herself many times over and regrets it. And one who sells themselves once and regrets it. I've met both kinds. It's like you're left with the question. Why are so many Jews called Murphy and Kelly. Last night I dreamt I socked Pricilla. Threw her to the ground for being unfaithful, getting pregnant with twins. I worried as the blows landed that I had hurt her. She shouted at me. Right while I went out the house for the last time. You're full of shit. Your deals are full of shit. And the people you try to make them with are full of shit. Jesus, it would make you join losers anonymous.

She found everything hid where I hid it. Still I might have loved her. If she didn't give me a toothache as soon as she came into the room. Our marital bed was like a wasteland. Neither touching the other through the night. Like she was miles away over the tundra. When it was just fourteen inches across to her skin. Jesus I could come to love my children. I took to shouting at my mother at an early age. She said eat. You're thin. The castle behind up there on the hill. Broods. Like it's watching down. The courtyards. The alleys. The cobblestones. Holy Jesus. Come beauty to me come. Old Europe is so wise to people's frailties. Guys exist to screw women and women exist to make them pay for it. Holy christ. There's the new moon in the sky. A sliver. So clean. Over the thousands of rooftops. The gold glinting towers. Uncle Werb took a picture of me in my first football uniform. Somewhere to leave your memories. Preserved by the houses and streets. If someone comes and tears them down, they are putting part of you to death. This is the way it must have been, just like this when my grandfather was a little boy playing. Maybe the worst thing my father and mother did to me without doing anything, was to make me Jewish. The fucking way I'm tripping over these stones, you'd never know I was descended from some of the greatest philosophers.

Around a narrow alley, in and out the winding ways of shining cobblestones. Schultz stopping. Pointing to the steeply pitched roof of an ancient building sunk down lower than the street.

"Your Lordship my rabbi scholar and poet ancestors officiated right in that synagogue there. They told other fucking Jews here what to do for a thousand years. On the ceiling, the star of David was invented."

"I'm sure it was Schultz. But I do wish you'd slow up. I must warn you. If indeed you do take up foxhunting and if you want to make an unpleasantly lasting impression in the field, you need only let your horse step on a hound while you are galloping past the master."

"Your Lordship, I am not fucking well foxhunting just yet, so just let me gallop past you this minute. And I can assure you that my horse won't step on a hound."

Schultz dragged back by his Lordship from climbing the wall and fence into this cemetery. Led then around the corner to a lady who sold them two tickets. The lady at the gate thought his Lordship looked like her son as she told them to hurry, that they were closing soon. Heading through the entrance of this ancient graveyard. All I can say her son must have been one great Jewish looking guy. Then his Lordship nearly fainted when she said that I looked like his brother. Today blond and black is the same color. Holy Jesus are things in two seconds getting fast familiar. Walled in here hidden away in all its own tumbling thousands of shadows. The evening shafts of light coming through the trees. The symbol of the Cohens, hands extended in blessing. The Levites, a jug pouring water. Stop here at this grave. Loneliness is a step towards death. Utter hysteria hit Al when he was about to sneeze for he could also be about to slip a disc. So be careful as I lean to pick a pebble up. Add it to all the other pebbles stacked on top of this tomb. And the symbol of Schultz. Could now be a bird fallen over on its side with a broken neck. But I'm not finished yet. And just like you'd imagine. There's nobody lying in here with a name like Al Duke. That imposter. I got to forget. Jesus, still in my head is a brain. Which could make good conclusions, rules and decisions yet. Every night I think of money. When I should be thinking of it in the morning. Criminality is the most efficient form of capitalism. But son of a bitch hell. Ask me. Loud as you fucking well can. Why did my stupid ancestors leave such a lovely place.

"Schultz, for god's sakes. Slow up. That's what I find most unacceptable in you, your total impatience concerning the more solemn things in life."

"Shit your Lordship, come on. I got to get to the oracle. For some spiritual communion. Before they close the place up."

"My god Schultz, you do have a soul after all."

"Of course I do. I'm not flint hearted all the time like you guys think."

Schultz followed by his lagging Lordship, rushing further along the narrow twisted gravel paths. The shifting serene shadows of light. Amid the tumbling askew gravestones. Jesus where is everything I need to discover. Before the lady shuts the gate. Holy Methuselah, hear my prayer. Lengthen my life. Which way to go. To find the rabbi. I'll study the Torah every night. I'll give to charity. Jesus what am I saying. In a second it could be I'll promise to observe Mitzvah of family purity and get circumcised. So many god damn stones. Right here. Like Uncle Werb told me. This is the famous rabbi. Write your trouble or request on a piece of paper. Like I could be that geriatric Al here asking, as he does women, Madam I possess three things in this world. An ugly body, a beautiful mind and loads of money. And you can't have the one you want of these without having the others as well. That is your problem, madam. But because you're gorgeous I hope you can solve it soon. And they do, they tiptoe into your bedroom while you're sleeping, and they take the money out of your pocket. Louella ratted on me. My wife kicked me in the balls. Roxana and Greta fell in love. Agnes went on the porno stage. Lady Lullabyebaby, in the sweetest way she could ever say goodbye, told me I had the kiss of death. Binky says masturbation is the supreme form of sexual pleasure. He's right. Life at best is just a Jewish joke. Jesus I'd need a filing cabinet to contain the questions to be pushed into the hole. For this old pops metaphysician in there to read. Lying in death wide awake. Cooking up solutions under the slab in your ancient rabbi mind. Your spirit I beg. I'm going to be the father of twins. But please don't tell me I'm guilty of fancy fucking. And don't tell me to go screw myself now. You lie there knowing so much. With a reservoir of wisdom. In which the big questions in people's lives get answered. If you can't tell me why I went into showbizz instead of diamonds and lingerie. Then tell me what holds up the world. An elephant. What holds up the elephant. A turtle. What holds up the turtle. An elephant. Hey holy shit, what holds up the last elephant. My boy, my child, listen just a second I'll tell you. It is another turtle. So don't ask more silly questions. It is elephants and turtles. All the way down.

But if you can balance on top. You can not only scratch your fanny but touch the moon. But don't count on anything.

> You bet
> Your sweet
> Rabbi ass
> I won't

J. P. Donleavy

was born in New York City in 1926 and educated there and at Trinity College, Dublin. He is the author of eight novels: *The Ginger Man; A Singular Man; The Saddest Summer of Samuel S; The Beastly Beatitudes of Balthazar B; The Onion Eaters; A Fairy Tale of New York; The Destinies of Darcy Dancer, Gentleman;* and *Schultz;* a collection of stories, *Meet My Maker the Mad Molecule; The Plays of J. P. Donleavy* (the plays included are *The Ginger Man, Fairy Tales of New York, A Singular Man,* and *The Saddest Summer of Samuel S*); and *The Unexpurgated Code: A Complete Manual of Survival & Manners.* Mr. Donleavy currently makes his home in Ireland, on the shores of Lough Owel.